Praise for Sara

'A slow-burn thriller with a great
characterisation where almost no ⌐
Tense and shocking.' Catherine Cooper, author of *The Chalet*

'An intensely gripping thriller, with astute characterisation, a
cleverly woven plot that keeps you guessing all the way, and a
story that is both suspenseful and moving. A hugely satisfying
read.' Philippa East, author of *Little White Lies*

'Sarah delivers such a smart and beautifully taut novel in *My
Perfect Friend*. Full of intrigue and delicious betrayal. Just how
I like my thrillers.' L.V. Matthews, author of *The Twins*

'A gripping read, exposing the dark lies at the heart of a
supposedly perfect life. Pacy, with well-drawn characters you
care about. The perfect thriller!' Louise Mumford, author of
Sleepless

'An incredibly tense psychological thriller that grips you from
the very first page. The suspense is utterly breathtaking.'
Victoria Dowd, author of *The Smart Woman's Guide to Murder*

'A carefully crafted, clever novel with plenty of twists, suspense
and red herrings. A sparkling and satisfying read.' Diane Jeffrey,
author of *The Silent Friend*

'A dark and clever thriller that kept me turning the pages late
into the night.' Sophie Flynn, author of *All My Lies*

'A really tense and atmospheric read with distinctive voices and
a satisfyingly twisty ending.' Mira V Shah, author of *Her*

SARAH CLARKE is a writer living in South West London with her husband, children and stubbornly cheerful cockapoo. Over fifteen years, Sarah built a successful career as a marketing copywriter, but her dream has always been to become a published author. When her youngest child started secondary school, she joined the Faber Academy Writing A Novel course to learn the craft of writing psychological thrillers. Sarah's debut published in 2021 and *The Ski Trip* is her fourth novel.

Also by Sarah Clarke

A Mother Never Lies
Every Little Secret
My Perfect Friend

The Ski Trip

SARAH CLARKE

ONE PLACE. MANY STORIES

HQ
An imprint of HarperCollins*Publishers* Ltd
1 London Bridge Street
London SE1 9GF

www.harpercollins.co.uk

HarperCollins*Publishers*
Macken House, 39/40 Mayor Street Upper,
Dublin 1, D01 C9W8, Ireland

This paperback edition 2023

1

First published in Great Britain by
HQ, an imprint of HarperCollins*Publishers* Ltd 2023

ISBN: 9780008608446

This book is produced from independently certified FSC™ paper
to ensure responsible forest management.

For more information visit: www.harpercollins.co.uk/green

Printed and bound in the UK using 100% renewable electricity
at CPI Group (UK) Ltd

For Chris
my number one ski guide

Prologue

1996

They don't have a normal handle on their front door, so Ivy curls both her hands around the brass knob and twists. It doesn't cross her mind that opening it up might be dangerous. They live in a Yorkstone cottage at the end of a narrow lane on the edge of a small village where everyone knows everyone. Danger is getting too close to the tractors or playing football outside Mrs Berry's kitchen window.

She expects that it will be her dad anyway. He usually gets back around now, when the sun has dropped too far for him to be able to read the cracks in the rockface safely. And he'll be in an extra hurry to get home today, she thinks, now that the storm has arrived, and gusting wind is howling down the chimney.

She pulls on the knob, but the door only opens a fraction before getting caught on the curled edge of their worn woven doormat. 'Hang on!' she calls out to the still-hidden figure beyond the door while dropping to a squat and yanking the mat. There's no response though, no teasing question about whether she wants him to freeze to death out there, so maybe it's not her dad after all. She straightens up and swings the newly freed door open.

'Hello, there. Is your mummy in?'

Ivy suddenly wishes she'd called for her mum in the first place. There's something in the man's expression – fake smile, tiny tremors in his cheeks – that makes her want to rewind time, go back into the living room, and keep watching the match; her dad's beloved team Leeds United (and by extension hers) trouncing Manchester City at Maine Road. The other man in uniform is staring beyond her, maybe at the framed photo on the wall, her mum and dad's proud grins as they summited the Matterhorn together.

But she can't run away from the situation. She needs to deal with it; that's what her dad would say. Like when he takes her to Rawcliffe boulder. *Work with what's in front of you.* So she nods to answer the man's question, then turns her head towards the kitchen and calls out for her mum. It only takes a few seconds for her to appear, but each one feels like an hour as Ivy holds on to the doorknob and chews the inside of her cheek.

'Hello? What is it? What's happened?' Her mum's voice is sharp and rapid.

'Could we come in, Mrs Hawkes? Talk inside?'

Ivy feels her mum's familiar callused hands rest on her shoulders, then pull her in close. She leans against the soft fabric of her mum's fleece jumper and listens to her racing heartbeat.

'Is it Calum? Is he injured?' her mum continues, staring at the men's faces, searching for clues.

'If we could just . . .'

'Jesus, please tell me,' she begs. 'I know the risks, Officer; I'm a climber too. If he's fallen . . .'

Ivy feels a strange sensation then, as though the air around her has doubled in thickness. The voices become muffled, and she's not sure she can stay upright; it's too heavy on her chest. But then a cheer rings out from the living room, loud and clear, and she clings to it. Leeds will have scored again, she thinks.

She can't wait to tell her dad when he gets home.

Chapter 1

The fall

Tom

Tom flails in the white abyss, his body plummeting towards the ground.

It's freezing cold. Harsh wind rips at the exposed patches of his skin.

He can't see anything – the thick cloud, the speed he's travelling, the crushing fear, make that impossible – but images start to form, nonetheless. First, the terrain he witnessed on his journey up the mountain. Sheer cliffs and rocky overhangs. The brutal, unforgiving side of nature. Not the orchestrator of his death, but soon to be his executioner.

Then other images.

Memories. Achievements.

The article in the latest *Annals of The Royal College of Surgeons* calling him a promising knee surgeon.

His new practice on Harley Street. His growing list of indebted patients.

How can it all be over so prematurely?

The moment of falling suddenly flashes in his mind. How the safety of packed snow disintegrated under his skis, the feeling of his stomach catapulting into his mouth as he dropped. The shock as he realised – a split second before it happened – that his life was coming to an end.

What could he possibly have done to deserve this?

There are the apologies he won't get chance to make, he realises as his wife's image finally, belatedly, comes into focus. Will she miss him? Will she hate him for leaving her, now, all alone?

And there are the secrets. All the small ones that protect the big one. Will they stay hidden, or spread like wildfire without him there to absorb the heat?

A dart of black below him suddenly punctures the blanket of white. Rock face, speckled with snow like bared teeth. Ready for him.

This is it, he thinks. His moment of reckoning.

Panic rips at his insides. Tears freeze on his cheeks.

He screws his eyes shut. Pushes all the images away. Prays for the black depths of unconsciousness. The protection of oblivion.

Eventually, it comes.

But it's a second too late.

Chapter 2

Ivy

Seconds pass as we duel with our eyes. I don't speak because I think silence gives me authority. Calum doesn't speak because he can't.

Eventually, I capitulate. 'Okay, one more story and then it is definitely sleepy time, okay?' He smiles triumphantly and leans forward, dragging a book from underneath a mound of soft toys at the bottom of his cot. As he proffers *The Very Hungry Caterpillar* towards me, I can't help marvelling at his tiny fingers holding the cardboard spine, the strength in his chubby arms matched only by the firmness of his expression. It's been a year – twelve months and two days to be exact – but I still struggle to believe I have a son.

'Mama,' he says. It's the only word he's mastered so far, and he uses it liberally, but tonight it's a clear instruction, so I take the book from his grasp.

'Lie down first, then I'll read,' I tell him, trying to claw back some control. He considers my offer for a moment, then shuffles along the mattress and lowers down onto his back. He's zipped into a baby sleeping bag and his feet lift as he lowers, as though the mechanics of his hips are stuck at ninety degrees. I dip my head and start reeling off the list of foods that the iconic caterpillar ate through. Calum grabs his toes and blinks at the star stickers on his ceiling. As I build to the denouement – the one green leaf, the cocoon – I watch Calum's eyelids grow heavy. 'Butterfly,' I whisper as sleep finally descends, then I kiss him on the forehead and slip quietly out of his room.

I pull Calum's door to and avoid the three creaky stairs as I head down into the kitchen. Other than a small utility room, the whole ground floor is open plan, and baby paraphernalia seems to be taking root throughout the whole space. Not that I mind. I bought the house five years ago when I first moved to London – the paradoxical luck of having a nest egg because someone you love died too young – but it never really felt like home until Calum was born.

I open the fridge door and hesitate for a moment before pulling out a half bottle of cava from the remaining few lined up on their sides. I feel a stab of guilt, popping a cork just for me, but I quickly banish it. They were a gift – a touching one at that – and it would be a shame to waste them. I fill my glass and take it over to the sofa, sinking down into the well-worn cushions. 'Cheers,' I murmur to the short line of birthday cards on the mantelpiece as I take a sip. I didn't host a party for Calum – there wasn't really anyone to invite – but I did bake a cake to mark the occasion, and we had a Zoom call with my mum.

I know some people would consider this sad, being at home on a Saturday night with only a sleeping one-year-old for company, but I'm used to it. I'm not an introvert exactly, but after spending the first week of Calum's life amidst the constant whir of a hospital ward, I craved solitude when I finally got him home. January quickly became April, and I realised we'd spent three months like that. Content in each other's company. We're a bit more sociable now – we've even made it to Yorkshire a couple of times – but those formative weeks have left their mark, and I'm happy with a Thai takeaway and good Netflix series on the weekend now.

Although life will change again soon, I remind myself as I take another sip. I love my job, it's a big part of who I am, and when I was pregnant with Calum, I thought a few months off work would be all I could handle. That I'd be back at Imperial University in September, ready for a fresh intake of new meteorology students, and craving the intellectual challenge of more research. But as the date loomed closer, I realised I couldn't face it. Maybe it was the trauma of my labour – blue-lighted to hospital with a ruptured placenta, emergency caesarean to save Calum's life – or the growing guilt for not providing him with a father. But I also didn't realise how intrinsically attached I would feel to him, as though leaving him in someone else's care could have physical consequences for us both. So I extended my maternity leave, and I'm now going back next month.

I'm a creature of habit, so I tap into Netflix with the remote control, and pick up my phone to find the Thai takeaway app. But as I look at the screen, I notice that Zoe has called. I stare at her name and the number in brackets beside it. Three missed calls. That's so strange.

Zoe and I were best friends at university, but that came to an abrupt halt at her twenty-first birthday party when she shouted abuse at me in front of everyone. We didn't speak for ages after that, but time moves on and memories fade. When I was invited to the opening of the new Peter Wilde laboratory at Exeter University a few years ago, I expected her to be there – she's his daughter after all – and it didn't put me off accepting the invite. I resolved to be civil, even friendly, but in the end, we got on better than that. Tom was there too, Zoe's husband who I also knew at university, and we managed to reminisce about student life without mentioning that terrible final night.

We swapped phone numbers at the event, but I didn't contact Zoe, and wasn't surprised that she didn't get in touch with me either. But then last winter, I got a text message from her, asking how I was. Calum and I were in our two-person bubble at the time, so it took me a while to respond, but eventually I invited her round for a cup of tea. She was surprised to see me with a baby, I think. But she wasn't the first to react like that, and she didn't do the infuriating thing of asking where his father was. She also apologised for how she spoke to me at her twenty-first birthday party, and that proved to be enough to kick-start our friendship. She's popped over a few times since then – including to personally deliver a crate of small bottles of cava at Christmas – and has supported me in other ways, like helping out with my mum. I'm starting to believe we can be proper friends again.

But we're not at the chat on a Saturday evening stage yet. And definitely not close enough to explain three missed calls in the time it's taken me to get Calum off to sleep. I tap into my voicemail but there aren't any new messages listed – only the one from my mum, unopened because I don't have the energy for that just now.

I continue staring at my screen. I should call Zoe back. She's clearly very keen to talk to me. And we were inseparable at university; that should count for something. But I'm tired, and not really in the mood to hear about her glamorous life this evening. Zoe studied liberal arts at university, but her capitalist instincts took over as soon as she left. Like me, her first property was funded by inheritance, but Zoe didn't stop there. Within two years of finishing her degree, Zoe had set up a property renovation business, and she now owns at least a dozen houses in Exeter and London. And there are plenty more that she buys, improves, and sells for an eye-watering profit. She spends her working week fine-tuning architect drawings, choosing different finishes, and courting prospective investors over swanky lunches. And that is not a world I want to hear about tonight.

I don't regret having Calum – far from it – but I'm not immune to the dreariness of the daily routines, especially at this time of year. Battling with the pram cover just to make the 500m journey to Sainsbury's Local. Pushing him on the swing with numb fingers. Not having a partner to take the pressure off every now and again. I'm not jealous of Zoe's lifestyle, but there are still times when I prefer to keep it at arm's length.

With nothing stronger than a twinge of guilt, I open the Thai takeaway app. Prawns in blankets and green curry, I decide. But I miss the correct tick box as the sound of the door buzzer makes me jump. I'm not expecting anyone, so it must be a delivery driver, but that's a pain because it means I need to go outside. I don't have a front door like traditional houses; there are sliding doors onto a small courtyard with a solid gate beyond that. I should be able to open it from inside the house, but the remote-control system broke a while ago – God, before I even had Calum – and I haven't got round to fixing it yet.

Rain is snaking down the glass, so I reach for the umbrella as the buzzer sounds again. 'Yes, all right, I'm coming,' I mutter. A rush of cold air hits me as I slide open the door and I tense my shoulders against it. Rain patters on the umbrella as I cross the courtyard. 'Hello?' I call out, suddenly wary in the dark night.

'Ivy!'

'Zoe?' A long-buried memory scratches at my temples and I feel an urge to back up, return to the warmth of my little home. The familiar Netflix logo glows at the edge of my vision through the glass doors.

'Let me in, please.' A sob escapes from Zoe's throat and I take a breath. *Work with what's in front of you.* I match up the two door latches and pull the gate open.

But I can't help taking a step backwards, because Zoe looks like she's come straight from the set of a horror movie. Her cheekbones are smudged with mascara and her hair hangs heavy either side of her face. She's not wearing a coat and in her thin, wet blouse, her body is more convulsing than shivering. 'Zoe?' I whisper hoarsely. 'What's wrong?'

'It's Tom,' she whispers, followed by a low moan. 'Ivy, he's dead.'

11

Chapter 3

Ivy

For a moment Zoe disappears, replaced by the memory of two policemen, and the invisible weight of Mum's hands on my shoulders. I waver, wonder if I might be sick. But I need to toughen up, remember that my friend is telling me she's lost her husband.

'Tom's dead?' I repeat. The idea is so surreal – a man with such vitality, who I've known almost as long as I've known Zoe, not alive anymore.

'He was skiing; he fell,' she whispers. Her head drops, her face disappearing into her upturned palms, and her voice becomes muffled. 'The weather came in, and he disappeared. The search and rescue team found his body.' I close my eyes, try to absorb the news.

There's been an accident, Mrs Hawkes. The storm came from nowhere, sixty-mile-an-hour wind gusts . . .

I don't know why Zoe has chosen me, but I need to move, to comfort her. She used to be my best friend, for Christ's sake. Like a robot, I drop the umbrella and reach out. She's cold and wet from the rain, and I force my arms to wrap around her. I feel stiff, but Zoe moulds her body into mine and we stand like that for a while, Zoe crying softly, me in silence.

Your husband was airlifted to Leeds General, Mrs Hawkes. But I'm afraid he was pronounced dead on arrival. I'm so sorry.

I screw my eyes closed, forage for an image of my son, drag it forward in my mind. I use the quiet drumbeat of rain against the stone walls to imagine the rise and fall of his chest as he sleeps. It works to a degree, just enough for me to remember where I am – London, not Yorkshire – and to realise that Zoe and I are both soaking wet. 'Let's go inside,' I whisper. 'You need to dry off.'

Zoe doesn't speak but she lets me lead her across the courtyard and in through the sliding doors. I find a large bath towel in the utility room and wrap it around her, then guide her to the sofa. My hands are shaking, and I wonder if she can tell.

'Can I get you something?' I ask. 'I don't have brandy or anything like that, but I could make you a cup of sweet tea. Or there's some of your cava open?' The insensitivity of my suggestion – sparkly bubbles to mourn a dead husband – thumps at my temples, but Zoe doesn't seem to notice. She's slumped on the sofa, staring through the glass doors, as though wondering if she preferred it out there, distracted by darkness and driving rain.

'I'm fine,' she murmurs eventually. It's a phrase people use to turn down hospitality, but tonight it sounds ridiculous, so far from the truth, and I feel a terrible urge to laugh.

I concentrate on breathing instead. In and out.

'Can I ask?' I whisper once I've collected myself. 'How it happened?'

She looks at me, startled. But before I get chance to panic, to ludicrously worry that I'd misheard her all along, her features slacken. 'I don't really know,' she says, her voice cracking. 'Julian wasn't making sense.'

'Julian?' Another name from my past.

'He was with Tom,' she whispers. 'On the ski run. They go on

13

a boys' ski trip every year, with Rob too. They're in Morzine this year. Do you know it?'

My skin fizzes. 'Rob and Julian?' I finally manage to ask. Two men I knew once but haven't seen for fifteen years.

'It's in France,' she continues, ignoring – or not hearing – my question. 'But near Switzerland. They were doing a final run when . . .' Her voice peters out and we sit in silence. I think about Calum and wish I could go and wake him up, draw comfort from his smell, his warm body. I'm so lost in my thoughts that I jump when Zoe starts talking again. 'Anyway, Julian said it was a white-out. Cloud so thick they couldn't see more than a metre or so ahead.'

'But surely that wouldn't faze Tom?' I bite my lip. It's not my place to say this. But I know what a good skier Tom is – a crowd of us went on a university ski trip to Andorra in the Easter of our second year – and it's hard to imagine that something as innocuous as visibility could kill him.

'They were in a neighbouring resort, Avoriaz.' Zoe sounds exhausted. 'And it was the first time they'd skied that run. They were really high up, Julian said. Swamped by cloud. They agreed to ski down, but lost sight of each other straight away. When they got to the bottom, Tom didn't appear, so they called the *pisteurs*.' Her voice trails off again and the tears flow more quickly. I look towards the staircase, wonder if Calum is okay, and blink away my own. I should go to Zoe really, hold her again. Comfort her.

'You know the fucking irony, though?' she suddenly spurts out, her voice louder and harder. My mouth is too dry for words to form, so I shake my head. I want to sip some liquid but there's only my half-drunk glass of cava in reach. 'It was a blue run,' she goes on. 'Not black, or off-piste. A simple fucking blue run. How can that be possible, Ivy?' Her voice cracks again and she drops her face into her open palms. She needs me, but my body is still refusing to move.

'How did Julian explain it?' I ask instead. Because she's right;

it doesn't make sense.

'He said that the white-out hid the piste markers. And that Tom must have veered off in the wrong direction and fallen.'

'Down a rock face?'

'The run curves around the mountain, apparently,' Zoe says. 'With a steep, craggy drop on one side.' She lets out a low moan, like a wounded animal, and crosses her arms at her midriff. 'There are barriers, Julian said, but Tom must have slipped through one of the tiny gaps.'

Slipped through a tiny gap. A thousand-to-one chance. Like the slab of rock that came loose in the punishing rain and fell on to my dad's head as he belayed his climbing partner.

Work with what's in front of you.

I draw courage from my dad's memory, then push off the sofa and sit down next to Zoe. I put my still-shaking arm around her shoulder, and draw her into my chest. Yes, our second chance at friendship is still new, but she needs me now.

'The police need me to go out there,' Zoe says in a quiet voice. 'So that I can bring Tom home.' She pauses. 'But I can't do it on my own.'

Chapter 4

Ivy

Realisation creeps in. Zoe wants me to go to France with her. My heart slows and my arm seems to work independently, rejecting Zoe, pulling away from her shoulder and folding over my midriff. 'Can your mum go with you?' I ask. 'Or Rebecca?'

'Bitter and twisted mother or goody-two-shoes older sister; is that the choice you're offering me?'

'What about Luke?' I ask. 'Is he back from travelling yet?'

'He's still in South America,' Zoe says, shaking her head. 'He doesn't even know yet. God, he'll be devastated when he hears. He adored Tom.' She turns towards me but instinctively I shuffle away. 'Ivy, it has to be you,' she pleads.

'Why though?' I can't help spurting out. 'We've hardly seen each other in fifteen years.' God, I sound callous. The woman has just lost her husband. But I can't accompany her to France to reclaim him. It's too intimate, too awful.

'Because you're one of us,' she pleads. 'You knew Tom in the beginning; you were there when we first got together. And you know the others too. Please, Ivy.'

I first met Tom at the MedSoc Christmas Ball in my second year of university after Zoe persuaded me to buy a ticket. She'd been secretly pursuing him for months by then, certain that he was the only man for her. And it turned out her instincts were good because they got together that night, and quickly became the perfect couple. I heard that their wedding was on Zoe's twenty-third birthday, which seemed a strange date to choose, given what had happened two years earlier.

I look back towards the stairs. 'I'm sorry, I can't.'

'Bring Calum too,' Zoe says, reading my mind even in her distressed state. 'He'll be the perfect distraction for me.'

I shake my head, relieved when I suddenly realise that I really can't go. 'Calum doesn't have a passport. It's on my to-do list, but that's as far as I've got.' I remember now, moaning to Zoe about it on one of her visits, my ever-growing list of chores. I want her to remember too, but maybe that's too much to expect.

'Oh God.' Zoe drops her head back into her hands. 'I'm scared, Ivy; I can't do it without you.'

On the day my dad died, Mrs Berry was drafted in to look after me, and Mum left with the two policemen. She didn't cry, or even hesitate on her way to their car. She didn't ask anyone to help her through her grief. But then Mum had a nervous breakdown six months later and has never really recovered, so her way doesn't have much to recommend itself. 'There must be someone else who can go with you,' I plead. 'You've got lots of friends.'

'No, there's only you,' Zoe says vehemently. 'Only you who knows me back to front, and what I've already been through. Please Ivy.'

Conflicting feelings flare inside me. Guilt. Fear. Duty. 'I want to come,' I lie. 'But how can I? There's no one to look after Calum.'

'What about your mum?' she asks desperately.

I wish I could ask my mum to help with Calum. But I know that the responsibility of caring for her grandson would be too much for her. I shake my head. 'She's too fragile. Always scared of some invisible threat. You know that. There's no way she'd agree to come.'

'It'll only be for a few days,' Zoe pleads. 'How about I talk to her? She knows what it's like to lose a husband suddenly; if I ask her, explain how much you being there means to me, maybe that will be enough to persuade her?' Peter did this to Zoe, I think. Making her believe that if she pushed hard enough, she'd get her own way. He may have left the family home when Zoe was 11, but his influence remained.

'No,' I say, too loudly, too quickly. I watch her face collapse with disappointment and my resolve instantly starts to slip. I assume that Mum wouldn't agree to help with Calum, but is that fair? Because Zoe's right – Mum would understand her grief more than most. 'Look, maybe I could call her,' I hear myself say. Am I really doing this? 'Talk it through. But if she's the slightest bit uncomfortable, I'm not pushing it, okay?' Zoe nods meekly, and we both turn to look at my phone, still resting on the sofa arm from my aborted attempt to order a takeaway. It feels like ages ago now, my hunger long since gone. I sigh and pick it up. 'I'll call her from my bedroom,' I say, suddenly wishing my downstairs space wasn't so open plan. 'I won't be long.'

'Thank you, Ivy. I know it will be hard, leaving Calum; I appreciate it.'

I hesitate for a moment, contemplate reminding Zoe that I haven't said yes yet. But instead, I just nod and walk quietly up the stairs.

'Mum?' I push the phone against my ear and drop down onto my bed. There's a picture on my bedside table and I stare at it. Calum and me. Do I stay for him? Or, if he was older, if he could talk, would he tell me to go?

'Hi, love, is everything okay? It's not like you to call this late.'

It's only nine o'clock, but I don't say this. And she's right in a way; I rarely call her in the evening when my patience has been worn away by a day of childcare. 'Calum and I are fine,' I start, cutting the energy supply to her anxiety. 'But I do have some bad news.'

'Oh?' Even in that one syllable, I can hear a tremor. My mum is always expecting disaster, but never ready for it.

'You know my friend Zoe?'

'Of course,' she says. 'What's happened?' A year ago, she might not have even recognised the name, but that's changed over the last few months. When Zoe first came to see me, and met 3-month-old Calum, she asked after Linda, and how I was coping with supporting her now that I had a new responsibility. Zoe has always known that Mum needs looking after, and could guess that I didn't have the time, or headspace, for it with a young baby in tow. When I admitted that I was struggling, she offered to help, and Mum has been touched by the attention Zoe has bestowed on her ever since.

'It's Tom, her husband.'

'Oh no,' she says, her voice lowering. 'I've never met him, but I've seen him in photos.' It reminds me that she came close to meeting Tom once. Sixteen years ago. When Zoe decided to make a surprise visit after a holiday in Scotland, with Tom, Peter and her brother Luke in tow. It could have been disastrous – them turning up unannounced, with my mum the way she is – but it wasn't. I managed to keep the men away, and Zoe seemed to know instinctively how to lighten Mum's mood. As the memories form, I feel fresh tears in my eyes. I can't believe Tom's dead. Or that Zoe is a widow at 35, the same age my mum was. Perhaps I do owe her. Maybe I've owed her since I walked out of her twenty-first birthday party and never looked back.

'Mum, I need a favour,' I say, in a more determined tone than she's used to. 'And you know I wouldn't ask if it wasn't important.' I push to standing, pick another photo of Calum off my chest of drawers, this one of him on his own, and say a silent prayer that he'll be safe. 'I appreciate that this will be hard for you, but I really need you to come and look after Calum for me.'

Chapter 5

2006

Ivy

'Right, feel a bit more awake now, lad?'

I can't help smiling as a boy wearing a Nickelback T-shirt further along the front row lurches back in his seat, eyes wide with shock, and wipes the droplets of water from his face. At least his gaunt skin has got some colour now, but the stale scent of last night's alcohol still gives him away. 'Sorry, sir,' he blusters, trying to work out whether it's appropriate for a lecturer to be flicking students with water from a half-drunk glass in 2006. 'I was studying late last night, must have dropped off.'

'Sure you were,' comes firing back. 'And it's Peter, not sir, remember?' The lecturer then looks up into the tiered crowd of students, his audience, and rolls his twinkling eyes. 'But that small interlude of dynamic precipitation does provide the perfect segue to our next topic: storms.'

My chest puffs out like a mating pigeon and my hand flies up, like I've been waiting for this moment since I was 9. Which I have. Although I'm glad I'm sat at the end of the row, and out of water-flicking range.

'Yes?' he asks, with only the smallest hint of irritation.

'Sorry to interrupt, um, Peter, but I didn't think storm was an official meteorological term?' I'm only pretending to be unsure; I actually know this for a fact. I've been reading books about the weather since I was 9 too.

'Ah, felled at the first hurdle,' he says, but with a smile that suggests otherwise. 'You're absolutely right. The word "storm" doesn't have an official definition in the meteorological handbook, largely because it is used too broadly for one to be of any value, but it is still a key area of meteorological study. Why do you think that is?' He's still looking at me, I realise. I swallow hard. Less confident now.

'Because storms are major weather systems?' I suggest.

'Yes and no. Storms are violent atmospheric disturbances, and so they introduce extreme weather conditions – whether that's rain, snow, high winds or most often a combination – but the reason it's so important to study them is because they can cause damage – to property, the environment, and to life. We need to be able to predict them in advance, and that means understanding the warning signs. Now how do we do that? Someone else?' He looks up to search the crowd, while I shift my gaze downwards. If my dad knew a thunderstorm was coming, he might have decided to climb Gordale Scar anyway. But it is more likely that he'd have heeded the warning and packed his gear away. But he wasn't given that choice. The afternoon forecast was for settled weather, with storms not due until later that night. Dad had no understanding that the towering clouds above him were cumulonimbus, or that they can hold as much energy as ten Hiroshima-sized atom bombs.

'Storms are caused by low pressure systems,' a voice responds from the back of the room.

'Excellent,' Peter says. 'Go on.'

'Well . . .' But the voice peters out and silence hangs in the air for a moment until someone fills it by sneezing. I try to push my lips together, to let someone else take the glory, but it's no good. Peter Wilde is the reason I came to Exeter University, his research into extreme weather conditions my bedtime reading for years, and I can't give up the opportunity to impress him now. I raise my arm again. He looks at me, one eyebrow raised, and I take that as my cue.

'In the British Isles,' I start. 'Low pressure systems are usually dictated by the jet stream. The bigger the temperature differential between the polar air from the north and the tropical air from the south, the stronger the jet stream, and the more intense the low-pressure system. The pressure gradient causes high winds, and the clashing between the different air masses causes heavy rain.'

'Textbook answer!' he calls out.

'Thank you,' I murmur with more than a hint of pride, feeling my cheeks flush as everyone in the lecture hall turns to stare.

'No, I mean you've read that in a textbook,' he clarifies. 'It's the bones, without the flesh; the bare facts without the story. There are so many other elements at play, terrain type, micro-climates, previous weather patterns.' He looks at my deflated expression and softens his features. 'But it's still the best response I've heard from an undergraduate in a while, so congratulations.' He winks at me – actually winks – and then turns to face the large screen on the wall behind him. He picks up a clicker, and a second later a PowerPoint slide showing an angry anvil-shaped cloud appears. I pick up my pen, and with my face still smarting, start to take some notes.

Half an hour later, Peter draws the lecture to a close and dismisses us. But as I step out of the front row, he beckons me over. 'Have you got a second?' he says, still smiling. I notice that one of his incisors is chipped and imagine him pulling off a beer bottle cap with his teeth.

'Well, you're a ray of sunshine, if you'll excuse the pun,' Peter says, walking back towards his lectern and gesturing for me to join him. 'I teach the master's here in Applied Meteorology and I expect that kind of knowledge from those students, but Environmental Science undergrads tend to be more interested in saving the planet than forecasting the weather.'

I feel awkward, it just being the two of us, but that's stupid. I chose this module – the changing climate of the British Isles – because he teaches it, so it would be crazy to miss out on a one-to-one conversation. 'I'm hoping to do the master's after my degree,' I explain, adding shyly, 'I've wanted to be a meteorologist since I was little.'

'Really?' He sounds surprised. 'Personally, I didn't have such a calling. For me it was joining the Navy when I was 18; I became obsessed by the weather out at sea. I qualified as a specialist officer in meteorology while I was there, and then started teaching once I left. Between you and me, I still prefer the research trips that I go on outside of term time, but teaching has its plus sides too. Like meeting future meteorologists.' He pauses for a moment, assessing me. 'So what inspired you? It's a pretty niche profession.'

'Um, well . . .' I don't want to tell him the truth. That my dad died because he didn't understand weather patterns, and so I owe it to him to learn. And that while other people are scared of spiders, or mice, I'm scared of menacing clouds and squally winds. And understanding them feels like the best way to overcome that fear.

'Fancy yourself as the next Carol Kirkwood, maybe? Is that it?' A small laugh drifts out of his nose, and I don't know how to respond. I want to pull him up on his chauvinism, deliver a smart comment, but I'm actually just struggling to breathe normally. I was a confident child, spurred on by two parents who believed anything was possible. But it was hard to keep that going after my dad died and my mum withdrew into herself. It wasn't so obvious before I left home – village life, familiar routines – but being at university has made me realise how underprepared for life I am.

Luckily, I'm saved from my internal battle by the door swinging open. We both turn to look as a girl about my age with long blonde hair swept over one shoulder walks inside.

'Zoe?' Peter says. 'What are you doing here?'

'I came for your lecture,' she says, frowning. 'Am I too late?'

'About an hour, but don't worry. You wouldn't have understood a word. And aren't you coming for supper tonight anyway?'

I look from one to the other, take in Peter's sparkly blue eyes, and see them superimposed on the girl's face. Embarrassingly, I feel a gasp form in my throat. I have read so many of Peter Wilde's books that I feel I know him personally. But I've never actually thought about him having a family. I swallow the gasp and manage to mumble 'hello'.

'Oops, sorry,' Peter says. 'This is my daughter – Zoe. She's a second-year student here at Exeter too, which we're eternally grateful for after the shenanigans she got up to at school. She's in the arts though, so perhaps that explains it,' he adds, with a wink in her direction. 'And I've realised I don't know your name?'

'Ivy,' I say, turning from Peter to Zoe. 'Nice to meet you.'

'Ivy? That's a cool name,' she says.

'My parents were climbers,' I whisper as a way of explanation.

'Even cooler.' Zoe leans against the lectern and guides her iron-straight hair behind her ears. She tilts her head and looks at me quizzically, as though she's never seen hair as unruly, or a face so free of make-up, as mine. 'What are you studying?'

'Environmental science,' Peter interjects before I get chance to answer. 'But Ivy wants to do my master's course after, don't you? None of this liberal arts rubbish.'

A flash of hurt darkens Zoe's face for a split second and then it's gone. She smiles and rolls her eyes. 'Oh, you're jealous,' she says. 'You'd love to spend your tutorials discussing the scourge of the media, or street culture in London.'

'Is that what you learn about?' I ask.

'I don't know.' She shrugs. 'Maybe.'

'Zoe doesn't consider lectures compulsory,' Peter explains. 'Like she thinks getting expelled from the exceptionally average Swindon Comprehensive school was a teenage rite of passage.'

'I was expressing my right to free speech,' she says primly.

'You spray-painted *Mr Mullins is a fucking psychopath* on the music building wall. A man you hardly knew, I might add.'

Zoe snorts, followed by a giggle. 'And I was very grateful that you saw the funny side of it, unlike Mum,' she adds, giving Peter a beaming smile. He shakes his head in mock exasperation, but it's obvious that he adores her. I can't help feeling a pang of envy, and wonder if my dad ever looked at me like that.

'Well, I suppose I'll be off then,' Zoe continues. 'As it looks like I've missed the main event. See you tonight, Dad.' Then she turns to me. 'It was nice to meet you, climbing Ivy.'

I only met Zoe two minutes ago, but I find that I don't want her to leave. I'm not sure if it's because she's the great Peter Wilde's daughter, or just that her energy is infectious, but suddenly I want to get to know her better. 'Do you fancy a coffee?' I blurt out.

'Sorry?' Zoe's brow crinkles in confusion.

I try not to think about how weird I sound. 'I, um, I have some free coffee vouchers,' I improvise. 'But I've realised they expire today. It's only if you're at loose end, but I'd hate them to go to waste.'

'So your shout, you mean?' She's still suspicious, but seems to be warming to the idea.

'Yes, definitely. Whatever you like.'

She hesitates for a moment, and my face reddens as I feel her eyes drill into me, then soften. She thinks I'm lonely, I realise. So desperate for a friend that I invite a complete stranger for a coffee. Perhaps there's some truth to her assumption too. I've blamed my lack of friendships so far at university on being too busy with my studies, too engrossed in my coursework, but I sometimes wonder which came first.

'I'd love a coffee,' she finally says. 'But can I pick the café?'

'Be warned, she'll choose one in the Arts department,' Peter offers.

'You're wrong, actually. I like Cross Keys,' Zoe says breezily.

Peter furrows his brow. 'On the St Luke's campus? That's miles away.'

'One mile,' Zoe corrects. Then she winks at me – like father, like daughter – and leans in. 'It's where the medical students hang out,' she says conspiratorially. 'And we all know that the best-looking men are doctors.'

Chapter 6

Zoe

Zoe turns off the engine, leans back against the headrest, and stares through the rain-splattered windscreen at her own front door. She's not sure she's got the strength to walk inside. Knowing it will be empty, and that Tom is never coming back.

Does that make her a coward? Masquerading as a successful independent woman rather than being the real deal? It used to be genuine – as a student she had more balls than most of the boys – but there's been a gradual decline as life has thrown a succession of hand grenades in her direction.

She had wondered whether Ivy might invite her to stay over, offer to sleep on Calum's bedroom floor, and give Zoe her bed. But her old friend seemed desperate to get rid of her once she returned from calling her mum. Perhaps Zoe can't blame her for that. Their second attempt at friendship is still in its infancy, as well as being loaded with unspoken truths.

After finishing university, the trauma of what happened at her twenty-first birthday party was still so raw that Zoe refused to apologise for the way she spoke to Ivy, even though Tom begged her to. Then their paths drifted, and they didn't see each other at all for years. Zoe guessed that Ivy would be at the opening of the laboratory named in memory of her dad; it made sense that his former student and Exeter University golden child would be invited, so she was prepared for it. Encouraged by Tom, she made the effort to talk to her old friend at the event, and gradually she relaxed. They relaxed. And soon they were chatting like the friends they used to be. It hasn't all been plain sailing since then, but now that Tom has died, she really needs Ivy by her side.

And she is very grateful that Ivy has agreed to travel to France, because it has to be Ivy that goes with her, even if it took a little white lie to persuade her. She and Tom were a couple for so long – almost all of their adult lives – and she can't imagine functioning, surviving, without him. Ivy is one of the few people who knew Zoe before they got together – who will remember the sassy arts student, the girl who wore her rebellious streak with pride, and revelled in her ability to not give two fucks. Ivy is the best reminder that a future without Tom is possible once she's worked through her grief.

A task that, at only 35 years old, she can't believe she's having to carry out for a second time.

Her father was her hero and, when he died suddenly, Zoe couldn't imagine experiencing a pain more disabling, a sense of loss more acute. But here she is, less than fifteen years later, mourning her husband in equally shocking circumstances, perhaps more so. Some might think she's cursed, or that she somehow must be to blame for so much misfortune, but of course she knows that's nonsense. This wasn't fate, or bad luck, or the devil's work. This is because she's drawn to men who like to take risks.

And no one knows how that can lead to tragedy better than Ivy.

She thinks back to when Ivy opened her front gate, the distress that radiated off her. Was she remembering her own father's death? It was a quarter of a century ago, but memories that terrible don't fade with time. A swelling of emotion billows inside Zoe's chest and she feels an urge to drive back there. To see Ivy again. But she mustn't. And not only because Ivy clearly doesn't want her there.

She can't bear to express the words, even silently in her head, but her hands drop down to her lower abdomen. She runs her fingers across the silk of her untucked blouse, from the hard curve of her hipbones to the softer flesh of her pelvis. It's enough for her eyes to sting again, for the blinking to prove inadequate in stemming the tears. Does she even want to be pregnant now? Only a few hours ago she was gently fizzing with anticipation, feeling ready, wondering whether it was worth doing a test or still too early. How quickly things can change. She thinks about Ivy, bringing Calum up alone. Pretending she loves the sacrifice of motherhood when any sane person can see how hard it is. Is that what's in store for her now too?

Her house is halfway along a quiet residential road behind Bishop's Park, and except on the days when Fulham F.C. are playing at home, there's very little foot traffic. So when Luke turns into their road, Zoe spots him straight away. Her little brother – 28 years old but still not comfortable in his own skin. There are seven years between them – Luke was the glue that was supposed to seal her parents' marriage back together – and Zoe has often felt more like his mother than his sister.

He had originally planned to go to South America for six months, a trip financed by Zoe that would take him from Mexico to Argentina. But in the end, he only made it as far as Cuba before deciding he wanted to come home. Maybe she should have told Ivy that he was back when her friend asked earlier, but that would have meant explaining why she didn't want Luke to go to France with her. How she can love her brother profoundly, and yet still know his qualities are not in holding her up.

And now she needs to tell her emotional, loyal little brother that Tom is dead. She watches him stub his cigarette on the brick wall, slip his key into their front door, and walk inside the house. She'll give him a few minutes, she decides. A chance to take off his trainers, pour himself a large glass of milk – a nightly ritual, even if he's been in the pub all evening – and settle in front of their enormous TV once he realises the house is empty.

She pictures him now – oblivious to how his life is about to take a harsh turn – and the image pulls at her insides, which in turn, makes her wonder again if there is a baby growing inside there. And if there is, whether he or she will grow up emulating Zoe as intensely as Luke does. When their parents split up, and Peter left, their elder sister Rebecca became a carbon copy of their mum: sensible, reliable, honest, but also risk-averse, and suspicious of anything that could be described as fun. Zoe was the opposite, rebelling against them, clinging desperately to the traits that her father represented. And Luke sat in the middle, wanting to be like Zoe, but lacking her talent to throw the cat amongst the pigeons.

Zoe sighs, closes her eyes, but she can't put this off forever. She climbs out of the car and slips inside the house. 'Luke?' she calls out.

'In here!' She guessed right; he's in the media room (which sounds fancier than it is; they just don't have the need for a playroom yet). She takes a deep breath and pushes on the door. He looks at her, his eyes wide and expression open, like a blank page waiting for her to speak. And yet there is something fearful, guarded, about his face too. Like he already knows she has something significant to say. 'Is everything okay?'

'It's Tom,' she starts.

'Has he fallen? Broken something?'

On her father's insistence, Zoe has skied every year since she was 5. At first it was a family ski holiday, and then it became the only guaranteed week she spent with him after he left. Tom has also skied since childhood, so it was easy for the habit to continue once Peter wasn't around to take her. But in all those years, Zoe has never allowed herself to lose the final frisson of fear, the recognition that she can never match the majestic might of a mountain range. She's certain that it's what keeps her safe, and also that Tom banished the fear a long time ago. 'It's worse than that,' she whispers.

Luke's lip trembles. 'What could be worse?'

Chapter 7

Ivy

I stare out of the small porthole window. I usually love the view from this height, observing the cloud cover below from the radiance of bright blue skies. From habit, I note that the clouds are *altocumulus stratiformis* today, a mid-level cloud that won't do anyone any harm. Not like the clouds that blinded Tom yesterday, most probably *nimbostratus*, dense and uncompromising. I turn away from the window, and the images it conjures up, and look at Zoe instead.

She's flicking through the in-flight magazine, but her fingers are shaking, and her eyes aren't tracking the words. She's been like this since she arrived at my house this morning. Pretending to be fine while leaking fragility. I couldn't deal with it then; I was too taken up with the loss I felt handing Calum over to my mum, who'd left Yorkshire at 5 a.m. to get to my house on time. Not a sad sense of missing him, but raw, physical loss. I might not have felt it quite as keenly if Mum hadn't look so terrified as she forced a smile and waved goodbye from the window, Calum tucked tightly against her side. But I couldn't expect her to exude confidence. I need to be grateful for her stepping up at all.

I look at my watch, calculate that I've been away from Calum for four hours. Not even half a day. Zoe didn't book us return flights – she said that was too much to get her head around – but we're going to be away for a few days at least. Does the pain of separation ease up over time? Or become more acute? I really hope it's the former, because I can't deal with anything worse than this. I look back at Zoe. My role on this trip is to support her; if I concentrate solely on that, maybe I can get through it. I take the magazine from her hand and slip my fingers between hers. She tenses for a moment, then shifts to rest her head on my shoulder.

'Why is this happening to me?' she murmurs, tears bubbling at the back of her throat. 'Why is it my husband lying in a French morgue?' She lifts her head up, twists in her seat to face me. 'Why didn't his friends look after him? If it was so difficult to see, shouldn't they have stuck together, kept him safe?'

I don't say anything, but her comments, her instinct to blame someone else, make me feel uneasy. Because I was Zoe's scapegoat when Peter died, on the receiving end of her vicious tongue. After she accused me of killing him in front of all the party guests, I knew our friendship was over. I'd finished my exams by then, so I changed my master's degree from Exeter University to Birmingham and resolved to never see her again. Listening to her edge the blame for Tom's accident towards Julian and Rob, I can't help wondering if I should have stuck to that promise.

'Why aren't you saying anything?' she pushes. 'Talk to me, please.'

But I'm here now, and I need to manage this. 'It isn't fair,' I start. 'You're right. But be careful what you say in front of the others. The three of them have been through so much together; for Rob and Julian, it must feel like they've lost a brother.'

Zoe sighs, looks down at her lap, chastened, at least for now. 'I know, you're right,' she mumbles. 'I think I'm scared. What if the police want to talk to me? My French is terrible; I won't understand what they're saying.' She looks up, tears glistening. 'And what if they won't release Tom's body? I need to bring him home.'

Tom's body. The flash of an imagined image sucker-punches me. I hold my breath for a moment, will myself to stay in control, then exhale slowly. 'It's going to be okay,' I say, trying to sound soothing. 'Tom died on their watch, remember? It's the police and mountain officials who should be answering your questions, not posing their own.'

'I don't want to be the difficult widow,' Zoe whispers. 'Mountains are dangerous places – accidents happen; I do know that.'

'That's true, but you're entitled to ask. It is strange after all,' I add. 'A skier as skilful as Tom dropping off a cliff.'

'What are you saying?' Zoe asks, her voice guarded.

I silently berate myself. The last thing she needs is me questioning the account she's been given. 'Nothing, nothing at all,' I say, back-pedalling. But her questioning stare shows I'm not off the hook. 'It's just hard to make sense of what happened without any witnesses,' I try. 'At least when my dad died, there were other climbers there, people to explain how he managed to fall from such a stable ledge.'

'But what other explanation could there be for Tom's fall?' Zoe's eyes continue to drill into me. God, what have I started? I scrunch my eyes closed, then pop them back open.

'Ignore me,' I say. 'I'm really tired and talking nonsense. Tom's death was clearly a terrible accident. And caused by bad weather, same as my dad's,' I add.

Zoe gives me a last look of suspicion, then relaxes her face. 'You do look tired,' she eventually says. 'Did you not sleep well last night?'

'Not really,' I admit. 'I think I was worried about leaving Calum.' I don't give Zoe the fuller explanation. That every time I closed my eyes, I found myself skiing towards a cliff edge, Calum in

34

my arms, going too fast, unable to stop. And that the only way to escape was to snap them back open and wait until my heart rate receded.

'Your mum will take good care of him,' Zoe says.

'I hope so,' I murmur. Zoe knows that my mum suffers from anxiety, and needs reassurance over everyday decisions, but not how crippling it can be when she's tested. I could never bring myself to confide in Zoe fully at university – I was too ashamed, I suppose – and I suspect my mum will have shown her best side during their more recent phone conversations too. 'I guess it's just been Calum and me for so long. It feels strange to be this far away from him.'

'It might do you both some good,' she observes. 'For him to be less dependent on you.'

I bite the inside of my cheek in silent protest. Zoe still doesn't get it. All she sees is the hard work, the sacrifices I make as a single mum. She doesn't know about the love part. 'Calum's a baby,' I say. 'He's supposed to be dependent on me.'

'And his father,' she counters. 'If he was involved, that is.'

I draw back, switch my stare towards the tiny window again. There's a break in the cloud cover and I can see the undulating waves of the English Channel below me. I should let Zoe's comment go. This is the first time she's ever hinted her disapproval of my family setup, and she's hurting at the moment. But I've sacrificed a lot to be here, and there's only so much I can take.

'Listen, I am very aware of what – or who – Calum is missing,' I start, focusing on the aeroplane wing, trying to draw something from its solidity. 'But he benefits in other ways. Like having me for his mother; I'll always be there for him.'

'I still don't really understand why you chose to have him,' she murmurs. 'I mean, Calum is gorgeous of course,' she adds, as though belatedly realising how callous she sounds. 'But when you first found out . . . did you not consider other options then?'

I shrug, try to keep it simple. 'I've always wanted to be a mum. And there was a child growing inside me.'

'But you weren't even 35; there was still plenty of time to have a family the traditional way. You know, meet someone, fall in love, get married maybe. Not drink too much cheap wine at a geeky conference in Finland and shag a weatherman from Canada.'

I still remember giving Zoe my account of how I came to be a mother when she turned up on my doorstep. There was no truth to my story, but it was an easy enough lie to tell; I'd been pedalling it for almost a year by then. The international conference in Helsinki, the free, well-stocked bar and Robert Pattinson lookalike from Vancouver. I'd wondered for a moment if she'd be the one to see through my lies – they say that friendships made at university create a special kind of bond – but she didn't question it, perhaps because she was too shocked that I'd chosen to go through with the pregnancy at all.

'It's all right for you,' I say quietly, still not daring to look in her direction. 'You don't want children.'

'How do you know?' she counters. 'Tom and I might have been trying to get pregnant for years.'

I flick my head around in surprise. When we were at university, Zoe would talk about having six kids, but she also said that she and Tom would live in a Scottish castle and learn the bagpipes. Since we've been back in touch, Zoe has shown no interest in Calum, and if I venture onto the subject, she claims she doesn't have time for kids, that her property empire is her true baby.

But now the chance for a family with Tom has gone, I realise. The seatbelt light flicks on above me and the plane takes a sudden dip. A voice crackles through the overhead speaker. *Ten minutes to landing.* 'And were you?' I ask as gently as I can.

But doesn't answer me. She looks down at her lap, slots the two sides of her belt buckle together, and pulls on the black tail. Then as the plane dips lower and we pass through the cloud, she adjusts her gaze to the window. I follow her lead. We stare into nothing, both of us surely imagining the same thing. Then we're below it, seeing snow-covered mountains in the distance and the vast Lake Geneva underneath us. The wheels drop with a droning sound, and we bump onto the runway. Finally, she turns to me.

'We weren't,' she says tightly. 'And now of course, we can't.'

Chapter 8

Ivy

We glide silently past digital posters of handsome men in sparkling Swiss watches, then both forget to speak French to the austere immigration official behind the Perspex glass booth as he gestures for our passports. We only have cabin cases – no bulky ski gear needed for this trip – so we bypass the baggage reclaim area with its piles of ski and snowboard bags and head for the *Nothing to Declare* exit lane.

As we wander past the line of tables, ignored by the smattering of staff on duty, I wonder how different it will be on our journey home. Will Tom fly with us? Or are there special flights for coffins? I picture him being dropped into an aeroplane hold by indifferent baggage handlers, lying alongside cargo boxes in the icy cold air. My face starts to crack at the thought. But I don't want Zoe to see me like this, so I turn my head. Tom was my friend too, but grieving for him feels wrong in front of her.

The arrivals hall is busy. Condensation drips down the bank of windows as dozens of transfer drivers in North Face puffer jackets and Oakley sunglasses hold up signs with bright company logos.

AlpyBus. PowderCab. Skiidy Gonzales. Ready to deliver their passengers to different ski resorts within a two-hour radius of the airport. Apparently someone called Nina is picking us up, so we wheel our cabin bags slowly past the throng of holidaymakers, our dark expressions out of kilter with their excited ones, and scour the landscape for any possible candidates.

'Excuse me?' A hand touches Zoe gently on the shoulder. 'Are you Mrs Metcalfe?' The woman speaking has cropped brown hair and wears the regulation puffer jacket, hers in a cobalt blue colour. She has no make-up on, but her face is tanned and her ears shimmer with a curved line of studs and hoops. I take in the rest of her, the vivid green eyes, the bulge of thigh muscles beneath skinny jeans. She has a word tattooed on her wrist, but it's impossible to read it beneath her jacket and I find myself intrigued to know what it says.

'Yes, I'm Tom's wife,' Zoe mumbles. 'Are you, um . . .' Zoe shakes her head, trying to dislodge the name.

'I'm Nina,' the woman says, helping her out. 'I run Tall Mountain with my business partner. Tom was staying in one of our chalets. I'm so sorry for your loss.' Her voice catches and she coughs. There are tears forming, I realise. The unnecessary level of emotion feels awkward, and I look away, but a moment later she recovers her demeanour and gives Zoe a watery smile. 'God, sorry,' she says. 'I just can't believe what's happened. This is Tall Mountain's first season, but I've been working winters in Morzine for years, and I've never had to deal with anything like this.' Her face tightens and she looks down at the floor. Zoe doesn't speak, but she stares at Nina like she's observing a rare animal in the wild. I need to cut in, move the conversation along.

'It must be hard for you,' I say, which is bullshit really, because Nina didn't even know Tom. 'But Zoe doesn't blame Tall Mountain. Accidents happen,' I add, although the explanation sticks in my throat again.

'Thank you, that's very kind,' she says. There's a hint of relief in her tone, and I wonder if this is all an act, an insurance policy in case we want to hold her company accountable for his fall. 'And look at me, making it all about us,' she continues. 'You both must be exhausted.' She gestures towards the lift. 'Shall we go? The car park isn't far but it's up a couple of floors.'

The instruction seems to reboot Zoe and she smiles and nods. 'Yes, thank you for picking us up. This is Ivy, by the way. An old friend from university; she knew Tom too.'

I nod my head in belated greeting. 'Nice to meet you,' I say on autopilot.

Nina pushes a path through the crowd of skiers, and a few minutes later we're all climbing aboard her minibus with its blue and grey Tall Mountain logo liveried on the side. The front seat takes three people, and we sit in a line, me nestled between them both. 'It's about an hour fifteen to Morzine,' Nina explains. 'The last half an hour winds up the mountain, so let me know if you feel sick at any point.'

Zoe first skied when she was in primary school. I was a late starter in comparison, but I've still racked up about ten weeks and a couple of long weekends since my inaugural trip to Andorra at university, so mountain roads don't faze either of us. 'We'll be fine,' I say. 'We have plenty of experience on roads like these. But thanks for checking.'

'Oh, you've been to Morzine before then?' Nina asks, misunderstanding my comment. Before I get chance to say no, that's not what I meant, Zoe touches my arm.

'You've been to this resort?' she asks, her forehead crinkling in confusion. 'Why didn't you say anything last night?'

'No, no, I haven't,' I say quickly, shaking my head and smiling broadly, as if to distract her from how my heart rate has ticked up under her scrutiny. 'All mountain roads wind, don't they? That's what I meant.'

As Zoe settles back against the seat, I focus on the view through the windscreen. We pass through a small town called Taninges and then start driving up the mountain, a zigzag of steep straights and tight bends. As we climb, the snow cover at the side of the road increases, and I stare in wonder at the thick icicles hanging down from rocks, waterfalls frozen until spring arrives. Tom will have made the same journey with his friends three days ago, no doubt itching to get to Morzine and clip into a pair of skis. If I could remove myself from the intense sadness of it all, there's something romantic about Tom dying doing the sport he loves most in the world. But I can't.

The tree branches are all blanketed by an inch or so of snow. They never stay like that for long, so it must have fallen recently. 'Was it snowing yesterday afternoon?' I ask. 'When Tom fell?' I feel Zoe shift in the seat beside me, and I wonder whether I shouldn't have brought the accident up. Maybe it's not my place to initiate conversation this trip. But it's too late now. And details have always been important to me.

Nina shrugs slightly. 'It started around then, I think. I remember that we had blue skies in the morning, then the winds picked up around lunchtime, and a storm came in at some point after that. I was in the office most of the day so wasn't paying much attention, and anyway, weather is so localised in the mountains that what was happening where Tom and his friends were skiing in Avoriaz could have been completely different to the weather I was getting in town. I do know that it was coming down heavily when mountain rescue started their search though. That's why it took them a while to locate Tom. Not that it would have made any difference,' she adds quickly. 'There's no way he would have survived the fall.'

I lean back against the headrest and wonder what it felt like. Every skier has imagined it, veering towards the edge of a piste, losing control, sliding over, then hurtling towards certain death. Like in my dream last night. But most people have the chance to stop it before impact, to wake up or switch off their imagination. How did Tom feel in those last few moments? Was he scared?

Angry with himself for making such a devastating mistake? Was he even conscious when he fell? There are so many questions that we'll never get answers to.

I think about my own dad. How his death was explained in excruciating detail at the inquest by the two climbers who survived the double tragedy. It was so clear in their minds, they said. Like film on constant replay. A storm had whipped up from nowhere, first gusting wind, then driving rain with thunder and lightning. One of them, the one who radiated arrogance from the witness box, had wanted to continue climbing anyway, but he was outvoted by the others, and they started to head back. My dad was belaying his partner's abseil down the rock face when the torrential rain dislodged a large slab of rock above him. My dad wasn't wearing a helmet (none of them were, none of them ever did back then) and it struck him cleanly. And his partner's death was collateral damage.

Zoe shifts in her seat again, but this time it's more of a lurch and I instinctively turn towards her.

'Stop the van!' she cries out suddenly, her scream reverberating around the enclosed cabin. I freeze with the shock of it, but Nina reacts immediately, swerving into a passing spot and braking hard. Then Zoe flings the door open and launches out of the van.

And I look on in surprise as she vomits all over the frozen mud.

Chapter 9

Two days before the fall

Tom

Tom leans forward, rests his forearms over the front seat. 'You look a bit green there, mate. Are you okay?'

'Oh God, I hate this bit.' Julian moans, rubbing his stomach and pushing a button on the passenger door. A jet of cold air rushes into the minibus as the window slides down. 'Give me the aftermath of drinking a vat of red wine over this misery any day.' He turns to the driver, a kid called Nico with a chequerboard buzz cut who frankly looks too young to be driving them anywhere. 'No offence.'

'None taken, mate,' Nico responds in an easy Antipodean drawl. 'We'll be in resort soon, so you can start putting your red wine theory to the test.'

'Can't wait,' Julian manages through gritted teeth.

'And then maybe a spot of backcountry heliskiing tomorrow. You up for that?' Tom says with a wink.

43

'You're joking, right?' Julian's face turns greener, if that's possible. 'It's illegal in France, remember.'

'I know, bloody killjoys,' Tom says, frowning. Some of his best skiing has been via a helicopter drop. Although he *was* only joking when he suggested it to Julian. When he was younger and on a junior doctor's salary, he could somehow justify spending a thousand euros on an epic day in the mountains, but now he's started to finally make some dosh, it doesn't seem to cross his mind.

But still, it's fun winding Julian up. 'There are plenty of options for heliskiing in Switzerland,' he says. 'Or we could get them to fly us into Italy?'

'I just don't think . . .' Julian stutters.

'I know, your knee,' Tom says, softening his voice; maybe he's gone far enough. 'It's fine, mate. I was only kidding. There's snow forecast, so all being well, we'll be able to enjoy the powder without having to leave the piste.'

'Right now, I can't imagine doing anything more ambitious than lying in a dark room,' Julian mutters.

Tom pats his friend on the shoulder, attributes the slight flinch to his friend's nausea, and leans back. They were introduced to Julian's sensitive stomach on their first ski trip together, sixteen years previously, when the coach travelling from Barcelona airport to Andorra was forced to stop. While Tom, Rob and Harry toasted the poor guy from their crate of Spanish lagers, Julian did the walk of shame up the aisle and then threw up by the roadside, in full view of everyone, including Zoe and her friend Ivy. A few things have changed since then, one being that Julian always takes the front seat.

'It still amazes me that a bloke who gets car sick decided to become a forensic pathologist,' Rob muses, choosing to show his concern by working a drum beat on the back of Julian's seat. 'The smell of decomposing bodies turns my stomach, so God knows what it does to yours.'

'Give me inert patients with predictable odours any day over your lot,' Julian mumbles, leaning towards the window and breathing in the fresh air.

'Blood, shit and vomit not for you then?'

'A&E has a special place in hell as far as I'm concerned. I don't know how you do it,' he adds, with poorly disguised admiration.

'I wouldn't have it any other way,' Rob says, dropping his hands and smiling with a new air of superiority. Tom knows what his friend is thinking. That he might not be a respected forensic expert like Julian, or on the path to infinite wealth like Tom, but he's got the most bragging rights as a doctor. While Tom's building up his private practice on Harley Street, and Julian's helping put away killers across the Thames Valley, Rob is busy on the front line. A&E at St George's Tooting, the largest hospital in London. Saving lives.

'Any talk about a move to consultant for you yet?' Tom asks tentatively. He knows that it's unlikely; the last time he spoke to Rob about work, the guy was still beating himself up, privately working off his penance for screwing up. Tom won't pretend the fuck-up wasn't significant, but one mistake shouldn't stall a man's career indefinitely. Especially when no one else at the hospital knows about it.

'What, pen pushing and wanky suits?' Rob shakes his head. 'That life is not for me. And anyway, the last thing the trust needs right now is me moving behind the scenes. We're so short-staffed in the department; there's at least one clueless locum on every shift. I know that place back to front; I don't reckon they'd function if I wasn't there propping things up.'

That's so like Rob, Tom thinks. Hiding his vulnerability behind bravado. Maybe he'll work on him during this trip. Remind him that everyone's allowed one mistake. Not that he's made one himself, Tom thinks. At least not in a work capacity. From the day he decided he wanted to be a doctor, when he first heard medicine was the hardest university course to get onto – craving first place has always been his Achilles heel – he has not put a foot wrong. Top grades, stellar extra-curricular achievements, character-building work experience, and a first-class medical degree from Exeter University. Then the hard work started. Head down, surrendering both social life and normal sleeping patterns, brown-nosing the right arseholes and never, ever, complaining. And it couldn't have worked more perfectly. Because he's now an orthopaedic consultant, with a burgeoning black book of wealthy patients with dodgy knees.

No, his screw-ups aren't work-related.

'All right, guys,' Nico says, pulling up outside a chalet built in local stone and wood cladding. 'This is Chalet Jouet. You go on in, and I'll get your bags.'

'We can carry our own . . .' Tom starts. But Nico has already jumped out of the van and slammed the door closed. He allows himself a moment of envy for the sprightly way the kid moves, then slides open the back door and enjoys the sound of snow crunching as his feet reach the ground. Julian beat him out of the van too – more desperation than fitness – and is now leaning against the wall of the chalet taking some deep breaths. It's been dark for an hour or so already, but the exterior lights are shining, and Tom watches the tiny water particles of his breath rise, then gradually disappear into the night. It excites him, the magic of it, and a thrill of anticipation rumbles through his body.

They ski as a trio every January. The tradition started when they finished uni, and they haven't missed a year yet. It's not the only time they see each other – they meet up for drinks in a certain south London pub regularly enough – but as their lives continue to diverge, this trip has proven vital in keeping their friendship on track. They take turns to choose which resort they go to, the only rule being that it has to be somewhere new. It was Julian's turn this year, and Tom was secretly delighted when his friend chose Morzine.

Because he *has* been here before. It was only a weekend break, but he's a fast learner when it comes to the mountains – in fact when it comes to most things – and he remembers a lot of the runs. He could tell Rob and Julian about his previous visit, but why give up the opportunity to appear instinctively brilliant? To make ski-guiding suggestions and be right every time? He doesn't mind admitting they're a competitive trio, and a little cheating never hurt anyone.

'You coming?' Rob asks, interrupting Tom's thoughts. He nods, and together they walk up to the thick oak door.

'Hi there, I'm Erin. Welcome to Chalet Jouet.' A willowy girl with long auburn hair and grey-blue eyes stands back from the doorway and the three of them shuffle inside. Nico follows, wheeling two cabin bags. He hoists Rob's compact rucksack off his shoulder and drops it on the floor.

'Right, that's me. Enjoy your trip, guys. And stay safe out there.' Nico gives them a languid thumbs up and retreats out of the chalet.

'So you've got two rooms on the first floor, *Chamois* and *Aigle*, and both rooms on the second, *Arbis* and *Tulip*,' Erin explains in a pleasantly lyrical Irish accent. 'All our bedrooms are named after local ski runs.'

'Four rooms?' Julian asks, frowning. 'But there's only three of us.'

'Oh, really?' Erin's brow furrows and she runs two fingers along her sharp jawline. 'So who's Harry?'

'What?' Julian drawls slowly.

'He showed up around an hour ago,' Erin says helpfully, oblivious to the shift in atmosphere. 'Hasn't said much, but he did the washing up for me.'

Tom claps his hands. 'Um, surprise!' he announces, with a mix of pride and trepidation.

'Jesus, Tom. Why the hell did you invite Harry?' Rob asks, horrified. 'After what he did to us?'

'Come on, mate,' Tom says, trying to placate him. 'I know Harry screwed up back at uni, but it's been nearly fifteen years, and he

47

used to be one of our gang, didn't he? A good laugh? And think about it, until everything went to shit, he was the nicest one of us all. Never complained, not even about us nicking his milk every flipping day. He's been trying really hard since he got back to the UK, retraining as a paramedic, reaching out to the three of us. All he wants is to say sorry, but he told me that neither of you have returned his messages. So I gave him our dates and the chalet details. And now you've got the perfect opportunity to patch things up.'

'But this is our boys' weekend,' Julian moans. 'I've got so much shit going on at home, I really needed these few days to be about the three of us. Not stoking up old dramas.'

'He's changed, I promise. It will be fun. Trust me?' Tom gives his friends his widest smile and the tension drops a notch. Thank God. Because he was beginning to question his decision. Harry first got back in touch a couple of years ago, an email and then a phone call. He was full of promises that he was a changed man, and Tom quickly accepted his apology – in truth, he's never quite managed to brush off the feeling that he let Harry down back then. But they haven't had much contact in the interim, only a few phone calls, and he doesn't really know whether Harry has recovered from the demons that poured petrol on his future medical career, and ruined a bunch of friendships at the same time.

'What's he been doing since he dropped out anyway?' Julian asks grudgingly.

'India for a bit apparently. Then France. Worked on superyachts out of St Tropez for a few years, then a couple bartending in Nice I think; he was a bit vague about that. Came back to the UK about two years ago – that's when he first contacted me – and he lives with his dad in Surrey now.'

Julian sighs. 'Not sure he deserved such a fun lifestyle after what he did.'

'At least he won't have been skiing for a while,' Rob offers. 'So we'll be better than him at last.'

'Exactly, mate,' Tom says, desperate for any positive spin on the situation. 'And Harry was always easy company, wasn't he? Before, you know . . .' His voice trails off. This time Erin seems to notice, and claps her hands to break the silence.

'Shall I take you upstairs, then?' she says, brightly. 'The living area is on the first floor, to make the most of the views. Dinner will be ready in about half an hour, but there's a carafe of wine on the table. And the owner of Tall Mountain is popping in too, so she'll be here soon. She wanted to make sure you arrived safely.'

They all follow Erin up the stairs, and when they reach the first floor, Tom discovers she's right. The view is amazing; and set off perfectly by a bank of glass. But Tom's focus quickly moves away from the floor-to-ceiling windows and towards the man stood in the centre of the room. Harry. The last time they were together, Tom was watching him implode, and wondering if the slim bones in his hand might snap from the compression he was forcing through them. But he looks different now. Fifteen years away from his friends has clearly been good to him. Tom walks up, takes Harry's outstretched hand, and smiles.

He doesn't know what he was worrying about. This is going to be a great weekend.

Chapter 10

Ivy

'Erin, can you get Mrs Metcalfe a glass of water please?'

I watch the chalet girl's hands shake as she reaches up for a glass and then holds it under the tap, fresh mountain water bubbling out. She looks young, maybe around 18 or 19, too young to be dealing with the shock of a dead client while also hosting his grieving friends, that's for sure. Erin hands the full glass to Zoe, but her eyes skitter away.

'Thank you,' Zoe whispers. 'I don't know what came over me; I'm not usually travel sick.'

'It's been a terrible twenty-four hours for you,' Nina says, leaning against the units in the open-plan kitchen. 'It's not surprising that you're reacting physically.'

'I guess,' Zoe says. I watch her drop her hand to her belly and stroke it softly. She must still be feeling rotten. I guide her towards the large L-shaped sofa, and we sink down into it together. The wall opposite is mainly glass with double doors onto a balcony, and I take a moment to digest the view. But then Avoriaz comes into focus directly ahead of us – the highest resort in the Portes du Soleil ski area, and the place Tom was skiing when he died – and I look away.

'Where are the others?' I ask. I thought Rob and Julian would be here, ready to comfort Zoe.

'They're at the police station,' Erin says softly. 'Nico gave them a lift. Apparently they need to hand over their passports while the investigation is ongoing, and give a statement.'

'A police statement?' Zoe asks, frowning. 'Why do they need to do that?'

'I'm sure it's just standard procedure,' Nina offers, reaching for a glass herself, and filling it from the tap. 'They'll want to know if there are any learnings they can take from your husband's accident, to make sure it doesn't happen again.'

'Well, that's good of them, I suppose,' Zoe says, sighing.

'Don't credit them,' Nina responds. 'This is all about damage limitation. No one wants to ski in a resort where people die on blue runs.' That paradox again, I think. The element that makes this so hard to accept.

'Oh God, I wish the men would hurry up,' Zoe moans. 'I need to look them both in the eye and hear what the hell happened up there.'

'You do know there's three of them,' Erin warns carefully. 'Julian, Rob and Harry.'

My head shoots up. I blink, then whip it hard left towards the window before anyone can see my expression. Shit. Harry? I won't be able to cope with seeing him. Not under these circumstances. Not under any circumstances. 'Harry's here?' I finally ask, somehow managing to keep my voice from cracking.

'Oh yes,' Zoe says vaguely. 'I forgot about that. Tom asked him to go along, as a surprise for the others.'

'I didn't realise they were still in touch,' I whisper, on autopilot, the heat from the log burner more oppressive than comforting now.

'They weren't for a good while,' Zoe explains. 'But Harry called

Tom out of the blue, maybe a couple of years ago now. He wanted to apologise for what he did the night of my party, and they've stayed in touch – vaguely, at least – ever since.'

My mouth is too dry for words to form, but luckily Zoe's attention is claimed by a noise below – the heavy front door opening and the sound of outdoor shoes on tiled floor. She looks scared suddenly.

'Sounds like they're back,' Erin says.

I can't look at the stairs, so I continue staring out of the window and listen to the sound of clumping footsteps instead. *Please don't let them belong to Harry.* A watery reflection appears in the window, and I breathe a sigh of relief.

It's hard to say whether Rob and I were ever friends at university. We hung out in the same group, and he was always good fun, but we never spent time together. Rob was a party kind of guy, always at his happiest in the centre of a group. It's been fifteen years, so it's an obvious thing to say, but he looks older. The basics are the same: curly brown hair, tanned skin, eyes that don't quite match in colour or size. But there's a haggardness about him now, like a once-coveted painting that's been bashed around in the back of a van for a while.

He looks at me and manages to turn his surprised expression into a nod of acknowledgement before shifting his eyeline to Zoe. And that's enough to set him off. We're supposed to be comfortable with men crying. But watching Rob brush angrily at his cheeks like a child unnerves me. I feel my own face pull at the corners. Is this when I break down? And would it be about Tom's death, or the thought of seeing Harry again? I dig my fingernails into my opposite hand and breathe deeply. Not here, not in front of everyone.

Another figure appears on the stairs before I have chance to prepare. But it's Julian, a man I definitely considered a friend once upon a time. Julian was quiet – like me – so it took us a while to realise that we got on, and by then he had Nikki's feelings to consider. But all the same, I liked him. We liked each other. He's aged too, but in a more subtle way. Skin slightly less pliant. The ghosts of creases at the corners of his eyes. He also looks embarrassed about Rob's outpouring, but puts his arm around his friend and guides him towards two chairs by the window. 'I'm so sorry, Zoe. There are no words.' He looks over at me, smiles a greeting. 'It's good to see you, Ivy. Just a shame that . . .'

'It's in such difficult circumstances,' I finish for him. People like standard phrases when talking about people dying, familiar tropes to lean on.

'How's Nikki?' Zoe asks, clearly needing to change the subject. Nikki studied biochemistry at Exeter and became a member of our group when she and Julian got together. She always seemed grateful to be given access to our inner circle, which I remember feeling flattered by. I lost touch with her – along with the whole gang – when I left Exeter, but I heard that she and Julian got married six months after Tom and Zoe.

'She's fine,' Julian mutters. He sounds defensive and I wonder why.

'And where's, um, Harry?' Zoe asks. She says the name like it's alien, unfamiliar, and it hits me how hard this trip must have been for him, trying to find some space in a friendship group that has reformed and tightened over the years. But also, that it's strange, Tom dying on the first trip Harry joined, after everything that happened on his last night at university.

Julian looks at his hands. 'He came with us to the station, but the police said he needed to clarify a couple of extra things,' he mumbles. 'They asked him to stay behind so Nico's gone back for him.'

'What things?' The words tumble out of my mouth before I can stop them.

'Yes, why are they singling Harry out?' Zoe asks guardedly.

'Because he's a liability?' Rob suggests. 'Christ, we haven't seen him in a decade and a half; we've no idea what he's been up to, he could be a serial killer for all we know.'

'You're being ridiculous,' Julian says. 'Harry told us exactly what he's been up to, and it's hard to be a serial killer when you're working on superyachts, monitored by state-of-the-art CCTV twenty-four seven.'

'We've only got his word for it though, haven't we? And it's not like he hasn't got form,' Rob adds. 'In a way.' I feel my cheeks burn. Neither Rob nor Julian knows the full extent of Harry's crimes that night, but I'm not going to start revealing them now. 'They asked me about him, you know,' Rob continues, still looking for a reaction. 'The police. I bet they asked you too.'

'And what did you say?' Julian asks.

'I lied, didn't I? Told them that I'd never known Harry to be violent.'

'Me too.' Julian breathes out a long sigh. 'He was one of us, wasn't he, once upon a time. Yes, he lost his head, but that was ages ago. We're hardly going to grass him up to the French police now.'

'Let's hope Tom's not turning in his grave,' Rob murmurs.

'He's not buried yet,' Zoe whispers, and that's enough to silence the room.

A few moments later it's broken by a thud from downstairs. This is it. I run my hands over my hair, try to tame its wildness, then lean back against the cushion and push my shoulder blades against it.

Harry takes an age to make it up the stairs and we all listen to each long, protracted footstep. Finally, he appears. He scans the room, until he spots me. His eyes widen, just like I knew they would. And then he looks back towards the stairs, as though he's contemplating running away. I hold my breath. If we're going to get through this, we both need to keep cool heads. I silently beg him to find the strength, then watch him take a deep breath and run his fingers through his dirty blonde hair.

The panic clears and he takes a few steps into the room. 'Sorry I wasn't here when you arrived,' he mutters to Zoe.

She shrugs. 'It's fine.'

'Why did they make you stay longer?' Rob asks, his tone suspicious.

'It was nothing important.'

'How about Erin and I make some coffees?' Nina interrupts. 'She's baked a cake too, banana and walnut, if anyone is hungry.'

'It must have been something,' Rob presses. 'Why won't you tell us?'

Harry sighs. With his attention elsewhere, I risk taking a proper look at him. Out of the three of them, he has aged the least since university, although he's also the only one I've seen since leaving, so maybe that's distorted my judgement. His dark blonde hair is in the same unkempt style and his body still looks too thin for its tall, broad frame, like Lycra stretched around a hanger. He must sense me staring because he flicks his head around, but I manage to look away before our eyes catch. I know I'm putting off the inevitable though, that he'll want to know about Calum. There's no way I could – or would want to – keep news of my son hidden away, so I can only hope that he respects my privacy, and the promise he made.

After what feels like an age, he turns back to face Rob and shrugs. 'They told me it was confidential,' he says, not quite meeting Rob's eyes. 'Otherwise, of course I would.'

Chapter 11

2006

Ivy

I stare at my image in the long mirror on the back of Zoe's door. 'And you're sure I look okay?' I ask. Black-tie events were never a thing in my village, nor at my comprehensive school in Skipton, and I've never worn anything this posh before. With my boyish figure, it's hard to work out how I look in this tight-fitting steel-blue dress.

'You look amazing,' Zoe reassures me. 'That dress really suits you. Dark hair, green eyes, porcelain skin. It's so deliciously Gaelic. Not like boring blonde-haired blue-eyed English girl over here.' She drops her bottom lip into a pout for a moment, then pulls it back into a smile. 'A friend from school had your colouring and she wore a lot of blue; that's why I chose that dress,' she adds.

I'm not sure when Zoe became my best friend at university. Our first coffee together – Zoe pretending not to notice when

I paid with cash rather than the promised vouchers – led to a night out at the students' union bar. That toppled into a hangover day – watching old DVDs in Zoe's student house and comfort eating buttered crumpets – and then Zoe invited me to join her intramural netball team. The rest of it – daily texts, lunch meet-ups, hanging out in each other's rooms – happened without either of us really noticing.

So when the MedSoc Christmas Ball loomed closer, it didn't feel awkward to admit that I didn't have anything appropriate to wear. And a few days later she turned up at my room with a Jack Wills bag. I felt self-conscious when I first put the dress on, but then Zoe lent me some strappy silver high heels to wear with it, and tonight, she's done my make-up, and spread glitter gel across my arms. I'm starting to think that maybe I look all right.

But I am still no match for Zoe, who looks incredible. She's wearing a full-length rose-pink dress with plunging neckline and diamanté straps. Her mix of gold and rose make-up makes her blue eyes stand out even more than usual, and her hair has been intricately styled at the hairdresser's this afternoon. I can't blame her for going to all this effort though. She's been desperate to impress Tom Metcalfe since she first met him – apparently at the end of our first year, before I knew her – and has been waiting all term for a moment like this.

'Shall we go then?' she asks. I smile, link my arm in hers, and we walk out of her room together.

'There he is,' Zoe shouts, as the Scissor Sisters' 'I don't feel like dancin'' thumps out of the speakers beside us. She nods her head towards one end of a long bar, and I follow her gaze. It's amazing that she's spotted Tom at all really, because the place is rammed and every man is wearing a dinner jacket. The only difference being what state of undress they're in – from those still looking smart, to the guy in an unbuttoned shirt with his bow tie knotted around his forehead.

From this distance, I can stare openly, but I still only recognise two of them – the now-famous Tom and the guy I often see him with. I think he's called Harry. While I haven't said anything to Zoe – because I know exactly how loudly she'd squeal if she knew – I have found myself daydreaming about the four of us double dating. Harry and I have never spoken, but my heart clicks up a gear whenever I spot him, and I have the contradictory urge to both jump into his path and run for the hills. Chemistry between couples is supposedly scientifically proven, so I'm putting my raised adrenalin levels down to that.

With a burst of it now, I grab Zoe's hand. 'Come on then,' I shout, and weave us both through the crowd towards them. It's not like me to be this bold, but it's easier when I've got a decoy willing to take the spotlight – and I'm sure the half a dozen vodkas have helped with my confidence. We arrive in front of them, and I breathe a sigh of relief as Tom gives Zoe a lazy smile.

'Hey, Zoe,' he says. 'Good to see you. You look amazing, as always.'

Zoe beams. 'Thanks,' she says, then gestures to me. 'Do you know my friend Ivy?'

Tom turns to me, and I find myself drawn to his eyes. I've never seen him up close, and I didn't realise how warm they would be. 'I've seen you around, but we haven't been formally introduced.' He holds his hand out. 'I'm Tom.'

I'm not used to shaking hands, but I take it. It's hot, but not sweaty. Three firm shakes and then he pulls away.

'Great night,' Zoe says. 'Have you been involved in organising it at all?'

Tom laughs. 'Because we're medics, do you mean? No chance.'

'He's got more important things to organise,' one of the lads I don't recognise says. 'Like how to survive four weeks of the Christmas holidays with his folks in Milton Keynes.' Then he laughs at his own joke, the curls on his head bouncing along with his shoulders, and takes a long swig from his glass, finishing his pint.

'That's an easy one,' Harry says. 'Milton Keynes has got the largest indoor ski resort in Europe.'

'Do you ski then?' Zoe asks. Out of politeness, she directs her question at Harry, but her eyes flit towards Tom. Skiing is Zoe's favourite sport and I'm sure she'd love it to be his as well.

'Yeah, kind of,' Harry answers. 'I was Surrey county champion actually, but it was on a dry slope. Tom is master of the snow, skied before he could walk and all that.' I watch Zoe's eyes grow wide, grand terms like 'destiny' and 'perfect for each other' shining out of them. But I can't help thinking that Harry is the real hero. Bristly plastic mats sound a lot harder to ski on than fluffy Alpine snow.

Clearly Zoe doesn't agree. 'Ah, that's crazy,' she squeals, taking a few baby steps in Tom's direction. 'I LOVE skiing. Which is your favourite resort?' She hasn't moved very far, but in this cramped room, the new sliver of empty space makes me feel abandoned. I watch her lean against the wall by Tom and clink her vodka and Coke with his pint of lager.

'Another drink?' the curly-haired man asks. His voice is slurring, but I imagine so is mine. Both Harry and the other guy nod their heads and tip their glasses in his direction. Then he turns to me. 'And you, Ivy? Can I interest you in an alcoholic beverage?'

'Vodka and Coke, thank you.'

'I'm Rob by the way, and this is Harry and Julian.' I smile nervously, then nod at them both while avoiding Harry's eye. 'Right, Tom looks otherwise engaged,' Rob continues. 'So it's three pints and a vodka. Back in a minute.' He twists on his shoes (which I realise are white Nike trainers) and mumbles, 'sorry, emergency,' a few times before disappearing into the crowd.

'Rob's got legendary speed at the bar,' Harry explains, edging towards me. 'And we keep feeding his ego, so he continues buying the drinks. It's a win-win.' I smile, rack my brain for some clever response, come up empty-handed so stay silent. 'I've seen you around, you know,' he goes on.

'You have?' I can't hide the surprise in my voice.

'Yeah.' He nods his head, then breaks out an embarrassed smile. 'Sorry if this sounds cheesy, but you kind of stand out. Especially your eyes, they're very striking. Okay so that is cheesy,' he adds lifting his hands in apology.

I stifle a giggle. 'Well, I like cheese,' I say with a shrug. I want to say more, but I can't think of anything, so I smile at him instead, willing my emerald irises to shine seductively. But a sudden movement grabs our attention. For a few moments we all stand and stare as a girl a couple of metres away starts jerking like a bad body popper, her arms and legs flailing, head dropped to one side, and eyes blank.

'Fuck, she's fitting!' Rob skids in, then thrusts the drinks into Harry's hands. 'Hold these!'

'Wait, what?' Harry wails. 'I am a fucking medic too, you know!'

But Rob's not listening. He reaches for the girl, but it's too late. Her legs give way, and she drops onto the concrete floor. Crack! Her head whacks on the hard surface. Her limbs are still twitching, but the movement has turned fuzzy in my eyeline now. I can only see her face. I stare, transfixed, as dark blood pools out from her blonde hair, and smears across the concrete as her head continues to shake. I'm aware that Rob is still shouting, barking out instructions, and that other people are rallying around, holding her head, calling an ambulance, pressing clothing against her wound. But I'm somewhere else now, unable to help. Freezing cold. Wind and rain pummelling me. I stare at my dad, the image I've conjured up a thousand times, his head bent and bloody against the rocky ledge.

'Hey, are you okay?' A voice in the distance. Harry. 'Ivy, you've gone really pale. Why don't you come with me?' Fingers curl around my upper arm; a palm cups my elbow. The grip is gentle, but I've got no strength, and I let myself be led away. It's a good decision. As soon as my eyes pull away from the girl, the image of my dad fades too. But I still feel shaky, and scared that I might burst into tears. I look up at the ceiling, blink frantically. God, what is wrong with me? He's been dead for ten years; I need to pull myself together.

'I'm so sorry,' I stutter, not sure how to explain my overreaction, wishing it hadn't happened in front of Harry.

'You looked like you'd seen a ghost.'

'I suppose I had,' I whisper. 'My dad died of a head wound. I wasn't there, but . . .' I don't know why I'm telling Harry this. I hardly know him.

'It's no wonder that scene freaked you out then.' His voice is comforting, heavy with both acceptance and understanding. I should feel distraught that this hot guy has witnessed my weakness, but I realise I'm glad he's here.

He pulls me gently towards him and I fall against his chest. I feel his warmth, smell the sandalwood of his aftershave. Then he leans down and kisses me. And I close my eyes and kiss him back.

Chapter 12

Ivy

'So, who's going to start?' Zoe asks quietly, dabbing the crumbs from her plate with her finger. I was surprised when she asked for a slice of Erin's cake – that she can eat anything at all with the ordeal she's going through – but perhaps it's helping to line her stomach after being sick on the way up here.

'Start what?' Rob asks.

'Isn't it obvious?' she counters. 'Explaining how my husband, the best skier I know, fell from such an easy ski run.' Zoe's face drops for a moment, but she pulls it back and lets out a slow breath. 'Please, just tell me,' she says in a gentler voice. 'What happened up there?'

Colour drains from Rob's face and he can't hold Zoe's imploring stare. He looks at Harry, but then changes his mind and turns towards Julian instead. The movement is so small that it's almost imperceptible, but I still catch it. The tiny shake of Julian's head. The silent message that passes between them. *Don't tell her that.* I wonder what they don't want Zoe to know, and then I feel dirty, as though I'm now complicit in their cover-up.

'The visibility was shocking,' Rob says eventually. 'Honestly, Zoe, I've never seen a white-out so dense. And we'd not skied that run before, so we had no idea that there was a sheer drop on one side.'

'But why didn't you stay together?' Zoe asks plaintively. 'If the conditions were that bad?' It's uncomfortable, listening to her beg for an explanation, while the three men stare at her, unable to think of one. I wish I could slip through the glass doors and hide on the balcony. Call my mum to check on Calum, or even swipe through the hundreds of photos I have of him on my phone. 'It would make more sense if you saw him fall,' Zoe goes on. 'I can imagine Tom wanting to take the lead; I know what's he's like. But for you to not even know what happened to him, to abandon him up there. I thought you were his friends?'

'Fucking hell, Zoe,' Rob shouts, pushing out of his chair. 'Talk about twisting the knife. Don't you think we feel bad enough already?' He rubs his palm hard across his forehead, then drops his arm and stomps into the kitchen area. Erin stifles a gasp as he gets closer, then backs up against the units, as though his grief might be contagious. 'Is there any wine open?' he demands. 'I need a drink.' She nods, and points to a carafe in the corner. Rob swings open a cupboard door, reaches for a glass, and then pours wine up to the brim. 'Anyone else?'

'Water,' Harry says. It's a demand, not a request, but Rob pours him a glass anyway.

Suddenly I'm desperate for the numbing effects of cheap chalet wine, served in a carafe because the five-litre cartons don't carry the same aesthetic. 'Wine for me please,' I call out. Rob's hands are shaking, and I worry that he's going to spill red wine on the sheepskin rug, but miraculously he manages to pass a glass to me without upset. As Harry reaches wordlessly for his drink, I notice an angry red welt on the back of his hand. I want to ask him about it – or more accurately, I want someone else to ask him, because I don't trust myself to speak to him directly – but he slides it back under the sleeve of his hoodie and the opportunity passes.

Rob has drunk half his wine by the time he sits down, but at least he seems calmer now. 'Look, we skied hard in the morning,' he says. 'We did the Swiss Wall, which is crazy vertical.'

'One of the ten hardest runs in the world,' Julian says ruefully. 'Moguls like mountains.' I shudder at the thought. Moguls are mounds of snow, created by hundreds of skiers following similar lines down the piste, and I've never fully got the hang of them. On most runs, moguls are flattened overnight, but on blacks, skiers are considered proficient enough to fend for themselves.

'And once we got into Switzerland, we wanted to cover as much ground over there as possible,' Rob says. He looks at Julian. 'Well, most of us did anyway. Then suddenly it was two o'clock, and everyone was starving. Tom really wanted to try this particular restaurant he'd been recommended, by Erin, I think.' He looks towards the chalet girl for confirmation, but she's stony-faced. I'm not sure she's even listening. He shrugs and continues. 'So we dropped back into France and went there for a steak.' He looks down at Harry, then down at his socked feet. 'We had a few drinks, toasted our amazing skiing – you know the drill.'

'So you were pissed when you left?' Zoe asks.

'No, nothing like that.' Rob looks pained. 'But maybe the alcohol gave us a second wind. We were late eating, and the weather was getting worse. We discussed heading straight back to Morzine but then someone suggested we do Clementine instead.'

'Clementine?' I ask, my voice hoarse with emotion, or maybe underuse.

'That's the name of the run,' Rob explains. 'It's a long cruisy blue, so it seemed like a good idea.'

I nod, not trusting myself to speak anymore.

'Who suggested it?' Zoe asks. Her tone is pleasant enough, but all of us realise the weight that sits behind this question. *Who suggested Tom ski to his death?*

'I'm not sure,' Rob mumbles, turning to face the window.

Zoe looks at Harry. 'It wasn't me,' he says tersely, before shifting his eyeline away from her. I wonder what's driving his irritability. Is this his way of coping with Tom's death? Or is it because I'm here? I think about the police holding him back at the station, his violence at university, and I desperately hope that it's not guilt making him behave this way.

Julian sighs. 'I think it was Tom,' he admits quietly, without looking at her.

'Tom's idea?' Zoe whispers, shaking her head slowly, like she can't believe he'd be that stupid, but also that it doesn't surprise her at all.

'The visibility was fine at the bottom though,' Julian continues. 'A bit cloudy, but nothing to suggest how bad it would be at the top. It was misfortune, Zoe, not recklessness.'

Zoe slumps against the sofa and it's as though the fight has gone out of her. Like something taut has snapped and she's lost all her strength. It's strange to see her so defeated, the girl who swanned through university with a wink and a smile, and suddenly I want to pick up the baton for her. 'And then what?' I ask. 'There were four of you. How did Tom manage to get lost on his own?'

Silence settles in the room, and I'm taken by how guilty they all look. So much so that I jump when my phone buzzes in my pocket. I feel Harry's eyes turn towards me as I reach for it. It's a message from my mum.

Have you arrived safely?
Can you call me?

I stare at the message. Why does Mum want me to call her? My stomach lurches in fear. But this is to be expected, I tell myself. Mum worries about everything; this will be her panicking about Calum not finishing his lunch, or crying when he woke from his afternoon nap. Of course I'll call her, to find out for certain, but it can wait a minute. It's not fair to leave Zoe to hear the explanation of Tom's death alone.

'Is everything okay?' Julian asks.

'Yes,' I whisper, looking at Zoe, the film of tears covering her eyes. 'You were telling us how Tom fell.' Julian bites his lip and looks at Rob. But Rob shakes his head in frustration.

'For fuck's sake, I don't know why we're acting like we're guilty of something.' He turns to face Zoe. 'It's fair to say we were all pissed off when we got to the top. It's a bloody long lift; it had started to snow a bit, and the wind was howling as we got higher. We were freezing cold and couldn't see jack shit.'

'Go on,' Zoe says.

'Well, Tom offered to go first,' Rob continues. 'Lead us down, just like you said he would. But to be honest, we'd all had enough of him bossing us around by then. So yeah, we argued. But then I skied off. And that was the last I saw of him.' He looks away, towards the window, his eyes filling with tears again. Zoe seems mesmerised by them, staring at Rob's face in profile, and the room falls silent.

'And what about you, Julian?' I eventually ask. 'Did you see Tom veer off in the wrong direction?'

'Of course not,' Julian snaps. 'Otherwise, don't you think I'd have called him back? It was freaky up there. Like pitch black, but white. I had to concentrate on getting myself down. Tom was always a better skier than me; I assumed he'd be fine.' He turns to look at Harry. 'You were hanging back with him I think?'

Harry entwines his fingers into a steeple, almost as though he's praying. 'I don't really remember. I'd got bored of listening to you guys squabbling by then, so I just chose my line and skied down.'

'I'm sure you were still with Tom when I left,' Rob muses. 'So you must have been the last one to see him alive. Is that what the police wanted to talk to you about?'

'Why?' Harry counters. 'Is that what you told them?'

Silence hangs in the air and I realise my phone is buzzing. I expect it to be another message, but my mum is calling me this time. My heart hammers. I need to get my priorities straight. I push off the sofa, walk over to the sliding doors, then breathe in the cold air as I press to accept the call.

Chapter 13

Zoe

Zoe lies on the bed and strokes the curve of her belly as it slopes down towards the duvet. She's never been travel sick before. Does that mean she's pregnant, suffering from morning sickness? Or is her stomach in knots because her husband is dead? Her period is now four days late, so she could find out categorically if she took a pregnancy test. But she didn't think to pack one – even though she's certain there's one in the bathroom cabinet at home – and she doesn't feel comfortable going to a French pharmacy and trying to explain what she needs.

She rolls onto her back, her belly disappearing into her spine, and stares at the skylight above her. Her father would be able to name exactly what clouds are floating past, Ivy too, but they're cotton wool to her. Long Latin words that don't feature in her vocabulary.

If she's honest with herself, she didn't 'forget' to bring a pregnancy test. She just can't cope with finding out what her future holds right now. Yes, she's more tired than she's ever felt in her life, but stress and grief could be to blame for that. And yes, she and Tom were having unprotected sex, but at 35, pregnancy doesn't carry the same sense of inevitability as it once did – back when she'd pop a morning-after pill if there was even a chance the condom had split.

She thinks back to the conversation she's just had with Tom's friends, men she's known since she was that laissez-faire 19-year-old. They all seemed so furtive. At first it set off some alarm bells, wondering what they might be hiding from her, but then realisation hit. She's not interested. Whatever happened up there, they didn't push Tom to his death; they're his best friends. So even if there was an argument, something they're not proud of in retrospect, what difference does it really make? Tom isn't coming back; that's the only thing that matters.

Ivy wouldn't let it go, though. Not that that's a surprise. Ivy has always been a fact gatherer, whether that's a detailed weather report, or a lengthy explanation of what she can expect from a night out. Even at Zoe's twenty-first birthday party, Ivy was the only one in full possession of the facts. That's why Zoe got so mad with her, and who wouldn't under the circumstances? But instead of apologising, or even arguing, Ivy retreated. And suddenly Zoe was the bad guy, even though she was the one grieving. Some people even had the cheek to remind Zoe that Peter's death would be upsetting for Ivy too, her mentor, the closest thing she had to a father figure. Incredible.

And then Ivy cancelled her place on the master's course anyway and left Exeter for good. Zoe never worked out whether that was down to their argument, or because the tutor Ivy idolised so much – the feeling irritatingly mutual – was no longer alive to teach her.

But either way, that was all a long time ago now, and their friendship has finally moved on to a new place. She needs to forget about the role Ivy played in her father's death.

Or more accurately, acknowledge that there wasn't one.

Zoe runs her hand over the perfectly made bed. She had

expected Erin to give her a choice of rooms when she asked if she could go for a lie-down, especially as Nina confirmed that she's moved the new week's guests into a different chalet. But Erin either wasn't that thoughtful or assumed that Zoe would want to be in Tom's room, because she brought her straight here. *Aigle*. The room that remains untouched from how her husband left it yesterday morning.

Zoe still can't decide whether Erin's call was the right one. Whether she's comforted or horrified to be surrounded by his things. She slips her hand under the pillow and finds the piece of material that she'd knew would be there. Tom always wore an eye mask in bed because he needed total darkness. She brushes the soft cotton against her cheek and wonders if he's there now, floating in black nothingness. Or whether there really is a heaven and hell. Because if there is, she knows where Tom would be.

With a sigh, Zoe picks up her phone and scrolls to the last message Tom ever sent her. She wishes it said something romantic, a grand declaration of love, or a confession of how much he's missing her. But it doesn't. Tom was too wrapped up in his own drama at the time to spare a thought for his wife suffering the January blues alone. As though him having a *massive moral dilemma* exempted him from caring about how she might be feeling. She drops the phone back onto the bed and lets out a loud sigh.

There's a light knocking at the door. 'Hey, it's Ivy. Can I come in?'

Zoe turns her head towards the voice, only then realising that her pillow is wet with tears. She runs her fingertips under her eyes to clear any residue mascara and pushes up to sitting. 'Yes, come in,' she calls out.

As Ivy perches on the end of her bed, Zoe notices that her hand is tightly gripping her phone. 'Is everything okay at home?' she asks.

'Um, I think so,' Ivy says, tapping the phone against her knee.

'Mum's a bit nervous about being in London, I think. She said something weird though.'

'Oh?'

'She took Calum to the park and apparently some guy came too close for her liking. And now she's got it in her head that Calum's in some sort of danger.'

Zoe's eyes widen. 'What?'

'I'm sure it's nothing,' Ivy says, pulling her face into a weak smile. 'You know, just Mum's anxiety playing havoc.' She blinks, then looks away, and Zoe wonders who she's really trying to convince. 'And anyway, it's not for you to worry about.' Ivy turns back to her. 'I can't imagine what you're going through at the moment.'

'Can't you?' Zoe asks. She watches Ivy try to hold her smile, her trembling lips making it difficult. 'Didn't you feel like this when your dad died?'

Ivy's eyelids drop a fraction. 'Yes, I suppose. It felt like my whole world had shattered. But I was only 9 so it took me a while to really understand the finality of it. It's different for you, with the clarity of adulthood. Losing Tom so suddenly must be devastating.'

Ivy's sympathy sounds so unequivocal that Zoe thinks she might cry again.

Because it's not deserved. Not really. Not anymore. Suddenly she feels an urge to confide in Ivy. Tell her what Tom, their marriage, had become. While she never stopped loving him (so her conscience is clear) that doesn't mean he was worthy of her affection, and she needs Ivy to understand that. 'You know, things weren't that great between us.'

'Oh?' Ivy catches her eye, then looks away again.

'I don't know why,' Zoe continues. 'But he'd become distant. Maybe he felt intimidated by how much I was earning, or perhaps he was stressed about building up his own practice. But I think he'd come to wish I was more of a traditional wife, baking banana bread and popping out babies, like Nikki does for Julian.'

71

'He never seemed . . .'

'But I couldn't sit around while he was working those ridiculous hours at the hospital,' Zoe continues, cutting Ivy off. 'I had to do something.'

'Of course you did.' Ivy pauses for a moment, biting her bottom lip as though she's weighing up whether to say more. 'So Tom wanted children and you didn't?' she finally asks. 'Is that what you mean?'

Zoe narrows her eyes. 'Why, did he say something to you?'

'No,' Ivy says quickly. 'I haven't seen him since that night in Exeter, the opening of your dad's lab.'

Zoe shakes her head in frustration. 'Sorry, of course you haven't. I'm not thinking straight.'

'I just remembered what you said on the plane,' Ivy tries again. 'That you weren't trying for kids. I didn't realise that Tom felt differently.'

'And you think that makes it okay?' Zoe's voice rises a few octaves.

'What do you mean?' Ivy asks, dropping her head to one side. 'Make what okay?'

Zoe sighs and drops her hands back to her stomach. She's watched pregnant women do this in the past and it's always annoyed her, but now her hand seems magnetically drawn to her middle. 'Tom was unfaithful,' she says at last, forcing herself to look into Ivy's eyes. 'He was drunk,' she explains. 'At least that's what he said. It was an NHS shift and it had been a stressful night – a car accident and Tom had spent hours resetting the driver's leg – and he'd gone to the pub with his team afterwards.'

'He slept with one of his colleagues?' Ivy asks, her voice squeaking with surprise.

'A locum, only there for the week, lucky for him. I smelled her on him the next morning, and when I accused him, he owned up without a fight. That was Tom all over, believing he could charm his way out of any predicament. He promised that he had no feelings for her, and expected me to both forgive him and not tell a soul.'

'God, Zoe, I had no idea . . .'

'Why would you? I didn't tell anyone,' Zoe whispers. 'I couldn't.' An image flashes up, a drunken night with Julian and Nikki, but she expels it with a shake of her head. 'But the worst part was, if he could have a one-night stand with a random doctor and not feel bad, what else might he be getting up to?'

'But you didn't leave him,' Ivy presses. 'So you did find a way to forgive him?'

'Yes and no. I wanted to make it work. I still loved him. But it was so hard to trust him again. I thought that maybe, in time, we'd get there. And now I guess I'll never know.' She gives Ivy a watery smile, then visibly jumps when there's a knock on the door.

'Sorry to disturb you,' Erin says in such a quiet voice that Zoe has to strain to hear. 'But the police are here. They want to talk to you.'

Chapter 14

Two days before the fall

Tom

'Any chance of the wine making its way back here?' Rob calls out from the other end of the table.

Tom raises his eyebrows in mock disapproval, but leans forward and pushes the carafe along the dining table, a thick slab of rustic French oak shimmering slightly under a thin wax coat. The carafe slides to a halt in front of Harry, who pours Rob a full glass. Harry, on the other hand, has only drunk water this evening, and Tom wonders if that's part of his recovery, or a sly way of ensuring a competitive advantage on the slopes tomorrow.

'Smooth move,' Nina says under her breath. 'I thought I was going to be mopping up red wine for a second there.' Tom turns to the woman sat on his left and pretends to be offended. 'You think I'd try a risky manoeuvre like that if I hadn't already perfected it? Gentleman first, entertainer second, I promise,' he adds, giving her his best choirboy smile. The chalet has five bedrooms, and Julian had been warned there might be other guests staying when he arranged their trip. But Harry took the fourth, and the fifth room didn't get booked at all. Which is lucky, because their style of banter isn't to everyone's taste.

'Well, that's a relief,' Nina responds, before turning to Erin who's hovering at the end of the table. 'Erin, can you get another carafe of wine?' The chalet girl's generous smile becomes a little fixed as she realises that it's going to be one of those nights. Drunk guests refusing to go to bed. A late finish, followed by a morning dealing with dirty wine glasses before she can get the porridge on. Tom feels an urge to change her mind. To tell her that the evening can be fun for her too if she gets involved. But saying something like that is clear proof that he's past it, so he limits himself to smiling when she hands him a full carafe.

'Where are we going tomorrow then?' Harry asks. 'Remember I haven't skied for years.'

'Yeah, we're definitely going to adjust our plans for you,' Rob mutters.

'I thought we should ski on the Morzine, Les Gets side tomorrow,' Julian says. 'Apparently it's a bit easier than Avoriaz, so we can find our ski legs.'

'Mate, we're not middle-aged beginners,' Rob reminds him, taking another mouthful of wine. 'We don't lose our ski legs in a year.'

'Well I appreciate it,' Harry says, raising his water glass towards Julian, who looks uncomfortable about being caught on Harry's side. Which is funny to watch, Tom thinks, but also annoying. Because why won't Rob and Julian give the guy a break? Yes, Harry fucked up. But it was a lifetime ago, and he's been trying to apologise for over two years. He's even shelled out five hundred quid for this trip, just to show them he's changed. How much more effort do they need?

Especially as neither of them were the one left with a fractured cheekbone. Or know half of what Harry did that night.

Although now he thinks about it, it's not just Harry who's suffering from Julian's bad mood; the guy hasn't been himself since they met at Heathrow. Whatever the problem is, Tom hopes he snaps out of it soon, otherwise it's going to be a long weekend.

'I think that's a good idea,' Nina says, breaking the silence. 'There are some lovely reds and blues in the Les Gets bowl, and if you want something more challenging, there's a black run down from the Chamossière lift.'

'Thanks, Nina,' Tom says, smiling. 'Sounds like exactly what we need on our first day.' She smiles back, and he may hold her gaze a moment too long, but luckily none of the others notice. When Nina first arrived at the chalet, he thought she looked familiar, and worried for a moment that they'd met during his previous visit to Morzine. The last thing he needed was someone blowing his cover after he'd managed to keep the trip a secret from his friends. But then he realised that it was just the image of her that was familiar. Nina looks like most other British women who make a life for themselves in the mountains. Healthy, tanned, and with eyes that speak of clandestine adventures.

'Annual first-day race on the black run then, yeah?' Rob suggests, his voice slurring now.

'I'm up for that,' Tom says. 'The way you're knocking back the *vin rouge*, you've got no chance.'

Rob snorts. 'A bit of fresh mountain air is all I need to blow the cobwebs away.'

'I'm up for a race,' Harry says, a new glint in his eye. 'If it's tradition. They say it's like riding a bike, don't they?'

'Ah the great Surrey champion, Harry Cooke, about to be blown off the mountain!' Rob looks longingly at the carafe of wine, his glass empty again, but he doesn't reach for it. Perhaps Tom's words have struck a chord.

'How about we don't race this year?' Julian suggests. 'Just enjoy a day on the slopes instead? If the forecast is right, it might be the only day of sunshine we get.'

'This is because you're a dad now, isn't it,' Rob says, nodding with the wisdom of someone who's drunk a litre of red wine. 'The weight of new responsibility holding you back.' Rob pauses a moment, his eyes narrowing in concentration. 'Hang on, didn't you have them last year?'

'The twins are 3 now,' Julian says, rolling his eyes. 'It's not about being a dad.'

'It's about his knee,' Tom says softly. He needs to tread carefully here. 'Not trusting it yet. But you'll be fine, Julian. I promise.'

'So you say,' Julian mutters.

'Yeah, well it is my job. You can trust . . .'

'Anyway,' Julian cuts in, clearly not wanting to talk about last year's injury. 'It's late. I'm going to hit the sack.'

'I'll be up in a minute, darling,' Rob offers, laughing at his own joke, and blowing Julian a kiss as he walks around the back of the dining table towards the winding staircase. Rob and Julian are on the top floor, Jack and Jill bedrooms under the eaves, while Tom and Harry's rooms are on the same level as the living area.

'Great,' Julian mutters, without slowing his pace. 'Just make sure you don't sleepwalk through the bathroom.'

Rob sighs at the space Julian has vacated. 'I suppose I better get some beauty sleep too.' He pushes back his chair, and it makes an ear-piercing screech on the wooden floor. 'Night, all.'

Tom's phone buzzes in his pocket and he pulls it out. It's a message from Zoe.

'Another glass, Tom?' Nina asks. 'Or are you calling it a night too?'

Hope you arrived safely.
How's your first night?
Gorgeous chalet girl??

Tom puts his phone back in his pocket. 'Maybe one more,' he

says. 'What about you, Harry?'

'Not me.' Harry drops his napkin on the table. 'I'm off to bed. See you in the morning.' Tom watches his old friend – little more than a stranger now really – lope off towards his room, and wonders what's going through his head. This Harry is so different to the one he knew at university. Tom wonders which is the real one – the talented medic who hid his anguish so well until he didn't, or the tight-lipped trainee paramedic who prefers water to wine.

'Am I okay to finish?' Erin asks. 'There's a band on at the Tibetan.'

'Of course,' Nina says, her silver tail of earrings catching the light as she nods. 'I'll finish up here for you.'

Erin throws her a grateful smile, then lifts her hand in a wave. 'Bye, Tom, see you in the morning. Breakfast starts at eight.'

'We'll be raring to go,' he calls out. And they will be too because that's how they always behave. Play hard, ski hard. Return home feeling ten years older.

The ambience feels more intimate now it's just the two of them. Tom leans back in his chair and smiles at Nina.

'It sounds like you've skied together a lot,' she says, taking a sip of her wine.

'Every year without fail. Well, Julian, Rob, and me. It probably sounds like we despise each other, but we go way back.'

'And no wives or girlfriends allowed?' For a heady moment, Tom wishes he could lie. Tell Nina he's single. Things have been a bit challenging at home lately and the pure wickedness of pretending Zoe doesn't exist is tempting. But that's ridiculous of course. He's wearing his wedding ring for starters.

'Strictly prohibited on this trip,' he says. 'Rob doesn't have one. Julian's wife Nikki skis, but she's on childcare duty this weekend.' He takes a deep breath. 'My wife loves to ski, but I take her later in the year.' He doesn't mention that she earns three times as much as him, and is therefore three times more likely to pay for

78

their holiday.

'You don't have kids then?' Nina asks.

God, this question again. He's sure it's being asked more regularly since he slid over the hump of his thirties. 'No, not us,' he says lightly, before appraising Nina more closely. She must be about his age. 'What about you? Any mini Ninas out there?'

She laughs. 'No, that lifestyle isn't for me,' she says, shaking her head. 'I think I wanted it once, when I was a wide-eyed kid: important job, gorgeous husband, 2.4 children and a designer dog. I got straight A*'s in my GCSEs; all my teachers thought I was the model student, until I fucked up my A levels. And that's when I realised I'm too much of a rebel for all that traditional family stuff.'

'Oh?' he asks, his intrigue growing. 'Any acts of rebellion you'd like to share?'

Nina's eyes sparkle and Tom wonders if she's about to tell him something juicy. He's already noticed the tattoo on her wrist – *Hendrix* – so she must have been quite a wild child at some point. A one-night stand with Mick Jagger perhaps? Or leading an armed bank robbery, *Point Break*–style?

'Off-piste skiing when it's a five-out-of-five avalanche risk?' she finally offers. Tom sighs. That makes more sense.

'Well, I envy you,' he admits, twisting in his chair to face her. 'Choosing to walk your own path rather than doing what society expects of you. Oh, and skiing pretty much every day of the season,' he adds with a grin.

'Yeah,' Nina says, returning his smile. 'That helps bolster my principles.' Her teeth are bright white, not stained by wine like his probably are by now. 'Maybe you should try it one day?'

'I'm not sure how my patients would feel about that.'

'I guess you'll have to make the most of your three days in Morzine, then?' Nina's small laugh rings out again, and he finds he likes the sound, perhaps more than he should.

Chapter 15

Ivy

Wow. Tom was unfaithful, had a one-night-stand with a colleague he hardly knew. I know it's not my place to judge him, but it's a shock all the same. Especially when I'm still reeling from that phone call with my mum. It must be her imagination playing tricks – babies from regular families don't get stolen in twenty-first-century London. Mum suffers from anxiety, and so she's bound to be hypervigilant in unfamiliar surroundings with such a perceived weight of responsibility on her shoulders. It's easy to see how she could jump to the wrong conclusions.

But still. Not being there physically, not being able to watch over Calum myself, is agonising. Except what choice do I have? I only arrived today. The police are here, and Zoe must have lots of conflicting feelings going on. How could I possibly leave her now?

I follow Zoe out of her room in a daze, and all these thoughts are still banging at my temples when Erin leads us back into the living room. Nina is now perched on the edge of the sofa. Harry has disappeared, and I can't help wondering if he's purposely avoiding the police. Julian and Rob are still sitting on the chairs by the window, the carafe of wine now balanced precariously between them. And two gendarmes – officers from the local police force – are standing in the centre of the room.

With a shaky voice, Erin introduces us, although she doesn't use their names, just says *Monsieurs l'agent*. She calls me an old friend of Tom's, which sounds wrong, but I accept the description with a polite smile. The gendarmes are both dressed in fitted navy uniforms, with simple bomber jackets zipped up to their chins. The tall one is young and seems nervous, his shoulders pulled back and Adam's apple quivering. The other one is about 40 and has a guarded expression, as though he's been briefed by his superiors and needs to remember his lines. *Do: show respect and compassion. Don't: admit culpability or sully the image of our town.*

But it's Zoe who looks the most scared when the older gendarme takes a step towards her, his strangely shaped cap clasped in one hand. 'I am sorry for your loss, Madame Metcalfe. This is a terrible shock for you, and for us too.' He lowers his head. 'I am Lieutenant Dufort, and this is my colleague, Lieutenant Intern Curtet. We are here to help you in every way we can.'

'Thank you,' Zoe whispers. 'But really, I just want to get Tom home, as soon as possible.' Her words feel like lotion on my skin. A day, maybe two. And then I can get back to Calum, and never let him out of my sight again. My fingers itch with the urge to text my mum, to check he's safe, but I can't go on my phone now.

'Of course, I understand. But there are some procedures we must follow first.' He sounds uncaring, but perhaps this is the French way. No-nonsense efficiency. 'Today we must register your husband's death. We will go straight away, if that is okay for you?'

'To see him?' Zoe asks, her voice rising in panic. 'His body?'

'No Madame,' the policeman says, the cap still scrunched between his fingers. 'To complete the relevant forms. Your husband is at the Legal Medical Institute in Thonon now. Your friends identified his body at the scene,' he adds a bit more gently.

Thank God. 'And then he was taken there by ambulance. It's a forty-minute drive away.'

'What?' Zoe says, her face crinkling with confusion. 'Why have you taken him out there?'

'That is where the autopsy will take place,' he explains.

'Post-mortem.' The words waft over, and we all turn towards Julian. 'In the UK it's called a post-mortem.' He gives an apologetic shrug. 'It's what I do for a job.'

'You're going to cut him up?' Zoe suddenly asks, as though her brain has just caught up. 'After everything his body has already been through! Why would you do that?'

'Zoe, I get that it's upsetting,' Julian says, sounding more professional now he's on his specialist subject. 'But every sudden death requires a post-mortem, in France like in the UK. It's a way of making sure Tom's death is recognised and remembered. That's important, isn't it?'

'Exactly. Thank you, monsieur.' Dufort nods proudly at Julian, as though he's personally coached him on what to say. 'And once the post-mortem is completed, assuming there are no anomalies, I'll be able to close the investigation. These gentlemen will get their passports back, and the funeral director in Morzine – Monsieur Durand – will be able to assist you in repatriating your husband. Now, I am sorry to hurry you, but the mayor has come in specially to carry out this duty. Can we go?'

Lieutenant Dufort offered to drive us to the *mairie*, but Zoe said she wanted some fresh air, so we're on foot instead. The two gendarmes, Zoe and me. Plus Nina. With hindsight, I'm not sure that asking Nina to come with us was the best idea – the way both her and Zoe visibly tensed when I suggested it – but I still think that having a friendly French speaker on hand is a sensible precaution. I know this is a habit of mine, using knowledge like a protective shield, but it's the way I'm built. It's why I tapped out a message to my mum while the others

82

were getting their coats on, asking her to send me a photo of Calum, evidence that he's okay. Mum must have had her phone in her hand because one came through moments later, my son sucking happily from a yoghurt tube. It doesn't mean Mum's fears are unfounded, but it was still good to see that – right now – Calum is safe and well.

It's past four o'clock now. The sun has dropped behind the mountains and the *cumulus fractus* clouds look like billowing smoke. Lined with cafés and bars, their windows all steamed up, the street is busy with people heading out for an après ski beer. Some are carrying skis on their shoulders, their feet double tapping in unclipped ski boots, while others are less encumbered with only helmets swinging by their sides. Most of these are stuffed with gloves, goggles, and neck warmers, and I wonder how many accessories will make it back to their accommodation when they stumble home later this evening, a few pints down.

I sense Dufort, who's next to me, stop walking, and I instinctively pause too. 'It's a beautiful view, isn't it?' he says, nodding towards the mountains. The famous apartment buildings of Avoriaz, designed to look like mountain rocks, are twinkling with lights and there's a pale pink bridge of sky underneath the darker cloud cover.

'It's majestic,' I murmur.

He looks pleased with my reaction. 'They rule us, you know. The mountains. Not everyone remembers that.'

'You mean Tom, I suppose?'

His brow crinkles. He starts walking again and I fall in step beside him. 'Yes, I imagine so,' he says, but there's a hint of uncertainty in his voice that makes my skin prickle.

'You think there could be another explanation?' I ask tentatively, not sure I want to know the answer.

He looks up at the sky, then down again. 'Could I ask how well you know Monsieur Cooke?' he eventually says. A breath catches in my throat. I suppose I should have expected this; it was Harry they kept behind at the police station after all. But I still feel sick at the thought of him being a target of suspicion.

'I met Harry – Mr Cooke – at university. The same time as Tom and the others,' I stutter. 'But I didn't know him very well.' It's both a lie and the truth.

'And since then?'

I look at my feet. I was always taught to be honest, especially to people in uniform. But if I admit to seeing Harry more recently, I'm not sure I'll be able to keep it a secret from Zoe and the others. And with everything that happened between us, I don't want them to know. 'We haven't kept in touch,' I say. 'Why do you ask?'

He stays silent for a while, and I watch his breath rise into the night air. Then his face transitions into a tight smile. 'No reason. I was only curious. Ah, we're here,' he says. I turn and look at the large building at the edge of a cobbled square. It's typically French with rendered walls and a line of windows, each one flanked with wooden shutters. The rest of our group is waiting outside. 'The mayor's officer is one floor up,' Dufort explains. 'He's already prepared the paperwork, with an English translation, so this shouldn't take long.' The younger policeman takes the lead, and we all traipse up behind him, then along a line of offices, all dark, abandoned for the weekend.

'*Bonsoir, Madame Metcalfe,*' a voice booms down the hallway. Then a man appears, tall and broad in a pale grey suit, with a protruding belly and comb-over hairstyle. Not French-looking at all. 'I am Monsieur Grorod, the mayor of Morzine. I am sorry to meet you in such tragic circumstances.'

'*Bonsoir,*' Zoe returns dully, not meeting his eye. 'Can we get this over with?'

Chapter 16

Ivy

The wood burner is on when we get back, and I kneel in front of it, staring at the flames licking at its glass door, and wishing I could curl up in a ball. This time yesterday, I was running Calum's bath and wondering what Netflix boxset to watch with my Thai takeaway. Now I'm in a different country, with people I share too much history with, trying to get my head around a barrage of bad news. Tom's death. His one-night stand. The police asking questions about Harry. And most importantly, my mum's fears about Calum. The photo she texted gave me the strength to get to the *mairie*, but the relief has long since vanished.

'Praying to the fire gods, are you, Ivy?' Rob slurs from behind me, before descending into drunken laughter.

God, Tom has only been dead for a day, and one of his supposed best mates thinks it's okay to get smashed and laugh at things that aren't funny. Rob was like this at university, skating over life's surface like nothing really mattered. 'I'm cold,' I say stonily.

'How did it go with the mayor?' Julian asks. His tone is more respectful than Rob's, but the purposeful way he enunciates each word exposes how much he's been drinking too. Zoe went straight to her bedroom when we got back, and Harry hasn't reappeared since this afternoon. I'm starting to wish he would. Even though it's awkward, and the police are asking all these questions about him. It's messy of course, there's no denying that, but we've been through a lot together, and instinctively – maybe incorrectly – I feel like he's an ally.

'Fine.' I continue staring at the fire. Mainly because I can't bear to look at either of them, but also because it's mesmerising, the way it flickers and dances. 'The mayor told us that the post-mortem will take place tomorrow,' I say. 'In Thonon, with Dufort attending.'

'I don't like it,' Rob mumbles. 'The police taking my passport. A pathologist cutting up Tom.' I imagine him giving Julian a disapproving look. 'Makes it feel like a crime when we all know it was an accident. How am I supposed to grieve for my mate when there's all this suspicion flying around?'

'Surely you want it investigated?' I ask, still staring at the fire. 'If someone pushed Tom, I assume you'd want justice for him?'

'He fucking fell, all right? Jesus, fuck!' Rob's swearing rings out in the otherwise quiet room and I turn to look at him, his angry eyes and ruddy cheeks beneath his three-day stubble.

'Why so defensive?' I ask.

'What, you think I pushed him?' Rob spits out, pushing up to standing. He teeters in his new position and grabs hold of the back of Julian's chair to stop himself falling. 'What the fuck are you even doing here, anyway?' he continues, jabbing his finger towards me. 'I'm pretty sure Princess Zoe banished you years ago.'

'Stop being a prick, Rob,' Julian warns.

'Quit acting like my mum!'

'Um, excuse me, dinner will be ready in five minutes.' Erin's Irish lilt cuts through the tension. 'So if you want to move to the table?' she continues hopefully. As the scent of something cheesy wafts over, I realise that I'm starving. All I've eaten today is cereal bars and a packet of Calum's rice cakes that I found buried in my bag.

'Thanks, Erin, it smells delicious,' I say, grateful for the distraction. 'But is it okay if I make a phone call first?' When I spoke to my mum earlier, I focused on reassuring her, reminding her that babies of badly paid academics don't get kidnapped. But since receiving Calum's photo, seeing his beautiful smile, I'm worried that I did too good a job. That I've reduced the threat level to amber when it needs to stay at red.

'Of course,' Erin says. 'It's tartiflette so I'll leave it in the oven until everyone's here.'

Making an effort to avoid both Rob and Julian's eyeline, I push off the floor. My room is adjacent to the living room, with only a thin internal wall between us, so I lock myself into the en-suite bathroom and perch on the toilet seat.

Mum picks up on the first ring. 'Hi, love.' She has a broad Yorkshire accent, and despite the tightness, its familiarity comforts me.

'Hey, Mum. How's Calum? Did he eat his dinner?' I find I need the sanctity of simple questions, predictable answers.

'Yes, I gave him the pouch you left. He gobbled it up.'

I feel my shoulders relax a notch. 'And he's behaving himself?'

'Oh, he's such a poppet. And I see so much of your dad in him. I'm still touched that you named him Calum, you know.'

'I know,' I whisper, smiling into the phone. But then Mum releases a deep sigh, like wind rushing through a tunnel, and I steel myself for what's to come.

'But I've got some bad news, love. I hate to tell you this, with you so far away, I mean I know Calum is my responsibility right now. But . . .'

'What is it, Mum?' I prompt.

'The man in the park.' She pauses. 'I think he followed us home.'

I close my eyes. My heart pounds with such ferocity that I can hear it in my ears. 'Why do you think that?'

'Because I'm sure I saw him again, outside. Watching the house.'

A shiver crawls over my skin. But I need to remember that my mum's fears are rarely, if ever, real. They're ghosts. Because she is still haunted by my dad's death, and how he only took up climbing because she persuaded him to. 'Are you sure?' I ask.

'Well, it was dark.' She sounds less confident already. I open my eyes. My mum still lives in the house I grew up in, at the end of a small village where no one walks past your window unless they're visiting you.

'Maybe it was someone else,' I suggest gently. 'London streets get busy.'

'Oh, maybe,' she says with a sigh. But then she rallies. 'But why would anyone stand outside like that and stare? He was smoking a cigarette, and the tip of it kept lighting up a patch of his face. I don't think he knew I was watching – I was upstairs in Calum's room – but he didn't move from that spot.'

I pull my knees into my chest and lean back against the cold cistern. The urge to be there, guarding my son, is primal. But how can I abandon Zoe when both of us know that Mum spends her whole life scared of nothing? 'Is he still there?' I ask.

'No. This happened a couple of hours ago. He was only stood there for a few minutes.'

'Listen, Mum,' I say, not wanting to dismiss her fears, but needing to reassure us both. 'I'm glad you told me, but I wonder if you're seeing threats that aren't really there because you care so much about Calum, and are so desperate to keep him safe.' My tone is soothing, but the truth is, I can hardly breathe. Am I risking my son's safety by downplaying my mum's concerns? And for what? So I can stay with a friend who once accused me of killing her father? 'Just make sure the house is all locked up,' I continue. 'And I'll be back as soon as I can.'

'If you're sure,' Mum says in a quivering voice.

'It will be fine, I promise.' I bite the inside of my cheek. 'I better go, Mum. Please tell Calum I love him.' I want to tell him myself, but I need to get off this call. To distance myself from her lurking anxiety. I splash some water on my face and stare at my reflection in the mirror, wavy dark hair escaping from its loose plait, green eyes the only flash of colour against my pale skin. Then I push off the sink and walk out of my bedroom.

The four of them are already sat down when I arrive at the table, and the only spare place is next to Harry. As I drop into the chair, our forearms brush against each other. I expect him to linger, to enjoy a few seconds of subterfuge, but he pulls his arm away. Even though we touched by accident, I feel stung by the rejection. Then I think about how difficult this must be for him. Me turning up out of the blue. The others asking after Calum and him not being able to. I suppose I deserve it.

'Wine, ladies?' Rob says, lifting the carafe.

I hold out my glass. I notice Zoe cover hers for a moment, then change her mind and release her hand. Julian fills it up, then proffers the carafe towards Harry.

'Not for me, mate.'

'Really? I thought you'd dropped all that healthy living rubbish?' Rob says. 'You were knocking the beers back yesterday.'

Harry bristles. 'That was a temporary blip,' he says quickly. 'I'm back on the water now.' I look towards the window and try to pretend I didn't hear that, or that I don't understand the significance of Harry falling off the wagon. On the day Tom died.

Erin arrives with the tartiflette and cuts it into six portions. As she dishes it out, I notice her hands are still shaking. The traditional Alpine comfort food – potatoes, bacon and melted cheese – smells delicious, but when I try to swallow a mouthful, it sticks in my throat. I take a gulp of wine.

'A toast!' Rob calls out, lifting his glass. 'To our best friend Tom. He may have been a competitive prick who would rinse his granny if it meant winning something, but still, we loved him. And we will fucking miss him.' We all watch as Rob closes his eyes and tips his wine back, his Adam's apple rising and dropping with each gulp.

'Why are you being such an arsehole?' Zoe asks. 'Tom adored you; do you really think he deserves that?'

Rob's features slacken with instant remorse. 'Oh God, Zoe, I'm being a total dick, aren't I? It's grief, I think. But that's no excuse. You're right, Tom was an absolute legend. He did love his mates, didn't he? He even forgave that idiot.' His eyes narrow as he nods towards Harry, who raises his eyebrows and mutters something indecipherable. Rob's emotions are swerving so chaotically that I have no idea what he really thinks. Can grief be like this? When my dad died, I felt nothing. No highs, or lows. Just a strange detachment that made normal, familiar things feel unreachable. But people cope with loss differently; that's what every counsellor I've ever met has said. Maybe this is Rob's way of handling Tom's death.

He looks up suddenly. 'Hey, we should watch the video!'

'What video?' Zoe asks.

'You want to see Tom, don't you? In all his glory?'

'I don't understand . . .'

'We took some footage on our first day,' Julian explains. 'Of us all skiing. I think that's what Rob's referring to.'

'I don't think that's a good idea,' Harry warns.

'What, because you look like a violent thug?' Julian murmurs.

'No,' Harry throws back. 'Because it will upset Zoe.'

'Rubbish!' Rob calls out. 'You'd love to see Tom skiing, Zoe, wouldn't you?' I want to scream at him – *of course she doesn't, of course it will be too painful for her!* – but I push my lips together and wait for her to say it instead.

'Yes,' she whispers. 'I'd love to see it.'

Chapter 17

One day before the fall

Tom

God, he loves this. Blue skies, bright sunshine, hard-packed snow crunching beneath his skis. Plus the exhilaration of travelling at eighty kilometres per hour without any protection (Tom's never been a fan of ski helmets). He pops off a ledge and enjoys a few seconds of airtime before his skis reconnect with the piste. Then he shifts his weight from one parallel turn to the next, racing past other skiers in his peripheral vision, until the final hard stop by the lift station. He leans on his poles and looks back up the mountain.

'Woo hoo!' Rob flies in next to him. As his edges dig in, an arc of snow sprays upwards, and Tom feels a few icy flakes drop inside the neck of his ski jacket. 'Oops sorry,' Rob says, winking in case Tom thought his apology was genuine. 'God, this is great, isn't it? Better than sex!'

'Better than your sex probably.'

'Ah, you're just jealous of my bachelor lifestyle, my impressive swipe-right record.'

Tom rolls his eyes, while secretly admitting Rob's got a point. 'Anyway, where are the others?'

As predicted, they all made it to breakfast by eight o'clock, even if they looked like shit and stank of alcohol (excluding Harry). After wolfing down Erin's healthy porridge, plus a massive plate of croissants, they headed off to the ski shop together, priming themselves for the worst part of the day. Squeezing soft feet into tight, rigid boots in a hot boot room surrounded by dozens of other skiers all reeking of yesterday's beer and garlic.

But they survived it, and as per Nina's suggestion, headed straight to the Les Gets bowl. He did wonder if he might see her here, but no luck so far. The four of them have been skiing together, more or less, for most of the morning, but now Tom can't see Julian or Harry.

'Oh, they'll be here in a minute,' Rob says confidently. 'Julian's being cautious, isn't he? I thought you said you'd fixed him? And it's hilarious seeing Harry ski like a beginner. He used to be better than you.'

'Bollocks,' Tom calls out before he can stop himself; he knows that Rob is just winding him up. 'And Julian's knee is as good as new,' he adds, this time with an air of pride. Because he is proud. He did a great job sewing up his friend's snapped ACL. 'Him skiing like a Sunday driver is about fear; it's in his head, not his legs.'

'There they are,' Rob says, pointing at two dots halfway up the slope, Julian in black, Harry in a light beige colour that almost blends into the snow. Tom and Rob watch their friends ski down the last section of the piste. 'You know, Harry seems to be improving pretty fast,' Rob says warily. 'Maybe we should do the race sooner rather than later?'

Tom shrugs. The sooner the better as far as he's concerned – he loves a race – but he doesn't share Rob's concerns about Harry.

The guy may have been vying for supremacy on the university ski trip, but his years by the sea must surely have messed up his ski technique.

'We're heading over to the Chamossière lift for the annual ski race now,' Rob declares when the pair of them reach the lift station. 'Come on.' He slides through the gates and the rest of them follow to the base of the four-man chair. Tom feels the familiar thud against his calf muscles, then drops onto the plastic cushion and pulls the safety bar down.

'We should do a recce run first, shouldn't we?' Julian asks. 'So we know the terrain before we race it?'

'Come on, mate,' Rob coaxes. 'It'll be fine. You trust me, don't you?'

'Not in a million years.'

'Nina says you can see the run from the lift,' Tom tries. 'And that it's straight and steep, so perfect for racing.'

'We'll do it your way, then, shall we?' Julian mutters, staring straight ahead. There's a real bitterness to his tone, not their usual banter at all, and Tom feels himself getting offended, then annoyed. What the hell has he done to deserve that?

'Easy, Julian,' Rob murmurs. 'No need to take your shit out on us.'

'Whatever,' Julian grunts, leaning forward over the safety bar. Behind his back, Tom catches eyes with Rob, but he just shakes his head slightly and looks away, so Tom shifts his eyeline to Harry instead. Is Julian's bad mood Harry's fault? Should Tom have known that their time-honoured friendship couldn't cope with the intrusion? Harry seems oblivious to the tension however, as though he doesn't think it's relevant to him. Perhaps it isn't. He supposedly came on this trip to work at their friendship, but he hasn't made any effort to ingratiate himself into the group so far – he doesn't drink, hasn't joined in with the banter. In fact, now Tom thinks about it, he doesn't understand why the guy asked to come along at all.

Twenty minutes later they're stood at the top of the Chamossière lift, looking down at the Les Creux black run.

'Guys, I'm not going to race,' Julian says decisively. 'Take the piss as much as you want, I can't risk my knee going again.'

Tom pauses for a moment. The friend in him wants to respect Julian's decision. But the doctor in him feels professionally responsible for pointing out that Julian is wrong to think that way. 'Your knee has healed,' he starts quietly. 'Don't race if you prefer not to, but don't blame it on your knee.'

'That's easy for you to say with two perfectly functioning ones!'

'I fixed it, Julian.' Tom forces himself to stay calm. 'And I bumped you to the top of the list so that you'd have plenty of time for rehab before this trip.'

'Well, I figured that's the least you could do, after causing my accident in the first place.'

This again. Tom sighs. He knows he should be more sympathetic, more apologetic, but accidents happen, and he's been saying sorry for a full twelve months already. 'Listen, your skis clipped mine, not the other way around. I controlled it; you didn't. You need to move on.'

'Move on?' Julian spits out. Beneath the helmet and goggles, only his cheeks are on show, but they're flushed with anger.

'Enough, guys,' Rob says, assuming the role of peacemaker again, which is fairly unfamiliar territory for him. 'Julian, why don't you ski down and film the race. I'd like some evidence of my win.'

'Gladly,' Julian grumbles, then drops onto the piste and skis – slowly – away.

'What the hell is wrong with him?' Tom exhales.

'Trouble in paradise I think,' Rob says. 'He made me promise not to tell you, but apparently Nikki's having an affair.'

'What?' Tom's heart rate ticks up a gear and his neck feels clammy all of a sudden. 'Why does he think that? Does he know who with? Has he confronted her about it?'

'All right, slow down. What's with the twenty questions?'

'Sorry,' Tom stutters. 'I just . . . I didn't know.'

'I guess I'm more of a natural confidant than you,' Rob says, trying to look nonchalant but still puffing out his chest.

'I don't remember you thinking that when you cried in my living room,' Tom counters quietly. The memory silences them both: that difficult conversation when Rob begged for repentance and Tom reluctantly gave it, and it's only when Harry speaks that the moment passes.

'Look,' he says, pointing to the bottom of the piste where Julian is waving his pole in the air. 'I guess that means he's ready.'

'Okay,' Tom says, trying to regain his focus. He takes a couple of deep breaths and stares at the piste, choosing his line. 'Right, let's start two metres apart. The piste is pretty clear so we can really go for it.' Rob and Harry slide away from him, one on each side. 'On my count, yes?' He takes another couple of breaths. 'Three, two, one, GO!'

He pushes hard on his poles and heads straight down the mountain to get some speed up before leaning into a turn. There are no big moguls, but the terrain is bumpy, and he needs to keep his knees relaxed and his vision alert. Rob is on his left, keeping up with Tom's pace, while Harry is a few metres behind on his right. Suddenly there's a kerfuffle, a cloud of snow and then Rob's shouting in frustration, his body sliding down the mountain.

But Tom can sense Harry catching up. And a couple of turns later, he's on Tom's shoulder. There's no fucking way he's letting Harry win this. Not after the guy persuaded Tom to include him on this trip and all he's done so far is suck the fun out of it. In fact, is this really why he came? Has he been secretly polishing up his skiing on a dry slope? Tom sinks lower, digs his edges even more aggressively, ignores the jolt of pain as his skis hit a mound of snow that he hadn't noticed. But still, Harry keeps up.

From the chairlift, the run looked like it had perfect visibility all the way down. But it's more undulating on the ground, and

95

there's a ridge ahead of him. Tom knows the rules. There could be a slower skier just beyond the ridge, out of sight from his current angle. He should slow down. But then Harry might win, and he can't let that happen. After all, what are the chances of anyone being there?

He hits the ridge. Harry's not with him anymore; he must have slowed down. But shit, there's someone in front of him! A fucking kid! For a split second, they catch each other's eyes, and Tom sees pure terror. But he's going too fast to turn. The kid screams, dives to one side, skis flying off on impact. Tom can't even say sorry. He's out of control, but he's been here before; he just needs to keep his balance. He surges on. And he makes it! The slope evens out and he pulls a sharp parallel stop in front of Julian. 'Jeez, that was close. Did you get good footage?' he asks, breathing heavily.

'Close? The boy dived out of your way!'

'Yeah, I know. Smart kid,' Tom says smiling, more pleased about winning the race than he's prepared to admit. But suddenly there's a noise behind him. And then someone shoves him in the back. He almost topples over, but regains his balance and twists around. 'Hey, what was that for?'

'You could have killed that kid,' Harry spits out, his eyes shining white with fury. It's the first time Tom's seen any emotion on the guy's face since he arrived, but right now he'd prefer blank Harry.

'It was an accident,' he shouts back, trying to regain his composure. 'The kid's fine.'

'You'll do anything to win, won't you?' Harry snarls. 'Trample over anyone in your way.'

'That's not true.'

'Yes it is! The only person you give a shit about is yourself.'

Anger bubbles in Tom's belly. It's not him who had to leave university in shame, or who detonated his medical career because he couldn't control his temper. That was Harry. And Tom was the one who was willing to forgive him, to include him on this boys' trip. 'I think you're forgetting why you're even here, Harry,' he says in a hard voice. And the warning seems to jolt Harry, because his expression changes – from anger, to realisation, then back to the newly familiar indifference. He looks away, then back again.

'Yeah, you're right,' he mumbles. And Tom feels his own anger receding as Rob tumbles into the group.

'Oh jeez, my arse is killing me. Caught my bloody edge, didn't I. Anyway, what did I miss?'

Chapter 18

Zoe

Zoe looks at her empty glass. She shouldn't have drunk a drop of wine, not when there might be a baby inside her. It was completely irresponsible. But now she wants a top-up, in fact she needs one after watching that video. God knows why she thought it would help: Tom's ruthlessness in high definition. And anyway, it's not like she's confirmed her pregnancy yet. She thinks of all those stories she reads, about couples who are desperate for a baby, and how often a late period ultimately ends in disappointment. She reaches for the carafe and pours another glass.

The image of Tom in the video, appearing over the brow of the hill, and straight into the path of an innocent teenager, keeps replaying in her mind. It was unsettling – the thought of what damage Tom could have inflicted if the boy hadn't reacted so quickly – but not surprising. Tom has always been like that where skiing is concerned. It was a drug to him, and like all drugs, it made him selfish. Willing to sacrifice others for his own gratification. Zoe included. And then at some point, that behaviour spread into the rest of their marriage. Did she see it coming? Or did it only become apparent when she found out that he'd fucked someone else? She feels like a fraud, defending him in front of the others, but it's how she's expected to behave. The grieving widow. Life is many shades of grey, but death is either black or white.

No one has spoken since the footage finished. Julian is kneeling by the TV now, unplugging the connecting cable from his phone. Rob – usually the one to fill a silence – is mute, staring at Harry. He was late to join the others after his fall during the ski race and, judging by the waves of fresh anger rolling off him, it doesn't look like he was aware of Harry's outburst. Zoe wonders what he's thinking now. Whether he's connecting the dots between Harry's temper, his presence on their boys' trip, and Tom falling to his death. Should she be thinking the same? Is it strange that she feels so passive? Or is it understandable under the circumstances?

Ivy looks exhausted. She's sat on the sofa with her legs pulled up and her chin resting on top of her knees, scrolling through photos on her phone. Zoe wonders if she regrets agreeing to travel to France. Probably. She's been arguing with Rob – Zoe heard them earlier – and has barely even acknowledged Harry. Julian's too drunk to engage with anyone. It's not like him to drink so heavily, and Zoe wonders what's caused it. Tom's death will have played a part, obviously. But he seems to have more than grief on his mind.

'I might go to bed,' she says wearily. It's a better choice than drinking the wine, even if she is unlikely to sleep.

'Yeah, I reckon we could all do with an early night,' Rob says, smiling weakly. He was hammered earlier – not that she was surprised about that; unlike Julian, heavy drinking is definitely in Rob's character – but the food seems to have sobered him up a little.

'Night then.' She pushes off the sofa and doesn't bother making eye contact with any of them before walking past the dining area and heading into her room.

She left her phone on charge during dinner, and when she

picks it up, she notices there's a message from Nikki. Finally. She can't pretend that she hasn't felt hurt by Julian's wife's – her supposed friend's – apparent lack of interest in Tom's death. She must have known since yesterday – Julian is bound to have called her – but it's still taken Nikki a full twenty-four hours to get in touch. She clicks into the message.

Such shocking news.
So sorry for your loss.
Lmk if there is anything I can do x

That's it? Where's the humanity? The warmth? Zoe flings the phone on the bed and swears under her breath. You really know who your friends are when tragedy strikes, and Nikki is not proving herself to be one of them. Which is strange really. Because Zoe thought they were close. Even with Julian and Nikki moving out to Berkshire, and then having the twins, they have all made an effort to see each other regularly. Nikki particularly loves the chance to visit Zoe and Tom in London for the weekend, the twins deftly palmed off to her parents. But she's acting more like a distant acquaintance now. Add that to Julian's drinking, and perhaps there's something else going on that Zoe doesn't know about. Could their marriage be in trouble too? Was getting hitched so soon after university a bad idea for both couples?

Not that she is married anymore, Zoe thinks, lying on her bed and staring up at the skylight. She hasn't pulled the blind down yet and the sky looks inky black above her. Like her mood. While Tom wasn't the perfect husband – far from it – it's hard to imagine life without him.

But maybe she should try.

While she would never have wished for him to die, and if she could roll back time, she would do so without question, perhaps this could be a chance for her. In time. To pick herself up and build a new life, without the burden of being in love with a cheating husband. To rediscover her strength, the attitude and energy from her university years. She runs her fingers over her belly, tries to ignore the flicker of fear it creates. Suddenly she wants to go home. To wrap everything up in France and return to her house, her work, normal life. To process possibly having a child in her future and get on with things.

She retrieves her phone (not to message Nikki, she doesn't deserve a response) and presses on her brother's number. It takes a few rings, but eventually he picks up.

'Hullo?'

'It's me,' she says, unnecessarily. 'I thought I'd call, check you're okay.' Zoe listens to Luke breathe heavily down the phone and wonders if he's crying. He was 14 when their dad died. She remembers breaking the news to him, her chest heaving with sobs as she tried to explain. He told her later that her grief upset him more than Peter's death. He enjoyed spending time with his dad, he'd explained. Listening to his stories, joining his adventures when he was invited. But he didn't love him. At least not like sons are supposed to love their dads. Not like he loved Zoe.

'Feeling a bit overwhelmed to be honest,' he admits.

'You've been through a lot over the last few weeks.' She remembers how Luke looked on the day he arrived back in London from Cuba. Knackered, shell-shocked, relieved to be back on familiar ground. It was clear then that Luke hasn't inherited their father's adventurous spirit. But she's still glad he found the courage to make the trip; you never know when experiences like that can prove to be useful.

'And you? Are you okay?' he asks, as though just remembering that she's the one who's lost a husband. 'How's it going in France?'

'Hard,' she responds. But she doesn't want him to know how tough this is for her. 'But manageable. Tom's post-mortem is taking place tomorrow, but the police said that's only a formality. There'll be a few other loose ends to tie up, but I'm hoping to fly home in a few days, maybe Thursday evening.' The clouds must have moved a little because a star has appeared above her, puncturing the darkness.

'Thursday?' Zoe can sense Luke counting the days. Maybe the hours.

'And you'll be able to do the things I mentioned by then?' she asks gently. She doesn't like to pressure him, but she wants her return to be as smooth as possible. And that means going back to a welcoming home.

'Yes, it's fine,' he says, his voice stronger now he's got tasks to think about. 'I've already made some headway.'

'That's brilliant, Luke. Thank you.'

'Honestly, you don't have to thank me. It's nothing compared to what you've done for me over the years.'

Chapter 19

2007

Ivy

They all seem so relaxed. Tom and Zoe are giggling, trying to push each other over in the snow – Tom with the upper hand, unsurprisingly. Rob's skiing backwards. Harry's sitting on the back of his skis checking his phone. Even Nikki and Julian – who are beginners like me – seem up for it. It doesn't make sense.

Or maybe it's me who's the weird one. Feeling like I'm going to be sick because Rob has suggested finishing off our day's skiing with a red run.

When Zoe first suggested that we go on the university ski trip to Andorra, my answer was a flat no. It's her favourite sport, and Tom and the others had already signed up, so I understood why she'd want to go, but it wasn't for me. For one, my mum would hate the idea, and I didn't see the point in upsetting her. And two, I was scared. I like sports in stable settings. Netball. Tennis.

Not sliding on snow and ice, and putting my life in the hands of unpredictable weather systems.

But then I found out that Nikki and Julian hadn't skied before and were planning on joining the beginners' group for lessons. And Peter kept telling me that witnessing Alpine weather first-hand would be good for my education. That was enough to convince me to pay the deposit, and before I knew it, I was getting on a coach to Gatwick Airport with forty other students – including my core group of friends – and making the fourteen-hour journey to Pas de la Casa.

I catch eyes with Zoe. Mine must give off some kind of distress signal, because she pulls away from Tom and skis over, her helmet clunking with mine as she leans in. 'Are you okay? Are you sure you're up for this?' she whispers. The whole group knows that I'm new to the sport, but only Zoe knows how petrified I am. I haven't told her everything, like how I've kept the whole trip a secret from my mum, but she knows enough to realise that this run will be difficult for me.

'I'll be fine.' I even manage a smile. Because I don't want to be the person who says no, the sole coward in the group.

'Last chance to take the lift down?' Rob turns to face us, the backs of his skis hanging precariously over the top of the ski run. My palms feel sweaty at the sight.

'God, I can't believe I'm doing this.' Nikki lets out a peal of nervous laughter.

'First pint is on me for any beginner who makes it to the bottom of the slope alive,' Tom promises, skiing over to Zoe's side. They've only been together for four months – since the Christmas MedSoc Ball – but it's been an intense romance and it's hard to remember a time when they weren't a couple. Tom is clearly into Zoe, but it's her who's changed. Nothing too dramatic, but she's a little more submissive now. Less cheeky. A bit slower to make a decision unless Tom's there to endorse it. I don't think it's his doing though, more that being in love, feeling content, has changed her personality.

'Not sure that's entirely comforting,' Julian murmurs in response to Tom's offer.

'Okay, let's do it!' Rob spins on his skis and drops onto the run. But my legs aren't working. I watch the rest of them follow him. Nikki with a squeal, Julian with a mumbled prayer, then Zoe and Tom in unison.

'You next,' Harry says. 'I'll stay at the back, make sure you get down safely.'

Being alone with Harry doesn't help my nerves either. I'd never had a one-night-stand before the night of the MedSoc Ball. In fact, I'd only slept with one other person, a boy I'd known since I was 7 who became my boyfriend in the long summer after A levels. But I didn't hesitate, or question it, when Harry took me back to his room, and gently guided the straps of my dress over my goose-bumped skin. It all felt too perfect. Physically, I wanted to be as close to him as possible. And after he'd talked me back from a panic attack, and I'd confided in him about my dad, we'd created this other, stronger, bond too.

It was the next morning when my viewpoint changed. It's amazing how the same body can go from irresistible to untouchable without any physical change. And I'm ashamed to admit, the only reason my desire vanished was because he took his turn to confide in me. As we lay in his single bed drinking mugs of sugary tea to stem our hangovers, he said that we were good for each other because we were both dealing with stuff. When I asked him what he meant, he started talking about his anxiety.

It began in his final year of school, a mix of worrying about getting his predicted A-level grades – and living up to his reputation as the cleverest boy in his school – and the enormity of being the single child of two doting parents, both doctors, with stratospheric ambition for him. As our ears grazed on the single pillow, neither of us willing to look at the other, he admitted that he should have dealt with it at the time. Told someone, opened up to his parents about his doubts. But instead, he chose to treat the condition himself, with a mix of obsessive studying, sport to tire his body, and drinking himself stupid at every party going.

When he got the top grades, and secured his place at Exeter, the anxiety went away, and he thought he was cured. But then he started his medical degree, and realised it was just lying dormant, waiting for life to overwhelm him again. The sheer volume of study. The exhausting clinical placements. The competitive nature of his peer group. And the constant gnawing fear of getting something wrong. In the winter of his first year, he forced himself to book a session with a university counsellor. He only made one meeting before deciding it was too embarrassing, too painful, to go back. But her words still stuck. Talk to someone. Don't deal with this alone.

And that's when he turned to face me and said how grateful he was that we'd found each other. How, with me by his side, he was certain he could cope with his condition.

None of this deserved my revulsion. I should have been supportive, like he'd been to me. But his confessions made me want to run a mile. For the last ten years, I've lived with someone shackled by their mental health issues – my mum – and I know the effect that's had. There's my own state of mind too: the scars, the fears, I carry from losing my dad. I need someone stronger than me, not weaker. Someone balanced and clearcut, not vulnerable and damaged. So I made my excuses, slipped out of his student house without the others seeing, and, hardly bearing to catch my reflection in the mirror, messaged him later to ask if we could just be friends.

And four months on, that's what we are. Theoretically, at least. Because the tension between us has never gone away.

I shake my head. 'Thanks, but I'd prefer to do it in my own time. You go.' I smile, a silent plea for him to take me at my word. That my request has no ulterior motive or meaning. He pauses for a moment, and I know he's wishing that things had turned out differently for us, then shrugs and drops over. I relax for a moment as I watch him ski without him knowing. His movements are so fluid that he makes it look easy; I still can't believe that he learned his craft on a dry slope in Guildford. But then reality bites once again, and my knees start to buckle.

'Can I give you a tip?' The voice has a French accent and I turn to see who it belongs to. A wiry man in a red ski jacket with grey hair and deep wrinkles.

'Sorry?'

'You look nervous. It won't be a good run for you if you're tense. That's why I sing.'

'Sing?'

'As loudly as possible. Try it.' Then he gives me a small salute – no helmet for him – and drops over, the sound of some unfamiliar melody trailing behind him.

Sing. It seems like a crazy idea, but right now, I'll try anything. I think of the right song for the occasion, then I murmur the first line to myself. It's perfect because I am both afraid and petrified. I smile at the analogy and drop over the edge.

As the song reminds me to grow strong, I dig hard with my edges. As I shout to turn around, I transfer my weight between the skis, as I was taught in my lesson. And when I'm singing about holding my head up high, I realise I'm halfway down the piste, and still on my skis. Thank you, Gloria Gaynor, I am surviving! And more than that, I am loving it. How can this be possible? How can I be enjoying the thrill of hurtling down a steep slope when I know the danger it holds?

I let out a yelp of laughter and lean into another turn. My muscles are taut, my eyes focused on the terrain in front of me, but I feel giddy too. Like the adrenalin has sparked the release of something that's been trapped inside me for years. I think of my dad. How his face would light up when he told me about his climbing trips. Reaching the summit of Ben Nevis one summer, then the Matterhorn in Switzerland the next. I haven't thought about these memories for years, but they're flooding back now.

Fuelling me as I fly down the mountain.

But suddenly I'm back in the moment because I can see someone familiar out of the corner of my eye. Nikki is sprawled in the snow on the opposite side of the piste. My stomach lurches as the fear makes an instant return. She's lying on her back, head down the mountain. I need to check on her, but that means crossing the piste, which seems busy all of a sudden. I look up, waiting for the right moment to traverse.

But then I see Tom above me. He's not with Zoe anymore; she must have gone on ahead – perhaps Tom's joke about the beginners staying alive has made him feel responsible, or maybe he was planning a slalom finish and wanted a captive audience. Either way, it's a relief to see him make a beeline for Nikki. He leans down, puts his hand on her shoulder, and talks for a few moments. Then he reaches for her legs and manoeuvres them into the right position for her to ski off again safely. He holds out a hand, and I watch her gingerly stand up. He gives her a hug, then she sets off, very slowly, with Tom staying with her, coaxing her along. There's something intimate about the scene that makes me feel like a voyeur, and maybe even jealous. Which is nuts. Tom is Zoe's boyfriend, her perfect match. Not even on the market.

I shake the feeling away and push off again.

Chapter 20

Ivy

Calum, NO! I scream it, screech it, with all the air I have in my lungs. But it's pointless. He's moving too fast. He can't hear me. CALUM! I throw myself onto the snow, scramble across it, tiny shards of ice scratching my face, and reach out. Yes! I grab his tiny hand. But it's not enough. His fingers are slipping; he's going to fall; I'm going to lose him.

I gasp. Sit up in bed. Scrabble for the light switch. Pick up my water glass and drink long, desperate gulps. It was a dream. Calum is asleep in his cot at home. He is safe. I repeat these facts to myself until my heart rate settles. There's no daylight framing the drawn curtains, but I know I won't get back to sleep now, so I reach for my phone to check the time. Six a.m. Technically morning here, but only five o'clock in London. I'm itching to call home, to get the reassurance I crave, but I know that's selfish. It's not fair to wake Mum up.

So I do the next best thing – the drug I've been inhaling for the last twenty-four hours – and click into my photos. I scroll through images of my son, stroke his features on the cool glass screen, linger on the one Mum sent yesterday, Calum's smiling, mucky face, and ten minutes later, I feel composed enough to get up. The duvet has crumpled around my middle, so I shove it further down the bed and climb out. I pull a hoodie over my pyjama top and slowly push my bedroom door open, praying that no one else has woken early.

Luckily the living space is empty. Breathing a sigh of relief, I pad over to the kitchen area with its dark wooden units, and flip down the kettle to make a cup of tea. The sky has turned from black to grey beyond the glass doors and the mountains look ominous under its cold glow. I wonder if I'll ever be able to ski again, or whether Tom's death has signalled the end of the sport for me, just like my mum never climbed again after my dad's fatal accident.

I take my drink over to the window and sink down onto the sofa. The sky has brightened a little and the silhouette of Avoriaz has got more detail to it now. As I stare at the same vista that Dufort pointed out yesterday, I replay our conversation in my mind, and wonder again why he asked about Harry. I hate the thought of Harry being involved in Tom's death, but I do know what he's capable of. How his anger can turn violent in the blink of an eye. And now the police are asking questions without knowing anything about his breakdown at university. Why would they do that?

When Harry reappeared in my life, he didn't reveal much about what he'd done since leaving Exeter, but he did mention living and working in France for a few years. Did something happen during that time? Could he have a criminal record here? I push off the sofa and go back to my bedroom, but only for a moment. Once I've got my laptop I head back, take a slurp of tea, and fire it up. I've always put greater value on fact than opinion, so if I'm going to start suspecting Harry of wrongdoing, at least I owe it to him to do the research.

When I first type Harry Cooke into the search engine, a line of images comes up — none of them of the Harry I know — plus a couple of Instagram accounts and a Wikipedia page. As I continue scrolling, I notice that a number of the websites are French rather than English — which makes sense because I'm in Morzine — but it's potentially skewing the information I get, so I return to the search box and add 'British national' to Harry's name.

Some of the websites don't change, but I notice a new link appear — thelocal.fr — with the headline: *Un Britannique emprisonné pour l'attaque sur un super-yacht*. I bite my bottom lip. I don't speak much French, but I can figure out that a British person has been jailed for attacking someone on a superyacht. I can't see Harry's name on the Google result, but why would the algorithm prioritise the article if he wasn't involved? And if he was, was he the victim or perpetrator? My finger hovers over the mousepad for a moment, then with a deep sigh, I click into it. I hit the 'translate to English' button in the corner and start reading.

Following the attack of American business tycoon and superyacht owner Mr Allen Brady, a British man has been convicted of aggravated assault. It is understood that Mr Harry Cooke was working for Brady at the time of the incident. Court papers reveal that, following an argument about working conditions, Cooke punched his boss several times and then pushed him overboard with no apparent concern for his safety. While the boat was moored up less than one kilometre from St Tropez harbour in calm waters, prosecution barrister M. Jalibert emphasised the level of danger Brady was put in as the incident took place late at night and the current was deceptively strong. While other members of staff acted quickly to rescue Brady, Cooke returned to his room, showing no remorse for his actions. It is understood that Cooke was heavily inebriated at the time of the incident, but Madame la jJuge did not consider this for mitigation. Cooke was sentenced to two years in prison and taken to Baumettes Prison in Marseille where he is expected to serve at least half of his sentence.

I lean back against the sofa cushion and feel my laptop slip to one side. Harry's been in prison? For hitting his boss and throwing him off a boat? I look at the date of the article: 10th February 2019. Nearly four years ago. Harry moved back to the UK in 2020, so if he did serve half his sentence like the article suggested, then those timings would make sense. Of course he'd want to leave France after being imprisoned there.

I close my eyes and imagine Tom falling from the mountain-side. Then the scene pans out behind my eyelids to include Harry watching on, with the wild expression that I remember from that night at university. It takes my breath away. Am I completely stupid for believing Harry when he said he'd changed? Was it all a big lie to get me to forgive him?

At Zoe's twenty-first birthday party, I felt like I'd unleashed a devil. That the trail of destruction Harry caused was somehow my fault. But so many years had passed by the time he got back in touch, those feelings had ebbed almost to nothing. If Harry wanted to see me to say sorry, then I was willing to listen. It could have ended there – a vehement apology, a genuine acceptance – but life isn't that simple.

And now this. Tom is dead. And Harry has served time in prison for assault.

Suddenly there's a noise downstairs, making me jump, and a few moments later, Erin appears at the top of the stairs.

'Oh hi,' she says. I can hear the disappointment in her voice, and I can't blame her. Having to prepare breakfast while making polite conversation with a grieving stranger can't be fun.

'I couldn't sleep,' I say, making it sound like an apology.

She nods her understanding while hovering in the space between the living area and the kitchen. 'It must be difficult for you,' she finally offers. I start to answer, to thank her for caring, but she hasn't finished. 'Accepting Tom's death when his fall doesn't make much sense.'

I blink. 'The mountains are dangerous places,' I say, but it feels more like a politician's answer than my own.

'Yes, I know.' She hesitates and I wait. 'The police asked me about Harry,' she finally adds. 'My impression of him. What his relationship with Tom looked like. Whether they'd argued at all at the chalet.'

I tense; pause. 'And had they?' I finally manage to ask.

'No. Not that I heard anyway, and I told the police that. In fact, I don't really understand why they're so focused on Harry. He seemed the nicest one of them all. Sorry,' she suddenly stutters. 'I know they're your friends, but . . .'

'Please, don't apologise,' I say, my voice gravelly. 'We were friends at university, but I've hardly seen them since. And even then, it's only really been Zoe.' That lie again. It rolls off my tongue so easily, but I can feel my cheeks getting hot.

'I didn't realise,' she says, wandering over and dropping down on the sofa, as though my distance from the rest of the group allows her to get closer to me. 'Why did you lose touch?'

I wonder how Erin would react if I told her. And whether Harry would still be her favourite then. 'I went to a different university to do my master's, then back up to Leeds for my PhD. The rest of them stayed in Exeter for a while longer, and then headed to London together.'

Erin nods along to my explanation. 'Was Rob your friend at uni?' she asks tentatively.

'We hung out,' I say. 'But we weren't particularly close. Why do you ask?'

'The police didn't ask me about him.'

I feel tiny electric shocks on my skin. I think about Rob's excessive drinking, his swerving emotions, the insults followed by the apologises. 'And should they have done?' I ask gently.

Erin runs her hands down her thighs. She's wearing leggings and there's a faint swooshing sound as her palms connect with the Lycra. 'Maybe,' she whispers reluctantly.

I stare at the blank TV screen so that I don't risk catching eyes with Erin and scaring her off. Even with the facts, the damning evidence, have I been too quick to label Harry the guilty party? 'Do you want to tell me instead?' I finally ask.

She sucks in a gasp. 'Sorry,' she blurts out. 'I've been holding this inside me since I heard that Tom died. I don't want to get anyone into trouble, but Tom deserves the truth, doesn't he?'

I knit my fingers together to disguise my shaking hands. 'Yes, he does,' I manage, but then my voice cracks and I have to cough to hide it. 'What happened?'

Erin exhales. 'It was Saturday morning. Harry and Julian had gone to the ski shop; Harry wanted new gloves I think. Nina had been over first thing, but she'd left by then.'

'By when?'

'When Rob and Tom started arguing. And I don't mean just disagreeing over something. They were really raging at each other. I couldn't see them because they were upstairs, in Rob's room, but from the banging around, I'm pretty sure it got physical.'

First Harry and Tom arguing on the ski slopes, now Rob and Tom fighting? And on the day Tom fell? I imagine the two strong men shoving and pushing each other, the noise it would create in this old wooden chalet. 'What were they arguing about?' I ask.

'I only caught snatches of it, so it was hard to tell. But it was how it ended that keeps replaying in my head.'

'Why? What happened?'

'I don't think they realised I was still here. They were arguing when they came downstairs, so I caught the last bit.'

'And?' I push.

'Rob was seething, his face bright red, like a fireball. And before he saw me, he screamed, "If you do this, Tom, you're dead to me, you understand?"' Erin sighs. 'At the time, I assumed he meant their friendship, you know?' She looks to me for agreement, and I nod, genuinely, because that's how I would have read it too. 'But the next time I saw Rob,' she goes on. 'Tom *was* dead. And in weird circumstances, falling from an easy run, no witnesses. I've been thinking about Rob's words ever since.' Her eyes well up, and she lets out a small laugh as she blinks the moisture away. 'While serving tartiflette to a potential killer.'

My chest swells as I imagine how hard the last couple of days must have been for Erin. She's still so young, and Morzine is a long way from her family and friends in Ireland. It's no wonder she was shaking when Rob went anywhere near her, especially with him being drunk and unpredictable. 'Why didn't you tell the police?' I ask.

She shrugs. 'They were only interested in Harry, and so I convinced myself that I was letting my imagination run wild.' She pauses, then looks at me sorrowfully. 'But Rob's behaviour since; well, I'm not so sure anymore.'

Chapter 21

Ivy

'Morning.'

I turn towards Zoe with a start. Could she have overheard our conversation? And why do I feel guilty at the thought that she might have? If there was a possibility that Rob pushed Tom, doesn't she deserve to know? But instinctively, I want to keep Erin's account of Rob and Tom's argument to myself while I process it – Zoe has form when it comes to singling people out for blame on a whim – so I attempt a smile instead. 'How are you feeling?'

'It's a beautiful day,' she observes, dodging my question. With the sun now above the mountains, the sky has turned a luscious deep blue, contrasting beautifully with the white snow. She walks over to the glass doors and peers through them. 'Maybe I should go out. Some fresh air might take my mind off Tom's post-mortem this morning.' As she says the words, her face contorts slightly with the effort of not crying, and I leave the sofa to join her by the window.

'What about a walk somewhere?' I suggest. 'Nina mentioned a lake yesterday, but I can't remember what it's called.'

'That will be Lake Chablais,' Erin calls from the sofa. 'It's not far from here and the scenery is stunning. It's the perfect place to distract yourselves. I can give Nina a call; I'm sure she'll be able to drive you up there.' A look of relief washes over Zoe's face, and I wonder if Lake Chablais could be the tonic I need too, to take my mind off Calum and my mum's fears. I hope so.

An hour later, we've attempted breakfast (a few mouthfuls of porridge for Zoe, half a croissant for me) and I've sucked as much reassurance as I can from a stilted phone call with Mum, and one-sided conversation with Calum. Neither Zoe nor I thought to bring walking boots, but Zoe has trail-running shoes on, and Erin thinks my trainers will be fine in these dry conditions. Nina arrives and we clamber into the minibus. 'It's not far,' she says, as though remembering how sick Zoe got yesterday. 'But it is cold up there, and sadly the café is closed for renovations, so call me as soon as you've had enough, and I'll come and collect you.'

'Is the lake frozen?' I ask, wondering if I should have brought an extra layer.

'Oh yes. They run ice-diving trips through the winter. You'll see a metre-wide hole at the north end of the lake on your walk. That's where they drop in. Apparently, it's pretty magical down there.' My parents tried ice diving once, on a short trip to Norway while I stayed at home with my grandparents. I remember them enthusing about it when they got back, how clear the water was, and how they saw so much wildlife because fish swim slower in cold water to preserve their energy. But I shudder at the idea now. I don't think of myself as claustrophobic, but I would not want to be stuck under a thick sheet of ice, however pretty the refracted light shining through it might look.

Ten minutes later, Nina pulls into a small car park next to a circular building with a sail-like roof. Erin was right, the view is breathtaking. There are steep cliffs either side of the lake, with frozen waterfalls snaking down the rock face towards a band of dark green conifer trees. The lake itself is covered in a blanket of snow, half in shadow, half sparkling under the sun's rays.

'Wow,' Zoe murmurs.

'Good for the soul,' Nina agrees. 'Enjoy your walk, and call me when you've had enough.'

We mumble our thanks for the lift and climb out of the van. A moment later, Nina swings back out of the car park and it's just the two of us. Without speaking, we find the hard-packed path beyond the car park and start walking, our legs moving in sync with each other. It's so quiet that I wonder if Zoe can hear the questions playing on a loop in my head. Did Tom fall or was he pushed? Could Harry have killed him? Or Rob? And most pressing of all, is Calum safe?

'Any more news from your mum on that man from the park?'

I take a breath. 'I'm sure it's nothing,' I start, trying to build some resolve. 'But Mum's now got it in her head that he was watching the house from the street last night.'

'Christ, really?' Zoe's eyes widen. 'Do you think there might actually be someone?'

I shrug, feel the corners of my mouth curl downwards. 'No.' I shake my head. 'No,' I repeat more vehemently. 'It doesn't make sense that there would be. Babies don't get kidnapped in Earlsfield.'

'And there's no chance that it could be, um . . .' Zoe pauses, tilts her face away from me. 'Well, that it could be Calum's father?'

My stomach lurches into my mouth. 'No,' I bark, then soften my voice, fall back on the familiar lie. 'He lives in Canada, and I didn't even tell him I was pregnant. This isn't him; it isn't anyone,' I add, feeling more certain. 'It's my mum being overly anxious, that's all.'

Zoe nods. 'It must be hard for you,' she observes. 'Trying to work out what's fact and what's paranoia.'

I look down at my feet, willing the tears to stay away. 'When I was little, she was up for anything,' I say. 'Always wanting to prove that women were as brave as men. Then we lost my dad, and the grief wore her down. It wasn't long before she saw danger everywhere.'

'I wonder if that will happen to me.'

I remember my reservations from earlier this morning 'Do you think you'll ever ski again?' I ask.

'Oh yes,' Zoe says firmly. 'Dad would turn in his grave if I gave that up.'

'Tom's fall doesn't make you scared that something similar might happen to you?' Zoe doesn't answer straight away, and we walk on in silence for a bit. The sunshine feels warm on my back, and I don't want it to go, but the path is leading us into the shade.

'Tom and I have always had a different approach to skiing,' she finally says. 'I know the risks and respect them. Tom was always more reckless than me. More like my dad in that way.'

I become conscious of my heartbeat as the seconds tick by. Zoe has apologised for the way she spoke to me at her twenty-first birthday party since we've been back in touch, but this is the closest she's come to acknowledging the role that Peter played in his own death, and I feel a long-buried weight lift slightly inside me. Now that Tom's gone, and Zoe and I are both single women, perhaps there is a chance for our friendship to strengthen into something meaningful again.

And that thought makes me wonder if I'm wrong to keep my suspicions about Tom's death to myself. 'And you don't have any questions about how Tom died?' I probe gently.

She shrugs. 'He always skied too fast; we all saw evidence of that last night. So I don't suppose I can be shocked that he died from the same vice.'

We cross the shadow line, and the temperature instantly drops. I zip my jacket up to my chin and shove my hands into my pockets. I can see the black hole in the ice where the divers have carved an entry point. 'And the police didn't say anything to you?'

'Only that they can't close the investigation until the post-mortem is done, but they don't foresee any issues with that after this morning.' She looks at her watch. Her expression darkens for a moment, then clears. As we pass a couple with a large, hairy dog, I wonder why Dufort didn't ask Zoe about Harry. Or if he did, why she hasn't mentioned it.

'And you don't mind?' I press. 'Not knowing exactly how it happened?' I know that I should stop pushing her, let her grieve the way she chooses to. I recognise that it's actually me who can't let it go rather than Zoe.

But I can't help it. That's why I'm a scientist, not a philosopher; why I predict the weather, not just talk about it. I need to know the facts. My grandparents thought I was too young to go to my dad's inquest, but it was before my mum became fearful of everything, and she wanted me beside her. I remember listening to the different witnesses explain in detail how the accident happened, especially the two climbers in Dad's group who survived. And even though I didn't warm to one of them, I remember how helpful it was. I even decided that I wanted to be a meteorologist while I was there, so that I'd be able to spot a storm brewing in plenty of time to avoid danger.

And I can't stand that we won't have that same clarity for Tom. That he disappeared into the cloud and the three people he was with can't explain it. Or perhaps won't.

But if Zoe is willing to accept it, do I owe it to her to try?

'Of course I mind,' she says, interrupting my thoughts. 'It's fucking heartbreaking.' Her voice cracks, and I listen to the rush of air as she takes one, two, three deep breaths. 'But if I focus too much on the why or the how, I swear I'll go mad.'

Tears sting as the enormity of what she's going through hits home. Their marriage clearly wasn't perfect, but they've been together since they were 19 years old. And now he's gone. Forever. I suddenly realise that I'm crying, and quickly wipe my cheeks.

'Can I ask you a favour?' she asks.

'Of course,' I manage.

'Can you stop bringing it up? All the unanswered questions? I know that I'll never find out for sure how Tom died. Whether he flew off in a blaze of glory, or edged over and stumbled.

Whether he called out for me in his last few seconds, or was too busy thinking about someone else. The not knowing is the hardest part of losing him, and every time you mention it, it hurts all over again.'

Shame pulls at my insides. 'I'm sorry,' I whisper.

'I know you think you're helping.' She pauses, bites her lip, strokes the front of her ski jacket. 'But I just want this trip over with. I want to take Tom home and begin to move on.' She pauses again. 'And get you back to Calum as quickly as possible.'

Chapter 22

Ivy

There's a grave expression on Erin's face when she opens the door, Nina having dropped us back from the lake, and I panic for a moment that she's going to say something about Rob. Assume I've told Zoe about his fight with Tom on our walk. But it's not that.

'Lieutenant Dufort is here,' she says in a conspiratorial voice. 'He just got back from Thonon.' My stomach lurches and I look at Zoe, but she seems more stoical now. Perhaps our walk has done its job.

'Thanks, Erin,' she says. 'Come on, let's get this over with.' We traipse upstairs in a line, Erin leading and me trailing at the back. I feel like I'm walking towards a firing squad, and my mood doesn't improve when I see Harry, Rob and Julian all perched on the sofa. Dufort is standing next to the wood burner with a mug of coffee in his hand.

'Ah Madame Metcalfe. I hear you've been up at Lake Chablais. It's full of colour in the summer, very beautiful, but there is something special about it in winter I think.'

'Absolutely. It was mesmerising. A wonderful place to clear your head, wasn't it, Ivy?'

Zoe looks to me for agreement and I nod. 'It was stunning,' I add, for something to say.

'And you've been at my husband's post-mortem,' Zoe goes on, a new quiver in her voice.

Dufort sighs, then gestures towards the dining table. 'Shall we sit down?' Zoe hesitates for a moment, then walks over and sinks into a wooden chair. Erin has moved into the kitchen – although I can tell from her body language that she's listening to every word. I hesitate – should I sit with the men or join Zoe at the table? – before the decision is made for me when Zoe beckons me over.

'Madame Metcalfe, the post-mortem confirms that your husband died from a catastrophic head injury,' the policeman says gently. 'No helmet was recovered at the scene, which fits with the three statements given by these gentlemen.' He nods towards the others.

'Tom wouldn't wear one,' Zoe whispers. 'He thought he was invincible.'

The policeman takes another mouthful of coffee, then places the mug lightly on the table. 'There were further injuries to your husband's body, but these were all consistent with the trajectory of his fall.'

'And nothing else?' Shit, I didn't mean to speak. I sit up a bit straighter, avoid Zoe's stare.

'There was some alcohol in his blood. But other than the injuries sustained in the fall, Monsieur Metcalfe was a healthy man,' Dufort confirms. 'And while any pre-existing injuries around the trauma sites would be impossible to detect at the post-mortem, there was nothing to suggest any third-party involvement in Tom's fall.'

'Lucky for you, Harry,' Rob murmurs under his breath.

'You were the one who wouldn't speak to him on Saturday,' Harry spars back quietly.

'Tom is dead, for Christ's sake,' Julian hisses. 'Stop bickering like little kids.'

'I think I should go,' Dufort says, pushing his chair out. 'Give you time to process your loss. I will be recommending that the police investigation be formally closed. Your husband's body will be transferred to the funeral director in Morzine this afternoon, along with his belongings.' He hands over a white business card with dark grey writing. 'This is the address. If you give him your insurance details, he will make all the arrangements for your husband's body to be repatriated to the UK. There are a number of steps that must be taken, but he has experience of this.'

Zoe takes the card, then slips it into her back pocket. 'Thank you for everything.'

Dufort turns to look at the men. 'And my colleague, Lieutenant Intern Curtet, will drop your passports off tomorrow. Then you are free to leave as you want.'

The police investigation will be formally closed. You are free to leave. Those sentences linger in my mind. It's what Zoe wants, and the police are the experts here. It's also a big step towards getting back to Calum. So why do I feel uncomfortable with it? Like I'm letting Tom down by accepting it?

Because no physical evidence of Tom being pushed doesn't mean nobody pushed him. And from what Erin told me, Rob did all but threaten Tom only a few hours before he died. The police only ever asked about Harry, but shouldn't they know the truth about Rob too? Before he disappears back to the UK?

'Let me see you out,' I say quickly. I know that I promised Zoe that I'd stop asking questions when we were at the lake, but I didn't promise to keep quiet about what I know. I keep my gaze firmly on the floor – away from both Zoe and Rob – and lead Dufort down the stairs.

'If you need anything at all, please call me,' he says as I push open the front door for him. I step outside and pull the door to.

'So you've decided that it was definitely an accident?' I ask

124

in a quiet voice. The balcony doesn't extend to the front of the chalet, but I know how far voices can travel in the stillness, and any one of them could be standing out there now.

'We've spoken to everyone involved, Madame Hawkes, and we're satisfied that there is no evidence of any criminal activity. So yes, it was a tragic accident.' He smiles, a dismissal, then turns to go. It feels like a now-or-never moment.

'I know Harry's been in prison,' I pipe up. He pauses, then turns back to face me.

'That is true. But Monsieur Cooke's final prison report describes his rehabilitation very positively. Alcohol appeared to be a trigger for him, and I understand he has addressed this. And there was no evidence of any disagreement between him and Monsieur Metcalfe.'

I'm pleased to hear him absolve Harry, provide the reassurance that I was right to forgive him when I did. But I can't let the policeman go yet. 'So what about the other two men in the skiing party?' I try. 'Have you considered whether either of them could be responsible?'

'Naturally, we've spoken with Messieurs Wakefield and Hill. They're both doctors, madame, and very good friends with—'

'Old friends,' I interrupt. 'I'm not sure they're good friends anymore.' I feel my phone buzz in my pocket – it could be a message from my mum – and an involuntary gasp slips out. But Dufort misinterprets my rising emotion and narrows his eyes.

'Madame Hawkes, if you have some information that you would like to share, please do so.'

I curl my fingers around my phone, itching to check it, but I have his attention now. 'I understand that Tom may have had a falling-out with one of them on the day he died,' I say.

'Which one?'

'Is everything okay here?' Julian's head appears in the doorway, followed by the rest of him.

'Yes, fine,' I snap.

'I was making tea, wondered if you wanted a cup?' He looks so apologetic that I instantly feel bad for my rudeness. None of this is his fault.

'Sorry,' I say. 'Tea would be good, thank you.' Then I turn back to the policeman, but with Julian there, the moment has gone.

'I have a meeting this afternoon that I must get back for,' he explains, but the intensity in his dark eyes shows me that I've aroused his curiosity. 'But if you have any concerns at all,' he adds quietly, 'please come and see me at the station tomorrow. I am very interested in what you have to say.' Then he turns slightly to take in Julian too. 'Goodbye, madame, monsieur. Again, I really am sorry that you've suffered such a terrible loss.' He lifts his hand in a short wave, then turns on his heels and disappears up the cobbled path.

'What were you talking to him about?' Julian asks.

'Nothing much,' I mumble, and scrabble to open the message from my mum.

Chapter 23

Ivy

We sit on the balcony and stare at the view. The cloud cover has increased since this morning, and the *stratocumulus lenticularis* clouds clinging to the mountains mean that Avoriaz is partially obscured. But it's still mesmerising. I wrap the blanket a bit tighter around my shoulders and take a sip of the hot cup of tea Julian has made me. He's doing the same in the adjacent chair, both his hands wrapped around the mug for warmth. Even though it's freezing out here, this is still the most relaxed I've felt since I arrived in Morzine.

Which might have something to do with the message from my mum.

Having a good day despite rain!
Have built a den with cushions.
Calum gorgeous. Such a cheeky laugh!
No sign of the man so might try park later xx

It's so good to hear her sound upbeat, even like she's enjoying herself. I wonder if this means I can risk the delay to going home that telling Dufort about Rob might cause.

'How are you coping with all this?' I ask Julian. 'You and Tom were friends for a long time.'

'Numb, I suppose. Like I can't really believe it's happened.'

It's another reminder of how similar Julian and I are, our matching approach to grief, and I feel a fresh wave of fondness for him. 'Could I ask you something?' I start tentatively.

'Yes.'

'Have you ever personally carried out a post-mortem on someone who's fallen to their death?'

He drops his head to one side in thought. 'Actually yes, a few years ago. A roofer who didn't have his harness attached. Such an unnecessary death. Why do you ask?'

'Did he die in the same way as Tom?'

'Um, from memory, I think his cause of death was a heart attack brought on by catastrophic blood loss rather than head injuries. He was wearing a hard hat.'

'Did the police get involved?'

'Yes, they always do when it's a sudden death.'

'And was there any suggestion the roofer was pushed?'

Julian straightens up in his chair and turns to face me. 'No, of course not. It was an accident. Why would you ask that?'

'But if there had been, or let's say you knew for sure that another roofer had pushed him,' I press on, 'would you expect the evidence found at his post-mortem to be any different?'

Julian sighs, shifts his eyeline away from me. 'I know where you're going with this,' he says. 'And yes, it is usually impossible to determine whether the victim of a fall was pushed, or fell accidentally, purely from post-mortem evidence. As gravity is such a key factor, the effort required to push someone off a roof – or a cliff,' he adds reluctantly, 'is unlikely to cause additional bruising to the body.'

'So Tom's post-mortem was pointless then.'

'No,' he says firmly. 'The pathology team would have looked for other causes, like neurological conditions for example, something that could have affected his balance.'

'There weren't any.'

'It's standard practice,' he explains. 'Sometimes you don't know what you're looking for until you find it.'

'But they didn't find anything with Tom!' I say, exasperated.

'Exactly!' Julian responds, matching my tone. 'Because he died the way the police theorised. By losing his bearings in the dense fog and skiing through the small gap between two safety barriers. Terrible. Tragic. But logical. You're a scientist – I don't understand why you're struggling with that.'

'Well, maybe I don't understand why you're not,' I counter, but that's not fair. He wasn't in the chalet when Rob had his argument with Tom. But Julian was a good sounding board at university, the most level-headed amongst us, and I'm desperate to share what I know with someone. 'Erin told me something this morning.'

'Oh?'

'About Rob. She said he and Tom had a massive argument on the morning Tom died, when you and Harry were at the ski shop.'

Julian's eyes flit towards the glass doors, then back to me. 'They argue all the time.'

'She said Rob threatened Tom.'

Julian narrows his eyes. 'So you think Rob, a dedicated A&E doctor, one of Tom's best friends, pushed him off a cliff because they'd had a falling-out?'

It sounds less plausible now. 'Maybe. We both know he's got a temper.'

'Rob's got a temper?' Julian lets out a short bark of disbelief. 'If you truly believe someone pushed Tom – which I'm sure didn't happen, by the way – do you really think Rob is the most likely culprit? Can you not remember as far back as fifteen years?'

I gnaw the inside of my cheek. Julian is right – Harry was out of control that night. And his conviction for assault a decade later shows that his violent behaviour wasn't a one-off. But he's had therapy since then, is finally putting his medical training to good use. And he promised me that he's changed. 'I'm just telling you what Erin said.' I hate how defensive I sound.

'Yeah, well, Erin shouldn't be spreading malicious rumours about innocent people,' he spits out. 'In fact, she didn't warm to Tom. Maybe she pushed him.'

I look at his face, the bitter anger in his expression. 'Why are you being like this?' I ask quietly.

'Like what?' He huffs, looks away. 'I'm not being like anything. I guess life is a bit shit at the moment.' He drops his head suddenly, closes his eyes, and runs his thumb and finger across his eyelids. But tiny teardrops leak out anyway.

I edge my chair in front of the glass door. 'What's happened? Is it work, or Nikki?' I ask.

'Having twins is hard work,' he whispers, brushing the tears off his cheeks and turning back towards me.

'I can't imagine. Just having Calum feels like a full-time job.'

He smiles, but then his face cracks. 'She's been sleeping with someone else, Ivy.'

My eyes swell in surprise. 'Nikki has?' I say, pointlessly. 'Are you sure?'

'Yes. I'm certain,' he says in a low, deliberate voice. 'But I have no idea what to do with that knowledge.'

'Oh, Julian, I'm so sorry. Do you know who with?'

He stays silent for a few moments, shifts in his chair. 'It's someone she works with,' he says eventually. 'A cocky son of a bitch who thinks he's better than everyone else.'

'I can't believe she'd do that.' But as I make the comment, I realise how ridiculous it is. I don't know Nikki anymore, or the state of their marriage. 'Have you asked her about him?'

'She's got no idea that I know. And I'm planning on keeping things that way.'

'What? You don't mind that she's been unfaithful?' I ask incredulously.

'Of course I fucking mind,' he spits out. 'But I don't want to lose her. I don't want our family to split up. I don't want to be that failed husband who only sees his kids once a fortnight. And I still love her; she's my wife.'

'But if you don't confront her, won't she continue to see him?' I ask as gently as I can. He doesn't respond, and I wish I hadn't said anything. I can see that he's in turmoil, still figuring things out. I reach out for his hand and squeeze his ice-cold fingers.

'No,' he finally says, so quietly that I only just catch it. 'I'm pretty sure it's over now.'

Chapter 24

Zoe

Zoe lifts one foot into the bathtub, then the other, and sinks down under the bubbles. The water is very hot – deliberately so, her bones still felt chilled from her walk around the lake – but now she wonders if the heat is bad for the baby. The one she still doesn't know for sure exists, she reminds herself. She sinks down further, lets the water roll over her shoulders, and closes her eyes.

Today was a big milestone. Tom's post-mortem completed. She can't think too much about what that would have entailed, like she can't let herself dwell on the injuries he sustained in the fall, or whether he was conscious at the point of impact. But she can be pleased that she's now one step closer to taking him home.

She was nervous about calling the funeral director, but it turned out there was no need to be. Monsieur Durand's English was perfect, and he explained what happens next clearly enough. Tom's body will be prepared by him personally, ahead of his journey to the UK. At that point in the conversation, he'd asked Zoe about what clothes to dress him in. She hadn't considered packing anything specific when she was getting ready to fly out, so she'll have to choose something from the wardrobe here.

Monsieur Durand also agreed to liaise directly with the insurance company (thank goodness) and with Geneva Airport regarding the flight and all the protocols involved in repatriation. Like the sealing of the casket under police supervision, although where they think Tom might disappear to over the Channel is beyond Zoe. The one problem is that only a select number of flights will accept caskets, and Monsieur Durand said it might take a few days to sort out. That panicked her – there's a flight on Thursday evening that she'd love to be on – and made her wonder if she could leave France without her husband. She doesn't like the idea of abandoning him, but she's also impatient to get home, to check on Luke, get back to work. And maybe take a pregnancy test in her own bathroom.

But either way, there are still a few more things to do before she can leave.

Like picking up Tom's belongings. The funeral director suggested Zoe drop by to get them – bringing his new set of clothes at the same time – and they agreed she'd go over tomorrow at ten. She wonders what belongings there will be. Ripped clothing. Mangled skis. Cracked ski boots. What will she do with them? Create a battered Arc'teryx shrine in his honour? But she can't be sentimental about it. She knows that the only sensible thing is to throw them away.

There will be Tom's phone too, she supposes. He usually keeps that in his inside pocket, cushioned by thick feather down, so it's even possible that it survived the fall. Not that it would be much use to her if it did; in all their years together, Tom has never told her his passcode. It didn't bother her for ages – in truth, it didn't even cross her mind – but that changed when she found out he'd slept with someone else. After that, the secrecy tore at her gut.

That surge of anger again. The bath isn't providing comfort anymore, and she pushes her hands against its hard base. Her back, now slick with bubble-bath residue, slides up the curved porcelain. She dries her hand on the towel draped over the toilet seat and reaches for her phone, which she dropped on the bathmat when she got in. As usual, she goes straight to WhatsApp. There's a message from Nikki which she scans – something about Julian not returning her calls, and her being desperate to know what's happening, as though she's the fucking widow – and scrolls down to Tom's name.

Like probably every married couple, there is a long thread of perfunctory messages between them. Favour requests, domestic instructions, memes with no explanation, and the odd *how's ur day?* When Tom goes on his annual boys' ski weekend, he usually sends her longer messages with details about the chalet (he knows she's curious about interior design) and how the day's skiing has gone. But not this year. He sent a quick message from the airport on Thursday evening – *Arrived safely but the transfer driver looks about 12, wish me luck!* – and then nothing until Saturday morning.

And that's the one she feels compelled to read now.

Which is all Ivy's fault. Because her supposed friend won't drop the idea that Tom was pushed off that mountain. The way she kept pressing Zoe on their walk, questioning how Tom could have fallen without anyone seeing him, and then asking Dufort if the post-mortem brought up anything else. She clearly only offered to see the policeman out of the chalet because she wanted to continue grilling him. He said earlier that he would be recommending that the police investigation be closed, but could Ivy have said something to change his mind?

And if she did, was it about Rob?

Taking a deep breath, Zoe looks down at her phone, and reads the message from Tom that she now knows off by heart.

Having massive moral dilemma.
Rob's been a fucking idiot.

We're talking off the scale idiocy.
Do I throw him to the wolves?
Or send his patients there instead?

And then, reluctantly, she scrolls a bit further to the final message in their shared thread. The one she typed back in response to her husband's question.

If Tom's phone is recoverable, and his code is somehow retrievable, it will be in his message thread too, she realises. How would she feel about Dufort reading her final piece of advice to her husband?

Would he think that she played a role – even indirectly – in his death?

She hopes it doesn't come to that.

And not only because she doesn't want the policeman to think badly of her.

She doesn't want Tom's death to be tarnished by the possibility of criminal intent. And more than that, she knows that any suspicion would mean a delay in her taking him home. She can't stand the thought of that. She knows that's a terrible thing to admit, that she should be more like Ivy, not satisfied until she has every last fact. But deep down, she knows Rob couldn't have killed Tom – they were best friends – and so why drag the whole thing out for absolutely no reason?

She looks down at her message one more time.

Honey, think of your own career.
If Rob's fucked up, it's not your job to protect him.
You MUST report him.

And then she chooses 'Delete for Everyone', drops her phone back onto the bathmat, and sinks into the bath until even her head is submerged.

Chapter 25

One day before the fall

Tom

Tom slides onto the tall wooden bar stool. As usual, they chose the most challenging ski run back into Morzine village, so it's a relief to finally give his overworked thigh muscles a rest. He reaches down to unclip his ski boots and rides the familiar – but always odd – sensation of blood rushing into his liberated feet.

'Pint?' Rob asks. And it would be Rob, because he appears to be the only one happy to talk to Tom at the moment. Harry is avoiding him, probably embarrassed by his violent outburst earlier, but lacking the grace to move on. It took him over a decade to face up to Tom last time, so perhaps that's not surprising. And it seems that the incident with the French boy hasn't helped lift Julian out of his black mood either. Lunch would have been pretty dull if they hadn't bumped into Nina outside the restaurant and persuaded her to join them. She'd recommended the *Grand Pre* the previous evening, promised that it did the best omelettes on the mountain, which turned out to be true, so it was nice to be able to shout her lunch as a thank you.

And at least she laughed at Tom's jokes, which was a bonus.

'You bet. And toffee vodka chasers all round?' Tom suggests, trying to lighten the mood. 'I think we've earned them.'

'Pint of Coke for me, thanks,' Harry says. 'And maybe a water chaser.'

Rob sighs. 'I hate to say it Harry, but you're not as fun as you used to be.'

'Some might say more fun,' Harry murmurs, as Rob pushes off the table and heads in the direction of the bar. Then with more effort than should be required under the circumstances, Harry turns towards Tom. 'Listen,' he says in a low voice, avoiding his friend's eyes. 'About earlier.' He coughs. 'I shouldn't have lost my temper with you.'

Not quite an apology, but something. And at least he's stuck around this time. Tom shrugs. 'Forget about it. I probably deserved it.'

Julian snorts in response, but doesn't follow it up. Instead, he turns to Harry. 'You know, I reckon you'd have won that race if it wasn't for Tom's sociopathic streak. You're sure you haven't skied in fifteen years?'

Harry shrugs, then looks down at the empty table, uncomfortable under the spotlight. 'Not since uni. But I enjoyed it today, getting back on the mountain. Finding my ski legs.'

'Maybe that's the real reason you came,' Julian ventures. 'Nothing to do with making up with Rob and I, just the chance of a ski holiday.'

Harry's eyeline shifts up. He looks from Julian to Tom, then back again. 'No, it's not that,' he starts. 'I came because Tom thought it would be a good idea. A chance to show you and Rob that I'm not the psycho you remember.'

Tom fixes a smile on his face; he's almost positive that it was

Harry who suggested he join the trip, not Tom inviting him, but life is busy, and he does have a tendency to get carried away.

'Yeah, Tom does like to think he knows best,' Julian responds, a new bitterness in his voice.

Tom's shoulders tense. He doesn't mind a bit of verbal jostling – in fact he positively thrives off it – but Julian seems to be properly pissed off with him on this trip and he doesn't understand why. It unsettles him. Yes, Julian can be a bit dull, but he's also reliable, a reassuring comfort blanket when Tom worries he's pushed his luck too far. It's never crossed his mind that Julian's loyalty might not be guaranteed. 'Your skiing looked great by the end of the day, mate.' Because no one is immune to compliments, he thinks. 'There's no way anyone could tell that you'd had knee surgery less than twelve months ago.'

'And I suppose you want credit for that too,' Julian says with a sigh. It's another jibe, but Tom thinks he can detect a slight softening in his tone. He starts to smile at Julian, to capitalise on his progress, but his attention is drawn away by his phone buzzing against his chest. He fishes it out and smiles more broadly at the newly arrived message on his screen.

But it seems to have the opposite effect on Julian because his expression hardens. 'Who's your message from?' he asks, but his question is drowned out by Rob dumping a tray of drinks on the table.

'The guy at the bar, Jerome, he owns this place,' Rob says, excitement dancing in his eyes. 'He makes his own toffee vodka, gave me a little taster, and I promise you, it is premium stuff.' He places a shot glass in front of each of them except Harry (who gets a disappointed eyeroll instead). 'To us,' he calls out. 'For killing neither French teenagers, nor each other!' Then he tips his head back and pours the mahogany liquid into his mouth. Tom and Julian follow suit and Rob's right; it does taste good. Tom has never understood why toffee vodka – a blend of two such loved ingredients – has never found a following outside of ski resorts.

Julian puts his empty shot glass back on the tray and picks up one of the pint glasses. He takes a couple of large gulps of his beer, then keeps both hands on the glass as he places it back down. 'Tom was just telling us who his message was from, weren't you, mate?'

'My message?' Tom asks, fumbling with his phone while taking a generous mouthful of his own drink. 'It was from Zoe,' he finally answers, making sure he doesn't look Julian directly in the eye, because that's exactly what a liar would do.

'You sure about that?'

The bar is full of stimulus – dance music throbbing out of the speakers, large screens showcasing extreme skiers emerging from avalanches, and the noise and stink of heavy-set men celebrating their day of exercise – but it all falls away as Tom processes Julian's words. A surge of guilt suddenly barrels through him and he feels exhausted. Why can't he be more like Julian? Sensible, honest. Not addicted to the relentless spinning of a Russian roulette revolver at his temple? He takes a long gulp and then turns to face his friend. 'Yes, of course.'

Julian raises his eyebrows, but chooses to glug a few more mouthfuls rather than give Tom a response.

'Jesus, Julian, you're putting me to shame.' Rob necks the rest of his pint without stopping for breath. 'Whose round is it next?'

'I'll go,' Tom says. He could do with some space – Julian looks like he might explode at any moment.

'I'll come and help,' Julian offers.

Fuck. That wasn't quite what Tom had in mind. 'Great, thanks,' he manages through gritted teeth. The two men walk to the bar in silence. It's busy, so they have to jostle for a spot. They stand, shoulders pushed up together, and stare at the barman whose attention is taken up elsewhere.

'I just want to know the truth,' Julian finally says, still not looking at Tom, his voice low and strained.

'What truth?' Tom tries to make his question sound offhand,

139

but the air is thick with tension, and he knows he's stepping into dangerous territory.

'That you're sleeping with my wife.'

'Fucking hell, Julian!' Tom splutters. 'Rob mentioned that you're worried Nikki's seeing someone else, but why on earth would you think it's me?'

'She's always fancied you. I knew it at university, really. But I chose to ignore it, figured it made sense for her to wish she was with one of the good-looking, sporty ones, rather than the geek who takes life too seriously.'

'Mate, she only ever had eyes for you.'

'I hoped she'd grow out of it. Thought she had,' he adds. 'Jesus, we have kids now. But clearly, I was wrong.'

'Julian, I'm sorry if Nikki is cheating on you, but I promise – on my life – that I'm not sleeping with her. I'm a married man too, remember.'

'Oh yeah,' Julian sneers. 'Because you've always been honest with your wife.'

Tom's heart rate ticks up. *Poker face.* 'I certainly have.'

'That is bullshit! Zoe even told me you've cheated on her.'

Tom swallows hard. God, it's hot in the bar. His bloody thermals are sticking to him like clingfilm. 'What did you say?'

'One weekend we were up, after too many glasses of red wine. You'd gone to bed by then, Nikki too, and Zoe and I stayed up talking. She was quick to deny it the next morning, blamed it on the booze, said that it was just a fear she had, not reality. But I could see she was lying. And I was suspicious even then, I suppose. I know how excited Nikki gets when we spend weekends with you, so I checked her phone – I don't think she realises I can. There was nothing dodgy in your messages to each other – you're far too smart for that – but I checked her calendar, and there were a couple of entries called Dr Love. So I tracked her location on those days. And guess what? She went to London, an address on Harley Street, trips she later denied making when I asked her what she'd done that day.' He pauses, catches his breath. 'And we both know you're a doctor, with a practice on Harley Street.'

'That's your evidence?' Tom asks incredulously, a jet of relief rushing through him. Julian's so-called proof is pathetic. He knows the other drinkers at the bar can hear they two of them. He can sense them looking away awkwardly. But he's got no choice; he needs to convince Julian that he's talking bullshit. 'A fake name linked to my profession – our profession, I should say – and a pied-à-terre vaguely near my practice?' he continues.

'And you flirting with each other all the time! And you cheating on Zoe! Don't try to wheedle out of this.'

'Julian, if you really think I'm having an affair with your wife, why the hell did you come away with me?'

'I don't know! Because I want to hear you admit it?' Julian hisses.

'Gentlemen, what can I get you?'

Tom looks up, flustered. Julian's accusations, his revelations, are still dominating his thoughts, and he'd almost forgotten that he was waiting to be served. The barman's hands hover by the shelf of clean glasses, one arm shining white under the overhead light, the other darkened by an intricate pattern of tattoos. 'Um, three pints, please,' Tom manages.

'Coming up.'

He watches the barman grab two large glasses, but then jumps as Julian slams his fist against the shiny metal bar and hisses, 'But you're too much of a liar to even do that!' It's loud, and a dozen heads turn towards them. Tom can't look. But then Julian pushes away from the bar, turns and, thank God, marches out.

Chapter 26

Ivy

I accept the second cup of coffee gratefully and stifle a yawn after another terrible night's sleep. I thought Sunday evening was bad, but last night was even worse. Zoe didn't make it to supper at all. Julian pushed his food around silently, maybe brooding over what Nikki might be up to at home. Rob hardly spoke either, just kept topping up his wine glass and staring at Erin, as though he knew what she's been saying about him. I'd asked Julian to keep our conversation private, but I should have guessed that his loyalty would be with Rob.

With neither of them saying much, it became clearer that Harry was giving me the cold shoulder too. I thought I'd be the one avoiding him, batting off his questions about Calum, but it seems that he wants nothing to do with me. Is he angry with me for the way we left things? Or protecting himself from more hurt? Or is it worse than that? Is he keeping his distance because he pushed Tom and feels too guilty to face me?

Whatever his reasons, the terse silence around the table was horrible, and I escaped to my bedroom as quickly as I could.

But I didn't find any solace there either. I phoned home hoping to have a decent chat with Mum after her earlier optimistic message, but her mood had nosedived. She'd been to Sainsbury's Local with Calum to buy a few bits for tea and was certain that someone had followed them there. She couldn't really describe the man, just gave vague details about him being quite tall and younger than her, and that he'd disappeared once she went inside the store. But the experience had terrified her, she said.

Of course I hardly slept after that. It's now been two full days since I left Calum, and all I can think about is getting back to him. Wrapping my arms around him and feeling his baby warmth.

And that means I need to stop dwelling on Tom's fall. I can't bring him back, so what's the point? Dufort is confident that Harry wasn't involved, and an argument between Rob and Tom proves nothing except that they're both a bit hot-headed. Perhaps I should be glad that Julian interrupted us before I had chance to tell Dufort about it.

Zoe's bedroom door opens, and I watch her walk over to the table. She looks even worse than me. Her face is pale, even tinged with green, and there are dark circles around her eyes. I think of Mum when my dad died. How broken she looked when she returned from the hospital in Airedale, and that was only half an hour away.

'Did you manage to sleep much last night?' I ask.

'Not really,' Zoe whispers. 'The bedroom feels haunted with Tom's things littered around. I just want to get back to London.' My own hopes echoed back to me.

'Would you like some breakfast, Zoe?' Erin asks. 'Or coffee?' Zoe shakes her head.

'You need to eat,' I say quietly.

'I'm meeting the funeral director at ten,' she says, by way of explanation. My heart rate ticks up. I never visited my dad at the funeral home, but it was on the bus route to my secondary school, so I passed it twice a day for seven years, and never once managed to do so without imagining him in there. I know what a big deal it is, and I can't let Zoe go by herself.

'I'll come with you, for moral support.'

Zoe gives me a weak smile, but then her features pull downwards. 'Oh God, I'm going to be sick.' She pushes off the chair and races into her bedroom. Moments later, the sound of Zoe throwing up filters through the walls. I look at my watch. There's no way she's going to be able to see the funeral director in an hour.

When the noise dies down, I knock at Zoe's bedroom door. 'I thought I'd call Monsieur Durand,' I say. 'Postpone your meeting so you can rest a bit longer.'

'I can't go, Ivy,' Zoe moans from inside the room. I push gently on the door and step inside. The blind is still closed, and I take a moment to adjust to the darkness. Zoe is lying on the bed, her legs entwined around the crumpled duvet. 'I feel terrible,' she goes on. 'I can't face it. Will you go for me? Please?'

I hesitate. But perhaps going on my own will be easier than being under Zoe's scrutiny.

'Everything's already organised,' Zoe pleads. 'Monsieur Durand just wanted me to bring some clothes for Tom – they're over there, on top of the chest of drawers – and give me Tom's belongings. But you can do those things for me, can't you? Please, Ivy?'

'Of course I can,' I whisper.

I arrive at the funeral director's at ten on the dot. It's the last in a line of units at the ground level of a modest apartment block on the edge of the town. There are wooden flower beds outside with hardy purple and green shrubs and a large sign running across the top of the main window. *M. Durand. Pompes Funèbres*. I take a deep breath and walk inside.

There's a small round table in one corner, surrounded by four chairs upholstered in a forest green velvet. In the middle of the room is a long oak counter with a desk behind it, and what looks like an office beyond that. There's an old-fashioned bell on the counter, but before I get chance to press it, the door at the back opens and a man in his fifties wearing a dark grey suit and ice-blue tie appears. 'Bonjour, madame,' he says solemnly. 'I am Monsieur Durand, and you must be Madame Metcalfe. I'm so sorry for your loss.'

'No, not me,' I say hurriedly. 'I'm Ivy Hawkes, a friend of Mrs Metcalfe's. Zoe isn't feeling well. She asked me to come in her place.'

'I understand,' he says, nodding. 'A loved one passing away is very difficult under any circumstances, but especially when the death was so unexpected. Please pass on my condolences.' He pauses for a moment. 'I think you have some clothes for me?' My arms are shaking so much that the bag is rustling against my skin. Zoe has chosen jeans and a sweatshirt for Tom. I'm sure it's the kind of thing he wore, but it still feels inappropriate somehow, even disrespectful. I wish I had a designer suit to give the funeral director instead, more the kind of thing that Tom wore to work. But it's none of my business. I hand the bag over.

'Thank you. Now, if you wouldn't mind waiting here a moment, I'll get Mr Metcalfe's belongings for you.'

As I watch him retreat to the office, I sink down into one of the velvet chairs. Tom is here, I realise. Perhaps in a room further back that I can't see, or maybe there's a basement. I imagine his cold corpse lying on an embalming table, the recent scars from his post-mortem on display. Then it's my dad lying there. Then both of them, side by side. My face crumples. God, why am I doing this to myself? I hide my face in my hands, let my cheekbones drop into the curve of my palms.

'Madame? Are you okay?'

I sit upright, wipe the tears from my cheeks. 'Sorry, yes.' He continues looking at me, concern etched into his face. I need to give him more of an explanation. 'It's a bit overwhelming I suppose. Being here.'

'Monsieur Metcalfe was a good friend of yours?' he asks.

No, not really, I want to say. But that wouldn't make sense based on my reaction, so I nod instead.

'It must have been such a shock for you all. For us locals too,' he adds.

'How do you mean?'

'It's just strange, that he fell where he did.'

'It was a white-out,' I murmur.

'Oh, I know, madame. But that mountain is often above the cloud line, and people have been skiing on it for decades. Monsieur Metcalfe is its first ever casualty.' He shakes his head. 'The mountains will always be a mystery, but your friend's death is especially hard to fathom.' He pauses, bites his bottom lip, then sighs. 'Perhaps it's not for me to say,' he continues. 'But it seems almost impossible that he could have fallen from there.'

I feel dazed as Monsieur Durand hands me Tom's things. He's talking to me about Tom's skis being stuck on the rocks, unreachable until the spring, and his ski boots needing to be sawn off because the clips broke on impact. That the rest of his clothes and his phone, which miraculously seems to have survived the fall, are in the bag. But I'm struggling to process any of it, because his earlier comments are on replay in my mind.

Monsieur Metcalfe is its first ever casualty.

It seems almost impossible that he could fall from there.

Chapter 27

Ivy

I stand on the pavement, my fingers gripping the bag of Tom's belongings, wavering with indecision. I could turn left. Go back to the chalet, check on Zoe, do what I can to speed up Tom's repatriation. Get back to the UK so that I can protect Calum from whatever threats, real or imaginary, might be out there.

Or I could turn right. Follow the River Dranse until I reach the police station on the outskirts of town and ask to see Dufort. Stir up a hornets' nest, alienate my old friends, delay my return home. But maybe get justice for Tom. Tears prick at my eyes as I weigh up the seemingly impossible choice.

I lean against the wall of the building, the local stone feeling cold and rough against the back of my head, and try to think more clearly. I don't want to make life harder for Julian with everything he's going through. And I'd be putting Harry – and his criminal record – back under the spotlight. I could be wrong about Rob too. I think about Zoe's stinging accusations at her twenty-first birthday party, how much damage they did. Am I considering accusing an innocent man now?

But if I go home without saying anything, I know that the uncertainty of how Tom died will eat away at me forever. Especially after everything he's done for me. A sob escapes from my chest, drawing the attention of an elderly lady walking past. I give her a weak smile and she returns it before looking away.

I believe in facts, and I need more of them before I can decide what to do, so I rummage in the bag of Tom's stuff until my fingers find his phone. I stare at it for a couple of seconds, marvelling that it managed to survive the fall. And then I wonder if I might be able to figure out his passcode. He's never revealed it to me since we've been back in touch, but there is one set of numbers that he could have chosen. Four numbers that would mean something to him. I could try it. Apple gives you three attempts before disabling the phone, so I've got nothing to lose.

Seeing Tom's home screen appear, and therefore discovering that I was right about his passcode, makes me more resolved to find the truth. So with a new energy, I open up his WhatsApp account. There's a special group for the trip – *Morski 23* – and I scroll through those messages, but there's nothing more incriminating than the ribbing I remember from our university days. I check the individual chats with Rob, Julian and Harry, but they've been quiet lately – perhaps that's to be expected as they've been in each other's company – and I don't find anything there to help me either.

Then I look at my own name on Tom's phone. It releases the catch on my emotions, and I have to breathe a few times to stay calm. I decide I don't need to check my own messages though. I remember every chat Tom and I have shared since he came back into my life, and looking at them now will only upset me. So I look at another name I recognise. Nina. If she's just the resort rep, why were they exchanging messages?

When Zoe told me about Tom sleeping with that locum doctor, I was stunned. I couldn't believe he'd do something like that, although I understood that I had no right to judge. But if he can be so casually unfaithful, could he have started something with Nina out here? She's definitely his type. And I remember her struggling to control her emotions when she met Zoe and me at the airport. Maybe she and Tom slept together. Then fell out. Maybe she followed him up in the lift and killed him.

I know my imagination is running wild, but I click into her name anyway. And then I exhale. There are three messages from Nina, but all of them are perfunctory. Answers to Tom's specific requests. A mountain restaurant recommendation, a bus time-table, and the name of a ski lift. Exactly what you'd expect from a professional resort rep.

But that leaves me back where I started, with no more evidence that Tom was pushed. Just a scared chalet host, confused funeral director, and gut instinct. I look at Zoe's name on Tom's phone and wonder if that might hold some secrets. I don't want to know intimate details about their marriage – I would never sink that low – but if Tom was worried about something, or someone, wouldn't his wife be the obvious person to confide in? If there was a clear threat, Zoe would surely have raised the alarm herself. But she's so grief-stricken – not sleeping, being sick, struggling to deal with her loss – that she could easily have missed something more nuanced about his mood.

I tap on her name, and before I have chance to reconsider, start reading. The last message is from Zoe, sent on Saturday morning, but it's been deleted, so the first one I can see is from Tom to her. And it's enough to set my heart rate rising again. *Rob's been a fucking idiot.* I listen to the thud against my ribcage, remember Erin's fearful explanation about the fight they had on the day Tom died. *Do I throw him to the wolves? Or send his patients there instead?* What does Tom mean by that? Is Rob making mistakes at the hospital? Did Tom threaten to expose him?

And did Rob react by pushing Tom to his death?

I think about how hard they all studied, how much they wanted to be successful doctors. And how Rob is still working at one of

149

London's largest A&E departments. Long shifts, high stress. No partner, no kids. A man wholly defined by his career. It makes sense that he'd go to extreme lengths to protect that.

I know I'm stoking up a fire, but I can't let this lie. I turn right, and head towards the police station.

'Madame Hawkes, please, take a seat.'

I've never been inside a police interview room in the UK, but I've seen enough TV shows to be confident they don't look like this. No scuffed walls or peeling linoleum here. I sink down onto the cushioned chair and try to relax.

'You mentioned that you have some information about Monsieur Metcalfe's accident?' Dufort prompts. I hesitate for a moment because the only word I really hear is 'accident'. It's like he's already made up his mind. But I've made this choice and I need to see it through.

During the walk along the river to the station, I decided not to mention Tom's final message to Zoe because I can't deal with having to explain how I know the passcode on his phone. I disabled the 'last seen' setting on Tom's WhatsApp account, and then turned the phone off completely. I can only hope that the fight Erin witnessed will be enough to get the investigation reopened. And then it will be up to the police to find the truth. 'I understand there was an argument,' I start. 'Between Tom and Rob Wakefield. On Saturday morning. Apparently, it got physical.'

'That's interesting,' Dufort says, nodding slightly. 'And Monsieur Wakefield told you about this?'

'No.' I shake my head. 'Erin told me, our chalet host. She overheard some of it, including Rob saying, "if you do this, you're dead to me".'

'And do you know what Monsieur Wakefield was referring to?'

I pause for a moment, wondering if I can slip in some details from Tom's WhatsApp message to Zoe. But I can't risk it. 'No, sorry. But it is quite a coincidence, don't you think?' I push. 'Them

150

fighting like that, then Tom falling to his death in mysterious circumstances hours later.'

'Not that mysterious,' Dufort counters. 'The visibility was very bad, and while I didn't want to make this point in front of his wife, the post-mortem revealed that Monsieur Metcalfe's blood alcohol level was 173 milligrams per 100 millilitres of blood. That's more than three times the drink-driving limit in France. That could easily account for him making this mistake.'

'But the funeral director told me that no one had ever fallen from that run before.'

A look of annoyance passes over Dufort's face, then disappears. He rests his elbows on the table and steeples his fingers. 'I spoke to Monsieur Wakefield.'

'I know,' I say impatiently, the adrenalin derailing my manners. 'He was here with you when Zoe and I arrived in Morzine, giving his statement.'

'I mean on the Saturday afternoon, in Avoriaz. I was alerted by the specialist search team when Monsieur Metcalfe's body was discovered and headed straight over there. Your friend Rob was very upset.'

'Well, wouldn't you be if you'd pushed your best friend off a cliff?'

'I was asked to take him away from the scene,' Dufort continues, his tone more measured than mine. 'He was making the process of removing the body more challenging.'

'Maybe he was trying to destroy evidence?' I know I'm pulling at imaginary straws now, but the less inclined Dufort is to take me seriously, the more I want to dig in.

He sighs. 'Monsieur Wakefield told me about the argument he had with his friend. And how devastated he felt knowing that he'll never get the chance to apologise.'

'But isn't that what a guilty man would say?' I push. 'He will have known that Erin overheard them, so he'd want to cover his tracks.'

'Perhaps,' Dufort says. 'But I believed him.'

'And that's enough?' I ask incredulously. 'Your opinion?'

'No, but if I trust him, then so will a jury. We might not have the same burden of proof in France as you do in the UK, but there is absolutely no hard evidence against Monsieur Wakefield. Maybe he did push your friend. Maybe He's been holding a grudge for decades and finally grabbed the chance when it presented itself. But argument or not, vague threat or not, I will never be able to prove it. And it would be wrong of me to use our limited resources to try.'

'So we'll never know,' I whisper, my vision starting to blur. 'That's what you're telling me?'

'I suppose so, yes. Sometimes we have to accept our limitations and move on.'

I sit back in the chair, processing Dufort's words, and thinking how much Tom would hate being constrained by anything.

Chapter 28

2007

Ivy

'Surprise!'

I look at the four of them in horror. I shouldn't really. This should be a welcome sight, a spontaneous visit from my best friend and her entourage during the long summer break. But Mum doesn't like surprises. And I don't like exposing my university friends to my mum.

'What? Um . . .' But I'm speechless. And powerless, I realise, as Zoe kisses me on both cheeks, then brushes past me into the cottage. I take a step back and watch helplessly as they all follow – Peter, Tom, and a teenage boy I don't recognise, but am guessing is Zoe's little brother.

'What a gorgeous home!' Zoe exclaims. 'I hope you don't mind us dropping by? We've been up in Scotland, wild camping in the cairngorms, Dad's idea obviously, and when we were driving back, I saw a sign for Skipton. And I was suddenly desperate to see you.'

'Great, yes, thank you,' I stutter. 'Come in.' Mum is in the kitchen, and I imagine her hiding behind the door, listening intently but not daring to come out. It's been over ten years since Dad died, but the legacy of losing him still defines her. 'Let's go into the living room,' I suggest, ushering them left, and away from the closed kitchen door.

'Well, this pit stop is certainly a cut above the usual motorway services,' Peter says, looking approvingly at the exposed local stone around the fireplace and the distinctive mullioned windows overlooking the back garden. 'Don't suppose I could get a coffee, could I? I've been driving for six hours straight.'

'Without a seatbelt,' Zoe adds, under her breath.

'They're too constricting,' Peter moans, rolling his shoulders, proving their potential for unruliness. 'I still remember when seatbelts were optional, bloody nanny state. And anyway, I didn't hear you offering to share the driving.'

Zoe shakes her head. 'That ancient jeep is like a tank,' she says. 'No way I'm lugging that around corners. Of course if it was the MG, then it would be a different story.'

'Sorry, doll, I love you too much to let you drive that car,' Peter says, shaking his head. 'Two-seater soft tops and effervescent young women are not a good combination.'

'Eurghh, such a chauvinist,' Zoe says, giving me a conspiratorial eyeroll. 'Luke, please make Tom your male role model and not your father, okay? Oh sorry, Ivy, this is my little brother Luke.'

'Hey, Luke.' He doesn't say anything in response but manages a self-conscious half-smile, which seems pretty generous for a 13-year-old boy under the spotlight.

'And Tom of course.'

'Hi, Tom.' I feel embarrassed about Tom seeing me here, in my childhood home. I prefer him knowing the Ivy who skis down red runs and drinks vodka shots. Not that his opinion of me matters.

'Hey, Ivy. Sorry for descending on you like this.' He sinks into the sofa and instantly looks at home. How does he manage to make everything look easy?

'It's no problem,' I manage, not quite looking at him. 'Honestly, it's great to see you all.' I realise I mean it too, now the shock has worn off and I've created some distance from my mum. When university finished for the summer, I stayed behind in Exeter for a couple of weeks to do some work experience at the Met Office (not the reason I chose to study in the city, but a nice bonus all the same). But I've been back home for nearly a month, and the boredom is starting to get to me. Last summer I found it easy enough to slip back into the old routines, but my second year at university has changed me, these friends have changed me, and this stifling existence isn't enough anymore.

'Is that your dad?' Tom continues, nodding towards a photo on the mantelpiece. I follow his gaze, then instantly look away, towards Peter, who's staring at the silver birch trees in our garden. Not quite trusting myself to speak without my voice cracking, I pick up the photo. It's of us all on holiday in Majorca, our three faces smeared with strawberry ice cream. It's not really how I remember Dad, but evidence of his climbing – even the photo of him and Mum having summitted the Matterhorn – is firmly banned now. 'Yeah, he looks like a good guy,' Tom muses. His assessment makes my eyes sting and I blink a few times. Zoe must notice too because she suddenly steps forward.

'Let me help you with the drinks,' she declares, clapping her hands. 'Is the kitchen through here?'

'No, really, I can . . .' I place the photo frame on the side table, but the tiny delay means that Zoe has already waltzed out of the living room, and I don't manage to stop her pushing on the kitchen door and walking inside. I feel a sense of my world collapsing in on itself and wonder for a moment if the high-pitched crash is its imaginary soundtrack, rather than a glass smashing, but then I hear Zoe's muffled voice.

'God, sorry! I didn't mean to startle you.'

I tumble into the kitchen. Mum is crouching down, picking up pieces of broken glass with shaking hands. Zoe is standing over her, hands covering her mouth, eyes wide with horror. A second later, she drops down. I assume she's going to start helping, but instead, she puts her arms around my mum and gently draws her up to standing.

'This is all my fault, and you are totally not clearing up my mess,' she says decisively, looking directly into my mum's eyes. 'I'm Zoe, Ivy's friend from university, and I've very rudely turned up uninvited. And with three strange men, which is even worse. I'm so sorry.' Genuine concern exudes out of her, and I feel a swell of love for my frivolous friend who keeps the best parts of herself hidden. She steers my mum towards one of the four chairs around the small kitchen table. Mum is 46 years old, but in this moment she looks both childlike and elderly.

'Oh, you have nothing to apologise for,' Mum says, her voice growing stronger now that Zoe has given some validation to her fear. 'It's lovely to meet one of Ivy's friends. Exeter is a long way from here, and I haven't had a chance to visit.' Mum works part-time from home and, thanks to Dad's prophetic approach to life insurance, doesn't have any money worries. It's not time or distance that has kept her away.

'I promise we won't stay long. A quick coffee and we'll be on our way.'

'Don't be silly. I'm a rusty host I'm afraid, but Ivy will look after you, won't you, love?' She turns to look at me, and I immediately feel guilty. I'm trying so hard to keep my friends away from her. But why? Because I want to protect her, or because I'm ashamed?

'Yes,' I say, nodding. 'Shall I make coffees all round? Or would Luke prefer a Coke?' I put the kettle on, then grab the dustpan and brush from under the sink and start sweeping up the fragments of glass. Zoe seems to have forgotten her earlier promise

156

to clear up the mess, but I can't complain – I haven't seen anyone new put my mum at ease so deftly in a long time.

'Will you join us, Mrs Hawkes? I'd love you to meet my dad. He's Ivy's tutor, but you'll know that already.'

'What's this?' Mum looks from Zoe to me, her fragile confidence waning as she tries to make sense of Zoe's words. I haven't told Mum about Peter, just like I haven't told her that I've wanted to study meteorology under him since childhood. She knows the basics – my degree, the career I hope to build – but I've never felt inclined to open up more than that. Mum believes that dreams get shattered, and I don't want to give her the chance to damage mine.

'It's nothing, Mum.' I try to sound offhand. 'Zoe's dad teaches one of my modules – that's how I met Zoe actually – and he'll be overseeing my dissertation next year.'

'And he's here?' she asks. Her question is laced with something unfamiliar. Curiosity. I bite the inside of my cheek. The truth is, I don't want her to meet Peter, or Tom. I have too many secrets now.

'He's a climber,' I blurt out. I know that doesn't accurately describe the academic meteorologist sitting in our living room who loves to sail, ski and explore wild places. But it is the surest way to put my mum off meeting him.

'Oh really? Interesting.' Mum's fingers creep upwards and she scratches her neck, the tell-tale sign that the message has hit home. She looks at her watch, and there are an awkward few seconds when none of us move. Finally, Mum looks up. 'You know, I would love to say hello, but I've just remembered that I promised to drop in on Mrs Berry, my neighbour,' she adds, turning to Zoe. 'She's not been well.' It's true that Mrs Berry has been complaining about a summer cold, but I doubt this warrants a home visit. But I've got what I want, so I give Mum an encouraging smile, and she takes that as her cue to leave. 'Bye then,' she calls out, then disappears through the back door.

'Your mum's nice,' Zoe says, turning to face me. 'But her anxiety does seem bad.'

'Oh, she's fine really. She's shy, so you're seeing her at her worst. Could you pass those mugs?' I add, hoping to change the subject.

'You're very loyal, aren't you? To your mum.'

'I guess we all are, aren't we? When it comes to family?'

Zoe shakes her head. 'Not always. I adore my dad – God you know that – but I know his love for me is conditional. If I did something he disapproved of, like refuse to shave my armpits, or become an accountant, he'd lose interest. I think that's why I value loyalty in my friends, like you.' She pauses for a moment. 'And Tom.' We catch eyes and I wonder if I see a warning in hers. 'I know that neither of you will ever let me down.'

Chapter 29

Ivy

I kick clumps of snow as I walk back along the river path. I can't believe the detective was so defeatist. That he basically admitted the case was too difficult for him to solve. Even though I heard echoes of my own mindset – the necessity of facts – it still felt wrong that he was so content to give up.

I'm still in a bad mood when I get back to the chalet, so it's not great to see Zoe sat at the outside table. The air is fresh, but the sun has made another appearance today, and Zoe's face is tilted towards it, her body wrapped in a thick blanket. I want to walk past her, go to my room, phone home. But I can't ignore her. 'Hey, Zoe.'

She turns, cups her hand over her forehead to avoid the sun's glare. 'You're back.'

I nod. 'Are you feeling better?'

'I've stopped being sick if that's what you mean,' she says staring at my midriff, the plastic bag held against my ski jacket, knowing what's inside. 'But Rob's in a foul mood. The police haven't dropped their passports round yet so he's raging. I think he's gone down there to demand them back.'

My stomach catapults. Rob's at the police station? What would have happened if I'd bumped into him there? Is there a chance he saw me without me noticing him?

'You've got Tom's things,' Zoe says, her voice catching, bringing me back to the present. I feel a rush of guilt and thrust the bag into her hands. Too late, I realise that Tom's phone is still in my pocket. I can't get it out now – how would that look? – so I pull my face into a sympathetic smile.

'Some things were too damaged to give back to you apparently,' I say. Suddenly I'm grateful that Dufort has washed his hands of this case, so there's no chance he'll be back to expose my lie. 'Tom's boots and skis. And his phone unfortunately.' But luckily, she looks more relieved than disappointed. I watch her carefully pull Tom's red ski jacket out of the bag and stroke the shiny material.

'Red for danger,' she whispers. 'That's what they say, isn't it?' But I can't help thinking something else. That dressed in red, Tom would have been more visible than the rest of them in the cloud. An easy target maybe.

'Shall we go inside?' I suggest. 'I walked back, and my toes are frozen.'

Zoe nods, then stands up, and together we walk towards the front door. 'Did Monsieur Durand mention anything about getting a flight for Tom?' she asks as we walk inside, warmth rising from the underfloor heating.

'Only that he would call you when it was organised,' I say, trying to remember the funeral director's final instructions as his doubts about Tom's fall reverberated around my head. 'I think he was hoping for Friday.'

'Three more days,' Zoe says mournfully. 'I'm not sure I can do it.'

Three more days wondering if Rob killed my friend, while desperately hoping that Harry didn't. And three more days away from my son, who Mum keeps telling me is being followed by a stranger. I'm not sure I can do it either.

'This is delicious Erin, thank you.' Julian catches eyes with the chalet host, then gives her an encouraging smile. It makes him look fatherly, and it hits me how old we've got, how long ago it was that we were at university together. It's crazy that I'm here at all, with people I've hardly seen in fifteen years. I slice off a chunk of lasagne but find I don't have the strength to lift it to my mouth. I still don't really understand why Zoe chose me to come with her.

Rob reaches for the carafe of wine and fills up his and Julian's glasses before passing it across the table. Harry and Zoe both refuse, but I can't resist. I take a long gulp and look at Rob who's also dissecting the food on his plate without eating any. 'So, Zoe,' he says eventually. 'I wrestled our passports back eventually.' I steal a look at him, to check if there's any accusation in his expression, but he looks guilty rather than cross. 'And Julian and I have booked flights for tomorrow.'

Zoe shrugs. I'm not surprised that she doesn't care – it's not like either of them have been a great support to her over the last few days – but my skin is fizzing. It makes sense that they'd want to go, but is Rob escaping justice? I take another gulp of wine.

'When do you leave?' Zoe asks.

'Tomorrow evening,' Rob says. 'It's a nine o'clock flight.'

'We need to get back to work, you see,' Julian adds, his tone more apologetic.

'What about you, Harry?' Zoe turns to look at him. 'Are you going too?'

Instinctively I look across at Harry and discover he's staring straight at me. The shock of it almost makes me gasp. He hasn't looked at me directly for two whole days. Why has he chosen now to change that? Because he can sense our time together coming to an end? Or because he feels more relaxed now that Dufort has closed the investigation? 'I came by train,' he says, not looking away. His face is heavy with regret, and I wish I knew what for. 'And I could only get a ticket back for Thursday.'

'Better hope the police don't change their minds about you before then, hey, mate,' Rob says, chuckling to himself as he reaches for the carafe.

'Or before your flight tomorrow.' Oh God. That just slipped out. I pick up my glass and pretend to study its contents.

'What do you mean by that?' Rob asks, his voice hardening.

I stare at the wine, the reflection from the light above me dancing as I tilt the glass. I'm supposed to be a dispassionate scientist who only deals in facts, and there is no real evidence that Rob pushed Tom. But Rob was always impulsive. Quick to act, slow to consider the consequences. If his career – his whole life really – was in jeopardy, it's not a stretch to imagine him lashing out and pushing Tom.

Fuck it.

'I mean that you keep going on about Harry, but it was you who argued with Tom on Saturday morning,' I say. 'And then he – the best skier I have ever known – fell from an easy ski run, that no one has ever fallen from before, a few hours later.'

'Oh God, Ivy! Please can you drop it?' Zoe pushes her plate away, a piercing clink chiming as her wedding ring slams against the porcelain. 'All of us have argued with Tom at some point, okay? Other than you, maybe. He was selfish, arrogant, uncompromising at times. But we didn't all kill him! In fact, the stupid mugs that we are, we all still loved him.'

'Hear, hear,' Julian mutters. Then he leans across the table and reaches for my hands. My heart is racing, and part of me hates them all, this clique who have ganged up to tell me I'm wrong. But I also feel lonely, cut adrift from my normal life, desperate to see my son, so reluctantly I let his fingers curl around mine. 'I know the opaqueness of Tom's death has been hard for you to accept,' he says gently. 'And I'm sure the memory of your dad dying in similar circumstances makes it ten times worse. But you

162

need to give this up now, this obsession with finding someone to blame, for Zoe's sake.'

I turn my head to look at my old friend, her tired, red-rimmed eyes pleading with me. When Peter died, she wanted to hold me accountable, even though everyone else understood it was a tragic accident. Has she learned from that? Is that why she's willing to accept Tom's death as blameless while I can't?

I shift my gaze towards Harry but he's looking away now, staring out of the window. I'm on my own. 'I just can't see Tom making such a big mistake,' I finally say, my voice quiet but steely.

'Oh, for fuck's sake,' Rob spits out. 'You want to be able to see it?'

'What do you mean?'

'Let's go, all of us.' Rob claps his hands, suddenly pleased with himself. 'Tomorrow's going to be another clear day, and it's our last one here.' He gestures towards Julian. 'We can ski the run together, and I'll personally show you where Tom fell, so that you can *see* it for yourself. Easy.' He gives me a wide smile, but it looks ugly to me. I don't want to ski with him. Or anyone. 'What do you think, Zoe?' he goes on.

'I don't mind,' she says, dropping her hands underneath the table. 'But if it will help Ivy make sense of it . . .' She shrugs in confusion, and it makes me feel sick. She doesn't understand why I can't let it go, why I care so much, but she's not challenging me or demanding answers. Perhaps she thinks she owes me. Even when I know that the opposite is true.

'You know what, I think I'd like to ski the run, one final time,' Julian says, nodding. 'Say a proper goodbye to Tom.'

'Well, that's settled then,' Rob says.

No it's not, I want to scream. *How the hell can I ski on the run where Tom lost his life?*

But if I believe he was pushed, then the run itself isn't the danger. It's the people Tom was skiing with.

The same people who want me to ski with them tomorrow, I realise.

Chapter 30

The day of the fall

Tom

'Morning, Tom, thought I'd pop in, check you're all having a good holiday so far?'

Tom looks up from his bowl of porridge. He wants to tell Nina that no, he's not having a good holiday so far. One of his mates nearly pushed him over yesterday, and another accused Tom of sleeping with his wife. Rob still seems to be enjoying his company, but all he wants to do is get pissed, so Tom's constantly hungover. And to top it off, it's 8.35 a.m. – he can see through the window that the ski lift is already moving – and none of his supposed friends have made it to breakfast yet. He smiles. 'Yeah, it's great, thanks. We had a big day yesterday – clocked up over fifty k – and we're heading over to Avoriaz today.'

Nina drops into the chair at the end of the table and reaches for a pain au chocolat. 'You'll love it over there, it's a much bigger ski area. And there's the infamous Swiss Wall on that side. Do you have a plan for where you'll head?' she asks, pulling off a chunk of pastry and pushing it into her mouth.

'Yeah, we're going to ski the Swiss Wall,' Tom says casually, as though of course they'd want to conquer one of the hardest runs in Europe. 'So I guess we drop over from Fornet?'

'You know the area well after one day of skiing,' Nina observes. 'Have you been studying the piste map or something?'

Tom feels his cheeks redden. 'Yeah, something like that,' he says, smiling through his faux pas. 'Although we're bound to get lost as soon as we get there. Maybe you could join us? You could be our guide for the day, and we'll pay for your services with a monstrously expensive Alpine lunch?'

Nina smiles as she finishes chewing the last piece of pain au chocolat. 'I'd love to – in fact my favourite restaurant in the whole Portes du Soleil ski area is close to the Swiss Wall – but I'm afraid I have to work today. It's transfer day in our other two chalets, so I need to be here to meet the new guests, and I have a heap of paperwork to get through.'

'Ah the downside of working in a ski resort, never having a ski holiday,' Tom says sympathetically. He noticed that Nina said 'our' again, and wonders who her business partner is. With the mystery person not showing their face yet, he knows Zoe would assume it was a man – making Nina do all the leg work – and Tom can't help wondering whether he's a boyfriend too.

Nina chuckles. 'Yes, something like that. And on that note, I'd better get going. Where's Erin by the way?'

Tom shrugs. 'This place is like a ghost town. Just a table full of food.'

'Did someone say my name?' Tom and Nina both jump as Erin appears at the top of the stairs, a small plastic barrel in her arms. 'I had to get some more red wine. This lot have gone through five litres already.' Tom's not sure whether he should feel proud or ashamed.

'Lucky it comes by the barrel, then,' Nina offers, smiling at Tom. It makes him like her even more, that she puts customer service above penny-pinching. 'Anyway, I'm off now,' she continues. 'Enjoy the Swiss Wall, Tom.' With a quick wave, Nina's gone, and crazily, Tom feels disappointed. He's only known her for two days, and she's already become his favourite person on this trip.

'I suppose I'd better go and rouse the others, or we won't get out today,' he says, sighing. He doesn't like playing the parent role – that's usually Julian's job. But it's their last full day in Morzine and he's desperate to get his skis on.

'Yeah, you're best heading out early,' Erin says. 'They're forecasting snow later. But it's only Rob who hasn't made it down yet, Harry and Julian had breakfast half an hour ago.'

'They did?' Tom says. The surprise makes his forehead crinkle but he quickly relaxes it; he can't entertain the idea of wrinkles in his thirties.

'Harry wanted some new gloves, so they've gone down to Intersport. I guess they'll be back soon.'

Julian must be softening towards Harry, Tom thinks. He supposes that's good news – it's what Harry came for after all – but he can't help wondering if they're bonding over a mutual dislike for him. He swears under his breath at the thought of it, then realises how loudly it came out.

'Is everything okay?' Erin asks.

'What?' he squeaks. 'Sorry, yes, I was thinking about lunch,' he says, making it up as he goes along, which has always been a skill of his. 'Nina mentioned that her favourite restaurant is close to where we're skiing today, but I didn't get chance to ask what it's called.'

'Ah, that will be Les Ancelles at Brochaux. She talks about it a lot.'

Tom beams, two birds and all that. 'Thanks, Erin. Right, I better get my lazy friend out of bed.'

Tom takes the stairs two at a time, then pushes on Rob's bedroom door. The double bed is unmade but empty, so he shifts his gaze to the connecting bathroom. The door is open, and Rob is stood in his thermals, leaning against the washbasin, drinking from a matt-black Chilly's water bottle.

'Feeling a bit dehydrated, mate?' Tom asks, pretending he feels fresh as a daisy.

Rob jerks around, eyes wide with fear. He mustn't have heard Tom come in. The metal bottle slips out of his hand and drops onto the tiled fall with a high-pitched crash.

'Jesus, are you okay?'

Rob drops to his knees, picks up the bottle, but the clear liquid has leaked across the floor. Fumes rise, stinging Tom's eyes. Not water then.

'Are you drinking vodka?' he asks, as calmly as he can. He knows Rob likes a drink, but it's not even nine o'clock in the morning.

'What the fuck are you doing in here?' Rob hisses. He straightens up, reaches for the bathroom door, to close it, but Tom's quicker, and blocks the door with his foot. He tries to put his hand on Rob's arm, show some compassion, but Rob helicopters it away from him. 'Get the hell out!' His face is screwed up in anger. He's furious about being caught, Tom thinks, not ashamed about what he's doing. Not anymore.

Tom remembers the time that shame brought Rob to his house, how he kept ringing the doorbell until Tom, bleary-eyed in the pre-dawn light, let him in. He'd sat on Tom's sofa and sobbed over the mistake he'd made. The old lady was dying anyway, he'd explained, but she passed away more quickly than she should, before her children got a chance to say goodbye, because Rob gave her the wrong dose of pain relief.

He then told Tom about the vodka tonic he'd drunk before his night shift started, and his fear that it had contributed. But he'd promised Tom that it was only one, a single measure, and drunk hours before he made the fatal error. And Tom had forgiven him – because that's what Rob came for, redemption – and reassured him that accidents happen when you're pushed to the limits. He told Rob that it wasn't the booze, wasn't his fault.

But was that the wrong call? Has he perpetuated a dangerous situation for the sake of misplaced loyalty?

'Mate, why are you drinking vodka before breakfast?'

'Christ, it's no big deal, okay? I'm on holiday.'

Tom hesitates. He wishes he was better at stuff like this. Wiser, like Ivy. 'And when you're not on holiday?' he chooses. 'Do you drink vodka when you wake up then?'

'Shut up, Tom.'

'And at work? Do you drink there too? Should I have reported you when I had the chance?' There. It's out. The hold Tom has over Rob.

Rob lunges forward, pushes Tom in the chest. 'You sanctimonious prick!' he screams. 'You try working fifteen-, sixteen-hour shifts, locums not turning up, the best nurses gone because they get paid better at Tesco!'

'And you think the answer is being constantly pissed?' Tom asks incredulously. 'What standard of care do your patients get from you?'

'I don't get pissed,' Rob spits out. 'I just have a few sips to take the edge off.'

'That is bullshit, and you know it. What happens when you fuck up again? Except next time it won't be an old lady with hours to live – you don't get that lucky twice. It will be a kid, or a pregnant woman, or a 36-year-old man who'll remind you of yourself forever.'

Rob runs his hands through his mop of curly hair, catches a glimpse of himself in the bathroom mirror, then looks away. 'Look, I'll stop, okay? If it means that much to you.'

'And you think it's that easy? That I'm just going to forget what I've seen, what you've admitted to?'

Rob takes a step towards him. 'Yeah, I do, actually. Because, for one, you're my mate, and secondly, this is none of your fucking business.'

'I might not be an emergency doctor, but I still have a responsibility to the GMC.'

'Are you threatening me?' Rob pushes at Tom's chest. Tom wasn't expecting it, and he loses his balance for a moment. His head cracks against the doorframe. Pain jolts through him, makes him angry.

'Mate, it's not a threat,' he hisses. 'I gave you a chance last time; you don't get two.'

Rob surges forward, but Tom is ready for him this time. He spins left, then rams his shoulder into Rob's back. Rob teeters forwards, out of the bathroom, then drops onto his hands and knees. He looks broken, a mess of inflated flesh and deflated ego. Tom shakes his head in disgust and walks out of the room. But it's not over. He can hear Rob getting to his feet and coming after him.

Chapter 31

Ivy

'So how are you feeling, Ivy?' Rob leans forward, rests his forearms on the safety bar, and twists his body around to face me. The movement makes the chairlift lurch to one side, and my stomach drops. I grab hold of the cold metal frame and push my back against the plastic seating.

'I'm fine,' I say icily, not meeting his gaze, not admitting that I feel sick with fear. Especially after my mum didn't answer my call this morning. I know that doesn't have to mean anything sinister; looking after a 1-year-old often takes both your hands and all of your attention. But last night I dreamed about a faceless man lurking in the alleyway next to my house, and I can't get the image out of my head.

The *Flosset* chairlift carries up to four people, but the queue at the bottom was chaotic, so we didn't get chance to organise ourselves into groups. The others spurted out onto the first lift, leaving me with Rob. There are two snowboarders sat on his right, big men staring at scratchy footage on a tiny GoPro camera, so Rob's leg is pushed up against mine. I feel trapped, and for a mad moment, I consider slipping underneath the bar and falling into the thick blanket of snow beneath me. The threat of broken ankles almost preferable to what's in store. But then the chairlift takes us higher, and snow is replaced by sheer cliffs, and the thought of escape mutates into images of Tom falling to his death.

'You look like you've seen a ghost,' Rob observes, before adding, 'Let's hope it's not Tom,' with a schoolboy snigger. He coughs. 'Sorry, that was inappropriate. Think I might be nervous too.'

'Maybe you shouldn't have suggested this particular excursion then,' I mutter, still not looking at him.

'What, and miss out on clearing my name with little Miss Ivy Marple?'

'Fuck off, Rob.'

'Stop suggesting I pushed Tom, and maybe I will,' he counters. I turn my shoulders away from him, and stare at the landscape instead, hoping he can't see my body quivering. The chairlift is a long one, and we pass steep rockfaces and craggy overhangs on our route upwards. I think about Tom, whether he crashed into the rock as he fell, or if momentum saved him from that fate. I wonder if we're sitting on the same chair that carried him, and what went through his mind on that final journey.

Finally, the top lift station comes into view, and as soon as I can, I lift the safety bar and ski away from Rob, and onto the plateau at the top of the run. I slip in next to Nina. 'Thanks again for coming with us,' I murmur under my breath. When I realised that I had no choice but to go with Rob's suggestion to ski Tom's final run, I got Nina's number from Erin and asked if she'd be our guide for the day – someone to dilute the charged atmosphere – and to my relief, she came back to me a few minutes later saying that she'd be honoured to.

'Not at all,' she says. 'It's the least I can do.' Nina has guided us all the way from Morzine via a network of relatively quiet blue pistes. I'm pretty sure there's a more direct route to this area, and I wonder if she's doing it for my benefit, sensing my nervousness and giving me the chance to find my ski legs before the main event. It worked for a while too, but unfortunately, the fear is back now.

'Are we going then?' Rob calls out, skiing a few metres ahead, then spinning 180 degrees so he's facing us. For all he said on the lift, he doesn't seem nervous, and I wonder if that's strange – or incriminating. If his friend really did suffer a tragic accident here, wouldn't he be more cautious? Although I have to admit, with full visibility, the piste doesn't look difficult or scary. And with Rob up ahead, at least I can keep him in my eyeline. I dig my poles in to set off. But in my peripheral vision I can see Zoe's shoulders rising and falling and I realise she's crying. 'Are you okay?' I ask.

'Sorry, sorry,' she mumbles. 'It all got too much for a moment, but I promise I'm fine.'

'You know, we don't have to do this,' Rob says, skating back up the slope. 'If it's too upsetting.' A burst of envy explodes inside me, and I bite my lip until it settles. *Zoe is Tom's wife,* I repeat silently, like a mantra. This is how it should be.

'Tom would want me to do this,' Zoe says eventually. 'And I know Ivy will feel better after seeing where he fell.' Everyone turns to look at me and I can see the big question hovering on all their faces, even Nina's. *Why do you care so much, Ivy?* I feel my cheeks burn as I look down at the hard-packed snow beneath my skis.

'Come on then,' Rob says, turning down the mountain again. Zoe goes next, then Julian and Nina, and I push on my poles to follow. But a hand grabs my arm. I instinctively pull away, but the shock unbalances me, and I teeter. Harry's eyes widen, realising I'm going to fall, and he reaches out with both hands. I know he wants to steady me, but instinctively I flail away from him. The momentum carries me over and I collapse in a heap. It doesn't hurt – I was hardly moving – but I feel powerless, with Harry stood over me.

'What do you want?' I shout crossly, trying to right my body.

'Jesus, Ivy. I just thought we should talk. I didn't mean . . .'

'You never do, do you?' I interrupt. My skis are crossed, and I can't get them into the correct position to stand up.

'Do you know what, forget it,' he spits out. 'It's you that said you wanted to be friends again, not me.'

I sigh, heave my leg into the air, and finally manage to flip my ski over. I push up to standing and take a long breath. 'I did,' I say in a kinder voice, although I still can't look at him. 'We are.'

His features soften. 'That night did something for me, you know,' he says, his voice low. 'I'd been trying to sort myself out for years, travelling, trying new things, and yet, it took something like that – messy and unplanned but also totally amazing – to make me finally feel good about myself.'

'Leave it, Harry, please,' I beg. Going back there makes me feel embarrassed, exposed. Even though I have Calum to show for it. But more than that, today isn't about Harry. I didn't want to come to this mountain, but now I'm here, I need to see where Tom fell. And check to see if there's guilt on Rob's face.

'Is that because of Tom?' he asks, his voice a mix of accusation and disappointment.

My heart jolts. I flick my head around, finally look him in the eye. 'What?'

'I saw his phone on Saturday.'

A gust of wind appears from nowhere, and I feel it brush across my cheeks. My heart is hammering against my ribcage, but other than that, I can't move. Did he see my message? I know the conclusion he would have drawn if he did. It doesn't matter that it's wrong.

'I told him to own up to Zoe,' he goes on. 'That she had a right to know.' His eyes harden again. Fear creeps up my spine because I can imagine how that conversation would have gone. Tom will have shut down, explained nothing, because Zoe finding out was his biggest fear.

'You don't understand,' I whisper, but it's got no strength to it, no conviction, because I don't want to tell him the truth either.

That was part of the deal, secrecy, and it would feel like a betrayal, even though Tom isn't here anymore.

As I take in Harry's wounded expression, the aggrieved look in his eyes, I feel my stomach clench. At university, Harry lashed out. And ten years later, he attacked a man badly enough to be sent to prison. Did he react similarly on Saturday?

Because there are other facts too, details that I haven't let myself dwell on because I didn't want to believe he could hurt Tom. The red welt that I saw on his hand the day I arrived. The fact that he was drinking alcohol on Saturday lunchtime when he's supposed to have given up. Because booze and violence are too closely linked for him.

Was it blindingly obvious from the start who pushed Tom?

I think of Calum. And of Harry's demons. Is this my fault?

Maybe he didn't plan it. It could even have been an equal fight – in the thick cloud, Harry would have had no way of knowing there was a sheer drop on one side.

Not like Tom, I finally admit to myself. The real reason I've found it so hard to believe his fall was an accident. He would have known about the cliff edge for the same reason I do. Because we've skied this run before. Together.

'Are you two coming?' Rob calls out from 50 metres down the mountain.

'Yes!' I shout back. I don't know what to do, whether Tom would care more about getting justice or keeping our secret, but I know I need time to figure it out, and space away from Harry. I pull my goggles down, then push hard on my poles to build some distance between us. 'Sorry,' I say breathlessly, pulling up next to Nina.

'The barriers are around this corner,' she warns. 'I'm not sure where the gap is – I've never noticed it – but you should prepare yourself for seeing where Tom fell. Is everyone ready?'

'I think so,' Zoe whispers. Then she clears her throat. 'Come on, we can do this.' She gestures for Nina to start skiing, and we all drop in behind, following in single file, like a scared ski-school snake. I can sense Harry at the end, hanging back, his shadow suddenly ominous, and I'm glad to feel the security of Julian between us. We follow the run as it curves around the mountain, then suddenly I see them. A line of wooden barriers in the snow.

And a gap. Thirty centimetres at the most. Could Tom have skied accidentally through there?

'Shit, I can't do this!'

I look up, twist with surprise towards the voice. But then he's skiing past me, fast, head turned away, refusing to look at the drop.

'What's wrong with Julian?' Zoe calls out, but to no one in particular, so no one responds. I'm too transfixed by the gap Julian has left, and how Harry is closing in.

Chapter 32

Zoe

'Shouldn't we at least follow him? Ouch!' Zoe jolts forward with a grimace as Ivy clatters into the back of her.

'Sorry!' Ivy calls out, flustered, digging in her poles to try and disentangle herself. 'I didn't quite stop in time.' As she nestles into the small space between Zoe and Nina, a stab of annoyance jabs at Zoe. Why does Ivy have to ski so close? The run is practically deserted now. And they're only here because she's so desperate to know all the gory details. But she plasters on a smile, nonetheless. 'Don't worry, it happens.'

'I'll go after Julian,' Rob calls out, his voice trailing behind him as he pushes off.

Zoe watches him go with relief. She couldn't cope with Tom's death causing another accident on this piste. 'Shall we?' she says to the others, gesturing down the mountain.

'Yeah, good idea.' Harry's voice, a gruff whisper, wafts over, and Zoe turns towards it. He looks strange. She wonders if the emotion of coming here has caught up with him too, and whether she should be worried about that. She didn't witness the havoc he caused at university, and Tom would never tell her what started it, but she saw the trail of destruction he left in his wake, so she's fully aware of his aggressive streak.

'Come on, let's find somewhere for lunch,' she coaxes. She wants to get Harry away from the scene, just in case. She pushes off, and relaxes a tiny bit when the three of them follow. Zoe would normally expect Ivy, the least experienced skier amongst them, to lag behind, but she seems to be skiing like her life depended on it. In normal circumstances, Zoe might see that as a challenge – and one she'd win – but she's not in the mood for racing today. Not when she's got so much to reflect on.

And maybe a growing embryo to protect.

Fifteen minutes later, they reach the bottom, and Zoe spots Julian straight away, standing by the door of a restaurant like a member of the King's Guard in civvies. 'Over here!' he calls out, lifting his arm in a kind of salute. They click out of their skis and stomp through the snow towards him. 'Sorry about that,' he mutters, his military stance wilting as they join him. 'I've never lost anyone important before. Turns out I'm not very good at it.'

'Don't you deal with death every day?' Zoe asks, genuinely curious.

'Death and grief are not the same,' he explains in a sad voice. Then he takes a deep breath. 'Anyway, Rob's got a table in here. We thought it would be best to avoid the restaurant we ate in on Saturday. Sorry, Nina, I remember Tom saying that *Les Ancelles* is your favourite.'

'Not at all,' Nina says. 'They're both great.' Zoe imagines the always-on resort rep giving Julian a reassuring smile, but chooses not to play witness to it, the falseness of it. Instead, she pushes on the thick wooden door, and enjoys the warmth that envelops her.

Rob is sat alone at a table for six, and his pint glass is already empty. Tom didn't explain exactly how Rob had screwed up in his final message to Zoe, but it doesn't take a genius to make the connection with his heavy drinking. Was he drunk in his A&E department? Did he make some terrible mistake? And with Tom not around anymore, does the responsibility of reporting Rob to the authorities fall to her? Zoe shudders at the thought. She's got her own shit to deal with; she can't cope with the task of ruining a man's career as well.

An hour later, the mood in the group has improved slightly. Ivy has hardly spoken, but Nina is doing a good job of making conversation with the men, and Zoe has finally managed to eat a proper meal – a rich and delicious spaghetti carbonara. The carafe of water that she's washed the salty meal down with is now sitting in her bladder, so she eyes the sign for toilets – Les Dames – and pushes to standing.

There was nothing to warn her. Not a dampness in her knickers, or a pain in her lower abdomen. Just a deep redness on the toilet paper, and more in the bowl. She blinks, breathes. Tries to control her emotions. But of course, she can't. She bunches up the bottom of her fleece jumper and pushes it against her mouth. And then she screams. A strangled, muffled cry of pain. For the lost baby. The phantom child that only existed in her mind.

Just like all the others.

Not a pregnancy at all; a week-late period.

Just like all the others.

Why does her body despise her this much? It knows how desperately she wants a baby, how that ugly desperation has fucked up her marriage, and how that still matters less than keeping her hope for a son or daughter alive. But still, it teases her. Lures her into the dream, the belief, the fairy tale of family life. Then a week or so later, it kicks her in the gut, stomps on her hopes until they're crushed to nothing.

She knows she could outsmart her body. Take a pregnancy test and find out for sure. But choosing to kill the dream is even worse than having it done to her. That's why she didn't bring a test to France. That's why she has a dozen packets in her bathroom cabinet, but has never opened one.

She also carries the weight of hiding how she feels. Pretending that her property-developer lifestyle is enough for her, thank you very much. Actually, she does love her job, but it's a lifeline, not a life goal. In the early days, before he showed his true colours, Tom suggested that she be more honest with people. Tell her friends that they're struggling to conceive and let them give Zoe the sympathy she deserves. Maybe that's when she should have realised what a selfish man he was. That he was willing to put her inadequacy on show to save him the burden of looking after her.

The truth is, it's her acting talents that have saved her. Her being so good at pretending her property empire is her true baby has stopped the invasive questions, the condescending smiles that try – but fail – to hide the sheer relief that they're not suffering the same fate.

But even more soothing than the acting she does for others, is the expectant-mother role she gets to play for herself over those special few days before her period arrives. Truly believing that motherhood is imminent, only nine short months away, is exquisite. Being able to completely block out the memories of the month before, is a skill that has served her well. Until the truth lands in her knickers. And she's devastated all over again.

After a year or so of trying, Zoe booked an appointment with a private gynaecologist (she couldn't walk into her local GP surgery about this) and asked what she should do. To Zoe's relief, the consultant didn't ask many questions, just booked her and Tom in for a myriad of tests. All of which, a couple of weeks later, confirmed them both as healthy. Of course Tom loved his above-average sperm count, but Zoe felt lost without a diagnosis. An explanation, coupled with a neat solution. The only way she could deal with the black hole of understanding was by focusing on the chance it gave them. If they could get pregnant in theory, then they could do so in practice too.

Except they didn't. And now the chance has gone.

She reaches into her pocket for a tampon – of course she brought one with her, she's an actor not a fantasist – and lets the curtain fall on her performance. Then she walks to the sink, douses her face with freezing cold water, and stares at her reflection in the mirror. When she was a teenager, she didn't consider her life difficult. Yes, her favourite parent left home when she was 11. And she made some questionable choices during her teenage years. But she stayed optimistic about her future – even being expelled from her secondary school turned out to be life-enhancing. So how did she end up here? Bitter. Resentful of every mother she meets. Willing to forgive a cheating husband on the off chance he might provide her with a child.

For all her dad's shallow attitude to women, he was always adamant that beauty is more than skin-deep. It was one of the few things they disagreed on – she felt her blue eyes, high cheekbones, and long blonde hair, were enough to earn her that badge of honour without any pleasant inner glow. But now she understands what he meant. Because whatever is broken inside her, is now seeping through her skin, covering her in a thin veil of grey misery. How can she continue pretending everything is fine when she looks like this?

Zoe pushes away from the sink, takes a deep breath, and walks out of *Les dames (damn, damn)*. She can't go back to the table though. Her ski jacket and helmet are draped over the chair, but getting close enough to collect it, having to explain to the others why she's leaving, especially to Ivy, is out of the question. So with only her fleece jumper for both warmth and protection, she stumbles, head down, to the front door and enjoys the rush of cold air over her burning face as she walks outside.

Chapter 33

2008

Ivy

It's one of those hot summer days when you can't imagine you'll ever need a coat again. I shift in my chair, peel my clammy thighs away from the leather, and try to lean into the path of the afternoon breeze weakly fluttering through the open window.

'So are you up for my proposal then?' Peter asks. He's sat behind his desk, opposite me, leaning back with his shirt sleeves rolled up and hands clasped behind his head. There are dark patches under each armpit, but he doesn't seem bothered about them being on show. *Of course I bloody sweat in thirty-degree heat*, he'd say if anyone dare comment. Peter doesn't do embarrassment, or insecurity, or adapting to other people's sensitivities. 'Hello? Earth to Ivy?' he prompts.

'Sorry,' I say. 'I think the heat's getting to me.'

'Well let's hope the temperature drops before tomorrow then. That's your last exam, isn't it?'

I nod my head. My final-year exams. Eleven down, one to go. Then a couple of weeks celebrating before a two-month work experience gig at Manchester Airport. All being well, I'll have earned a first-class honours degree in Environmental Science and will be back at Exeter doing a master's course in meteorology by September. Tom, Julian, Rob and Harry will be back next term too, continuing with their Medicine degrees, and Nikki has chosen to do a master's as well. Zoe is hanging up her academic boots, but there's no way she'll stray too far from Exeter while she and Tom are still joined at the hip.

'Anyway, to go back to what I was saying, the job I'm offering you for next term. I've been invited by the University of Wisconsin–Madison to join their AWS programme this summer – basically spending six weeks in the Antarctic observing the effects of climate change on weather patterns. So I'll be returning to Exeter in the autumn with a monstruous amount of data, and I was wondering if you wanted to be my terribly paid research assistant?'

'Me?' I ask. I should be flattered – a research job on a prestigious international project never goes to a master's student, and I can think of half a dozen PhD students who would bite Peter's hand off for it – but this type of work doesn't excite me. However much I try to broaden my interest, all I actually care about is forecasting the weather. Normal weather that's going to impact regular people, not penguins or elephant seals. Getting commuters to work safely, holidaymakers off without a hiccup.

And making sure climbers aren't blindsided by bad conditions.

'Yes you, Ivy,' he says, rolling his eyes. 'Although if you don't accept soon, I might change my mind.'

For a fleeting moment, I hate him. The way he teases me, but from behind a wide smile so that I'm not allowed to take offence. I wonder how he'd react if I told him to stuff his job. That I only pretend to like him to get access to his big meteorology brain. But the moment passes, and I remember who he is – my mentor, my best friend's father – and I see things more pragmatically. Yes, he's a chauvinist, an older man with outdated ideas, but I'd be crazy to let that get in the way of me achieving my goals. 'I'd love the job, thank you,' I manage.

'Excellent,' he says with an air of smugness. He drops his arms (finally) and leans forward over the desk. 'I think that brings all my outstanding business to a close. Now I just need to root out my merino thermals – not a pleasant thought on a day like today, to be honest – and get on that plane to Chile.'

A knot of tension forms between my shoulder blades. The way Peter's talking, his trip sounds imminent, but it can't be, because Zoe's twenty-first birthday party is still a week away. And she'd be devastated if he didn't make it to her big coming-of-age (her words) celebration. 'When do you leave?' I ask, covertly crossing my fingers underneath the seat.

'Next Sunday. Crack of dawn. I'll probably head up to Heathrow on the Saturday, stay in one of the airport hotels so that I can have as long as possible in bed.'

'What about Zoe's party? That's on Saturday. She told me you were going.'

'Oh bollocks.' He exhales. 'It completely slipped my mind. I'm like a kid in a bloody sweet shop when someone invites me on a research trip.' He sighs, rubs the heels of his hands along his jawline, then clicks his fingers. 'I'll take her for a drink, explain, she'll be fine about it.' He leans back in his chair again, clearly satisfied with his solution. And he's right, in a way, because Zoe would give him her blessing. I imagine her brushing the news off with a deferential shrug, accepting the conciliatory vodka tonic, maybe even pretending to herself that she doesn't care.

But it's not right that her dad – her hero – isn't there on her big day.

When I turned 21, last October, we celebrated in our local pub. Nothing fancy, just a group of mates and a willingness to drink Jagerbombs on a school night. There were loads of people

I could miss, but it was my dad I pined for. I wanted him to see how the unruly mass of 9-year-old potential had turned out. My dad had a good excuse for being a no-show – he'd been dead for nearly twelve years. An early flight the following morning is pathetic in comparison.

'I think you should change your plans,' I say, more meekly than I intended. 'Zoe will be gutted if you're not there.'

'Oh God, don't guilt-trip me,' he groans, screwing up his nose. 'I need to be at the airport around 6 a.m., and it's a good three-hour journey from here.'

'At least come for a few hours,' I try. 'You could still book a hotel room near the airport. Leave by ten, be in bed by one.'

'Who wants to go to a party knowing you need to leave by ten?' he wails incredulously. 'Especially when you've got to drive so can't drink.'

God, the selfishness of him. I fix on a smile and try to think strategically. 'Look, I was actually hoping you'd do a little speech for her,' I try.

'A speech?' He leans forwards slightly, cocks his head to one side. 'At the party?'

'You could do it earlyish, as long as it's after everyone's arrived. Zoe would be so grateful, and you're a brilliant public speaker. I'm sure everyone would love it.' I'm hoping a man with his ego won't be able to resist so many compliments in one sentence.

'Oh maybe you're right,' he says eventually. 'It would be a shame to miss it, I suppose, and I'd be honoured to say a few words.' A cool sense of victory loosens my shoulders, and I have to concentrate on not smiling too broadly as I silently congratulate myself.

Until he winks at me, and the smile dissolves anyway.

Even though the air is heavy with afternoon heat, I breathe it in. It's good to be outside again, absorbing vitamin D, away from Peter's office. On average, Exeter has 195 hours of sunshine in June, and it feels like we've had our monthly allowance already.

With my final exam tomorrow, I should go to the library for one last cramming session. But the thought of sticking to another plastic chair is too much, so I head in the opposite direction instead. I'll find a quiet patch of lawn, I decide, in the shade somewhere, and read through my notes for the millionth time.

I slip around the back of the Biosciences building – there's a tiny pond behind there that's reputed to have two terrapin inside, although I've never seen them – and almost trip over Harry's feet. 'Harry?' I splutter, the surprise of seeing him slouched against the red brick wall escaping out of my mouth. He jumps to his feet, shoves his hands into the pockets of his jeans. He looks caught out, and his eyes flit past me as though scanning for an escape route. 'So what brings you over to Streatham Campus?' I ask more cautiously. The Medicine buildings are over a mile away.

He blinks, but still won't look at me. 'Meeting with my tutor,' he finally offers. 'She was giving a lecture in Biosciences, so asked me to do it here.'

I hesitate as the awareness sinks in, then look away myself. If Harry had met with his tutor in the medical department, there's every chance his fellow students would notice. Normally it wouldn't matter, but in exam season, a summoning might draw some unwanted attention.

'And everything's okay?' I don't really want to get into this. I want to find a quiet place to study. But Harry and I are friends, sort of. We have history, and I suppose I owe him this.

'Why do you ask?'

I look up. Our eyes lock. 'Sorry?'

'Well, it's not like you give a shit about me, is it?'

'What?' I stutter, even though his words don't lack clarity. 'Of course I do. We're friends, aren't we?' I know I'm being unfair. Harry hasn't wanted to be just friends with me since we slept together eighteen months ago. It's me who's labelled our relationship, unilaterally, to suit my wishes. But in all this time, he's never complained, at least not directly to me, so his accusation is a shock. I watch him blink away tears, then twist his neck to break eye contact. When he looks back at me, his eyes are dry.

'Sorry, I'm being a dick.' He gives me an apologetic smile. 'Yes, we're friends. Just a bad day, you know?' The muscles in his face are twitching now. The effort of smiling. 'Anyway, I better get going,' he continues. 'I've still got a couple more exams to sit so I need to hit the books.' He turns, his shoulders hunched, and walks in the direction of the campus exit. He looks broken.

'Good luck with them!' I shout, hoping to lift his mood, his shoulders, something. And it works in a way, because he slides one hand out of his jean pocket to wave goodbye. The movement is swift, casual, but my breath catches in my throat. Because his knuckles are red raw. An open wound, clearly fresh too. And speckled with the fine dust of red brick.

Chapter 34

Ivy

If I lean far enough through the window, and twist my neck, I can see the narrow road into town from the chalet. Except for a small dog tottering towards the glow of restaurant lights, it's empty, but I stare anyway, hoping that sheer desperation will be enough for Zoe to appear, wandering back towards the chalet, unharmed.

'Try not to worry,' Julian says from behind me, and I twist to face him. He's perched on the edge of the sofa, alert, as though he might leap up at any moment. There's a charcoal-grey cabin bag at his feet and a rucksack balanced on top.

'What?' I say incredulously. 'Zoe walked out of the restaurant without telling us four hours ago and we haven't seen her since. She's grieving her dead husband, and you don't think I need to worry?'

'Her skis and boots are here,' he reminds me. 'So she got down the mountain safely. And Harry's gone to look for her. I'm sure he'll bring her back soon.'

The idea of Harry out there, searching for Zoe, terrifies me. What he might say to her. What he might do. I wanted to look for

Zoe myself, after we got back and realised the chalet was empty, but Harry jumped in before me, and I couldn't risk him suggesting we search together. So instead, I watched, defeated, as he headed off towards the main road and the sparkly lights of town.

I push away from the window and drop down into one of the armchairs. As I stare at Julian's miniature suitcase, its bulky arrogance, my frustration grows. 'It's all right for you,' I prod. 'You and Rob will be on your way home soon. It's no wonder you don't care where Zoe is.' Nico is due to pick them up in half an hour to drive them to the airport to catch their evening flight. Which means it will only be me, Zoe and Harry left in the chalet. And to make matters worse, it's Erin's night off.

'Don't guilt-trip me,' Julian counters. 'You know what I'm going through at home; I need to get back, see Nikki and the twins.' As Julian mentions his family, a deep ache pulls at my chest. I want to go home too, hold Calum, protect him from whatever threat might be out there. But I can also see Zoe falling apart and I don't want to abandon her. 'And the weather's coming in,' Julian continues. 'If we don't get out tonight, there's a chance we'll be stuck here for days.'

'What?' A shiver rattles through me.

'Have you not seen the forecast?'

I grab my phone off the coffee table and click into Meteo France. I'm a weather girl; this is what I've trained for, what I teach. How did I not know there was a storm coming? I usually check the forecast religiously, but I've been so distracted. I don't bother with the pretty symbols, but I scroll down to the background information. Wind coming from a north-easterly direction, speeds of 30 kilometres per hour, gusting to 50. A low-pressure weather system, originating in Russia; one hundred per cent cloud cover, heavy snow inevitable. It's already snowing in Austria and Switzerland, and it's expected to arrive in France in the early hours of Thursday morning. No thunderstorms, thank God, but seventy centimetres of snow predicted in Morzine.

My neck jolts as a loud bang above me pulls my attention away from my phone. Rob is stood on the upstairs landing, his bedroom door slammed shut behind him. He looks angry, glaring at us over the banister. It could still be him, I think, the killer, getting rid of Tom to save his career. He had a reason to hate Tom at least as much as Harry did. But then it was Julian who acted the most suspiciously on the ski run, freaking out when we got to the place where Tom fell. Could he have pushed Tom? Maybe he was lying about Nikki's lover being someone from work. Maybe it was Tom. He's clearly capable of it, after what Zoe told me about his one-night stand.

God, that's nuts. Of course Tom wasn't sleeping with Nikki.

Of course it wasn't Julian who pushed him.

Maybe I'm the crazy one.

Could I have got this whole thing wrong? Has the stress of Tom dying, of Mum's fears about someone following Calum, messed with my head so much that I'm creating a bank of killers where there are none? Yes, Tom has skied that run before, but everywhere looks different in a white-out. He could easily have got confused.

I shake my head in desperation, but nothing gets clearer.

'Bloody flight's been cancelled!' Rob shouts down, making me jump. 'I just got an email, heavy snow in Geneva apparently.'

'Already? Shit,' Julian spits out. He pushes to standing and storms over to the window, staring out, as though he can fend off the snow with his glare. 'I can't believe they can't fly in snow!' he wails. 'This is the Alps for fuck's sake. I need to get home!'

Is this level of frustration normal? Or a sign of guilt?

Stop it, Ivy. Stop it.

Rob sighs and clomps down the wooden staircase. 'All right, chill out. It's an inconvenience not a catastrophe. I'm sure they'll be up and running by tomorrow. How about we go for a beer? Drown our sorrows?'

'Jesus, Rob, when did you become such a bloody alcoholic?'

'What did you call me?' The mood shifts, tightens, like the

air has been sucked out of the room. But Julian doesn't seem to notice, or maybe care.

'What? Offended by the truth?' He snorts out a derogatory laugh, as though the band of tension inside him has finally snapped. 'You're always pissed, mate. Do you not think people notice? Tom certainly did.' Without warning, Rob barrels over and lunges at Julian. Julian lifts his hands to fend his friend off, but staggers under the force of Rob's shove and careers into the dining table. His eyes narrow with fury; his hands clench into fists. Cool, sensible Julian preparing to punch his friend. Where has all this violence come from?

But now isn't the time to reflect. I need to stop them hurting each other.

'What the fuckity fuck's going on?!' a slurred screech rings out into the room. I turn towards it, to Zoe, who's standing at the top of the main stairs. Or, more accurately, swaying dangerously. Instinctively I reach for her, but she pulls away, grabs hold of one of the dining chairs instead. I look behind her, expecting to see Harry, a look on his face that says, yes, I told her. Even though he's got the whole thing wrong. But there's no one there.

'Are you okay, Zoe?' Julian calls out in alarm.

'Whoa, she is seriously smashed,' Rob adds unhelpfully. But at least it's stopped them fighting.

'Where have you been?' I ask tentatively. 'Did Harry find you?'

'Harry?' she asks, her eyes flicking left and right, suddenly aware she's under the spotlight. 'Why would Harry find me?'

'He went to look for you when we got back and realised you weren't in the chalet. Why did you leave the restaurant by yourself? Where did you go?'

She blinks a couple of times, then her shoulders lower slightly. 'I've been to a bar on the high street,' she says. 'A swanky one, way too good for all of you. I met a guy,' she adds, a new belligerence in her tone. 'I mean, a gentleman.' She raises her hand and points her finger at me. 'Definitely not the type to cheat on his wife.'

As I feel the symbolic sting of her pointed finger, I search for any sign of accusation in her face, to see if Harry has got to her, but thank God, there is none. She must be talking about Tom's one-night stand with his hospital colleague.

'How about I help get you to bed?' I say gently. It's not even seven o'clock, but the state she's in, she needs to sleep. Zoe has been very restrained until tonight, which is quite an achievement with all the stress she's been under, so I can't blame her for finally giving in. Especially after the strange vigil we took part in today. She doesn't answer, but she allows me to put my arm around her shoulders and guide her towards her bedroom.

'The funeral man called me,' Zoe murmurs. 'It's all confirmed. Tom goes home on Friday.' Two more nights, I think. Time for the storm to pass. Less than the three I've already been here for. And if Julian and Rob get away in the morning, and Harry too, by train, maybe I can do this. It means I won't get justice for Tom, but I'm exhausted now. I want to get home, see my son, put this awful trip behind me. Dufort isn't interested in pursuing the case. And if the only way to expose Harry is to come clean about my relationship with Tom, and potentially devastate Zoe in the process, maybe it's better to let things lie.

Once I've got Zoe into bed, I'm going to call home, ask Mum to put the phone next to Calum's bubbling lips so that I can hear his voice, his own special way of speaking. My tummy flips at the thought as I push open Zoe's door, guide her towards the bed, and pull the duvet back. As soon as I sit her on the edge, her torso curls and sinks until her head hits the pillow. I lift her legs to straighten her out, then pull up the cover. She's asleep in seconds.

I cross the now empty open-plan living space to my own room – Rob and Julian must have patched up their differences and gone for a beer after all – and pull out my phone to make the call home. But as soon as I do, I notice there's an unread message from my mum, so as I pull the door closed behind me, I click into it.

Sorry. I can't do this anymore.
Someone's watching us.
Calum's in danger!
YOU NEED TO COME HOME.

Chapter 35

Ivy

I stare at my phone. I need to call her back. But what do I say? *Sorry, Mum, but a storm is fucking with your life for a second time.* Rob said that flights aren't taking off this evening, and with another seventy centimetres of snow on the way, how can that possibly change by morning?

But I can't ignore the message either. Has something else happened? Or are those anxious voices in Mum's head just getting louder? With shaking hands, and a tightening in my chest, I press on her number.

'Oh, love, thank you.' She's quiet, but I can still hear the tremor in her voice. Trying to sound brave when inside she's crumbling. Until this point, I'm ashamed to realise, all my fears have been for Calum; my urge to go home has been about protecting him. But she's the one who's really suffering. Because I dragged her away from everything that's familiar, cut her loose from her safety net.

'Mum,' I say.

'I know you think I'm crazy,' she starts.

'No . . .'

'That I'm scared of my own shadow.'

'I don't, Mum.' I sink down onto the bed, wonder if I'm being honest. 'Tell me what's happened. Where's Calum?'

'He's here, with me, he's fine,' she stutters. 'But I'll need to put him to bed soon, and I'm scared to let him out of my sight.'

'The doors are locked though?' I check. 'So no one can get in?'

'The doorbell rang,' she whispers. 'And your intercom buzzer thing doesn't work.' I scrunch my eyes closed and silently swear at my laziness for not getting it fixed. For forcing my mum to leave the house every time the doorbell sounds. 'So I went outside,' she continues, 'but no one was there. Oh, Ivy, I thought that man had outsmarted me and somehow got to Calum. I raced back inside, and thank God, he was where I left him, strapped into his highchair. But it made me realise how it could happen, how one little mistake could lead to me losing him – you losing him too.'

Waves of panic swirl around me, but I can't let them in; I need to stay strong. 'Are you sure, Mum?' I ask, trying not to sound sceptical. 'That you're being followed, and that it was him ringing the doorbell?'

'God Ivy, I wish it was my anxiety talking. But I promise it's not. I keep seeing him, everywhere I go. He has to be following us, it doesn't make sense otherwise.'

My head throbs as I try to process what she's telling me. I've never felt watched by anyone when I take Calum out, so if it's not Mum's imagination, it must have started after I left for France. And who would suddenly be interested in my son? Perhaps it's really Mum they're after, a vulnerable older woman pushing a pram, an easy target for a robbery. But if that's the case, why haven't they attacked her already?

'Can you tell me anything about him?' I ask. 'His ethnicity? Hair colour? Is he broad or slight? Does he have any tattoos or piercings?'

'I don't know,' she wails. 'I never get a good look at him. He's just there, lurking, with a hoodie pulled up to hide his face. He's white, I think.'

'But how can you be sure it's the same man if you don't know what he looks like?' I hate pushing her like this, but I need to know if they really are in danger. Especially as I can't think of anyone to ask for help. I was a workaholic before Calum was born, and a hermit for the first few months afterwards, so I've never made any local friends. I've been away from work too long to ask a colleague, and the other friends I've collected over the years live too far away. I could ask a neighbour, but I don't know any of them well, and I worry that another stranger in the house would make Mum's anxiety worse. Mine too, perhaps.

'It's how he behaves that's familiar,' she whispers, sending shivers down my spine. 'The watching, the hanging back. Somehow both uninterested and threatening.'

'Do you think you should call the police?'

'And say what? I'm scared of a man who I can't describe, who has never spoken a word to me? No, I just need you to come home, Ivy. I'm sorry to ask this, because I know exactly what Zoe is going through right now, how devastating it is to lose a husband, and with her being so kind to me lately, but I can't do this anymore.'

I listen to her short, chaotic breaths and know that she's crying. What have I done? I should never have given her the responsibility of looking after my most precious thing. It's not fair. Whether there's a genuine threat or not, she thinks there is, and that's what counts. 'Of course, I'll come home. As quickly as I possibly can. But there's a storm here, Mum, and it's grounded all flights. I'll find a way to get back tomorrow, I promise,' I hear myself say. 'But I need you to be brave for one more night.'

'I'm not sure I can,' she whispers. 'I'm bad luck, Ivy.' I close my eyes again. There it is. The belief that she is somehow responsible for Dad dying. The guilt that has kept her tethered to her narrow existence for twenty-seven years.

'You're not, Mum,' I say. 'Please, I need you to be strong.' She doesn't answer, and as I listen to her uneven breaths, I say a silent prayer for everything to work out. For Geneva airport to clear the snow, for me to be on one of the first flights out, for Mum to keep Calum safe tonight and not lose her mind in the process. 'Just one more night,' I say again, silently begging for her to accept my plea.

'Okay,' she finally whispers. 'One more night. And I'll do what I can to keep him safe. But, Ivy?'

'What, Mum?'

'Please promise that you won't hate me if anything goes wrong.'

Chapter 36

Ivy

Tom's hand reaches for me, but I hesitate a second too long, and then he's falling. I fly forward. It's too late to save him, but I need to see, to own, the damage I've caused. Except it's not Tom dropping off the cliff, it's Calum. NO! I try to jump too, to suffer for my indecision, but someone is holding my ankles. I fight, scrabble, but I can't get away. Who is it? A man in a hoodie. I can't make him out. Then he lifts a phone, the screen lighting his face. It's Harry. There's an image on the phone. Except it's not his, it's Tom's phone. Our secret on the display.

I sit bolt upright, suck in a scream. Hair is stuck to my face and my body feels clammy from sweat. I don't remember falling sleep. I remember climbing into bed after finishing the call with my mum, firing up my laptop and checking flights to London. There were plenty of options, and I booked one for midday, hoping that would give them enough time to clear the overnight snow and still get me be back to Earlsfield before it gets dark. But it didn't make me feel any better because I knew that was the easy part. The rest of it – navigating the storm, telling Zoe I'm leaving without her – is where the obstacles lie.

With my appetite non-existent and my head buzzing with barely contained panic, after booking the flight I pushed the laptop to one side, shuffled down the bed and closed my eyes, hoping for the oblivion of sleep. But my mind kept whirring. Why did I agree to come to Morzine in the first place? Was it to look after Zoe? Or because I felt a duty towards Tom?

And what has my decision cost? Is it that the pressure of responsibility is too much for my mum, or is Calum really in danger?

I lay there for hours, staring at the ceiling, feeling the dampness of tears dripping down my temples. But I must have fallen asleep at some point for the nightmare to come. And now it's the middle of the night, and I'm wide awake. I reach for my phone to check the time, but as soon as I pick it up, an image from my dream flashes across my mind. Tom's phone and the incriminating evidence on its screen.

After I told Zoe that Tom's phone had been destroyed during his fall, I hid it in the first place I could think of – under my clothes on the top shelf of my wardrobe. But there are no locks on any of the doors. What if Zoe comes into my room when I'm not here and finds it after I told her it hadn't survived the fall? And worse than that, she might know Tom's code. If she can open his phone, she could easily discover our message history.

I need to get rid of the damn thing. As soon as it's light, I'll take it out, to one of those industrial-sized bins on the main road that no one would ever rifle through. It's a good plan, and I feel calmer for making it.

But the composure doesn't last. Because the more I think about it lying there, the damage it could do, the more desperate I am to get it out of the chalet. Maybe the nightmare has made me feel more agitated, but I can't rest until I've removed all risk of Zoe finding out that I have it.

Fuck it. I push back the duvet and pull on my jogging bottoms and thick fleece jumper. I burrow my hand under my clothes until I find the cool slab of glass and metal, then drop it in my pocket. It's two o'clock in the morning, so it's likely there'll still be a few people on the street – the hardcore revellers who prioritise partying over skiing – but I'm sure no one from my group will be up. Zoe has a lot of excessive drinking to sleep off, and I heard Rob and Julian stumble upstairs to their bedroom a couple of hours ago. Harry's room is at the front of the chalet, but Julian messaged him about Zoe turning up soon after she arrived, so it makes sense that he's been in bed for a while too.

My confidence in my own logic dissolves as I push open my bedroom door, and my heart hammers against my chest as I peer into the living room. But it's empty. I let out a long sigh of relief, then head carefully to the stairs. In my socked feet, I can move almost soundlessly, and the tension eases as I reach the ground-floor entrance area. I sit on the wooden bench and pull on my trainers. Again, I wish I'd brought more appropriate footwear – especially as I can see a layer of fresh snow on the ground through the window – but luckily it's not far to the bins. I grab my ski jacket and push open the front door.

Tom's phone feels heavy in the pocket of my joggers, but I like the sense of purpose it gives me. I head left out of the chalet, away from the town centre. The sky is draped with black cloud but there's enough artificial light to illuminate my route. There aren't any bars in this direction, but there are a few small hotels, and I keep my gaze firmly fixed on the road as a collection of men stumble back from a night out.

The sound of Tom's phone falling into the cavernous bin makes me feel both relieved and sad. I'm glad that I've removed any chance of Zoe coming across it, but casting it aside is another reminder that Tom's dead. I let out a sigh, an unspoken acknowledgement of what we've all lost, and close the big circular lid. With my task completed, I head back down the road towards the chalet. But something catches me eye. Zoe's room has a small balcony, which overlooks a pedestrianised cut-through that spurs off the road I'm stood on. From this angle, I can only see one corner of it, but I'm sure there's someone sat in a chair, looking out towards town. I can't see their features, but it must be Zoe. I imagine her waking up, mouth dry and head pounding, and thinking fresh air might help. Or maybe she's been lying awake for hours too, desperate thoughts whirling around her head.

As I stare at the dark shadow, I realise I've stopped walking. There's no way she can see me from her position, but if she hears me, or senses my presence, she could turn around, lean forward slightly, and I'd be right in her eyeline. I know that means I should move more quickly, get back inside before she catches me, but the fear of being discovered has glued my feet to the road. And something else. As I watch her, an arm coming up, her head dropping from one side to the other, I realise she's talking to someone on the other side of the balustrade. Someone I can't see. Who could it be? But I can't satisfy my curiosity because that would mean getting too close. With a small sigh, I walk carefully towards the main chalet door instead and slip inside. I sink down onto the seat to pull off my trainers, the material already damp.

Suddenly the door swings open.

'Ivy? What are you doing up?'

I suck in a breath. 'Jesus, Harry, you scared me.'

'Seems to be a habit of mine,' he throws back.

'Well, whose fault is that?' I stand up, my thigh muscles tightening as though preparing to run. We glare at each other, neither of us speaking. Part of me is scared. But I also want to stand up for myself. A lot has happened since Zoe's twenty-first birthday party.

'I didn't push him, you know,' Harry says, finally breaking the silence.

'Really? So how do you explain the red marks on your hand?'

His eyes widen for a fraction of a second, then narrow as he shoves his hands further into his pockets. 'You think that proves my guilt?' he asks, his voice hardening. 'Did you not consider that it might be about my grief?' The comment takes me back fifteen years, to our chance meeting behind the biosciences building at university. But he must work out what I'm thinking because he shakes his head. 'It's ice burn, Ivy. From scrabbling through the snow to get to Tom once the search and rescue team found him. I didn't want to believe that my best friend was dead.'

'Best friend?' I spurt out incredulously. 'After what you did to him at university? And you didn't even stick around to apologise. You ran away, didn't contact him for years.'

'Shut up, Ivy! You can't take the moral high ground anymore!' He raises one arm and I gasp, skitter backwards. Memories of his anger at university make my eyesight blur. I clatter upstairs, run into my room. But there's no lock on the door, so I still don't feel safe. Trying to hold back the tears, I pull my duvet and pillow off my bed and race into the small bathroom. I flick down the lock and sink to the floor, my whole body shaking.

And all I can think is I wish Tom could be here.

Chapter 37

2008

Ivy

'Well, what can I say except haven't I done well?' Peter looks adoringly at Zoe, who returns the gesture, then he twists back to face his audience, some of whom who reward him with a smattering of applause. Not me though. I choose to smile at Zoe instead, to remind her who tonight is really about.

'Now I know what you're thinking,' he continues. 'That I don't look old enough to have a 21-year-old daughter, and I take your point.' He pauses to let the groans of laughter play out. 'But actually, I am beyond proud to claim this one. Zoe Lisa Wilde, my middle child, and dare I say my favourite, is beautiful, beguiling, and much to everyone's surprise, about to become a Bachelor of the Arts.' He turns back to face her. 'The world is your oyster, kid. And I have no doubt you'll be washing it down with champagne very soon.' He lifts his flute and winks as he tips it in her direction.

'Thanks, Dad,' Zoe says, lifting her own in response and taking a sip. She's wearing a navy-blue full-length dress with a high neckline and floating pleated skirt. She looks stunning, but also more grown-up than usual. As though she's marking her twenty-first birthday with a leap forward in maturity.

'Although that hasn't always been the case,' Peter continues, giving her a mischievous look then sharing it with the audience. 'There was a time when Zoe's mother was so worried about her, that she even sought advice from me.' Zoe smiles awkwardly as the crowd titters and I feel a rush of sympathy for her. It's not her fault that Peter left the family home, or that her parents couldn't be in the same room as each other without spitting vitriol. It's no wonder she went off the rails for a while.

'I still remember the phone call,' Peter muses, as though he's about to share a funny anecdote. 'Shock, horror. Zoe had been expelled from the exceptionally average Swindon Comprehensive School. Who would have thought that this smart young woman had it in her to spray obscene graffiti on the walls of her music block?' He bursts into raucous laughter, and it proves infectious. Soon all the guests are giggling too, even me, because it is weird to think that easy-going, vivacious Zoe was ever that angry. 'But listen, she pulled it back,' Peter says, his voice serious again. 'Changed schools, worked hard, and got into – yes, I'm biased – the best university in the country. So hats off, Zoe, my darling. You're a bloody star. Now stop listening to me drivel on, and go and enjoy your birthday party.'

He lifts his glass one more time, then beams as applause rings out around the room. And full credit to him, I suppose. He does know how to entertain an audience, and it was good to see Zoe visibly bask under his warm words. And it's only nine o'clock, an hour before he's due to leave, so there's also plenty of time for them to continue celebrating her milestone together. I can't help feeling pleased with myself for making it happen.

With the speech over, the DJ cranks up the music and the crowd disperses, to the bar, the dance floor, or through the open French doors into the hotel garden. I watch Tom fling Zoe around while Rob attempts some breakdancing move in front of a crowd of onlookers. Nikki and Julian are dancing too, unobtrusively, away from the spotlight. The hot weather has held all week though, and I'm thirsty, so instead of joining them, I wander over to the bar. It's busy, and I shuffle between two black dinner jackets to secure a spot.

'Oh, Ivy, hi.' Even though it's slurred, I recognise Harry's voice and my heart sinks. I hadn't realised he was one of the men I'd muscled in next to. Reluctantly, I twist to face him.

'Hey, Harry.' I pause, take in his glazed eyes, the sheen of sweat across his forehead. It's only mid-evening and he already looks wasted. 'Are you okay?'

He shrugs. 'Never better,' he mumbles, before adding, 'Want a drink?' as an afterthought. The bottleneck at the bar means our arms are touching, and I feel uncomfortable, but my body is trapped. 'Just a water, thanks,' I say. I've had a couple of glasses of fizz already and I want to keep my head tonight.

He stares at me for a moment, disappointed, then turns back to the barman. 'Two vodka and Cokes, mate. Doubles.'

'No, I don't want—'

'Ivy, it's your best friend's twenty-first,' he interrupts. 'Quit being so sensible.'

I check my watch again. Perhaps he's right. As he watches the barman prepare the drinks, I study his face. Zoe was adamant that her party be black tie, and the dinner jacket and loosely knotted bow tie suits Harry. But I can see it's a costume. A glamorous cover, while the inside pages are littered with bad news. I think about the last time I saw him, his raw knuckles. I don't want to delve, especially not tonight, but I also feel an impulse to check he's okay.

'I'm going outside,' he says, then adds, 'Wanna come?'

I look through the windows. There are plenty of guests on the terrace, enjoying the cooler temperature out there. Maybe I should go, just for five minutes; that's what a friend would do after all. I nod and follow him through the French doors.

I assume we'll sit at the first empty table, but Harry walks the length of the terrace and chooses one in the far corner. I suddenly feel nervous, being so far away from everyone, but that's stupid. This is Harry, I remind myself again, my friend. I sit down and the Provençal-style iron garden chair feels cool but unforgiving beneath the sheer material of my dress. Harry raises his glass in a silent toast, and I watch him take a large gulp.

When it's clear that Harry isn't going to speak first, I ask the first question that pops into my head. 'So, how did your last two exams go?'

He places his drink back on the table. The wound on his knuckles has almost healed, just a few speckles of a scab and new pink skin. He looks into the distance, then flicks his eyeline back to me. 'I didn't sit them.'

'What?'

'There was no point. I've failed the year anyway.'

'Are you sure? How do you know? But not turning up for your exams at all? Is that sensible?' I stumble over my words, flustered.

He grips his glass tighter. 'Look, I fucked up one of my first exams, okay? As in, really fucked it up. I didn't know one of the early questions, an easy one, and everything spiralled from there.'

'But you can re-sit that one! Why would you not take the others?' I know my voice is too loud, that even with the distance, people might hear. But I can't believe Harry's being so self-destructive. Then suddenly his hand whips up, and Harry slaps his own cheek. I gasp. The hand disappears under the table. It's so quick that I might think I'd imagined it if it wasn't for the reddening mark on his face. I blink, but my throat is too constricted to speak.

'Because my tutor wants me to give up,' he answers, as though nothing's happened. 'She said that being a doctor is highly stressful.' His pitch rises, like he's imitating her voice. 'And therefore not suitable for someone like me.'

'But everyone has off days,' I say weakly. 'Any one of us could freeze in the moment, leave a paper blank.'

'Yeah well,' he says, looking away. 'I didn't leave it blank.'

I fall silent as I imagine the SOS signals that he might have scrawled across his exam paper. And though I hate myself for it, I can't help wondering if his tutor is right.

'Although I don't know why I'm telling you any of this,' he mutters, before releasing an ugly laugh. 'Last time I confided in you, you did a runner.'

'I'm sorry,' I whisper. 'I was scared. I didn't know how to help you.' But my apology is a lie. Because I've never regretted leaving him that morning, and his behaviour tonight has only strengthened that belief. In fact, I want to repeat it, run away again. Lady Gaga's 'Just Dance' has started playing and loads of guests are shifting inside. I feel isolated out here with Harry. On the frontline of his crisis.

'So why did you come outside with me tonight then?' he pushes. 'If you're so scared?' He sounds accusatory, bitter. I eye the French doors in the distance and wonder if I should just get up and go.

'Because you enjoy messing with my head?' he goes on. 'Is that it?'

'Don't be stupid,' I mutter. 'I guess you looked like you needed a friend.'

'I have lots of friends, Ivy! Haven't you noticed? All those gullible idiots who think I'm a good guy because I'll go out and get pissed with them. Or because I never argue, never complain, even though that's only because I'm scared that if I start, I won't stop. No, what I need is someone I can confide in, someone who knows the real me and still sticks around. I thought you might be that person, but then I made the stupid decision to show my hand.' Another slap rings out, lightning fast like the first.

'Stop doing that!' I yell.

'Why should I? What do you care?!'

'Of course I care!'

Suddenly he pushes his chair back. Three steps and then he grabs me.

'No, Harry.' I try to shake my head, to tell him he's got the wrong idea, but he's holding my face in his hands. My cheeks burn against his palms. He curls his fingers into my hair, digs at my scalp, pulls me towards him. I suddenly realise that he's not going to stop, that I need to scream, to get help, but it's too late. His lips push against mine. A kiss to him, but an assault to me. I clench my hand into a fist, and punch him hard at his chest, but he doesn't even seem to notice. His tongue pushes harder into my mouth. I try to twist away from him, but he holds on tighter. I feel strands of hair break away. The sting brings on a surge of anger, and I punch him again, but lower this time, where I know it will hurt.

And it works, because he draws backwards, tears forming in his eyes.

And then he slaps me. Slaps me so hard that it feels like a breeze block against my skull. My brain judders, my head whips round, my body follows. I fall from the chair; my eyesight blurs with tears. He towers over me.

'STOP!'

I look up. Tom. Rage and confusion on his face.

'What the fuck is going on?!' he screams.

But Harry doesn't answer. He twists away, then jumps off the raised terrace and runs into the garden.

Tom looks at me, then back at Harry's disappearing figure. He's in shock. I wonder how I look, whether there's a handprint on my face. Suddenly I feel ashamed. Did I cause this? 'Go,' I say.

'Are you sure?'

'Just go.' Tom hurtles after Harry and within seconds they've both vanished into the darkness. And then I hear the crack of wood snapping, like a gate being kicked down.

Chapter 38

The day of the fall

Tom

'Guys, that was epic, wasn't it? Vertical drop, moguls like mini mountains. We're bloody legends for skiing that!' Tom looks at their hard, unresponsive faces and feels a rush of annoyance. What has he done to deserve their hostility? He loves these men, even Harry who hit a fucking woman, for Chrissakes. He has shown them nothing but loyalty, generosity and forgiveness over the years. He's kept Rob's shameful secret, patched up Julian's knee, brought Harry back into the fold. And yet it seems that he is still the villain. Well, fuck them.

'Oh whatever,' he mutters. 'I'm starving, and Erin said that this is Nina's favourite restaurant, so I'm going in. Join me or not, I really don't care.' Tom pulls open the thick wooden door of *Les Ancelles* and clatters over to the maître d' in his ski boots.

'Good afternoon, sir,' the man says, clocking Tom's Britishness instantly. 'You'd like a table? For how many people?'

Tom turns back to the door and sure enough, Rob and Julian have followed. He waits a moment longer, then Harry appears too. Tom tries not to sound smug when he answers the man's question with: '*Quatre, s'il vous plaît.*'

'*Trés bon.* Follow me.' It's busy – always a good sign, Tom thinks – and they weave their way past a few full tables before the maître d' finds an empty one in the corner. There's a window beyond it overlooking the piste, with a dramatic cliff face and frozen waterfall behind. It's a beautiful backdrop, but the piste is busy, and it's the colourful ants that hold his attention. Some take controlled, measured turns, while others swish down with ease. One skier in an electric blue jacket is particularly good, and he watches them for a moment, before turning his attention back to his table.

As they sit down, Harry on his left, Rob and Julian opposite, the slight man with salt and pepper hair hands them a menu each. Tom has a flick through. Pan-fried scallops, grilled fillet steak, tiger prawns in garlic butter. Not your average mountain fare, but why not push the boat out. They deserve it after the morning they've had.

He'd never worried that the Swiss Wall would outwit him, but he had wondered whether his technique might take a hit. Everyone knows that getting down the mountain is one thing, while doing it stylishly is quite another. But he rose to the challenge, proved he's still got it, and he only wishes there was some video footage of his performance to boast over once they're back in the UK. He's pretty sure Julian won't feel the same way though. The poor guy got the fear at the top, then proceeded to ski like a granny for the rest of the run. Long traverses; short, panicked turns; a few out-of-control moments riding the moguls like a bucking bronco. Tom hopes he came across as empathetic, but it was hard to do it sincerely with all that waiting around.

Rob, on the other hand, skied like a kamikaze pilot, attacking the moguls without hesitation, bouncing back up when he fell as though he was made of rubber. Onlookers might have called him a daredevil skier, but Tom knew it was just his way of expelling the anger. Harry was in a world of his own, hanging back, away from the group. Just as he starts to make progress – going shopping with Julian earlier – he seems to lose interest in rekindling their friendships. The trip will be over soon, and Tom is only more confused about why the guy wanted to come.

'A waiter will be along in a moment to take your order, but in the meantime, can I offer you an aperitif on the house?'

'You certainly can.' Tom beams at the polite Frenchman, and it does the job because less than a minute later, a waiter appears – a carbon copy of the maître d' except twenty-five years younger – with a tray of shot glasses. He places one in front of each of them. Tom senses Harry preparing to say something – to turn down the free drink – and he places his hand on Harry's arm. Gifts from strangers should never be snubbed; someone will drink it.

As Tom's about to reach for his glass, his phone buzzes inside his jacket, so he unzips the pocket and reaches for it. He doesn't wear reading glasses – he's only 36; he doesn't need them – but in the wood-darkened room he can't make out who the message is from. Without thinking, he clicks into it, then instantly realises his mistake. He jabs at the blue arrow in the top left-hand corner, but it's so bloody small. It takes a few attempts before the photo mercifully disappears, but her name is still at the top of the messages. Ivy Hawkes.

It's not surprising that it's from Ivy. He accidentally deleted the message she sent him last night – too flustered after Julian probed him about it in the bar in front of everyone – so he'd asked her to resend the photo. He didn't consider the risk that another message might bring. He finally thinks to swipe the app closed completely, but he's sweating and flustered. He picks up the small glass and knocks back the fiery liquid. 'A round of beers?' he asks desperately, but the waiter doesn't pick up the inflection.

'Yes sir, and I'll give you a few minutes to choose your meal.' He pivots on his heels, then heads for the bar.

Tom peers across the table, anxious to know whether Julian or Rob clocked what came up on his phone. But neither of them shows any sign of intrigue or curiosity. Perhaps their refusing to hold eye contact with Tom is finally working in his favour. Then he turns his head towards Harry. And his heart sinks. The guy's face is smarting with anger, and betrayal.

Tom smiles sheepishly, but Harry looks away, then picks up the shot glass and knocks back the *genepi*. And when the waiter arrives with the beers a few moments later, Harry is the first person to take one off the tray. Tom watches with unease as he sinks half of it in one go. While Tom rarely turns down a drink himself, especially after the thrill of a challenging ski run, he knows what alcohol can do to Harry. He's witnessed it first-hand. It may be nearly fifteen years ago, but the image of him slapping Ivy is still so clear in his mind. And what came after.

When Harry ran into the garden, Tom was in two minds whether to follow him or stay with Ivy, but when she told him to go, he ran. Because whatever Harry had done, Tom knew the guy deserved his help. For all the times Tom had ignored the signs. Because if he's honest with himself, he'd always suspected that Harry had his demons. Those nights when they got loaded together, and Harry would switch from life and soul of the party to mute in seconds, then disappear off by himself. And the next morning, the fresh grazes Tom would see on his knuckles. Harry always put it down to a drunken mishap on his journey home, but it was the same story every time; and after a while, it didn't wash.

But still, Tom would let it go. He was busy – making sure he was the top-performing medic in their year took effort – and it was always easier to pretend everything was fine.

The hotel was about a mile from their student house, and Harry sprinted all the way. Even with his regular gym visits, Tom struggled to keep up, and when he arrived home, Harry was already in his room. Smashing it to pieces. Tom tried to stop him, but Harry was raging, disgusted with himself, and with his anger came an extraordinary strength. It was impossible to prevent him splintering his wardrobe with a punch, swiping his books off the shelves, throwing his desk chair against the wall, or turning on Tom when the room was trashed. In all the chaos, Tom had no idea that Harry's punch fractured his cheekbone – something only an X-ray two days later revealed.

But that still wasn't enough for Harry. He ran onto the landing and then barged into Rob's room, pushing over his TV, kicking his guitar until it splintered. And then into Julian's, throwing his books out of the window, smashing the photo of him and Nikki on his bedside table. He was screaming and shouting the whole time. How he'd been kicked off the course because he was a headcase. How disappointed – no, fucking traumatised – his parents were going to be when they found out their only child couldn't cut it as a doctor like they'd both managed to do for nearly thirty years. And how he knows he's not deserving of Ivy's love, but still desperately wants it. Tom could only watch, and make sure Harry didn't turn his need to destroy things onto himself.

Eventually Harry ran out of energy. He sank to the floor, head in his hands, and quietly sobbed. Tom knew it wasn't all over at that point, that Ivy might well contact the police. And even if Harry avoided a criminal investigation, he'd still need professional help. But the imminent danger had passed, and Tom remembers the relief he felt as he finally persuaded Harry to drink a coffee and get lost in a Marvel movie. That's when he'd called Zoe with some fictitious explanation for why he'd had to leave the party. Of course that all went to shit a couple of hours later too. And when Tom returned home for the second time in the early hours, this time with a crushed girlfriend in tow, Harry had gone.

'It's not what you think,' he whispers in his quietest voice, once he's sure Rob and Julian are too invested in the menu to hear him.

'Does Zoe know?' Harry asks, in a hard but equally low voice.

212

Tom silently thanks his old friend for keeping things discreet, although he's not sure why Harry's extending him the courtesy.

'No.'

'Do you not think she deserves to?' Harry continues, another whisper.

'It's complicated.'

'Seems clear to me.'

'Have you two chosen?' Julian looks up from the menu. 'I'm going to have the steak.'

'Me too,' Rob grunts, taking a swig of beer. He hasn't spoken to Tom, or even looked him in the eye, since their argument this morning. When is he going to work out that he's taking entirely the wrong approach? That if he wants Tom to keep his mouth shut, he should be apologising, not acting the victim?

'Steak sounds good,' Tom says shrugging. He's losing his appetite to be honest, but he knows his energy stores need replenishing if he wants to ski well this afternoon.

'Harry?' Julian prompts.

Harry takes another gulp of beer. 'Nothing for me,' he says, looking out of the window.

'What?' Julian asks. 'You can't not eat after the morning we've had.' A veil of realisation drops over his features. Then it transitions to embarrassment. 'Is it because it's expensive? Listen, I can shout you a meal, Harry. And don't be awkward about it. Jesus, life's too short for that.'

Harry gives Julian a withering look. 'It's not the money,' he says scornfully. 'I'm just not hungry. Hey, waiter! Another pint over here when you've got a sec.'

Chapter 39

Zoe

Zoe stares at the murky dawn sky as she nurses a mug of lukewarm coffee, the sun too low to give the heavy snow clouds even a hint of brightness. She usually likes her coffee milky, latte her standard order at home, but this one is making her feel sick. She wishes she'd made it black instead. Or even opted for a peppermint tea. Yesterday was a difficult day, but she can't wallow in her misery forever. There's still too much to do.

'How are you feeling?' Ivy asks. Her tone is soft, but her body language is tense. It's only seven o'clock but she's already showered and dressed, as though she's got somewhere to be. Zoe is showered too, but for different reasons. Ridding herself of yesterday's dirt. And now she's dressed for comfort in salopettes and a thick Lululemon fleece hoodie.

Zoe considers how to answer Ivy's question. Heartbroken, she wants to say. Like the last morsel of goodness that she was clinging on to in this whole fucking mess has been ripped out of her. And on top of that, her head hurts, her eyes aren't working properly, and she might throw up at any minute, for all the wrong reasons. But Ivy wouldn't understand. 'Fine,' she murmurs instead. 'Bit rough, I suppose, but I know it's self-inflicted. Thanks for helping me get to bed by the way. I appreciate it.' Ivy looks relieved rather than gratified, and Zoe worries for a moment that they had a falling-out last night. But she shakes the feeling away. Even hammered, she wouldn't risk offending Ivy.

'Listen, don't blame yourself for this,' Ivy says kindly, lifting one hand and resting it on Zoe's arm. 'You've just lost your husband; it's no wonder you got a bit carried away with drowning your sorrows. I only wish you didn't do it all by yourself. You disappearing like that scared the life out of me.'

Zoe looks up from her mug, surprised at how genuine Ivy sounds, then gently pulls away from her touch. 'Sorry,' she whispers, shrugging her shoulders. 'It all got on top of me, I suppose.'

'And, um, did you have trouble sleeping after I put you to bed?' Ivy continues, picking up her empty mug, and placing it on her crumb-flecked plate. Ivy's tone is offhand, but there's a stiffness to it that makes Zoe pause.

'I was a bit restless,' she offers carefully. 'Got some fresh air at one point. Why do you ask?'

'Oh no reason,' Ivy says, pushing to standing, and picking up her used crockery. Nina had explained that Erin starts later after her day off, so they're fending for themselves for another hour or so. 'I always sleep terribly when I've drunk too much as well. At least you can rest today though, before you fly home tomorrow.' Ivy twists away from the table and walks towards the kitchen.

Zoe straightens up. 'Before we fly back, you mean?'

'Um, about that.' Ivy's voice is muffled as she bends down to fill the dishwasher, so Zoe has to strain to hear her. 'I've booked a plane ticket; I'm flying back today.'

'But you can't,' Zoe bursts out, trying not to sound needy, but failing.

'I'm sorry, Zoe. I know I'm letting you down,' Ivy says, standing upright up and picking a cloth out of the sink, still not looking in Zoe's direction. 'But I need to get back to Calum.'

Panic starts to claw at Zoe's insides. She can't let Ivy go, she needs her here, in Morzine. Tom's body is being flown home tomorrow, so it's only one more day. 'But look at the weather!' she tries. 'Even if flights start taking off again from Geneva, there's no way you'll get down the mountain.'

'I know it won't be easy – I called Nina first thing and she wasn't comfortable asking Nico to drive me – but I've managed to book a seat with Skiidy Gonzales. Apparently they use special tyres or something. My flight's at midday, and so far it's showing as being on schedule. I'm getting picked up in an hour.'

'Please don't go,' Zoe says, tears threatening to fall. 'I can't travel back by myself, not with Tom in the hold, freezing cold. Please don't force me to do that, Ivy.'

Ivy's face creases, and Zoe feels a rush of relief. Her pleas are working. Her friend isn't going to leave her. But the feeling is short-lived, because Ivy's expression hardens. 'I'm sorry Zoe, but I really need to get back to Calum, to be there for Mum too. But listen, why don't you come with me? It's not like you need to be on the same flight as Tom. Monsieur Durand has arranged everything, and the casket will go through completely different security checks. I could book you a seat on the same flight as me, right now, what do you say?'

Zoe stares at Ivy. She makes it sound so simple. All Zoe needs to do is pack up her things – Tom's too, she supposes – and leave this nightmare behind. It's what she's wanted since she arrived after all, to get back to the UK and start to put the few remaining pieces of her life back together. Her business. Her brother. The home she loves. No baby yet, but the dream doesn't have to be over forever.

But she can't go today. There's still one more thing that she must do. Which means she needs to persuade Ivy to change her mind. 'I know it sounds silly,' she starts. 'I know Tom's dead and doesn't know any different. But I promised him, his memory, that we'd do the journey home together. I'd love to fly back today, with you, but I can't let him down.'

Ivy doesn't respond at first, but Zoe can tell she's got something to say, so she waits, the knot in her stomach tightening, until Ivy takes a long breath in and finally starts speaking. 'And do you think he deserves it?' she asks quietly. 'After what he did to you?'

From nowhere, a burst of rage fills Zoe's insides and she has to swallow hard to stop it escaping as a tirade of abuse. How dare Ivy comment on her and Tom's marriage? On how Zoe should handle his infidelity? What right has she got to have an opinion?

But Zoe knows she needs to hide how she really feels. What she wants more than anything is to persuade Ivy to stay, and shouting at her is not going to help with that. She rolls her shoulders. 'Maybe not,' she says, staring out of the window, not daring to look Ivy in the eye. 'But I don't want to forgo my principles, my beliefs about marriage, just because he did.' Silence hangs between them for a while, and Zoe finds herself mesmerised by the falling snow. How on first glance each flake looks big and clumsy, but on closer inspection, is actually a mesh of tiny, intricate patterns.

'I get that,' Ivy says, finally breaking the silence. 'And respect that you feel that way. But I need to leave today.'

'Do you really not value our friendship at all?'

'Oh, Zoe, it's not that! Mum is petrified that someone's going to take Calum. What if it's true? How can I ignore her?'

Zoe blinks. 'This is about what Linda's been saying?' she asks incredulously. 'About being followed? I love your mum, Ivy, but are you really putting her paranoia before my grief?'

'She might be right,' Ivy whispers, but without much conviction.

'But who would even want to take Calum?' Zoe presses. 'Kidnapping is what happens to billionaires or royalty, not people like us!'

Ivy looks up at the ceiling, as though searching for some divine guidance, then back again. 'Look, I know it's probably nothing, just a figment of Mum's imagination. But she's exhausted, Zoe.

Genuine threat or not, she needs a break.'

'Well, can't someone else help?' Zoe asks. 'Someone local who could take Calum for a few hours? You must have friends.'

Ivy turns to face Zoe, but then changes her mind and looks down at the floor. 'I don't really have close enough friends for that,' she admits. 'It's mainly me and Calum.'

Zoe pauses for a moment, temporarily knocked off course. She assumed that Ivy would have a solid social circle, but why? Zoe made friends on her behalf at university, and Ivy was always reserved around new people. It makes sense that she doesn't have a tribe of friends to lean on now. But she needs to find a way to persuade Ivy to stay another day. 'What about a neighbour then? Or a work colleague? Christ, there must be someone who can take him for a few hours!'

'You don't get it, do you,' Ivy says quietly.

'Get what?' Zoe asks, her voice slowing down, low but persistent warning bells sounding from deep within her.

'What it's like to be a mother.'

Chapter 40

Ivy

I shouldn't have said that. From Zoe's demeanour, Harry can't have got to her last night, thank God, but I've managed to screw things up myself. Even if Zoe doesn't want children, it's the worst thing to say to a woman whose body clock is ticking away, whether she cares about it or not. 'I'm sorry,' I mumble. 'That came out wrong.'

'Oh?' Zoe's eyes bore into mine. They feel like two laser beams, scorching hot, burning my irises. 'Because it sounded a lot like you think you're better than me now that you have a kid,' she continues icily.

'No, it's not that,' I plead. God, I just want to get home to Calum, and with Zoe's blessing if possible. Why has this conversation become so complicated? My wording was clumsy, but it's not as though Zoe wants children. 'I just meant that it's impossible to understand the protective instincts of being a mum until you are one,' I say, trying to keep my voice measured. 'Like we can never truly know how we'd react if there was a natural disaster, or a terrorist attack.'

'You're comparing motherhood to terrorism?'

'No!' I reach out for Zoe's arm, but she whirls it away. 'I'm trying to explain why I need to go home. Why I can't call on someone I vaguely know to look after my son.' I hesitate, drag the lie out yet again. 'I know Calum came along unexpectantly. But he's the best thing in my life, the only thing that really matters. It's my job to keep him safe and I can't let him down. Please understand that my putting Calum before you isn't a reflection of our friendship, it's about how strong our relationship is, as mother and son.'

But the more I try to explain, the more entrenched the anger on Zoe's face becomes. How can I be doing such a bad job of this? The atmosphere feels thick with emotion, and as fat snowflakes layer up on the windowsill, I suddenly can't breathe properly. All I really want is to count the minutes until my transfer bus arrives, then get back to the UK as quickly as I can and put this whole, awful trip behind me. But I can't leave Zoe like this, so furious with me. Can I?

I watch her run her hands up and down her padded trousers, listen to the rustling sound it makes. 'You don't know half of what I'm going through,' she mumbles softly, not looking at me.

'So why don't you tell me?'

Zoe looks up. There's such raw emotion on her face that I suddenly feel awkward. As though I've accidentally walked in on her naked. But I force myself to hold her gaze, to try and project something comforting back. I think for a moment that it works, that she's going to reveal some buried secret, but then she changes her mind. And suddenly she's running for the stairs to the ground floor, then taking them two at a time.

'Zoe?' I call out. 'What are you doing? Don't go out in this weather!' I lean over the banister, just in time to see her whip a jacket from the closest hook, Julian's I think, and slam the front door behind her.

'Shit,' I mutter under my breath. I'm desperate to be on my

flight home, but I can't let her go off by herself, again, especially in such heavy snow. I canter down the stairs, grab my jacket, and pull on my pointless trainers. I hesitate for a moment, maybe I should wake the others up, get them to help with the search. But they always make things worse, and I can't face seeing Harry, so I pull open the door and step out into the snow.

I can't see Zoe from the gate, and there are footprints in both directions, so I have to make a choice. I pick right, towards town, but it's slippery underfoot, and to keep myself upright I have to tread carefully. Zoe's trail-running shoes are much more grippy than my trainers, so she'll be faster, and she had a head start. She could be anywhere, I realise with frustration.

As I reach the first roundabout, I try to call her, but it rings out; I don't even know if she took her phone with her. I turn up the volume, just in case, then shove my phone and my freezing hands back in my pockets – I didn't think to bring gloves – and walk further into town. I poke my head inside shops and cafés, scan the few skaters braving the open-air rink, and check down various touristy streets. But I can't spot her anywhere. I check my watch. It's been nearly half an hour since she ran off.

Maybe I should give up? Go back to the chalet, finish packing, wait for the transfer bus. Give the task of finding Zoe to someone else. God, I want to. But deep down, however easily I can justify the different choices I've made over the years, I know I owe her.

I could try the footbridge. When we drove into the town on Sunday afternoon, I remember Nina pointing out the *François Baud* suspension bridge, a striking construction that sits over the *Dereches* river and links each side of the valley. Its height will give me a great vantage point over the town, and maybe I'll get lucky. I head towards the Super Morzine cable car where the bridge connects with the road. The area is busy with liveried minibuses dropping chalet guests off, and as I get closer, I realise that I recognise one. It's the van we drove up in. Tall Mountain emblazoned on the side.

I knock on the window, expecting to see Nico, but it's Nina who turns her head at the noise. Her eyes widen for a moment, then fall back into place as she opens the window. 'Ivy? Is everything okay?'

'Not really. Are you busy now? Could I ask a favour?'

'I've been dropping off guests, mad people who still want to ski in these conditions. But this is my last drop, so I'm free now. What do you need?'

'I've lost Zoe again,' I say desperately. Like the rest of us, Nina had been concerned about Zoe when she disappeared from the restaurant yesterday, but I'd messaged to say everything was fine after Zoe turned up at the chalet yesterday evening. 'She got upset this morning – I upset her,' I clarify. 'Then she ran out of the chalet. I'm supposed to be leaving soon, back to the UK, but I need to make sure she's okay.'

'You're leaving?' Nina asks, looking up at the white sky, then back to me.

'I know Nico couldn't drive me in these conditions, but I booked a transfer with Skiidy Gonzales,' I explain. 'They're picking me up from the chalet at nine.'

'That's strange,' Nina says, her forehead crinkling in confusion. 'Have you looked at your emails recently? Checked if they've cancelled? There's been a small avalanche onto the road to Geneva and no traffic's getting through.'

'You're kidding,' I moan, looking up at the sky myself, silently begging for it to stop bloody snowing. I haven't checked my emails for at least an hour, which explains why I haven't heard the news.

'But I think I might know where Zoe is, if that helps,' Nina continues.

I look back at her. 'You do?' I ask. I should feel relieved, but the truth is, I feel numb. The only thing that really matters is getting home to Calum, and it looks like that's not going to happen any time soon.

'At least, I might do. My first set of guests wanted to be

dropped at the Ardent cable car, which is five minutes beyond Lake Chablais. The bus from town had just pulled in at the lake bus stop, and I was stuck behind it while a passenger got off. I remember thinking she looked like Zoe. I didn't actually think it was her, because this woman was wearing a black ski jacket, and I remember Zoe's being emerald green, but now that you've said she's missing. Well, with hindsight, I think maybe it was her.'

'At the lake?' I ask incredulously. 'In this weather?'

'I was distracted,' Nina says apologetically. 'Those guests are hard work. But you're right – it's not ideal for her to be up there by herself in these conditions. Come on, jump in, we can be there in less than ten minutes.'

I slip and slide my way around the front of the minibus, my heart thudding at the thought of Zoe up there, alone, upset. I climb into the passenger seat and yank the seatbelt. A second later, Nina slams it in reverse, and then we're heading out of the town, clumps of snow exploding on the windscreen.

Chapter 41

The day of the fall

Tom

Tom pushes the door open and blinks. It's bright outside compared to the cosy lighting of the restaurant, but the patches of blue sky from this morning have disappeared, replaced by heavy white clouds. It looks like the forecast for snow later is correct, which means there'll be fresh powder for their last day on the mountain tomorrow. For all the shit he's going through with his mates, the skiing on this trip has been epic.

In fact, he might even be able to count the whole thing as a success if he can find a way to convince Harry to keep his mouth shut. He knows that Julian won't be able to stop himself confronting Nikki about her alleged affair when he gets home, and whatever that means for their marriage, Tom assumes Nikki will put him in the clear. Which means Julian will be knocking on his door with a grovelling apology soon.

And those lunchtime beers have made him feel better about the Rob issue too. Because he's decided that instead of taking Zoe's advice and reporting Rob to the GMC, he's going to pay for him to go into rehab, and dress it up as stress rather than addiction to protect his career. Rob won't like it at first, being told what to do, feeling indebted to Tom, not having access to a drink. But in time, he hopes Rob will appreciate the intervention, maybe even feel like he owes Tom one.

So Harry is his only problem. And while it was a shock when Tom first realised he'd seen the photo from Ivy, he gradually decided that it might not be a disaster. Harry lives in Surrey for a start, and is training to be a paramedic in Guildford, so there's no chance he'll bump into Zoe in Fulham. And while Harry might be angry with Tom at the moment, would he really choose to inflict permanent damage? After the loyalty Tom showed him on the night of Zoe's party? Tom could have stayed with Ivy, but instead he chose Harry. Followed him home, made sure he didn't hurt himself, settled him down when the chance came. He didn't go to the police either, or try to track Harry down after he did a runner. Would the guy really ruin Tom's marriage after all that? Especially when any feelings he had for Ivy must be dead and buried by now?

'Looking at the map, I think we can ski all the way to Ardent from here and then get the ski bus back into town,' Julian says, before clipping on his helmet and kicking his toes into his bindings. Tom's heart sinks. Finishing skiing mid-afternoon is what old people do.

'Well, I'm not ready to go back yet,' Rob counters, scrabbling with the sleeve of his jacket until his watch appears. 'It's only half past three. This time tomorrow we'll be waiting for our transfer bus to the airport; I want to ski until we're chucked off the mountain today.'

'Harry?' Tom asks, feeling buoyed up by Rob's comment, even if the guy isn't technically speaking to him. 'What do you want to do?'

Harry gives him an intense stare. 'Well, I assume you want to do another run,' he says, with an edge that makes those few innocuous words sound slightly menacing. 'And we wouldn't want Tom Metcalfe to not get his way.'

'Um, okay, great, thanks,' Tom says, clapping his hands in an attempt to banish the unease. 'You okay with that Julian? Three against one? Democracy rules?' He pulls his poles out of the snow and pushes his boot toes into his skis, pretending not to notice Julian's stony silence. The binding doesn't catch at first, but after a few attempts he's rewarded with the familiar dull click, even though it still feels a bit odd. 'There's the *Flosset* lift over there,' he says, pointing at the chairlift directly opposite. 'Apparently there's a cruisy blue down from there called *Clementine*.' He looks up at the sky, which appears even heavier than it did a few minutes ago. 'We should get going; the weather's definitely coming in.'

Ten minutes later, the four of them are stacked together like penguins, skis dangling beneath them, snowflakes settling on their clothing as the chairlift rises slowly up the mountainside. When they first set off, the stunning views made up for the falling temperature and strengthening wind, but for the last two minutes they've been stuck in the cloud and now Tom can't see a thing. He shivers as the cold wind curls around his neck. It's at times like these that he wishes he wore a helmet. Not for protection – he's too good a skier for that – but for warmth.

'Fucking hell, this is taking forever,' Rob grumbles, his voice stuttering as he tries to stop his teeth from chattering.

'We must be near the top by now,' Tom offers, but it's a feeble attempt at optimism. He's cold, and his lunchtime drinking is already morphing into a hangover.

'Another one of your great ideas, Tom,' Julian mutters, his voice muffled by the snood he's wearing over his mouth. Despite the weather, Tom feels a sudden heat rise from the pit of his stomach. Why do they all think they can treat him like a punchbag? What has he done to deserve any of this? He's never claimed to be perfect, but none of them are. He doesn't whinge like Julian, or get drunk and kill patients like Rob. And he certainly doesn't hit women. Yes, he's got secrets. But isn't everyone entitled to a private life?

'Do you know what, Julian?' he starts. 'You can fuck off. It's no wonder Nikki's shagging someone else when she's married to a mean-spirited prick like you. And Rob, you can be as pissed off with me as you like, but you're the screw-up here, the alcoholic, not me. And as for you.' Tom twists his body to look at Harry.

'What Tom?' Harry asks, but it's a warning, not a question, his piercing stare making the message clear. *You mention what I did to Ivy, and I'll tell Rob and Julian what I saw on your phone.* But Tom is done with feeling ashamed. He hasn't broken any laws, unlike Harry, and as long as Zoe never finds out, he hasn't hurt anyone either.

'Why not? What the hell do I owe you?'

'What are you two talking about?' Julian growls. 'Come on, don't leave Harry out of your friendship annihilation.'

Tom hesitates, the story hovering on his lips.

'Shit!' Rob calls out. Tom whips his head around to see the top of the lift station almost upon them. It wasn't there a moment ago, but the cloud is so thick that visibility is down to a couple of metres. In one fluid movement, he slides his skis off the footrest and pushes up the safety bar. A second later, his skis connect with the snow, and they all come tumbling off the lift together.

With a cold wind stinging his face, Tom surveys the mountain. Except for the four of them, everywhere is white. No contours or shading, no dark objects to give the landscape any context. He's skied in white-outs before, but nothing so completely pervasive as this. To steady himself, he looks back towards the chairlift. But it doesn't help. The structure is visible, but the chairs seem to appear from nowhere. The world beyond those few metres has disappeared. And as the chairs get sucked back into the abyss, all of them empty, he feels like he's been abandoned.

'Which way is it, do you think?' Julian asks, his anger gone as fear creeps in.

Tom takes a deep breath. He's the most experienced skier here, and he's done this run before (not that he'd admit that). He should show some leadership. 'I think it's this way,' he says, pointing with his pole. 'Everyone stay close and follow me.'

'What if we don't want to follow you?' Harry pipes up. 'Julian is the most cautious skier, I think he should go first.'

'Thanks, Harry,' Julian says slowly, as he tries to work out if it's a compliment.

'Julian?' Tom asks incredulously. 'He's just told us he doesn't know the way!'

'I vote Julian too,' Rob calls out. 'And remember, democracy rules!'

'Oh whatever,' Tom mutters. 'Let him dig his own grave.' With his senses still on high alert, he watches Julian push off and Rob follow. He expects Harry to go next, but he seems to be waiting for Tom.

'After you,' Harry says eventually. Tom feels an involuntary shiver rush through him. He doesn't like the idea of not having Harry in his eyeline but he's not sure why. What does he think the guy's going to do? So he shrugs, digs in his poles, and skis in the direction of Rob's fading silhouette.

Chapter 42

Ivy

Nina stops at the entrance to the Lake Chablais car park. 'Sorry, I can't go any further. The snow's too deep – the van will get stuck.'

'It's fine,' I say breathlessly, unclicking my seatbelt and pushing open the door. The vents have been pumping out hot, damp air since we left Morzine, and even though it's freezing outside, it's a relief to get out of its path. 'I can walk from here.'

'I'll wait for you,' she says. 'If Zoe's upset, it's probably better for me to keep my distance, let you two talk in private. But this way I can drive you both back to the chalet as soon as you've persuaded her to leave. You don't want to be stuck out here in this weather.'

I nod and smile my gratitude, conscious that Nina is going way beyond her job to help us. Then I twist out of the van and my feet immediately sink into the snow, above my ankles. The snowfall is more dense here than in town, and with steep cliffs all around the lake and thick tree cover, I feel isolated, at the mercy of the weather, like Dad was. The thought unnerves me, but Zoe is out there somewhere, alone, upset, and I need to find her.

I flip my hood up and pull on the drawstring to stop snow seeping inside my jacket and down my neck. It's better, but the soft icicles still scratch at my cheeks. I drop my head and push on through the snow, up the side of the empty car park, my trainers already soaking wet, until I find the path where the ground is a bit more solid. The heavy snow fall makes it hard to see, but the extra height gives me a better vantage point, and as I stare at the monochrome vista through pinched eyes – black lake, charcoal trees, grey skies and matt-white snow – I see that the place is deserted.

Except for one person in a black ski jacket.

Stood perfectly still in the middle of the snow-covered lake.

I run along the path as fast as my wet, smooth-soled trainers will allow until I'm in line with Zoe. Then, as carefully as I can, I clamber down the bank until I reach the edge of the lake. It's vast, more than a kilometre in length and three hundred metres wide, and the whole thing is covered in a thick layer of snow. My logical brain screams that it's safe to walk on, that snow wouldn't stick if there was any water seeping through, and anyway, Zoe has already made the journey. But my legs refuse to move. The thought of the ice cracking, of being submerged, of drowning in freezing cold water is so terrifying that I'm rigid. Except for my heart, which is battering my ribcage with such ferocity that I can hardly breathe.

This is my mum's influence, I think. Catastrophising. Missing out on life because she's hamstrung by unfounded fears. Haven't I moved on from that way of thinking? Isn't my life better, richer, for taking a few calculated risks over the years? Gingerly, I step onto the frozen lake. It doesn't move. No cracks or tremors. I suck in another breath and take a few more footsteps.

As my terror gradually ebbs, and my breathing becomes a bit more regular, I turn my focus to Zoe. She must know I'm here, but she hasn't acknowledged my presence at all. I walk further onto the lake. But as I get closer, my panic starts to rise again as I realise where she's standing. Right next to the dive site, the perfectly circular hole in the ice, and surely the most vulnerable place across the entire lake.

'Zoe!' I call out when I get within five metres of her; I don't want to go any further. 'What the hell are you doing out here?!'

'Hello, Ivy,' she says, looking up, unsurprised, as though she's been waiting for me. 'Come closer. It's safe, I promise.' Her voice is calm now. I should be relieved after our argument at the chalet, but it sounds ominous in this setting. 'I found this place so peaceful the other day,' she continues. 'I wanted to come back, find my composure again.'

'But it was sunny on Monday,' I remind her. 'It's blizzarding now. You're soaking wet; you must be freezing. Nina is waiting for us, up there, at the edge of the car park. Please, Zoe.' I reach out my hand towards her, but I still don't move my feet. I can just make out the water lapping against the edge of the ice hole in my peripheral vision.

'Come here, Ivy.' She beckons me over. 'I want to ask you something.'

I remain rigid for a few seconds, but finally succumb to her pleading eyes and shuffle towards her. I stare down at the black water and feel my knees tremor with a new weakness. 'What did you want to ask?' I whisper, not taking my eyes off the water, as though it could suck me under if I don't stay alert to its threat.

'What was it like?' she whispers.

'What was what like?' I ask back, confused.

'Finding out you were pregnant.'

I swallow hard. Of all the questions I thought she might ask, this didn't feature. And I'm not ready for it. Can I admit that, even though it was scary, it was also the best day of my life? A suppressed dream come true? Would that tally with my pregnancy being the surprise result of a drunken one-night stand at a conference in Helsinki? 'Why do you want to know?' I say instead, playing for time.

'Because I can't imagine it,' she murmurs. Then she lets out a long sigh. 'Except that's wrong because I do imagine it, every month, from the day I ovulate until my period turns up, usually late. A few days maybe, a week sometimes.'

'But I thought . . .'

'And I sometimes wonder if the reason I'm not given one, a baby that is, is because I'm imagining it incorrectly. That my daydreams are too selfish, that I'm lost in my own joy about becoming a mum, and not thinking enough about the baby and their happiness.' She turns her face skyward, as though she's talking to the mountains, or the snow. Or perhaps she thinks Tom's up there. My eyes smart with tears at that thought, and my ribs spasm with the effort of not sobbing.

'I had no idea,' I finally manage. It's a whisper and I'm not sure she can hear me. But she must do because she turns towards me.

'Really?' she asks, searching my face. 'You had no idea at all?'

I feel exposed under her scrutiny and tilt my face away. 'I thought you didn't want children. You have your business . . .' But I tail off, because why should that stop her wanting a family as well?

She stares for a few more seconds then finally looks away. 'It's okay,' she says, her voice robotic. 'I hid it from everyone. Only Tom knew how desperate I was. We had tests,' she adds.

'Tests?' I focus on my breathing. Long, slow breaths. My body is still trembling, and I wonder if I might fall over. My feet are like dead weights, glued to the ice; I need to lock my knees but they're so weak.

'We were fine,' she exhales. 'No explanations, no treatments. Just pointless advice like, take a holiday, see an acupuncturist, change your diet. Or my personal favourite, try to put it out of your mind for a while.' She laughs suddenly, a hard bark that explodes like a firecracker in the snow-blanketed silence. 'And then I found out that you had Calum.'

'I'm so sorry.' I shouldn't be apologising for my son – it's not his fault that Tom and Zoe couldn't conceive – but as I think about Tom knowing of Zoe's struggles, her desperation for a baby, and not telling me, I feel like I could suffocate with the shame of it.

'Thank you,' she says stiffly. 'For apologising.'

'Well, I . . .' I shift from foot to foot, look up towards the car park and wish that Nina's van was in view. The reassurance that this awful awkwardness will be over soon.

'We should probably go back now, shouldn't we?' Zoe says, answering my prayers. 'Find a way to get you to Geneva.'

'Really?' I ask, gratitude spilling out. 'You don't mind me leaving?'

'I shouldn't have guilt-tripped you. Being here, amongst all this natural strength and beauty, has made me realise that.'

'Thank you.'

She smiles at me, beams, and it reminds me of the Zoe from university. The one I proudly called my best friend for nearly two years.

'I'll call Nina,' she continues. 'Tell her we're coming up. It will give me a chance to apologise too, twice I suppose, for running out on you all yesterday, and dragging her out here this morning.' She pulls one side of her mouth down. 'I guess I have a lot of grovelling to do.' She pushes her hand into her jacket pocket, then a look of realisation wafts across her face. 'Oh shit, I haven't got my phone. This is Julian's jacket, not mine. My phone must still be on the coffee table back at the chalet.'

'It rang out when I called it earlier,' I say unhelpfully.

'Have you got Nina's number in your phone? Could I use yours to call her?'

I hesitate for a moment. I've archived my chats with Tom (I couldn't quite bring myself to delete them) so she couldn't come across those by accident, especially as she only wants to use the call function. And anyway, what excuse could I give for refusing? 'Yeah, of course,' I say, trying not to sound nervous. As I pass her my phone, our fingers touch, but they're too cold to feel any sensation. Telling her my passcode brings a sting of shame, the memory of me checking Tom's messages before throwing his phone into a French bin to hide our secrets. And the distraction it brings, coupled with the bad visibility, means it takes me a while to notice. But then I do, and fear lurches in my belly.

Because Zoe isn't calling Nina.

She's scrolling through my messages.

Chapter 43

2008

Ivy

There's an abandoned glass of fizz on the windowsill and I take it. Not because I want a drink – even though part of me craves its anaesthetising effects, I also want to be sober, alert – but because I want something to hold. A party prop to grip onto. I take a pretend sip and practise smiling at a girl I don't know as she walks past. She smiles back. No look of shock, no *oh my fucking God has some guy just assaulted you?* My cheek must be red raw – it's still smarting – but the low lighting is clearly hiding the damage. I take a deep breath, then walk further into the crowd of guests.

The hotel calls this private space their ballroom, but luckily it's smaller than the name suggests, and I reach the door in less than a minute. As I slip into the empty corridor, I feel hot tears trying to escape, but I blink them away.

I push on the heavy wooden door of the ladies' cloakroom,

avoid the mirror above the washbasins, and slip into a cubicle. I sit, fully clothed, on the toilet seat and lean my head back against the fake wall hiding the cistern. Why the hell did I go outside with Harry? I knew he was drunk. I saw how stressed he was the other day. And he's never hidden how he feels about me. Why did I take such a risk? I close my eyes but all I see is Harry's furious expression, the brain-shuddering pain of his open palm, so I flick them open.

Some people would tell me to go to the police. Say that Harry has committed a serious crime and needs to be punished, taught a lesson, rehabilitated. But there's no way I'm doing that, not now, on Zoe's special night. I just need to cut him out of my life. Move on.

I want to go home really, get into my pyjamas and pull a duvet over my head. But I can't leave yet. It wouldn't be fair on Zoe. Tom chased after Harry and could be gone for ages, and Peter is leaving the party early for the first leg of his journey to Antarctica. I need to stay.

With a deep breath, I stand up, brush down my dress, and unlock the cubicle door. There are two girls at the washbasins reapplying their lipstick – friends from Zoe's course who I vaguely know – and when they see me in the mirror, they pause, their eyes widening. Instinctively I shift my gaze to the mirror too. Shit. In this brighter room, the mark of Harry's hand is more obvious. A glaring red patch across my left cheek. But I can solve this; I have my make-up bag with me. Zoe and I came to the hotel early to set up, so I finished getting ready in these toilets.

The actual cloakroom with people's jackets and bags is a small area next to the door. It was manned when guests were arriving, but it's empty now, and I scoot over the counter to retrieve my make-up bag. My jacket is hanging up too, and even though the air is still warm, I pull it on. The subtle weight of the material feels good on my shoulders, as though it will give me a layer of protection. Ten minutes later, my cheek is layered with foundation, my mask in place, and I'm as ready as I can be. I head into the corridor, and almost walk straight into Peter.

'Ivy! Bloody hell, you nearly gave me a heart attack.'

'Sorry, I was in the . . .' I narrow my eyes, drop my head to one side. 'Are you okay, Peter?'

'What?' he asks, scrunching his nose scornfully. 'Of course I'm okay! It's my beautiful daughter's birthday party. Why on earth would I not be okay?'

I nod my head as though he's making perfect sense, but I also peer into his eyes, which aren't quite focusing. 'Are you still planning on driving to Heathrow tonight?' I ask.

'Yes. Hotel's booked; flight's on time so far. I'll be in Chile by tomorrow night. God, I love my life.'

I look at the glass of fizz in his hand. It's almost full, but I'm not convinced it's his first, or his second, or even his third. 'That's great, Peter, your trip sounds amazing. Listen, I couldn't ask a favour, could I?'

'Anything for you, Ivy – you know that.' I worry that he's going to wink, but luckily, he just grins instead. 'What do you need?'

'I couldn't have that glass of fizz, could I?' I say, pointing at the drink in his hand. As with my last glass, the one I must have left in the cloakroom, I don't want to drink it. But this time I have a different motivation for making it mine.

He crinkles his forehead in confusion. 'You want this?' he says, holding the glass out. I take the opportunity, and gently manoeuvre it from his grasp. 'Thank you, Peter, I appreciate it. I'm absolutely parched.' I put the glass to my lips, take a fake sip, then smile with equally fake gratitude. I know Peter, and if I'd suggested that he should stop drinking because he was driving, he'd have accused me of nagging, or being boring, and downed it in one go. This way I have a small chance of convincing him that he's being gallant.

There's silence between us as he eyes the glass in my hand with hardening intent, and I gradually realise that my idea isn't going to work. That any moment now, he's going to point me in the direction of the bar – which, I have to admit, is less than twenty metres away – and demand his drink back. I start to edge away, in case I can escape before he gets chance to reclaim it, but my movement catapults him into action.

'There's a bar behind that door!' he exclaims. 'Get your own bloody drink, Miss Hawkes.' He lays both hands on the glass – one around the flute, the other at the stem – and drags it towards him. There are a few other people in the corridor now and I have no choice but to let go. 'Honestly, I know students are lazy,' he continues, shaking his head. 'But this proves you have a particular talent.' He takes a large gulp, then looks back at me with raised eyebrows. 'Anyway, I need to head off soon, so I should probably find Zoe. Have you seen her?' I shake my head, not trusting myself to speak. 'Maybe she's on the dance floor,' he goes on, cocking his head to one side, listening to the music filtering out from the ballroom. 'She loves the Pussycat Dolls, just like her father!' He winks then, but at least it's a final gesture because he twists away from me and disappears into the main room.

As I stare at the now-closed door, I think about the glass I didn't manage to confiscate. I imagine him necking the fizz so that he can dance with both hands free. Then getting into his car and thinking he's perfectly capable of driving the three-hour journey to Heathrow. Too arrogant, too enthralled by risk, to recognise his stupidity. Well, fuck him. He's a grown man, the master of his own destiny.

Let him crash his precious MG for all I care.

Chapter 44

Ivy

'Are you going to call Nina?' I ask hopefully, itching to grab my phone back from Zoe, but not wanting to escalate the situation. She's typing now, not scrolling anymore, and I pray that she's just decided to message Nina instead.

'No,' she says. Her voice is still quiet, but there's a new purpose to it now. The atmosphere has changed too, thickened, like the snowfall, but I'm not entirely sure why. Maybe it's my imagination. The isolation of this place, the threatening weather, the freezing temperatures. Maybe it's playing tricks on me.

'Well, what are you doing then?' I ask meekly, as though it's not my privacy she's riding roughshod over.

'I'm sending a message to Linda.'

Her words drop on me like snowflakes, freezing for a moment on my exposed skin, then melting into me as I process what they mean. 'My mum?' I whisper. 'Why are you messaging her?' I could reach for my phone now, I think, swipe it off her, check what she's written. But I don't move. It's like I'm waiting for her to give me a rational explanation, to reassure me that I don't need to panic.

'She's scared, thinks someone's following her and Calum.'

'I know! That's why I'm trying to get home.'

'Well, I have a solution for her.'

'What solution? And why are you telling her, not me? Please, let me have my phone back.' I reach out, but I'm still tentative, too polite, and Zoe shrugs me away.

She pauses her wriggling fingers, taps at the screen for a final time, and looks up. But instead of giving me the handset back, she grips it more tightly, her knuckles growing even whiter with the effort. 'Because I'm not sure you'd approve,' she says.

'What?' I say breathlessly, I'm already shivering, but her remark makes the sensation more acute. 'What do you mean? Give me my phone!' I demand, more assertive now. I reach out again, but she whirls her arm away and I hesitate, my own arm extended. I want it back, but I'm even more desperate for an explanation. 'Please tell me what you've done,' I beg.

'Why, don't you trust me?' She smiles, a slight curling of her lips that might look pretty in different circumstances, then hardens her expression. 'I've told Linda to expect Luke,' she says. 'That he's in the neighbourhood and is going to help her out, take Calum off her hands because you can't get back to London today. That he's one of your best friends who Calum adores, so she mustn't worry.'

Luke? Zoe's brother? I shake the image of a shy teenage boy out of my head. 'Luke's in South America,' I whisper, my brain refusing to process what's happening. That Zoe's pretending to be me, lying to my mum, convincing her to hand my son over to a stranger. And that Zoe's brother is going to walk out of my house with Calum, and my anxious, paranoid mother will feel nothing but relief.

'That was a lie,' she explains, her voice oddly calm. 'He's been back for a while. I just didn't want anything getting in the way of you coming to Morzine.'

That she's been lying to me from the start to get what she

wants isn't that surprising – she's Peter's flesh and blood after all – but it doesn't explain what she wants with my son. 'But why do you want Luke to have Calum?' I warble. The thought of my son being wheeled out in his buggy, oblivious to the sheer wrongness of it, is driving cracks into my voice.

She doesn't answer me at first. She checks her watch, then stares through me, as though weighing up how to respond. But suddenly her eyes snap into focus. 'Maybe it's because you don't always know best, Ivy. Remember how my dad died? How you decided not to bother saving him?'

That terrible night again. Memories start to swirl, but I shake them away. I will not feel guilty about Peter's death. He brought it on himself. But the memory of Zoe's face that night, contorted in anger, creeps forward in my mind. 'Have you told Luke to take my son to punish me? Is that it? Because you still think I'm to blame for Peter's accident?'

'Perhaps I'm doing you a favour, Ivy. Have you thought of that? Luke would do a much better job of defending Calum, protecting him from this mystery assailant you keep talking about, than your mum would. She'd be useless, wouldn't she? Crumble at the first sign of trouble. You know that. And yet you still left him in her care. You think you're this amazing mother, but I'm not sure you are.'

'I left him for you,' I remind her through clenched teeth. 'Because you begged me to.'

'I did, didn't I?' she says, her voice suddenly smug. 'You know, you have no idea what true sacrifice is. Not like me. I'd do anything for my child. If I had one,' she adds.

'And you think Calum is better off with Luke than my mum? He's a total stranger!'

'Luke is my brother. He does what I say. Of course I think Calum is better off with him.'

And with those words, the realisation crashes onto me like an avalanche. My son's safety isn't in Luke's hands, it's in Zoe's. That shouldn't be scary – our friendship goes back fifteen years – but somehow it's terrifying. 'Calum's my son, not yours,' I say. 'You've got no right.'

'Really, Ivy? No right at all?' Her eyes drill into me and she takes a step forward. My breathing gets shallower. Did Harry get to her last night after all? Was it him leaning over her balcony, telling her what he thinks he knows? I instinctively move backwards, away from her, but I slip in the snow. My left foot slides from under me, closer to the hole in the ice. I draw it back underneath me, but the slip makes my heart race. My feet are wet and I'm freezing cold. Zoe has my son, and the most likely explanation is too horrific to bear thinking about.

I picture Nina, sat in the warm van, oblivious to what's happening. Only half a kilometre away, but unreachable in this terrain with this weather. And then I imagine my mum, reading my WhatsApp message, how happy she'll feel when she thinks her ordeal will soon be over, that there's someone else – someone stronger and fitter, less scared of life – to take over the reins. And then Luke ringing the doorbell. I remember how sweet-faced he was as a teenager. Does he still look like that? Will he be easy for my mum to put her faith in?

Tears roll down my cheeks. I feel helpless.

But there is a way. I just need to get my phone back. Then I can call Mum before Luke gets there. And call Nina, ask for her help. I start to reach out, but the sound of two dings, almost in unison, one loud in the silence, the other more muffled, makes my heart jump. And when I stretch forwards again, Zoe has turned her back on me. I put my hand on her shoulder to twist her round. She holds steady, but I pull harder, and finally she succumbs. But she's holding two phones now. More lies. Mine is in her outstretched hand, like she's reading a message, her own phone is against her ear, a tinny voice fizzing out of it.

'That was a voice note from Luke,' she says, her eyes shining with a new power. 'He's got Calum. Linda was very grateful apparently.'

A low moan crawls up from my belly. I fight the urge to double over with the pain of it. Instead, I lunge more forcefully, grab at my phone, but Zoe's quicker. She lifts it high in the air. Then lets it go.

And I listen to the loud plop as it drops into the dive hole.

Chapter 45

2008

Ivy

Someone is screaming. It's Zoe. I recognise her voice, but I can't see her. The music cuts out and the lights go up. There she is, sinking into a chair, people gathering around her. I push my way through the deepening crowd until I reach her side. There's someone in uniform too, a police officer.

The room starts to spin. My vision blurs. Memories from my childhood swirl.

Hello, there. Is your mummy in?

Can I do this? After everything I've been through tonight? Do I have the strength?

Because without anyone saying a word, I know exactly what's happened.

Peter left an hour ago. I watched him drive away, the roof of his soft top concertinaed at the back, pop music blaring through the small speakers. I didn't care at the time whether he'd make it to his destination. But as I look at Zoe now, her broken expression, it's different. All those wandering thoughts, those vague predictions, have come true.

I gently drop my hand onto Zoe's shoulder. 'What's happened? Are you okay?'

'Ivy?' She grips my hand with both of hers, twists her body until she's facing me, turning away from the police officer. 'She's saying stuff, about Dad, but it can't be true, can it?'

'I don't know,' I whisper, even though I think I do.

'I understand how hard this must be for you to take in,' the police officer is saying, her accent local and strong. I catch the name badge on her shoulder – Constable Willis. 'If it brings any comfort, the paramedics are confident that your father died instantly. He won't have suffered.'

Peter is dead. The news I was half expecting threatens to overwhelm me. My mentor. The man who inspired me to become a meteorologist.

Zoe's father.

'How did Mr Wilde die?' I ask.

The police officer looks at Zoe and seems to take her silence as consent to share the details. 'We were called to the scene of a road traffic accident on the Honiton Road out towards the M5,' she says quietly. 'There was only one vehicle involved, a racing-green MG Roadster. It skidded out after a tight bend and collided with a tree. The impact caused the car to roll into the adjacent ditch, and the driver was thrown from the vehicle as it flipped. There was a witness – a cab driver who was a few hundred metres behind – and he called the emergency services. We were on the scene in three minutes, but Miss Wilde's father had suffered catastrophic head injuries and there were no signs of life when we arrived.'

I don't want to think about how Peter died, or the impact his death will have on Zoe. I know too much about how it feels to lose a father. So I focus on the practical side instead, try to draw some strength from the facts. 'Peter only left an hour ago. How did you find Zoe so quickly?'

Constable Willis sighs. 'It turns out that the cab driver's passenger was Ivan Hall, one of the party guests. He recognised Mr Wilde from a speech he gave earlier this evening.' She turns back to Zoe. 'Your father has been taken to the Royal Exeter and Devon Hospital, Miss Wilde. Would you like me to take you there now?'

Zoe's expression turns from disbelief to horror. 'No!' She shakes her head. 'I mean, yes, but I need to find Tom first.' She looks around the crowd of onlookers. 'Can someone get hold of him?' A dozen phones get pulled out of pockets and bags. I imagine the ding-ding-ding of messages that Tom is about to receive. I wonder if it will be a welcome reprieve from Harry's anger or too much to cope with in one night.

'How about I give you a moment?' Constable Willis suggests. 'I can wait outside until you're ready. And take as long as you need.' She smiles at Zoe, nods at me, and turns to go.

'Thank you,' I whisper to her retreating frame.

'My dad is dead,' Zoe murmurs.

'I'm so sorry.'

'On my birthday.'

'Oh, Zoe . . .'

'He was here. Standing next to me, telling everyone how amazing I was.'

Adrenalin is coursing through me; it feels like electric sparks on my skin. But I need to hold it together, for Zoe's sake. 'He was very proud of you,' I manage.

'But it doesn't make sense! How can he be here, larger than life, the soul of the party, and then not here at all?'

I think about the knock on our door when I was 9 years old. How I thought it was my dad coming home. Returning from a day's climbing to catch the end of the football match, just like he'd done so many times before. And then, in a flash, how the world I knew vanished. 'It's risky, I suppose, driving with the roof down, and no seatbelt on.'

'He always has the roof down! And he hates wearing a seatbelt,' she moans. 'I know that's dangerous, but these roads are so familiar to him. He's lived in Exeter for ten years. How could he have missed a bend?'

I bite the inside of my cheek until I taste blood. But it's not enough distraction to stop the images coming. Peter's unfocused eyes, the glass in his hand, the tell-tale signs that he'd drunk too much. Me taking his glass away, him grabbing it back. But I can't have been the last person to see him. 'He was looking for you when I saw him. Did he find you?' I ask.

She looks at me for a moment, then her face creases. 'I didn't say goodbye, Ivy!' she cries out. 'I was on the dance floor, he came over, but my phone rang. It was Tom. I didn't understand why he was calling me, why he wasn't here at the party, so I turned my back, took the call. And when he rang off, Dad was gone. I missed my last chance to speak to him, didn't I?'

My eyes are hot with tears, but I have no right to cry. 'You could never have known. You have nothing to feel guilty about.'

'He didn't want to come to my party, you know. He didn't want to drive to Heathrow that late at night.'

Something crawls over the back of my neck. I scratch it away.

'But he came, for me, and now he's dead.'

'This isn't your fault, Zoe.'

'Oh? Even though he was only here because of me? Driving late because I guilt-tripped him into coming? This is my fault, Ivy. I killed him.'

'That's crazy. It was an accident.'

'Caused by my neediness.'

'Caused by his drinking!' My words ring out and I feel the impact of them around the room. I shouldn't have said anything. I know it will come out at some point, at the post-mortem, or the inquest. But it's too much for Zoe to deal with tonight. 'I'm sorry, ignore me.'

'He only had one glass – he promised me he wouldn't have any more,' she says, but her tone is imploring, not defiant.

'Maybe,' I whisper. I wish I could take my comment back, but I learned young that mistakes can't be erased. All we can do is make the best of the consequences.

'But you wouldn't say it unless you knew,' she pushes. 'Did you see him drunk?'

'I bumped into him,' I say with a sigh. 'In the hallway. I tried to take his drink off him.'

'You tried?'

'He wouldn't let me – you know what he's like,' I plead.

'What he *was* like!' she shouts. 'Before he died because you didn't stop him drink-driving!'

'Zoe, you can't blame me.'

'You knew he was drunk. And you still let him get in his car, his convertible sports car, to make a three-hour journey in the dark. That's practically murder!'

'Don't say that.'

'He would be alive now if it wasn't for you,' she hisses.

'Zoe, that's not true . . .'

'Yes it is! You killed him! Get the fuck away from me, you're a murderer!' She's screaming now and I don't know what to do. I should leave, but I can't move. I should defend myself, but I can't speak. A circle of accusing faces stare at me. I wonder if I'm going to faint.

'Zoe?' A voice in the distance.

'Tom! Oh, thank God!'

I watch Zoe run into his outstretched arms, bury her head deep in his shoulder. Then I slip away, into the garden, and out through the same gate Harry escaped from a few hours earlier.

Chapter 46

Ivy

My heart booms in my chest, but I force myself to sound calm. I need to convince Zoe to change her mind, to tell Luke to take Calum back to my mum. 'Why did you drop my phone into the water?' I ask.

'Because you don't need it. I've sorted everything.'

Boom, boom. 'Let's head back then,' I try instead. 'To Nina's van. If I make my flight, Luke won't have to look after Calum for too long.' I know it's a fantasy, that there's a darker reason behind Zoe interfering in Calum's care, but I need to keep pretending. Otherwise I might disintegrate into a thousand pieces. A million regrets.

'I think we're fine, just the two of us, having a chat.'

My fake composure explodes. 'Fine? We're soaked through!' I shout. 'Stood in the middle of a frozen lake with snow hammering down. And my son has been taken by a complete stranger. I'm nowhere near fine!'

'Maybe I mean relative to how you're going to feel soon.'

Zoe's cold, quiet tone douses my anger in an instant. Fear

crawls up my neck. I came here to save Zoe, but do I need saving from her? And if I'm in danger, then what about Calum? I think about his downy head, his big eyes, always flicking left and right, absorbing everything around him. Where has Luke taken him? Would he hurt him? Does he even know how to care for a baby? 'What do you mean?' I stutter.

'Why do you think I lured you out here?'

My mind freezes, then clears. I can't hide from it anymore.

Zoe knows.

And she wants to destroy me for it.

I look at the hole in the ice, the black water lapping at the edges. I feel the remoteness engulfing me. I need to get away from her. To run. Get back to the van, use Nina's phone to call my mum. It's a plan, but I need to move. I twist to go, but my feet slip in the snow, I can't get any traction with my stupid trainers. Then it's too late. Her hands are on me, her gym-built arms pulling me down. A mix of her strength and my rubbish footwear give her the edge, and then I'm on the ground, and she's on top of me, pinning me against the freezing cold snow, her legs trapping my arms.

'You know, I could just about deal with you fucking my husband.'

'I didn't. I wasn't. I promise,' I stutter. But I know how it looks.

'But having his baby?' Zoe goes on, her voice seething with anger. 'Do you know how that felt, when the first time I saw you together, you had this huge belly?' She pushes back the hood of my jacket and stares at my face, as though wondering how Tom could ever choose me over her. Not that he did. I start to speak again, to explain, but she covers my mouth with her hand.

'Don't you dare try and talk your way out of this,' she hisses. 'It was New Year's Eve 2021 when I first saw you together,' she goes on. 'Over a year ago now. I'd found out about the two of you ages before, but I'd wanted to pretend it wasn't true. If I confronted Tom about being unfaithful, I'd have to throw him out, wouldn't I? And how could I get pregnant then? But when Tom told me there was an emergency at the hospital, when I was ovulating and we were supposed to be seeing the new year in together, I'd had enough. So I followed him. He didn't sleep with a colleague from work by the way – I made that story up, to piss you off. I mean, why should you get to grieve purely, when my own grief was so compromised? No, there was only you.' She winds a few strands of my hair around her fingers and pulls. The pain is sharp, and I feel a tearing at my scalp, but a second later she releases the pressure.

'But when I sat in my car outside your house,' she goes on, 'I had no idea what was about to hit me. And then you opened the gate, my one-time best friend, and you had this belly. All round and perfect. And God it hurt. Finding out you were carrying my husband's child. When I'd been trying so hard to make one for us.'

Tears are rolling down her face now, and despite everything, I feel a rush of sympathy for her. And disgust at myself. But she's the attacker now, and I need to get away. Her hand slips away from my mouth and I take my opportunity. 'You've got it all wrong, I swear,' I plead. 'I never meant to hurt you.'

'You took my husband from me.'

'Please, Zoe, let me explain.'

'NO!' Her hand drops back on my mouth, pushes down. With her free hand, she pulls something out of her jacket pocket. It's an avalanche transceiver, a heavy slab of hard plastic. 'Have you ever been ice diving?' she asks, but it's rhetorical – she knows I can't answer. 'My guess is probably not. I imagine it's too scary for you.'

I can't see the hole anymore, but the memory of its cold black water is imprinted on my mind. I imagine being submerged. The chill hitting me. The panic as the water drags me away from the opening. Looking at the ice but not being able to break through.

'I did it once,' Zoe continues. 'In Tignes Le Lac, with my dad. God, it was cold. I pretended it was fun, but I hated every minute of it. I doubt you'll have the same experience though; without a dry suit, you'll be unconscious in seconds.' She taps the transceiver against my forehead. Thud, thud, thud. It doesn't hurt, but it's solid, heavy, and my panic rises as I imagine the damage it could do with real force. 'You do know that you need to die, don't you?' she adds, almost apologetically.

A gasp erupts in my chest and flies out, through Zoe's fingers. 'I wriggle underneath her. She's straddling me, I can't get away, but it's enough to dislodge her hand. I squeeze my eyes closed and scream as loudly as I can, from deep inside my chest. It's guttural, but it carries, bounces off the mountains. Surely Nina will hear it? I look towards the car park, pray for Nina to walk over the brow of the hill, look down towards the lake, her eyes growing large with shock as she sees what's happening, then charge across the ice to rescue me.

But no one comes. And then Zoe shoves something in my open mouth. It's soft and woolly, and I gag at the feel of it. 'Shut up!' she hisses. 'No one is coming to save you, okay? No one can even hear you.'

With my mouth stuffed full, I can't breathe properly. My body convulses under her weight.

'I know I'll have some explaining to do,' Zoe continues. 'Tom dying first, then you a few days later. But it's the only way. And I've got it all worked out. I'll say that I was suicidal, that this lake had a profound effect on me – I set the story up when I talked to Dufort on Monday – and I wanted to end my life here. I'll tell them you were trying to stop me from jumping. That I was distraught, and it all happened so quickly. One minute you were there, and the next you were floating under the ice. I tried to save you, but it was too late. When the moment comes, I'll run for help. And I guarantee they'll believe me, because I'm a fucking brilliant actress. I've been honing my skills for all the years I've been trying to get pregnant.'

Tom dying first, then you a few days later. Does that mean she killed Tom? She can't have pushed him; she wasn't even in

France when he died. But it all sounds planned. I think about the mystery person by her balcony last night, then Harry appearing in the chalet a few minutes later. Of course it was him. I think about how he joined the boys' ski trip. Did Tom invite him, or was it Harry's idea? Could Zoe have been pulling the strings even then? I think about the red mark on Harry's hand that he tried to explain away. His drinking on Saturday. It's all so obvious. Why did I hide from it? But did Zoe take advantage of Harry to get what she wanted? Or are they equal partners?

'Not that I'll be childless for much longer,' she adds quietly.

I think about Calum in Luke's clutches, and my fear intensifies even more.

'I've been a good friend to your mum, since Calum was born, haven't I?' she says. 'Getting those broken tiles on her roof fixed after that storm. Organising for a meter to be fitted when her energy bills sky rocketed. Buying her a new mattress when her back was bad. She trusts me, owes me, even.'

Understanding creeps over me. Has Zoe been planning this act of revenge for that long? I scream in frustration, a muffled bray, but then I can't replenish the oxygen and my chest convulses. I wonder if I might suffocate.

'Linda will be torn apart by grief when you die,' Zoe says, her voice so calm, it's like she's been rehearsing this speech for months. Perhaps she has. 'Two tragedies in one tiny family. I would feel bad, except that's exactly what I've suffered, isn't it? What you and Tom have forced me to suffer anyway.' She glares at me, then looks away, towards the water. 'There's no way your mum will be able to parent Calum, especially after the fright she's had over the last few days.'

There's a new note of pride in her voice and I realise with horror that she's set this up too. The man my mum was so scared of. He does exist. Zoe sent him there specifically to frighten her, to make doubly sure that Mum would be happy to give Calum up. Who was it? Mum said she never got a good look at him. Could it even have been Luke, the man who transformed into Mum's saviour when she read the message from my WhatsApp account?

'I'll offer to look after him for her, while she deals with her loss. But we both know she'll never get over it. The overworked authorities will love a neat family connection, so before you know it, I'll be able to adopt him. I may not have been able to give Tom a child, but this way, he'll be giving me his. It's almost as good.'

I shake my head. 'No!' I try to shout. 'Not his!' I just about manage.

'Don't lie to me! I know Calum is Tom's son,' she hisses. 'Okay, I didn't know for sure on that New Year's Eve. But I waited until he was born. Then I pretended I wanted to revive our friendship. You took your time coming back to me – I had to be patient. But eventually you invited me over. I didn't really need any more proof after that – I could see Tom shining out of Calum's face – but I still took his milk bottle so that I could do a DNA test. Even after being so certain, my heart broke when the results arrived a few weeks later. But now I'm grateful. I get to raise Tom's child, something I feared would never be possible.'

I scream with frustration. Wool fibres stick in my throat. I need to explain, but I can't speak.

Zoe pushes away from my neck, then lifts her arm, her fingers still gripping the transceiver. And with a sense of inevitability, I watch it come crashing down on my skull.

There's a flash of searing pain.

Then nothing.

Chapter 47

Ivy

I know that I'm cold. Scared. But nothing else. My head pounds. My eyes won't open. But I don't know where I am.

All I can see are images, memories. My son. Splashing in the bath. His determined expression as he crawls towards a toy. How peaceful he looks when I kiss him goodnight.

There are other memories too.

Like the night Calum was born.

I thought I'd lost him. That my worst fears about my diagnosis of placenta previa were coming true. My first reaction had been acute embarrassment when I felt the warm gush of fluid drip down my thighs. But that turned to horror when I realised it wasn't my waters breaking a month early, but my placenta rupturing. I had stared at the mass of blood as though it was an alien rather than a medical emergency. I don't know whether I would have found the strength, the cognitive function, to launch into action. Or if I would have continued staring, rigid with shock, starving my child of oxygen as the placenta continued to break down.

I didn't get chance to find out because Harry did it for me.

He phoned 999. Gave me towels, water. Kept me calm. Promised me that everything would be fine. Thirty minutes later, Calum was born by emergency Caesarean section in Chelsea and Westminster Hospital.

Harry. The man who had fallen for me, then assaulted me. The man who had let anger control his life for over a decade.

I only let him in on that cold night in January because Tom had asked me to. And by that point, it was hard to say no to Tom. He'd turned up at my house on New Year's Eve on the way to the hospital with a request. Harry wanted to say sorry. He'd apologised to Tom soon after returning to the UK, for punching him, for smashing up their student house when his self-loathing boiled over, and he'd tried to apologise to Rob and Julian too. But what he really wanted was a chance to see me, to explain, so that he could finally lay his most evil demon to rest. Tom promised me that Harry had changed, grown up, had therapy. And over a glass of alcohol-free fizz (Tom was working, and I was pregnant, but it was New Year's Eve) we arranged for Harry to visit a couple of weeks later.

And Harry did apologise. Profusely. He explained that he no longer drank alcohol, that it was a trigger for him losing control. That it had taken a while, but he finally felt at peace with himself.

And then he admitted that he still loved me. Had never really stopped. That he hoped fifteen years was long enough for me to draw a solid line between his violence and the man he had become, and would I give him another chance? Sat next to him on the sofa, both of us with a mug of hot chocolate warming our hands, it had even seemed possible. But then he'd said *baby steps*, and the phrase had made me think of the baby growing inside me. And I knew then that anything happening between us was impossible. So I made my excuses. I told him that life was complicated enough, that I had to focus on my pregnancy, and adapting to life as a single mum. And I meant every word at the time.

But later, when I lay in my own blood, thinking I'd lost Calum, clinging to Harry's competence, his skills as both a student doctor and trainee paramedic coming to the fore, those thoughts became confused. When Harry held my hand, I didn't pull away. And when the paramedic asked me if I'd like him to travel in the ambulance with me, I didn't hesitate before saying yes. For those terrifying minutes on the way to the hospital, he suddenly meant the world to me, and I felt an overwhelming urge to tell him everything. That continued in the hospital too, and when he leaned over to say *good luck* before I was wheeled into surgery, I kissed him.

But then hours later, with Calum safely in my arms, scared of how close I came to revealing everything, I had to let him down all over again.

Because I couldn't be with Harry knowing that Tom was Calum's biological father.

Especially as I'd promised Tom to never tell a soul.

But there was never anything romantic between Tom and me.

In fact, I've never succeeded at romance with anyone. I don't know why, whether it's because I'm married to my work, or scared of relationships after losing my dad, or if it was just never meant to be. But by 34, I hadn't chalked up a single long-term relationship. And my body clock was ticking. For as long as I can remember, I've wanted a child, someone to help keep the world breathing when I no longer can. It was an embarrassing longing when I was a feminist teenager. And two decades later it was becoming an unreachable dream. As I spent evenings alone at home, I began researching, fact-finding, and I discovered a whole world of modern women who were choosing to sole parent. Why not me? After all, I was healthy, solvent, owned a house with two bedrooms. And I was brought up by one parent so I knew it could be done.

When I started my journey into intra-uterine insemination, I'd assumed I would use a sperm bank, and had researched the merits of shipping it from places like Denmark or Canada. But when I began reading donor profiles, comparing big eyes against square jawlines, sensitive and creative types versus resilient or clever men, it all got too much. My child was going to be half them. How could I possibly gauge enough insight from one page on a website?

And then I was invited to the opening of the Peter Wilde laboratory at Exeter University. Seeing Zoe for the first time since her twenty-first birthday party was less difficult than I feared, but seeing Tom again was genuinely a pleasure. He had saved me that night after all, and I'd never had chance to thank him. He'd done much more than that too, showing Harry compassion when many would say he didn't deserve it, and then coming back for Zoe when tragedy struck. Tom was clever and athletic, generous, and funny. He was loyal to his wife and ambitious at work. He was handsome. It didn't take me long to realise Tom would be the perfect sperm donor.

We swapped numbers at the event, we all did, and I called Tom the next day. We met on a bench in Hyde Park during our lunch break – him from his Harley Street practice, me from Imperial University – and I blurted it out. He said he'd think about it, and two days later he phoned me at work and said yes. But he had two conditions. The first one was absolute secrecy, which suited me fine. I'd already decided that I didn't want anyone to know what I was doing. I couldn't bear the questions, the assumptions, the litany of opinions on the challenges that lay ahead. My mum's entrenched fears. And the second condition was that he wanted to use a clinic overseas. As a fledgling consultant with a growing practice on Harley Street, he couldn't be sure that news of his donation might not find its way to his colleagues, or even worse, his wife.

With Tom offering to pay for this extra guarantee of privacy, I agreed, and a few weeks later he booked into a clinic in Geneva. From a medical perspective, I didn't need to go with him, but he asked if I wanted to be involved and I found that I did. Not up close of course. But it was a significant part of my unconventional journey to motherhood, and it felt right for me to share in the experience.

When Tom first told me he'd added on a weekend's skiing in Morzine, I said I couldn't join him. It felt disloyal to Zoe, even though I'd only seen her once in thirteen years. But the more time Tom and I spent together, the more I realised that it was our friendship that had survived. Not mine and Zoe's. The way she spoke to me at her birthday party, how she played her part in forcing me to leave Exeter, I owed her nothing. So I booked a budget hotel room close to his lavish four-star affair and we had a couple of days on the slopes. And I remember skiing *Clementine* together, and even commenting on the sheer drop to the side of the piste.

It was February then, a few months before I got pregnant with Calum on my second attempt. The visibility was perfect, bright blue skies and sunshine, but freezing cold air temperatures. I remember sitting on the chairlifts, shivering in the cold, my teeth chattering.

My clothes wet, dampness seeping into my bones.

Snow falling. Black water beckoning me.

But no, that's not right. I'm remembering it wrong.

I hear a voice, not words, but a breathy gasp of exertion. I feel the sensation of being dragged. I prise my eyelids apart. Slowly realisation creeps in as I regain consciousness. Zoe. The lake. Her pulling me towards the dive hole.

I kick out. 'No!' I scream. But it's muffled; the mass of woollen material is still stuffed in my mouth. But my hands are free now, I realise, Zoe no longer holding me down. I pull it out – a beanie I half recognise – and throw it away. 'Zoe, please! You've got it wrong! Yes, I should have told you, but Tom and I were never lovers.' I continue lashing out with my feet, but my head is so dizzy, I can't pull myself up.

'Bullshit! DNA tests don't lie!' She steels herself against my kicks, winds both her arms tighter around my ankles, continues dragging me. My head is still throbbing. I need to create some drag with my arms, but she's got all the momentum, and all I do is flick clumps of snow into the air.

'You're right that Tom is Calum's biological father,' I call out, desperate to make her understand before it's too late. 'But not in the way you think.'

'What other way is there?' she shouts incredulously. 'You can't talk your way out of this!'

'He donated his sperm! That's all. I wanted a baby and I asked for his help. I had no idea you were even trying! Now I understand why he was so determined to keep it a secret from you. He wanted to help me, but also protect you. He was stupid, yes, but he loved you, Zoe. I promise you that!'

Chapter 48

Ivy

Zoe freezes. I sense her brain whirring as she processes my words. I consider using the opportunity to kick my legs free, but instinctively, I decide this isn't the right time to fight. I want to show Zoe that I'm on her side. For her to let me go voluntarily. I mustn't think about Tom, how he might already have paid the highest price for her jumping to the wrong conclusions.

For our secrecy.

'I'm sorry we didn't tell you,' I whisper. 'If we'd thought for a second that you might find out another way . . .'

'You're lying,' she stutters, gripping my legs tighter. 'Lying! Do you think I'm going to believe your bullshit IVF story?' Her words are decisive, but her eyes expose her. Even in the blurred grey light, I can see the confusion shining out of them. The seeds of realisation that she's got this all wrong.

'You have to believe me,' I plead. 'Tom has only ever loved you.'

'No, no, no.' She shakes her head but drops my legs. They thud onto the frozen ground. I'm cold, my body battered, and I'm not sure I can move. But gingerly, I push up onto my forearms. My head is spinning, my stomach churning, but I manage to slither backwards, away from the hole, away from Zoe.

She runs her hands through her bedraggled hair. 'That's not true,' she says, trying to claw back some control. 'I was sure something happened between you and Tom at my twenty-first birthday party.' She nods, warming to her story. 'He was always so secretive, so guilt-ridden, whenever I asked him what sparked Harry's rampage. It was jealousy, wasn't it? Of you and Tom? And then you meet again thirteen years later and take up where you left off.'

'There was never anything between me and Tom. Ever. And yes, we stayed in touch after your dad's lab opening, but not for the reasons you think.'

'My dad,' she continues, her eyes glistening with anger and tears. 'Another man who put you before me. Ivy Hawkes, Peter Wilde's perfect young protégé. A scientist, doing a proper degree. Unlike his daughter, the pointless arts student.'

'No, Zoe. Peter adored you.' I feel on stronger ground here. My relationship with Peter was transactional at best. 'Yes, he wanted to mould me in his image, but he saved his affection for you, and only you.'

It seems to hit a nerve because Zoe suddenly folds over and slumps to the ground. Against the wind and driving snow, I can't hear her sobs, but I can see her body convulsing. I wonder if I should take my chance, run away, but she's the only person who knows where Calum is. I need to stay, persuade her to give him back to me.

'I blamed you for my dad's death,' Zoe suddenly moans through her tears. 'And now I've accused you of sleeping with my husband when you weren't.'

I don't know what to say. That we shouldn't have kept it from her? That it was unforgivable for Tom to be my sperm donor when Zoe was so desperate to get pregnant? But why should I make her feel better when she's killed her husband, attacked me, and taken my child?

'I just want to get Calum back,' I say, as calmly as I can manage. I know I need more than that – safety, justice for Tom – but right now, my son is the priority. If I can persuade her to instruct Luke to take him home, I can start to work out the other stuff.

'I don't know,' she mumbles, dropping her head into her hand. 'That's not the plan, Ivy. I need to keep him.'

'No, please,' I gasp.

'Zoe? Ivy? What's going on? Are you both okay?'

Relief rushes over me. Nina. The one person who can get us out of this nightmare. 'Nina,' I sigh. 'Zoe's not feeling well. We need to get back to the chalet.' I try to push to standing but my legs are wobbly, and I sink back down.

'Okay,' Nina says, her voice guarded. Her eyes dart between us as she tries to work out what's really going on. 'Do you need a hand getting up?'

'We're fine, Nina,' Zoe says, her voice stronger, as though Nina's presence has fortified her. 'This is between Ivy and me,' she continues. 'You don't need to get involved.'

'Don't listen to her,' I plead, through chattering teeth. 'We're not fine. Nowhere near it. I think she might even have killed Tom.' My mouth fills with saliva, like I'm going to be sick, but I need to ride out the nausea. I swallow hard. 'And she's taken my son,' I continue, slowing it down, breathing through my words. 'At least, her brother has. In London. Please, Nina, you've got to help me.'

Nina looks at us both in shock. It must be hard for her to take it all in. But she reaches out one arm and I take her hand. She's wearing woolly gloves and I feel a rush of comfort as her fingers curl around mine. My vision blurs as tears pool in my eyes, but I can just make out a shadow in the distance.

A dark form, growing larger. Standing behind Nina. Grabbing her shoulders.

I scream as Harry pulls Nina backwards. The hood of his jacket is up, obscuring half his face, but I can still see the seething anger, the way it contorts his features. A rage still familiar after fifteen years.

Did I know from the moment I saw him that Harry had pushed Tom? Deep down in my gut? Or was it only when I found that article online? Did I bury that truth because he showed some compassion on the night Calum was born? Made a declaration of love?

Am I that pathetic?

Nina lets out a loud gasp, tries to twist away, but she loses her balance and drops into the snow. Harry tries to sit on top of her, but Nina is strong and fast, and she whips away from him, rising onto all fours. She crawls away, but he grabs the hood of her jacket, concertinaed at her neck, and pulls it backwards. The zip is up high, and I can see it cutting into her throat, strangling her. She lets out a few choking sounds. Shit, I need to help her.

I push up to standing. My head throbs. I can't feel my feet. I stumble towards them. I'm not much of a threat, but the movement distracts Harry, and he turns towards me. And as his hold on Nina's jacket loosens a notch, she takes her chance. She must have already noticed the transceiver nestled in the snow, discarded by Zoe a few minutes earlier, because she lunges forward and grabs it in one swift movement. When Harry notices, he pulls harder on her jacket, but it's too late. It's in her hand. She swings her arm around and smashes the heavy block into his forehead.

Harry rears back, releases Nina's jacket, lifts his palm towards the cut. For a moment I wonder if I look like him – my face is too cold to tell if it's bleeding – but then my focus is back with Nina. She's breathing heavily, but her eyes are bright with indignation, like she's furious with Harry for thinking he can get the better of her. A stupid sense of feminine pride swells in my chest, until I see Harry shake the pain of his head wound away, and then run at Nina, his six-foot two-inch frame towering over her. She tries to hit him again – the device is still in her hand – but he's ready for her this time. He blocks every attempt, until finally it slips out of her grip. Then he barges into her side, knocking her off balance. She falls again. She kicks out with her legs, but he punches her hard in the face. Once, twice.

She falls still.

I gasp in horror. How could I have possibly believed Harry when he said he'd changed? How could I have let him into my house, listened to his words of comfort, kiss him? I feel sick, violated. I let out a strangled cry and run at him. My head pounds, my arms and legs won't work properly. But I still lash out with my fists. Pound his arms, his back, his chest. 'You fucking bastard!' I scream. 'Tom was the only one who forgave you! How the fuck could you kill him?'

But he's either not listening, or he doesn't care. Because he doesn't say a word. He just folds his arms around my body like a straitjacket. I look at Zoe, her closed, unreadable expression. Then my knees buckle, and I drop to the ground once more.

Chapter 49

The day of the fall

Tom

Tom puts in a turn and his right ski skids out from under him. He wobbles, almost loses his balance, but manages to pull it back just in time. He stops, takes a breath. 'For fuck's sake,' he mutters to himself. What is wrong with him? He's only skiing a bloody blue run, but he can't find his mojo, slipping and sliding all over the place. Unable to cut even a half-decent turn. It doesn't help that he can't see much further than the tips of his skis in this white-out. He was supposed to be following Rob and Julian, but they disappeared into the fog minutes ago.

He hasn't seen Harry pass him, so he supposes that at least he's still behind somewhere. Although if Harry chose a different line down the piste, a few metres to the left or right, he could easily have skied past without Tom even knowing. Perhaps he is here alone after all. He's usually more than happy to rely on himself, but right now he feels a bit uneasy, stuck in the thick cloud, very aware that there's a sheer cliff somewhere close by. He remembers the piste from when he skied it two years before, on his sneaky jolly (that he only half got away with) after doing his good deed for Ivy in that clinic in Geneva.

Not that it feels like a particularly laudable act anymore. When Ivy asked for his help, he and Zoe had been trying to get pregnant for a while. A year or so, maybe two. But it hadn't seemed urgent at the time, at least not to him, so he'd decided it shouldn't stop him helping his old friend. Because he likes helping people. Some might call it just another competition, battling for first place in the altruism category, but he doesn't see it that way. And while he isn't a psychologist, it was obvious to him that Ivy losing her father at 9 years old had impacted her ability to form meaningful relationships. If she wanted a baby, and just needed a bit of sperm to help her along the way, then where was the harm?

Although he wasn't quite that obtuse, because he did decide to keep his involvement in Ivy's baby-making a secret from his wife, and everyone else. Zoe is the impatient type – when she decides she wants something, she has to have it straight away – so of course she was getting frustrated when her period kept appearing. But they'd had the various tests, and there wasn't a medical reason why they couldn't conceive, so he always figured it would happen at some point.

Except it didn't. And two years on, Zoe is inconsolable when another month rolls by and there's no baby. About a year ago, he'd decided that he couldn't bear to see her upset anymore, and suggested they start the process of IVF. He knew it wouldn't be plain sailing, and nothing was guaranteed, but they could afford it, and it would be something positive for them to focus on. But to his surprise, Zoe refused. Apparently, she was still clinging to the idea of a natural pregnancy. And as the year progressed, she seemed to become both more devastated about not getting pregnant, and more entrenched in her refusal to consider other options.

And with it, she pulled away from him emotionally. Not that he's ever properly admitted that. He's let himself believe that it was work getting in the way – him growing his private practice, Zoe's business going from strength to strength – but if he forces himself to reflect, those were excuses, not reasons. He needs to try harder, he realises. Listen more to what Zoe wants.

Except now he's also got to navigate Harry having seen the photo of Calum that Ivy sent. He and Ivy aren't in touch very often anymore, and they were both clear that Tom wouldn't have a role in Calum's life (she doesn't need to know that Calum's birthday, the day Tom officially became a father, is the passcode for his phone). But she understands that he's curious, and so sends him the odd photo when Calum hits a particular milestone. Today's photo – of Calum on his first birthday – happened to be a selfie featuring Ivy too, so clearly Harry jumped to a different conclusion. But with Zoe's deepening torment about staying childless, Tom isn't sure which would be worse – her thinking that Tom's having an affair with her best friend from university, or knowing that her husband has fathered someone else's child.

No. Whether through charm, bribery or threat, Tom needs to make sure Harry keeps his mouth shut.

He takes a deep breath and sets off again, but he's so unbalanced; something's definitely not right. It's his skis, he realises. His bindings are too loose. That's so strange. They were fine when he skied the challenging Swiss Wall this morning, which means someone must have tampered with them at lunchtime. He was first in the restaurant. Did the others loosen them off as some kind of joke? Then he remembers that Harry was the last one in. Bastard. It's not a huge problem because he's got his ski toolkit with him – he always carries it – but faffing about with his skis is the last thing he wants to be doing, stuck out here by himself. The snow is getting heavier too, and the wind is still howling. Even the thought of removing his gloves is depressing.

'Is everything okay?'

Tom gasps, even though the voice is familiar. 'Jesus, you scared me,' he says. 'Creeping up on me like that.'

'Inevitable in a white-out, I guess,' Nina says, shrugging her shoulders. 'I saw you on the lift a few chairs ahead of me, so I was hoping I'd catch you up. Do you need any help?'

Tom lets out a sigh of relief. He doesn't need help exactly, but it's nice to have some company. 'Oh, my so-called mates clearly thought it would be funny to loosen off my bindings at lunchtime, so I need to tighten them up. Anyway, what are you doing here? I thought you were working today.' Nina is wearing a helmet and goggles, so Tom can only see half of her face. But he still senses something strange in her expression. An intensity that he's never noticed before. He wonders if she's nervous about the conditions too, and that thought sends a fresh tingle of fear down his spine.

'Transfers went like clockwork,' Nina explains. 'So I had time for a few runs. I guess it's lucky I did,' she adds, gesturing towards Tom's skis.

'My knight in shining armour,' he offers with an ironic smile, and for some reason, Nina gives him a similar one back.

'Listen,' she says after a few seconds of silence. 'Why don't we go to the edge of the piste to sort your skis out. In this visibility, being right in the middle of the slope can be dangerous. A skier could come out of nowhere and wipe us both out.'

'Yeah, I know piste etiquette,' Tom says, with a touch of impatience. Surely Nina knows how experienced he is? 'But I don't have a clue where the edge of the piste is in this cloud.'

'Follow me then,' Nina pushes on her poles, and Tom does the same. He lost Rob and Julian in seconds; he's not making that mistake again. A few moments later, he can just make out a dark-coloured structure. A wooden fence of some sort. Nina performs a neat parallel stop next to it, and he attempts the same thing. But his skis still aren't reacting as they should, and they slip from under him. He falls onto his knees, one ski beneath him, the other sliding away. He feels exposed, his legs stretched in different directions.

'Oh bollocks,' he swears, feeling his face blush despite the driving snow. He needs to bring his errant leg back towards him, but it's not moving, as though it's stuck against something.

'Here, let me help you,' Nina says, unclipping her skis.

'No, I'm fine,' Tom says testily. God, this is embarrassing, especially as Nina ignores him. She leans down, pushes on the binding of the ski that's underneath him to release it, then pulls the ski away. That's better, he realises. At least now he can stand up on that foot, move it closer to the other one.

'Does that help?' she asks. There's a new hardness in her tone, which Tom doesn't understand. He looks at her in surprise. Then he lets out a loud gasp as Nina throws his ski into the void.

'Why the fuck did you do that?!' he screams. This run is over 10 kilometres long; he's screwed with only one ski. The thought makes him stumble. He's unsteady, tottering on one ski boot, his other ski still caught on something. His goggles have steamed up too with all the exertion. And the snow too, the cloud, he can't see a bloody thing. He reaches out towards Nina. She's a lunatic, for throwing his ski, but right now she's ballast, something to tether himself to.

He feels Nina's weight against him. 'I did it for my best friend,' she finally answers. 'For the same reason I loosened your bindings when you were enjoying your posh lunch. Because I owe her. And so do you.'

And Tom's split second of relief turns to excruciating fear as she pushes him hard.

His ski releases from the wooden barrier at the edge of the cliff.

And his body follows it over.

Chapter 50

Zoe

'Nina!' Zoe gasps. She looks down at the ground where her friend is lying unconscious in the snow, then her eyes flick up towards Harry. 'What have you done to her? You're a fucking madman!' She needs to check on Nina, but she can't get too close, in case Harry attacks her too.

God, what is he doing here? Everything is going wrong. And it had all started so perfectly – even the weather's been on their side – but not anymore.

Was it all for nothing?

Or is Tom's deception, his contempt for her feelings, the baby he failed to give her, enough to justify what she's done?

Not that it matters anymore.

She's come too far, done too much, to turn back now.

Especially now Luke has Calum. She can't lose another baby.

She sinks her hand into the pocket of her ski pants and her shoulders drop a centimetre with relief. Yes, it's still there. Her dream might be damaged, but it's still achievable. And even if things turn really sour, she still has her contingency plan. That's why she sent Luke on a recce to Cuba after all.

She just needs a moment to think, to adjust. Nina is the best friend she's ever had. But she's also strong, fearless. She will be okay.

'You're the mad one!' Harry cries out. 'I saw you, dragging Ivy towards that hole. You and Nina were going to drown her! Thank God I worked it out in time. Erin traced the van via GPS, and thankfully I managed to hitch a lift here, even in this blizzard.'

'What?' Ivy stutters. 'What's going on?' She's still crouching on the ground. Like an injured tiger ready to pounce, Zoe thinks, except she doesn't know who her enemy is. 'You killed Tom,' Ivy says in Harry's direction, but with more confusion than conviction. 'You thought that he and I were having an affair, so you pushed him, out of jealousy, or principles, or because you lost your temper again. And now Zoe's persuaded, or blackmailed, you into helping her kill me.'

'No, Ivy,' he says, shaking his head and opening up his palms. 'I think Nina killed Tom. Yes, I found out about your affair on Saturday, at lunch, a couple of hours before Tom died. And yes, it was a shock. But I didn't kill him for it. It's none of my business, is it?'

'I wasn't sleeping with him,' she whispers, staring intently at Harry as though she needs him to believe her. 'Calum was conceived via IUI. Tom was my sperm donor. I shouldn't have kept it a secret, but I promise that's all it was.'

'Really?' Harry says, and there's so much hope in his voice that it makes Zoe feel faint. He's still in love with Ivy, she realises, like Tom was once in love with her. Tears prick at her eyes as she thinks about what she's lost, what she's thrown away. But she can't dwell on those things, she mustn't let regret blur what she needs to do now. To survive. To finally be a mum.

'But why would Nina kill Tom?' Ivy asks. 'It doesn't make any sense.' She's still crouched down, Zoe notices. Perhaps the head wound has affected her balance. That's good, she thinks; it means Ivy is still weak. If she can overpower Harry, she's sure the rest will fall into place. She knows that convincing the French police of two accidental deaths instead of one will be hard, but she's determined to make it work, and Nina will help her. Her oldest friend hasn't let her down yet. She looks at her, still motionless in the snow, and fights the urge to go to her side.

'I think,' Harry says, looking at Zoe with disgust, 'because Zoe asked her to.' She stares back at him with equal antipathy. He's not so perfect. Tom might not have told her what started Harry's violence at her party, but she saw the results. The destruction.

'But why would she do that for Zoe?' Ivy asks incredulously, still miles behind Harry. And she's supposed to be the clever, big-deal academic. In different circumstances, Zoe might enjoy seeing Ivy so clueless.

'Because they're friends,' Harry claims. 'I overheard them talking together last night on my way back from town, just before I saw you. Zoe was on her balcony and Nina was leaning on the balustrade, encouraging Zoe to sober up, to remember that today was going to be a big day, but that Nina would be by her side, like she's always been.'

'I thought that was you,' Ivy murmurs. 'Talking to Zoe.'

'I didn't think it through at the time – my head was elsewhere.' A look passes between Harry and Ivy, a shared understanding, and Zoe feels another stab of anger. She should do it now, she thinks. Shut him up. Punish him for Nina. But her head is spiralling with unwelcome thoughts, and her limbs feel like lead.

'But when I woke up,' Harry continues, 'I realised what their conversation meant. Zoe and Nina knew each other; they were friends. And why would Zoe pretend otherwise unless she had something to hide? When you kept questioning how Tom could have fallen off that mountain, I was too blinkered by jealousy, or self-pity, to listen properly. But when I forced myself to put that aside, I realised you were right.'

'Not according to Dufort,' Zoe reminds them, a jolt of pride giving her voice a new strength. Not everything has gone wrong. 'He's already closed the case.'

'So I looked at the Tall Mountain website,' Harry goes on, ignoring her. 'Nina told us that there were three chalets in the group, but when I checked properly, the other two have fake addresses, and the photos are copied over from someone else's Airbnb listing, two properties in Aspen. The only one she really manages is the chalet we're staying in, and you can't book for next winter. The whole business is a sham.'

'Are you saying Zoe and Nina set the whole thing up?' Ivy asks, her face contorted in shock. 'But how did they get Tom out here in the first place? Don't the guys organise that amongst themselves?'

'It was Julian's turn to book the trip this year,' Harry explains. 'I asked him this morning why he chose Tall Mountain. And guess who the initial recommendation came from?' Harry looks directly at Zoe. She wants to punch the triumphant expression off his face.

'But even if they are friends, why would Nina do all that for Zoe?' Ivy continues, scavenging for the facts like usual. And that's when Harry's tone, finally, registers defeat.

'I don't know,' he admits. 'Maybe Zoe's paying her, or maybe their friendship runs deep enough. But after everything Zoe's done, and knowing they're friends, it must have been Nina who pushed Tom.' They both turn to stare at Zoe. Ivy looks shocked, confused, while Harry's face has hardened. Zoe hesitates. The pair of them will die out here; she's going to make sure of that. So why not tell Ivy that she was never Zoe's best friend, not even close?

'Yes, our friendship runs that deep,' she starts, testing the sound of the secret she's kept for twenty years. 'Nina and I went to school together, Swindon Comprehensive. My dad was my life back then, my absolute hero, and when Mum threw him out, I felt abandoned. My sister was a bitch, Luke was a tiny kid. But Nina looked after me. Let me scream at her if I needed to, bunked off with me when it all got too much. There was nothing she wouldn't do for me.' She pauses for a moment, thinking back to that time. She remembers how angry she felt, but there was something liberating about feeling that way. As though her ill treatment gave her a freedom to behave as badly as she wanted.

Like it's doing now.

'So I returned the favour,' she continues. 'Listened to Nina's outbursts about her strict upbringing, her psycho father who'd hold back food, sometimes even water, for a night if she got less than an A* in anything. And her piano teacher – Mr Mullins, her dad's choice – who smacked her hand when she got the wrong key. Then one day she had a meltdown – who could blame her – and spray-painted the music block. I knew her dad would have killed her for that, actually physically murder her, so I said it was me.'

'That's what got you expelled,' Ivy whispers.

'My sacrifice saved Nina's life, and she never forgot it. She even got a tattoo for me. Hendrix – he sang "Wild Thing", you see? And I was Zoe Wilde. I told Nina that she didn't owe me anything, that I wanted to help, that that's what true friendship means. But she wouldn't let it go. And so, when I asked her to search for Tom after I discovered he'd gone on a secret trip to Morzine, she didn't give up until she found him.' Zoe takes a breath. 'And you.'

Zoe can still remember the crevice that opened up on her kitchen floor and threatened to swallow her whole that Saturday morning, nearly two years ago. Tom's colleague Sam calling with an urgent referral, on the landline because Tom's mobile was switched off. Zoe had explained that Tom was at a conference in New York, that the reason he was uncontactable was because he'd still be asleep. But then Sam had thrown the hand grenade – *A conference? Tom's diary says he's on annual leave?* – and Zoe had buckled, the phone slipping out of her hand as she mumbled something about passing the message on.

Tom had owned up to his lie the moment she called him. At least, in part. He told her that he had been feeling stressed, overworked, and needed a few days to himself. A chance to rip up the mountains around Morzine and release his pent-up energy. He'd feared she wouldn't approve, hence the fictitious conference. He was truly sorry.

While a secret solo ski break might sound implausible to some, Zoe knew it was the kind of thing Tom would do. So she could take him at his word. But Nina was living in Morzine. She had been for years, and knew every bar and most of the bar staff. It wouldn't hurt to ask her to look for Tom, to double-check he wasn't with someone else. Another woman. Zoe crashed to the floor for a second time when Nina's photo came through on her phone. *Is this Tom? He's been with this woman all evening.* That first humiliation felt almost intolerable, but there was worse to come.

'It wasn't what you think,' Ivy mumbles. 'Tom wanted to use a fertility clinic in Geneva, somewhere far away from his practice. He suggested tagging on a couple of days skiing somewhere close by. As friends.'

Zoe sighs. She's exhausted. 'I don't care anymore, Ivy. Sex and lies, or just lies. I know that the pair of you ruined my life, that Tom fathering Calum ripped my heart out.'

'So you murdered him?'

'All I wanted was a baby. At first I thought it would be easy, then I found out that it was hard. But I stepped up, dug in, like my dad taught me. To fight through the tough times. So I fought, and prayed, while Tom skied and lied. And he got Calum, and I got nothing!'

Zoe lets out a strangled cry for everything she's lost and everything she never had.

Then she pulls the Swiss army knife out of her trouser pocket, flicks it open and charges at Harry. She's never stabbed anyone before.

But she doesn't hesitate before driving it deep into his flesh.

Chapter 51

Ivy

'No, no, no, no,' I chant, like a mantra, as I scramble over towards Harry. I know I should be more afraid of Zoe. She's out of control. But I need to do what I can to help Harry after everything he's done, coming here, trying to rescue me. And at least she doesn't have the knife anymore. That is stuck in Harry's midriff, its deep red handle the worst kind of camouflage as blood seeps out of his wound. Zoe is sitting back on her heels, a strange expression on her face.

I take off my jacket and bunch it around the knife, pushing down to try to slow the flow of blood. I can feel the hard outline of his phone in his pocket and for a split second I wonder if I have time to grab it, to call for help before Zoe has chance to stop me. But with a crushing sense of defeat, I realise that the phone won't work. It's right next to his wound and will already be clogged up with his blood. 'Harry?' I say in as calm a voice as I can manage. 'Can you hear me?' I stare down at him, willing him to speak. Even as adrenalin courses through my body, I shiver in my thin jumper as the biting wind whips around me.

'Yes,' he finally whispers back, his voice weak but clear. 'Keep pressure on. Ten minutes to clot. Keep me warm.'

'I will, I promise,' I say, the words catching in my throat.

'I don't know why you're bothering,' Zoe says quietly from behind me. 'No one's coming to save him. Whether he bleeds out in five minutes or half an hour, it makes no difference.'

'You fucking bitch!' I scream, twisting my body towards her while keeping my hands pushed against Harry's torso. 'What happened to you? When did you become this evil?'

'I'm not evil!' she shouts back. 'I'm hurt, broken, pushed beyond my limits by the people who are supposed to love me.'

'And Harry?' I throw back. 'What terrible injustice did he do to you?'

She blinks, grabs her bottom lip with her teeth, then flicks it back out. 'He shouldn't have come here; he wasn't supposed to be involved. But you saw him punch Nina. He's no saint.'

My hands feel sticky, which means Harry's blood has worked its way through my jacket. He came here for me, and he's going to die here. Just like Tom died for agreeing to be my donor. I'm the problem. My friends are dying because of me.

And now Zoe has my son too. If I can't do anything else, I need to save him.

'Listen, Zoe, whatever you were planning, it's over. You won't get away with killing both Harry and me, especially as Erin knows he was looking for you. If you go through with this you'll end up in a French prison, probably for the rest of your life. And who wins then? But if you call for an ambulance, help Harry survive, a good lawyer will be able to blame it on stress and grief. Get your sentence suspended. And if you call Luke now and tell him to take Calum back to my mum, I promise not to breathe a word about Nina pushing Tom, or your part in it.'

'I will get away with it,' she says, trying to disguise the warble in her voice with a forced cough. 'Dufort has always been suspicious of Harry. Nina's injuries will be enough to convince him that Harry killed Tom, then attacked Nina when she accused him of it. Harry asking Erin for Nina's location fits perfectly with him hunting her down. It makes sense that I had to stab him to save her. And it follows that, in my current state, having to perform such a violent act made me feel even more suicidal, so you drowning in the proceeding chaos still fits.'

'You're living in a fantasy world,' I say, trying to sound brave, while inside I'm reeling. Because there's a chance she's right. As the beautiful grieving widow with a loyal sidekick, she might just get away with triple murder. I push harder on the wound in frustration until I see Harry grimacing. Shit, I'm taking out my fear, my horror, on his injury. 'Sorry,' I whisper.

'She won't,' he says. 'She won't.' His face is pale and clammy and despite the cold, there's a thin layer of sweat shining on his forehead. These are signs of shock, I realise, which means his body is being starved of oxygen. A burst of resolve explodes inside me. I can't let him die. But I can't wait for Zoe to find her conscience. I need to get hold of her phone, which means overpowering her first.

I pick up Harry's left hand, then his right, and place them either side of the knife. They're freezing cold, but mine are warmer now, and I lay them on top of his. Four hands pushing against the wound. My heart thuds against my ribcage. I look into Harry's eyes. They're glazed, unfocused, but they still manage to communicate a message.

You can do this. Don't be scared.

Work with what's in front of you.

'Push down,' I whisper. 'Use every bit of energy you have left.'

He gives me a tiny nod. I take a deep breath.

Then I turn and pounce.

Chapter 52

Ivy

I lunge for Zoe's jacket. I've never hit anyone in my life, but if I can drag her down to the ground, I can rummage through her pockets, get her phone, call for help. But she's too quick. She twists away from me, helicopters her arms to break my grip. Anger flares on her face. I have no choice. I clench my fist and swing it towards her jaw. Pain shoots up my forearm, but I don't care, because I make contact. Zoe's head flings back. I watch on, wide-eyed, as her eyes roll in pain.

But I need to do it again. Keep hitting her until she falls. Like Harry did to Nina.

For Calum's sake.

But slam! Her knuckles connect with my cheekbone. My head snaps away from her. Nausea swells in my belly. She hits me again. My head spins, but I stand my ground this time, manage to grab her arm with both hands. She tries to break free, pummels my ribcage with her free hand. I crease over in pain, but don't loosen my grip. I take a breath, then scream, emptying my lungs, and use the force of the echo to surge forwards. Distracted by the noise, she stumbles backwards. I take the opportunity, diving on top of her as she falls.

She writhes underneath me, desperately trying to push me off. I hold each of her arms down, just about manage to stay in control. But it's taking all my strength, and I need a free hand to frisk her for a phone.

'Get the fuck off me!' she screams. She rears up with her chest, then flings her head forward, slamming it into mine. I feel blood spurt from my forehead, the wound from the transceiver opening up. Oh God, it's too painful. I can't see, I can't think. I've lost all my strength. She's trying to flip me over, I realise, regain her dominance. I need to stop her. I let go of her arms but start punching her body, trying to ignore the explosions of pain as she gives me the same treatment.

My fist slams against something hard. Her phone. If I can get to that, know that I can call for help, I'm sure that will give me the strength to fight her. I rip at her jacket, reach inside her breast pocket. Yes! I manage to pull it out, but the pain, the freezing wet snow, means my fingers aren't working properly. It skitters out of my grasp. For a millisecond we both stare at it perched on a mound of snow, then we lunge forward, scratching and hair pulling, using every possible means to get to it first.

But in our scramble, the phone slides further away. Towards the ice hole. It's my only chance to save Calum. I can't lose this race. I pull up onto my knees, steady myself, reach out to grab it.

But I'm more vulnerable in this upright position. Zoe barges into my back. I tip forward. The phone skids again. Slides. Drops. 'No!' I cry out, my bare hand following it along the snow. She barges again. My hand drops into the freezing water. Burns with intense cold. I suddenly realise the danger I'm in. Fuck, no. Not this.

My knees buckle, but my torso tenses, twists away from her. Her midriff is right at my eyeline and I fling my arms out and grab hold of her waist. My only instinct is to get her off me, to give me a chance to move away from the hole. But as I throw her to the side, I realise what I've done.

She tumbles into the water. Shock shining on her face like a caricature.

For a split second I think it's over, but then I realise she's holding on to my jacket, and the momentum is too strong. I lurch forward, fall in on top of her. Splash! Then I'm sinking under the water. Fuck, it's cold! Too cold. My head bobs up. I gasp. Start gulping the air. Hyperventilating. I reach for the edge of the ice. But then I'm being pulled back under. By Zoe, or the current, or my limbs turning to lead weight in the freezing temperature.

Water engulfs my face again. My chest heaves, pulsating with the impulse to gasp for air. But somewhere deep in my mind, I know I need to fight the urge, to hold my breath, not let the water enter my lungs. I need to kick my legs, escape the water's clutches, stop myself from sinking into the abyss. Find a way to get back to Calum.

But the ice-cold temperatures are freezing my brain.

I can't feel Zoe at my side anymore. Has she escaped? Climbed out? Will she take pity on me? Pull me out too?

Or has she been swept away, caught under the ice?

I don't know. I'm not aware of anything but the deathly cold driving its way under my skin, into my brain.

And my son. If I stop to look, there are images of him everywhere. Swimming around me. His gorgeous face, his beautiful smile. The way his lips purse when he's cross, and spread when he wants to be kissed. I'm warmer now, thank God. I can stop kicking.

I can rest.

Chapter 53

Ivy

A light shining. A voice. A language I recognise but don't understand.

Rapide! Aidez-moi à la sortir!

A sensation. Being dragged through water. A new lightness around me.

Couvrez-la de couvertures. Vérifiez quand l'ambulance arrivera. Je vais faire la RCR.

Hands. Blankets. Warmth. More muffled words. A jet stream of air into my lungs. Life being breathed into me. But something blocking it. Then pressure on my chest. Rhythmical. Bang, bang, bang. The blockage dislodging.

My eyelids fling open. I stare at the dense cloud cover above me. *Nimbostratus.* Snow clouds, my mind registers. Morzine. Lake Chablais. Drowning.

I retch. My body flings itself over. I throw up lake water and bile, shivering uncontrollably. My head screams in agony. My body feels like a thousand kilos of lead weight. But still, something dances inside me.

I'm alive.

'Madame Hawkes, it is me, Lieutenant Dufort. The ambulance is two minutes away. *Dieu merci, to va bien.*'

I look at the police officer, the creases in his forehead, and try to smile my gratitude for him saving my life. I don't know how he found me, but I don't care right now. Something has gone right at last. Then I broaden my outlook. There are so many of them. Men and women in tight navy uniforms, moving frenetically on the snow like ants around split sugar.

My awareness clicks up a gear. Of course they would be here in numbers. Harry has been stabbed. Nina is unconscious. And Zoe?

My eyes dart back to the ice hole. The water is calm again, but still black, ominous. Realisation lurches inside me. 'Zoe,' I whisper, my voice raspy. 'Zoe fell in too.'

Dufort's eyes flit away from me. 'I know, your chalet host, Erin, told us who was up here when she first called, on Monsieur Cooke's instructions I understand. And then he, Harry, explained what happened when we got here. I'm afraid we haven't been able to locate Madame Metcalfe,' he says hesitantly, seemingly unsure about how I'll take the news. Perhaps Harry has also told him that our falling in wasn't an accident. 'She must have floated under the ice,' he continues. 'We've called for a dive team, but sadly it will only be a search and recovery operation now. You'd only been in the water for a minute or so when we arrived, but the body's cold-shock response is profound. I imagine Madame Metcalfe suffered a heart attack and that's why she drowned so quickly.'

Zoe's dead. And I feel nothing. Neither pleased to be rid of the woman who almost killed me, or upset that my once best friend has lost her life. Then my mind processes how Dufort found out about Zoe. 'And Harry?' I ask, twisting my neck, but I can't see him. 'He spoke to you?' Not only still alive, but able to talk. That must be a good sign.

'He's lost a lot of blood but he's being well cared for by my officers. He's alert and relatively stable. Only showing limited signs of shock. Between you both, you did a good job of stemming the bleeding.' He looks over towards the car park and I follow his glance. Three red ambulances are lined up in the snow. 'The paramedics have arrived now,' he says. 'They will take both of you to the main hospital in Thonon and Monsieur Cooke will go straight to surgery. The surgical team there are expecting him. And Madame Sampson will be taken to the medical centre in Morzine,' he goes on. 'Her injuries are less severe.' Nina. Soon I will need to tell Dufort what she did, but not yet. I'll wait until he asks.

I look over towards the car park and see a crowd of paramedics marching towards us, big bags of equipment slung over their shoulders, three of them also carrying a folded-up stretcher each. The slippery surface of the lake clearly isn't an issue for them in their heavy black boots. Soon I will be cocooned in a warm hospital room, I think, surrounded by medical professionals like them, being monitored for secondary drowning, concussion, kept safe.

I have escaped death.

But this isn't over. Not while Calum is still with Luke. I have no idea whether Zoe's brother is a willing conspirator, or an innocent pawn in Zoe's master plan. But either way, I need to get my son back with my mum again.

'There's something else,' I start, still trying to find my voice, my rising adrenalin at odds with my exhausted body. 'My son.'

'What about him?' Dufort asks, narrowing his eyes in concentration. He's no longer trying to fob me off, the man tasked with limiting the backlash from Tom's tragic fall. Finally, he's fully listening.

'My mum is staying at my house, in London, looking after him while I'm out here. But Zoe's brother has taken him.'

'Your son has been kidnapped?' he says, his voice hardening as he demands clarification.

'Not exactly,' I say, frustration starting to bubble inside me. At Dufort for not immediately understanding, and at myself for allowing Zoe to take my phone in the first place. 'My mum thought Luke was a friend of mine, helping out,' I explain. 'Zoe sent a message from my phone pretending to be me. It was all part of her plan. Kill me, make Calum an orphan, adopt him. Get everything she wanted.'

'Do you know where he has taken him?'

'No idea, no.' My voice cracks.

'Look, I can get in touch with the British police through Interpol. And they can contact the appropriate police force and ask them to investigate. But I'm not sure that's the best way to handle this. I think it would be quicker for your mother to call 999 from within the UK, and then they will act immediately. Are you well enough to call her? You can use my phone.'

Two paramedics arrive by my side as Dufort hands me his phone. '*Bonjour, madame,*' the male one says. It seems too polite, too routine, for such terrible circumstances, but I mumble the greeting back as I start dialling my home phone number. To my shame, I don't know my mum's mobile number off by heart.

'*Madame Hawkes est anglaise,*' Dufort says, his voice clipped, professional. 'So we should speak in English.'

'Okay,' the paramedic says, nodding.

'Her airway was blocked when we first pulled her out,' Dufort explains. 'But I performed CPR and chest compressions and it cleared. Since vomiting, she has been breathing and talking normally. We have wrapped her in blankets, but she is still very cold. There is also a head wound.'

'Madame Hawkes,' the man says, covering me in a bright foil hypothermia blanket. I nod, try a smile. I have Dufort's phone by my ear, listening to it ring, praying that my mum picks up. 'My colleague and I must do some preliminary checks before we can move you,' he goes on. 'And then we will get you hooked up with some oxygen and into the ambulance as quickly as possible.'

'Thank you,' I mumble.

'Hello?' A familiar voice at the other end of the phone. Relief sweeps over me.

'Mum?'

'Ivy? You sound strange. Is everything okay?'

I take a deep breath. It hurts my lungs, but I still hold it in for a few seconds, gather myself. 'It's a long story, Mum, but I'm fine. I just need you to do something for me.'

'Oh?'

'Don't freak out, but I need you to phone the police.'

'The police?' she repeats, her voice already wavering. I wish I didn't have to involve her, risk shattering her fragile shell. But I have no choice.

'Mum, I know you thought I wanted Luke to take Calum, but Zoe stole my phone, sent the message.' My chest hurts with the effort of talking. I pause, close my eyes, take another breath. 'I can't explain properly now, but Zoe got Tom killed. She wanted Calum for herself. She's dead now, but I don't know where Luke's taken him.'

A gasp down the phone, then silence.

'I need you to get him back, Mum.' She still doesn't speak. I swear at myself. I've pushed her too far; of course she can't handle this. I should have told Dufort to go via Interpol.

'I've put Calum in danger?' she finally asks, her voice hoarse with worry.

'You could never have known.'

The line goes quiet again but it's a different kind of silence this time.

My mum has cut me off.

Chapter 54

Linda

Linda wills her fingers to unfurl. The handset of Ivy's rotary-style telephone is back in its cradle now – she dropped it down when she couldn't cope with listening to her daughter anymore – so there's no point in continuing to grip it. But she knows that as soon as she lets go, she will need to act. To take steps to save her grandson. And she's not sure she can.

Except she must. It's her fault that Calum is in danger, not Ivy's; her unwillingness to take responsibility for his welfare that led to this. God, she was so grateful when she read the message she thought was from Ivy. *Big storm. Still can't get back. But have arranged for Luke – Zoe's little brother – to take Calum, give you a break. Calum knows (adores!) him. He'll be with you asap. Let me know when he's collected.*

When the door buzzer had gone, she'd been in two minds about answering it – what if it was the same phantom door knocker from the night before? – but her desire for help had overridden her worries and she'd warily stepped into the courtyard and opened the front gate.

She'd recognised Luke from a photo Zoe had texted to her once, a family barbecue, and she'd found that familiarity reassuring when he prised Calum out of her arms and strapped him into the buggy. Calum had looked a bit doubtful about the exchange, but he hadn't cried, and Linda had taken that as a good sign. She'd sent Ivy a quick message without a hint of suspicion.

But it turns out she was wrong. When Ivy called Zoe a killer, a kidnapper, Linda's first instinct was to push back, tell her that it couldn't be true, that Zoe was a lovely girl who would never do anything so violent or cruel. But Linda knows that Ivy is never wrong. Her daughter only ever deals in facts, so if Ivy says something without a caveat, then it must be right.

And now Zoe is dead. How did she die? Please God, don't let it be at Ivy's hands.

But of course it wasn't. Ivy isn't capable of killing. Linda would know if she was.

She releases the handset and drops her forehead into her clammy palms. Ivy wants her to contact the police. She imagines them turning up at the house, like they did twenty-seven years ago with bad news about another Calum. Is history repeating itself? Will the news about her grandson turn out to be as catastrophic as it was about her husband? And her to blame for them both? She pictures two police officers sitting on Ivy's sofa, dubious expressions on their faces as she explains that yes, she willingly gave her grandson away to little more than a stranger. And yes, she needs them to bring him home for her.

She can't do it.

But she can't just sit here and pretend it's not happening either.

She needs to admit it to herself. The truth that has been scratching at her brain since Ivy called.

She knows exactly where Luke has taken Calum. And he has no idea that she knows.

She hadn't been spying on Luke when she went outside moments after he left. She'd wanted to check that he'd closed the gate properly, that there was no way an intruder could get in. But she'd overheard him talking on the pavement, presumably to Zoe on his mobile phone, confirming that he would take Calum to Zoe's latest renovation project in Southfields, only a couple of miles away, as per her suggestion.

And Linda remembers Zoe telling her about that property on one of their phone calls, how she'd converted the loft room of the end-of-terrace house into a nursery and then blown her budget by decking it out with toys from Hamleys. And she even remembers the street because it includes the first part of her name – Linden Gardens. There can only be two end-of-terrace houses on the street, and it must be easy to identify which one of those has been renovated recently.

So all she needs to do is go there and demand Calum back.

That's all she needs to do.

Linda stares at the newly painted front door and wonders if her knees are going to give way. She got the bus here. Ivy would have wanted her to hail a cab and tell the driver to step on it. But Linda appreciated the slow but steady trundling, the regular chimes and wheezing as the driver made his stops. It gave her time to build some resolve. To remind herself that she hasn't always been a coward. That she has climbed both the Matterhorn and Mont Blanc, and how many women born in 1961 can say that?

But still, this feels like a bigger challenge.

She steps forwards, lifts the pewter door knocker, then slams it against the door. One, twice, three times. And – incredibly – each time it drops something stirs inside her. *Bang*. Calum is her grandchild, Ivy's son, the namesake of a remarkable man. *Bang*. Zoe had no right to take him, pretend he belongs to her. *Bang*. How dare Luke treat Calum like a possession, to be swapped around like an eBay purchase?

The door opens and Linda's breath catches. She feels sweat leak from her armpits, her neck become clammy. But she's not running away this time. She can't use her husband's tragedy as an excuse to hide away any longer. 'I've come for Calum.'

'Oh hi, Linda,' Luke says, rubbing his shorn head to hide his discomfort. He manages a watery smile, but his eyes dart behind her. He's checking to see if she's alone, Linda realises, so he's not an innocent pawn in this. 'How did you know I was here?' he continues. He tries to sound pleasant, casual, but Linda can tell it's forced.

'It doesn't matter. Can you bring him out?' Deep down, she knows it's not going to be that easy, but she doesn't know what else to do. He's stood in the doorway, blocking her entry, and she's not strong enough to push him aside.

'He's asleep, settled. I'll drop him back later, like we agreed,' Luke says. 'And I better get back to him now, so . . .' His voice tapers off. He edges the door. Linda takes a deep breath.

'If you don't let me in,' she warns. 'I will scream at the top of my voice that you're a convicted paedophile who's kidnapped my grandson.'

'What?' Luke's eyes widen in shock. Zoe probably told him that she would be easy to manage, a pathetic little mouse.

'It looks like a lovely road. Are you ready for the neighbours to hear that?' she keeps going. She'll do it too, and that tenacity must be reflected in her expression because after a moment's pause, he pulls the door fully open and, ignoring the obvious danger, she pushes inside. Calum's buggy is in the hallway, but there's no sign of him. She thinks about how long it took for Luke to answer the door and realises with a sinking feeling that Calum's probably in the loft room, the nursery Zoe created. It's so deep inside enemy territory, but what choice does she have?

Four big steps take her to the stairs. Then she grabs hold of the banister and starts clattering up to the first floor.

'Hey!' Luke shouts out from below her. She can sense him following but doesn't pause. She races along the landing and takes the next set of stairs two at a time. Her breathing is laboured by the time she reaches the loft room, but she doesn't care. She never thought that Calum was in any physical danger, but seeing him unharmed, in the clothes she dressed him in, the relief is almost overwhelming. She reaches forward to pick him out of the playpen, but freezes at the sound of Luke's voice, now hard and menacing.

'You can't take him, you know.'

Linda turns to face him. 'Why not?' she asks, half feigning ignorance, half challenging him to admit the truth. But he doesn't say anything. He just walks towards her, his expression darkening. Her face pulls taut, her knees weaken, and her chest tightens.

But she stands her ground.

Chapter 55

Linda

'Listen, Linda, I'm not sure how you found me, but you really need to leave now.'

'That's good, I want to go.' Linda hopes the churning fear in her gut doesn't show on her face. 'Calum and I will be on our way.' She wants to pick her grandson out of the playpen, act assertive, waltz out of the room with her head held high. But to do that, she'd need to turn around, and losing sight of Luke feels dangerous. Not to mention that she hasn't shown that kind of fearlessness in a quarter of a century.

Luke lets out a short laugh. 'No, that's not what I meant. Calum is staying with me.'

Linda hesitates. Luke is bigger than her, stronger. He could fell her with one swipe. But he's young. And there's a hint of something familiar in his expression. Fear.

'On your sister's orders?' she tries, gripping the playpen frame more tightly. She steals a look at Calum, for a sense of purpose, then turns back to Luke and adds, 'Do you usually do what a murderer tells you?'

'Zoe is not a murderer,' he throws back, his face screwing up in disgust.

'Really? I heard that she killed her husband.'

'That's bullshit! He's the murderer. Destroying their marriage, killing Zoe's dream for a baby, the thing she wanted most in the world, and then torturing her all over again by having one with your daughter. Zoe told me all about it, last Saturday night, before she went to France. So yeah, he deserved to fall from that mountain, but it's not Zoe's fault.'

'He didn't fall, Luke!' Linda shouts, not willing to let Luke's claims about Tom being Calum's father derail her. 'Someone pushed him, on Zoe's instruction, the same way you've kidnapped Calum.'

Luke leans forward, as though he's going to lunge at her, but his feet don't move. 'You're lying,' he spits out. 'And I haven't kidnapped Calum; I'm keeping him safe. You're not fit to look after him.'

Linda eyes his curled fists, then looks back at his face. She can't overpower him physically, which means she needs to break his resolve, his loyalty towards his sister. 'Is that the fantasy Zoe spun for you?'

'It's not fantasy,' Luke hisses. 'Ivy doesn't love Calum – that's why she was willing to leave him with you. She was obsessed with Tom, and that's the only reason she went through with the pregnancy. For him. Now Tom's dead, she'll neglect her son, just like she abandoned Zoe, her best friend, when our dad died. Zoe thinks she might not even bother coming back from France.'

A rush of dread fires up Linda's spine. It's not rational. She knows Ivy is alive and Zoe is dead. But even hearing the words, the image they conjure up, is enough to cause a physical reaction. 'There's something you don't know, Luke.'

Luke blinks. The muscles in his neck tense. His head seems to vibrate with tiny tremors. Linda prays she's doing the right thing. 'What are you talking about?' he spits out.

'It's Zoe who's not coming back.' She pauses. He suddenly looks so young, vulnerable, and it makes Linda realise that he's a victim too. Manipulated by his older, self-serving sister. She softens her voice. 'I'm sorry, Luke, but Zoe's dead.'

'No,' he mumbles, then louder 'NO! NO! NO!'

Calum bursts into tears. Linda aches to reach for him but she can't, not yet. 'All this . . .' she wafts her hand around the room ' . . . it's over. And I promise that Ivy does care about Calum, more than anything in the world.'

'You're fucking lying!' he screeches. The noise bounces off the walls. Linda's breathing gets shallower. This is what she feared. Luke's grief turning violent. Him attacking her, hurting Calum, to soothe his own pain. A line of sweat trickles down her face. Calum's cries get louder. Her eyes grow hot with tears.

'Gumma!' Calum suddenly shrieks. 'Gumma!'

Grandma? Is he calling for her? Relying on her to save him?

'You know I'm not lying, Luke,' she says, her voice finding a new strength. 'You need to accept the truth.' She twists around, lifts Calum out of the playpen, her shaking arms hardly slowing her down, and turns back. 'If I were you, I'd get as far away from this mess, Zoe's vile plans, as you can,' she adds. Then she takes a deep breath and walks past him towards the door. Their shoulders catch for a second, but it's his that yield.

Chapter 56

Ivy

'Are you ready?' Julian asks, his voice gentle, like he's talking to a relative of one of his pathology patients. Even though I have nothing to grieve about – I'm back to full health, Harry is convalescing well and planning a visit soon, *baby steps*, and Calum is with my mum again – I find I can't speak. My throat is too full of emotion. So I nod instead, smile, and blink away the tears that have been stubbornly refusing to dry up over the last week.

'Come on, guys,' Rob says. 'I'm all for being polite, but if we don't shove our way into the line, we'll be stuck on this plane forever. And I have my first AA meeting to attend,' he adds proudly.

Julian rolls his eyes at me, but gives his friend's arm a clandestine squeeze before shuffling out of his seat and into the walkway. Then he creates a barrier for Rob and me to do the same. With our cabin bags retrieved, we follow the other passengers off the British Airways flight from Geneva and into the airport.

'How will you get home from here?' Julian asks as we join the queue at immigration.

'Black cab,' I say. I would never normally choose such an

expensive mode of transport, but I haven't seen Calum for eight days, and I'm desperate to get home to him. I couldn't make my flight last Thursday – even though the avalanche onto the road was one of Nina's lies to keep me in Zoe's clutches, I was hooked up to machines in Thonon Hospital when it took off – but I booked one as soon as I was given the all-clear to leave.

Once Rob and Julian heard what had happened from Dufort, they sacked off their rescheduled flight so that they could visit Harry and me in hospital, and then waited for me to be discharged so that I didn't have to travel home alone. Erin was theoretically out of work by then, one of her bosses dead, and the other in police custody after a night's observation in hospital, but she still turned up every day and cooked them breakfast and dinner.

When Mum put the phone down on me as I lay shivering by Lake Chablais, I assumed my frantic plea had broken her. I was so sure that she wouldn't be able to help that I didn't even bother calling her back; I just demanded that Dufort contact Interpol and fretted that it was all taking too long. When the paramedics wheeled me away, I still thought that Zoe's brother had Calum, and that getting him back was far from guaranteed. With my phone at the bottom of the lake, it took another couple of hours for the news to filter through. That my mum had saved Calum. Found out where he was, forced Luke to give him up. I still can't quite believe it.

'What about you?' I ask. I know that Julian is looking forward to hugging his kids, but also nervous about seeing Nikki again, and deciding whether to confront her about her affair.

'Nikki's coming to collect me apparently,' he says mournfully. 'I offered to get the tube and train, but she wouldn't hear of it.'

'That's good, isn't it?' I offer. 'A sign that she values your marriage?'

He shrugs. 'I don't know. Even if Nikki does regret being unfaithful after everything that's happened, I'm not sure I've got it in me to forgive her. To deal with constantly wondering whether she might do it again. When I thought she was sleeping with Tom, I could direct all my hatred towards him. But now I know it's someone else, some other doctor with a Harley Street practice, I feel even angrier with her.'

'Just promise me you'll talk to her about it,' I say. 'I know first-hand how dangerous keeping secrets can be.'

'Madam?' An immigration official gestures to a newly free kiosk and I walk over, position myself correctly, and stare into the camera. My image stares back at me. Is this okay? Can I look myself in the eye after the carnage that I've been party to over the last few days? I blink, but don't look away. It was Tom's choice to keep his involvement in Calum's conception a secret from Zoe, and his idea to tag on a ski weekend in Morzine after our visit to the fertility clinic. And I didn't owe Zoe anything. Not after she accused me of killing her dad in front of every guest at her twenty-first birthday party. Without a shred of evidence that I had anything to do with it.

The glass screen splits, and I'm in the UK officially. Then Rob, Julian and I walk past baggage collection – we all have cabin cases so don't need to stop – and through the 'Nothing to Declare' customs exit. Rob looks at his watch, then gives me a big hug. 'Sorry I've been such a jerk on this trip.'

'You've had a lot going on.'

'Yeah, no excuse though. It's time to stop blaming everything on my stressful job and crack on with sorting myself out.'

'Well, I make a mean hot chocolate if you ever fancy popping over.'

'An addiction to chocolate sounds like the perfect alternative to alcohol,' he says with a wry smile. Then he gives Julian a short but tight hug and disappears into the crowd.

There's a wall of people waiting in the arrivals area, but I raise my eyeline above their heads to look for the taxi sign.

'Ivy?' I drop my gaze. Nikki is stood by the metal barrier, a scruffy blonde child in each hand. 'What a terrible thing you've been through,' she says. The gentle sympathy in her voice is enough for a short sob to escape my lips. Then I feel her arms around me, the children cast off towards their dad, and I can't stop the tears from falling again. I haven't seen Nikki for fifteen years, but sometimes I think she was the nicest one of us all. It's hard to believe she's seeing someone behind Julian's back.

'Hi, Nikki, thanks for picking me up,' Julian says eventually, unfurling himself from the twins. His voice is formal, robotic. 'I would have been happy to make my own way back.'

'What? And force me to miss out on my big moment?' she answers, gently letting go of me and beaming at her husband.

Julian's forehead crinkles. 'What do you mean?'

'Well, I know, under the circumstances, that this is highly inappropriate,' she says, an apologetic giggle escaping from her lips. 'But I wasn't to know that one of our friends was going to kill another one of our friends and then die herself after trying to drown her ex-best friend.'

'Nikki, I'm really tired . . .'

'Ta-dah!' Nikki whips down the zip of her puffer jacket and pulls it open. Julian stares, wide-eyed. I blink, then start sniggering like a teenage boy. 'I'm sorry I've kept them a secret,' she continues. 'I thought it would be a nice surprise, and you being away for a few days gave me time to have the operation without you knowing about it. You're mad, aren't you?' she continues, her voice starting to wobble. 'I can tell by your face. It's just that I haven't felt myself since I had the twins and I thought breast implants . . .'

'What's the name of the surgeon?' Julian interrupts.

'Oh, um, Mr Hussein. But I think of him as Dr Love. Because I thought it would, you know, help our love life,' she adds sheepishly. 'Not that it needed fixing. What? Why are you looking at me like that?'

'Oh God, Nikki!' Julian wails, but he's laughing too. Then he wraps his arms around his wife. When the kids start bundling on top, I take my opportunity.

'Bye, Julian,' I call out.

'Don't be a stranger!' he calls back.

The taxi rank is outside the main arrivals door, and excitement starts to bubble again as I head towards it. I've FaceTimed on my new phone with Mum and Calum daily since she rescued him, but it's not the same as seeing him in real life. Holding him again. I wait for the automatic doors to slide open, and then I gasp.

'Mumma!'

'Calum?' I squeak.

'Thank goodness we found you in time; the traffic was terrible.'

'Mum? What are you doing here?' I scrabble for the clasp of Calum's buggy, then lift him out, breathe in his sweet milky smell. 'I missed you so much,' I whisper. I hug his warm body against my chest and close my eyes.

'We got an Uber here. It's really easy, you just need to download the app. And we took one to Deen City Farm yesterday. Calum loved it.'

My eyes grow damp again. 'You sound like the mum I knew before Dad died,' I whisper.

She looks at me, tears welling up in her own eyes. 'I took my time getting here though, didn't I?'

'Grief is different for everyone,' I say gently. 'There is no standard.' I allow myself a moment to reflect on the way I dealt with it, the time and energy it took for me to find peace. Then I push the memory away. It's all in the past.

'I thought it was my fault,' Mum says. 'That Calum – the only man I've ever loved – died because of me.'

'I know you did. But it wasn't. You were a victim of Dad's death, nothing else.'

She nods, gives me a half-smile. 'Saving *your* Calum, finding the courage to stand up to Luke. It felt good,' she admits quietly.

With Calum in the crook of my arm, I lean over and wrap my spare one around her shoulders. 'He's *our* Calum, Mum, not mine. Our flesh and blood. And I'd love you to play a bigger part in his life.'

She drops her head into my neck. We're both quiet for a moment and I can sense her mind whirring beside me. 'Does that mean I can buy him presents?' she eventually asks.

'What?' I pause to catch up. 'Of course you can.'

'Even extravagant ones?'

'You can buy him whatever you want.'

She smiles, releases a sigh of relief. 'That means you'll be happy about Sugar and Spice then.'

'Sugar and Spice?' I repeat, a little nervous now.

'At the farm yesterday. Calum fell in love with two of the guinea pigs. I just couldn't help myself . . .'

Epilogue

2008

Ivy stares at his retreating figure and feels a sense of peace descend. She's done it. Twelve long years after making the promise to herself, and to her dad at his inquest, she's taken the final step.

Peter Wilde is going to pay for what he did.

All that hard work. Tracking him down, becoming a meteorology enthusiast (although that proved serendipitous), doing well enough in her A levels to get a place at Exeter University on the course he taught. Befriending his daughter. Putting up with his misogyny and horrendous ego for three years. Keeping her mum away from him when he came to her house uninvited, in case she remembered him from the inquest. It has all led to this night, and an opportunity to take revenge. Yes, it means Zoe will lose her dad on a night designed for celebration. But while she might not know it, Ivy is doing her a favour. Removing the most toxic influence from her life.

It might not work of course. The scientist in her wishes it was more guaranteed, but life can't always be black and white. And somehow, rolling the dice feels appropriate on this occasion. So she hopes that Peter's inability to refuse a drink, coupled with the Valium she's just dropped into his champagne glass, the one she knew he'd demand back, will be enough to cause him to veer off the road on his journey to Heathrow. And that the convertible sports car that he insists on driving without a seatbelt will lack the protection to save his life.

And if not, then she'll try again. And again, until he's dead.

If she's honest with herself, it probably isn't what her dad would have wanted. He'd say something like *everyone makes mistakes*, or *climbing is so addictive, it makes us all selfish*. But he hasn't had to cope with losing both his parents like she has – one physically and the other mentally. He hasn't had his life turned upside down by the cruel silence of one man.

Up from Swindon for the weekend with a climbing buddy, Peter Wilde may have been less experienced than her dad at scaling the different rock faces in the Peak District. But he was a meteorologist. He could read the weather, see the deadly *cumulonimbus* clouds forming overhead. He knew there was a major storm on its way. And yet he chose not to warn the group. He decided – all by himself – to take the risk. And then he walked away unscathed while two men lost their lives. Including her dad.

She might not have hated him so intensely if he'd shown some remorse at the inquest. If he'd looked upset, or guilty, or resolved to change his ways. But it had been the opposite. As he'd stood in the witness box and given his statement, he'd been smug. As though surviving the double tragedy was proof of his superior status.

Ivy listens to the Pussycat Dolls pulsating through the thin walls, Peter no doubt drinking his sparkling wine and thinking he's the best dancer on the floor. And then, despite everything that's happened tonight, she smiles.

Because who's the superior one now, Peter Wilde?

A Letter from Sarah Clarke

Thank you for reading *The Ski Trip*.

This book started as a *whodunnit* but grew into a tale of revenge and a warning about how keeping secrets can have terrible consequences. Zoe was a cold-blooded killer – she planned a double murder over thirteen months – but do you feel any compassion for her situation? And does it differ at all from Ivy avenging her father's death by causing Peter's?

I'd love to know what you think of Tom too. Did you see him as the altruist he believed himself to be, unfairly treated by his friends? Or was he arrogant and self-absorbed? Is it possible he was both? And do you think Nina helped Zoe purely out of loyalty, or did she have her own issues with arrogant men?

I'd love to hear what you think about all of these questions. You can reach me by email at sarah@sarahclarkeauthor.com or via social media. I am on Twitter as @SCWwriter, and on Facebook and Instagram as @sarahclarkewriter. And if you enjoyed *The Ski Trip*, I would be hugely grateful if you could spare a few moments to write a review. It really makes such a difference.

If you like short stories, I have written one called *The Morning After* which you can download for free by joining my mailing list. You can also follow my publisher @HQstories for lots of book news and great giveaways.

Happy reading,

Sarah

A Mother Never Lies

SOME TRUTHS CAN'T BE TOLD.

I had the perfect life – a nice house, a loving
husband, a beautiful little boy.

But in one devastating night, they were all ripped from me.

It's been fourteen years, and I'm finally ready to face the past.

I'm taking my son back.

He just can't know who I am . . . or why we were torn apart.

A nail-biting thriller packed with twists and turns.

Every Little Secret

From the outside, it seems **Grace** has it all.
Only she knows about the cracks in her picture-
perfect life . . . and the huge secret behind them.
After all, who can she trust?
Her brother **Josh** is thousands of miles away, and he and Grace
have never been close – he was always their parents' favourite.
Her best friend **Coco** walked away from her years ago, their
friendship irreparably fractured by the choices they've made.
And her husband **Marcus** seems like a different man lately.
Grace can't shake the feeling that he's hiding something.
But when her seven-year-old daughter makes a troubling
accusation, Grace must choose between protecting her child
and protecting her secret . . . **before she loses everything.**

A totally addictive and gripping suspense novel.

My Perfect Friend

Beth has the perfect life. She has constructed
it carefully over the last eighteen years.

But one night she makes a choice that risks everything.

When **Kat** sees an article about that night
online, buried memories begin to surface.

She and Beth were friends once.

Things ended badly then, but now she
has a chance to make them right.

Kat introduces herself to Beth.

Not as her old friend, but as a stranger.

Beth has no idea Kat isn't who she says she is.

But then neither is Beth.

Acknowledgements

I fell in love with skiing in 1995 when I did a ski season after finishing my degree, and it's not an exaggeration to say it changed my life. Five months in France led seamlessly to a winter in Queenstown, New Zealand, and by 1999 I'd racked up five ski seasons – and multiple letters from my dad telling me to get a proper flipping job.

I heeded his advice eventually, but my love for the sport never faded and in 2009, with a husband and young family in tow, I went to Morzine – and fell in love again. We've been back many times since then, so when a fellow author suggested I set a book outside of London (thank you Mira Shah), it was the first place I thought of.

The landmarks I mention in Morzine are real, but in case you know the area well, I did change a few names where 'bad' things happen (and you wouldn't go to the François Baud footbridge to spot people). Also, in real life, the piste security team work very hard to keep the mountain safe – in Morzine and all ski resorts – and there aren't gaps between safety barriers that you could fall through.

I want to start my acknowledgements with a big thank you to Gina (and Marcus) at Reach for the Alps. Your help in the early stages of my planning *The Ski Trip* was invaluable. Thank you Emma and Sandrine at FB Freeride for being my local French experts, Jerome at the Crépu for 'lending' me your bar, and Nick and Anna for letting me use Chalet Jouet.

Away from Morzine, thank you Liv Thorne for your insight into sole parenting – I loved your book *Liv's Alone*. My meteorology knowledge comes entirely from Google, but as our current classification of clouds is based on the work of an amateur meteorologist from 1803, there might be chance for me yet. Thank you Kate for inspiring Ivy's home – I'm sure you wouldn't have left it so long to fix your door entry system.

Thank you also to everyone at HQ and especially Seema Mitra for your attention to detail, and my amazing editor Cicely Aspinall whose ability to spot my supposedly invisible fudges is uncanny – once again, the book is much, much better for your input. Thank you also to my agent Sophie Hicks for championing *The Ski Trip* and making me feel excited about my future as an author.

The longer I inhabit the world of book writing, the greater the number of amazing authors there are to thank. Thank you to everyone who read and quoted on *My Perfect Friend*. A special thank you to Catherine Cooper for reading an early version of *The Ski Trip*, and Lucy Martin, Jac Sutherland, Alex Chaudhuri and Katy Brent for your constant positivity and support. Thank you to my non-author friends too – and particularly Teresa, Rachel, Sam, Jane and Jo for giving me a boost when I needed it.

I'd also like to thank my readers, especially those who have taken the time to review my books. From the early reviews from the book blogging community to every reader who has taken the time since. Reading your positive comments reminds me how honoured I feel to do this job.

And finally, my family. Thank you Dad – still the first to read a draft. And thank you Scarlett, Finn and Chris. Morzine will always be our special place and this one is for you.

Dear Reader,

We hope you enjoyed reading this book. If you did, we'd be so appreciative if you left a review. It really helps us and the author to bring more books like this to you.

Here at HQ Digital we are dedicated to publishing fiction that will keep you turning the pages into the early hours. Don't want to miss a thing? To find out more about our books, promotions, discover exclusive content and enter competitions you can keep in touch in the following ways:

JOIN OUR COMMUNITY:

Sign up to our new email newsletter:
http://smarturl.it/SignUpHQ

Read our new blog www.hqstories.co.uk

🐦 https://twitter.com/HQStories

📘 www.facebook.com/HQStories

BUDDING WRITER?

We're also looking for authors to join the HQ Digital family!
Find out more here:

https://www.hqstories.co.uk/want-to-write-for-us/

Thanks for reading, from the HQ Digital team